Cass

MW01611042

"Imaginati... delightful cha...... ......al adventure and a captivating plot, Stokes again captures young reader's attention with another dangerous, action-packed adventure..."
— Gail Welborn, Examiner.com

"As in her first book, Elise Stokes proves herself to be a master of suspense for tweens and teens with her ability to unfold a mystery with shocking twists and unexpected turns, all the while entertaining the reader with story lines of high school drama, relationships and pending romance..."
— Stephanie Laymon, Five Alarm Book Reviews

"Elise Stokes has done it again...This is by far turning out to be one of the most amazing and well-written, middle grade to young adult series I have ever read...This book has it all, wild adventure, non-stop action, hilarious banter, family value and love, teenage angst, and excitement at every turn...simply stunning and beyond superb!"
— Kitty Bullard, Great Minds Think Aloud

"(Elise Stokes) imagination for thinking up a superb plot is better than most and packaged air-tight, and colorful, bigger-than-life characters are becoming her trademark..."
— Michelle Isenhoff, Bookworm Blather

"This book was just as exciting as the last...events are fast-paced and high energy. I wouldn't change a thing with the ending. This book is highly recommended..."
— Krystal Larson, Live To Read

"Cassidy is too much for one book to handle. Stokes had to unleash her again for a second book. If you thought she and her friends took you on a wild ride before, you have no idea what you are in for when you crack open *Vulcan's Gift*..."
— Amy Eye, The Eyes for Editing

Praise for Elise Stokes
Cassidy Jones and the Secret Formula

"I was hooked from the beginning...The plot was generally original, the climax was pretty epic, and the story had some complex concepts that were explained incredibly well. Not only that, but Stokes painted vivid pictures in my mind with her fantastic use of imagery..."
— Gabbi, Book Breather

"Everything about this book sucked me in completely...nail-biting action scenes kept the story flowing at a perfect pace, pulling me along on the roller-coaster ride that was Cassidy's life. She was a complete kick-butt heroine who pulled out an arsenal of moves and weapons..."
— Kristin, Better Read Than Dead

"I was absolutely intrigued from the very beginning of this story and simply could not put the book down...Elise Stokes ranks up there with other YA masterminds! This is a definite must-read book!"
— Kitty Bullard, Great Minds Think Aloud

"Can I vote now for a movie on this series? With the adventure, the mystery and Cassidy's super powers, Elise Stokes has delivered everything that a young reader could hope for..."
— Stephanie Laymon, Five Alarm Book Reviews

"Man, did I love this story... I liked stepping out of the love triangle of a lot of books these days and even giving the vampires and werewolves a break. Just a great, fun story."
— Cheryl, Lady Techie's Book Musings

"Elise Stokes is a wonderful storyteller. Her characters are rich, believable, as well as relatable...There is adventure, excitement and overall enjoyment with this read..."
— Jen, Jen's Book Den

ELISE STOKES

Cassidy Jones
and
Vulcan's Gift

BOOK TWO

JACE
Publishing LLC.

JACE Publishing LLC,
15600 NE 8th St., Suite B1, 287,
Bellevue, Washington 98008

Edited by William Greenleaf, Greenleaf Literary Services

Cover by Kelly Carter, Mad Spider Studio

ISBN 978-0-9881851-0-4

Publishing LLC.

Printed In The United States Of America

For my mother and best friend,

Lynne Shoblom

Contents

Prologue

Rory Michaels sat in a wingback chair studded with aged brass nails, staring morosely at the dying embers in his study's fireplace. The embers were remnants of a fire that had burned bright and vibrant, as he once had, too.

"I have lived too long," he whispered into the silence.

His gaze dropped to his hands folded neatly in his lap, displaying wrinkles and other imperfections marking his years. Examining them, he mused about the vastness of their experiences. With his hands, he had muscled a plow through hard, rocky ground; cupped the face of his young bride; and gripped an M-1 rifle, his finger easing the trigger back. They had held the heads of dying comrades on blood-soaked soil, cradled the fragile body of his newborn son, and meticulously mixed metal compounds that would one day lead to his fortune.

A single hand had swung a forging hammer, shaken the hands of presidents and world leaders, and helped carry the caskets of loved ones to open graves. And now a single hand had struck the face of a deceiver, a deceiver he had loved like his own. His palm still felt the sting.

Tormented, he reflected on the confrontation that had just transpired.

When the deceiver had entered his study half an hour earlier, Rory had a moment of doubt as he looked into the blue eyes that had always shone with kindness and affection.

However, he had the facts, had them verified, and knew the insidious bloodline this one descended from. There was only one reason this person would be in their midst.

"Here you are, Rory." The deceiver had handed him a cut crystal snifter with a shot of brandy, smiling a smile that had once warmed his heart, as the brandy would do. Rory sipped the brandy, relishing the comforting burn in his throat. After the sip, he downed the shot. It was time to get this over with.

"Let me take that for you, Rory."

Releasing the snifter into the deceiver's hand, he had silently watched the deceiver walk to the granite-topped bar and rinse the glass in the small bronze sink. Grabbing a dishtowel, the deceiver carefully dried the snifter. "What is it you'd like to discuss with me?"

Rory heard the steel cords in the deceiver's voice. He had never heard them before, and he wondered what other new discoveries he would make this evening.

The deceiver returned the glass to the shelf over the bar and slowly turned around. "I'm all ears."

Rory marveled at the transformation in the blue eyes, turned hard and cold like glass. "You have your grandfather's eyes," he observed, a bitter taste coming into his mouth. "His were edged with madness, too."

"He was a great man," the deceiver said, as though they were in agreement.

"He was a menace," Rory corrected harshly. "Do you understand the evil he planned to unleash with this so-called gift from Vulcan?"

"Perfectly, *dieb*."

"How dare you call me 'thief'!"

"That is generally what someone is called who takes something that doesn't belong to them," the deceiver replied in a lethal tone. "It is *mine*, and I want it *now*."

Rory let out a humorless laugh. "It is the Devil's, and that is where it has gone."

"You're lying. Not even you, oh righteous *dieb*, would destroy the recipe for ultimate power."

"Your eyes will never look upon it."

A slow, cruel smile curved the deceiver's mouth. "Over your dead body?"

With a burst of fury, Rory launched at the deceiver, striking a hand across the face he had once cherished. The deceiver took the blow, and turned eyes full of mocking hatred back on Rory. The lips held a cruel smile.

Rory felt ready to collapse. "Get out," he whispered hoarsely, returning to his chair.

"This isn't over," the deceiver vowed, moving toward the door.

"Yes, it is."

The smile widened. "Yes. It is." With this puzzling response, the deceiver stepped out of the room and pulled the door shut.

Coming out of his thoughts, Rory noticed that the last of the embers in the fireplace had burned out, being reduced to ashes. Contemplating the deceiver's last statement, he realized that he had underestimated the motivation of this individual. When he had called the meeting, he'd been sure this was a case of a lost sheep in need of a shepherd's staff to hook its neck and navigate it to the right path. He had anticipated repentance, but instead learned the sheep was a wolf in disguise.

With this sad realization, Rory's heart clenched with grief, and then it quite literally clenched.

Pain riveted through his chest. "Brandy," he wheezed, clawing wildly at his heart. "What poison is this?" Gasping for air, he fell forward and collapsed to the floor.

"My child," he panted, rolling in agony. "You've murdered me."

One

Old Joe

I was standing at the base of the Space Needle, staring up conspiringly at the saucer housing Sky City Restaurant and an observation deck over five hundred feet above, when a homeless man approached me from behind. I recognized his scent from my midnight jaunts through Seattle's dark alleys, but had never come face-to-face with him before.

"Ol' Joe knows when somebody is up to no good," he said to me. His voice was deep and melodic, and he spoke with a Southern twang.

Running my gaze down the white-painted beam of the Needle's northern leg, I thought, *Joe is right. I am up to no good*.

The previous weekend, amber-hued lights had been strung from the tall antenna erected up top in the shape of a Christmas tree, as they were every first Saturday after Thanksgiving. I had admired the festive sight from my kitchen window my entire life and had always wondered what it would be like to sit under the warm, glowing "tree." Would it seem like a Christmas tree close up, or would it just look like dozens of lights strung from an antenna?

I had every intention of finding out.

Turning around, I looked up at Joe. He had salt-and-pepper dreadlocks, a gray goatee beard, and a brown, aged face lined by the hardships of his life. Tall and thin, he wore an oversized Pacific-blue Seahawks jacket. The jacket was grimy looking, but Joe had pride. You could see it in the way he held himself, and his round, dark eyes had wisdom in them, the kind learned from mistakes. Presently, they looked very scolding.

Tipping back his dreads, Joe stared down his nose at me, eyes bulging out in a knowing way. "That's right," he said, hands on his hips. "I am talkin' to *you*."

I wanted to assure him that I wasn't up to anything too terrible, but couldn't very well tell him that in my fourteen-year-old girl voice. He probably figured I was young, judging by my slender 5'5" frame. His tone, however, led me to believe that he thought I was male—an extremely misguided male. I could see where he would jump to this conclusion. A person wandering Seattle Center at one o'clock in the morning dressed head-to-toe in black and wearing a ski mask wasn't usually a girl.

The only nonverbal response that sufficed was a quick nod of acknowledgment. After bobbing my head, I turned away and lifted my chin to the saucer, lit up and looking ready for takeoff, hoping he'd get the hint and mosey along. No such luck.

"Now, none of that," he continued to scold. "You turn them green eyes back here."

Exhaling a resigned breath, I did what he asked.

He twirled a hand at my face level. "I don't like the looks of this here getup. You plannin' on rollin' somebody?"

Assuming he meant "robbing," I shook my head emphatically.

Joe puckered his full lips, evaluating me. I was careful not to fidget so I wouldn't look guilty. After seconds of scrutiny, his stern expression eased, and he slowly nodded, his coiled beard moving with the motion.

"I see," he said in a sagely way.

I had no idea what Joe saw, though I was pretty sure it wasn't a mutant. Not that he would even know what a mutant was, since I was the only one in existence. According to Professor Serena Phillips, that is, the world-renowned geneticist responsible for mutating me into a superbeing with wicked strength and speed, ultra-enhanced senses, and the abilities to learn fight moves just by watching them and rapidly heal from any injury.

I'd even risen from the dead once.

Now that's not fair, blaming Serena for being infected, I chided myself. It wasn't as if Serena had told me to sit on that rickety stool prior to my dad interviewing her, nor did she knock over the beakers of her gene therapy experimentation, Formula 10X. How could she have possibly known her soupy concoction of animal DNA would create a strange retrovirus? Einstein, Crick, and Watson combined wouldn't have seen that one coming!

And shouldn't you be a tad more grateful about the personal sacrifices she has made for you? My guilt deepened as I reflected on all that Serena had given up to help me—what she and her son, Emery, had given up. I couldn't decide which had gotten the rawer end of the deal: Serena, who had closed the doors to her Wallingford University laboratory so she could squirrel away in her basement day after day and secretly study my mutant virus with the next-to-nothing hope of developing a vaccine? Or Emery, the fifteen-year-old college-graduate genius, who had put Stanford on hold to enroll at Queen Anne High School, where he masqueraded as a ninth-grader of average intelligence in order to keep an eye on me?

It really was a toss-up.

"Pay attention," Joe demanded.

Coming out of my head, I stared at him. Bending over, he brought his face to mine. "Mind you, Green Eyes," he said, tapping his temple next to his right eye, "Ol' Joe is watchin'."

I nodded respectfully. I really liked Joe.

He studied me a moment more before straightening up and turning away, ambling nobly across the grass toward the garden sculpture called *Moses*, where he had set up sleeping quarters in the crevice underneath the black-painted steel sculpture. Walking, he called over his shoulder, "I got eyes on the back of my head."

I nodded, but Joe couldn't see me—unless he really did have eyes on the back of his head.

I watched him crawl into the dark crevice, and adjusted my vision so I could observe him tugging a pile of dingy blankets over himself. Playing with my hearing, I picked up his rhythmic breathing and listened to it discriminately for a moment. When he snorted a snore, I smiled. Old Joe was already catching z's.

"Glad you're on duty, Joe," I said to myself, doing a quick scan. Only he and I were currently in the near vicinity. "Hope all your eyes are shut."

Stepping up to the Needle's beam, I pressed my palms to the cold steel flanges jutting out from its sides. The chill penetrated to the bone. I pushed my feet against the flanges, creating opposing forces, and used the friction my tennis shoes and hands created to defy gravity and move rapidly upwards. Within a minute, I heaved myself onto the saucer's roof, 605 feet above the ground. Crawling past a lightning rod, I settled underneath the amber tree and gazed up at it triumphantly.

It did resemble a Christmas tree close up.

As I yanked off the ski mask, a strong wind gusted off Puget Sound. The icy blast whipped my cascading dark red hair into a frenzy and bit through my windbreaker and sweats like needle-sharp teeth.

"Oh, geez," I chattered, curling into a ball and wrapping my arms around my knees. The Needle swayed at least four inches. When the squall died down, I stuffed the mask into my windbreaker pocket and raked long, tangled locks off my face, tucking them behind my ears. Then I twisted around so I faced Elliot Bay.

The bay reflecting city lights looked like a sheet of black glass. *Looks can be deceiving*, I mused. *And none more than my own*. Scooping up a lock of hair, I observed it contemplatively. It was the same color as my mom's. Her name is Elizabeth. I also inherited her wide-set eyes, nose, and fair complexion. My twin, Nate, and six-year-old brother, Chazz, inherited these traits, too. My blond-haired, blue-eyed dad, Drake, would appear to be the odd one out in our family, when in actuality I am. My family doesn't know this, though. They don't have a clue what happened to me the day I fell off a stool in Serena's former laboratory eight weeks ago, and I plan to keep them in the dark, along with the rest of the world. If my secret were to get out, my life would not be the only one in danger.

When gruesome visions of being sliced and diced on a surgical table formed in my head, I moved my mind to more pleasant thoughts, primarily to volunteering this weekend at SnOOZe, Catamount Mountain Zoo's sleepover fundraiser. Carli Cooper's mom was the zoo's curator, so Carli and I, along with our other two best friends, Miriam Cohen and Bren Dawsen, had participated in SnOOZe since the second grade, first as "campers" and now as "big buddies." This year I'd be Chazz's big buddy.

SnOOZe was a blast, but not the sort of thing teenage boys volunteered for. Try as I might to explain this to Emery, I had not been able to prevent him from volunteering, too. I suspected his motivation to commit himself to a weekend of rambunctious kids was concern that I would answer "the call of the wild," lose my mind, and swing with the monkeys or something, but each time I'd challenged him on this, he had avoided giving me a straight answer, something he was very good at doing.

He is so fessing up! I vowed, rooting around in my sweats pocket for my beloved iPhone. The weekend the Phillipses had moved into the rental across the street from my house, I was given two cell phones: a bare-bones, *blah* one I could hardly text with from my parents, and a hot-pink iPhone with all the bells and whistles from Emery. After Arthur King Junior had abducted my dad, my parents had decided it was

9

high time Nate and I had cell phones for emergencies. Secret communiqués and state-of-the-art GPS apps had inspired Emery's gift, which only he and Serena know about.

As my phone dialed up Emery's Droid, I tapped my fingernails against the steel roof. He picked up after the second ring.

"Is anything wrong?" was Emery's greeting.

"No, I'm just calling to say hi. So, hi."

"Hi, Cassidy," he replied with some relief. "You do realize that it's almost two in the morning?"

"Two?" I was shocked. It seemed like no more than ten minutes had passed since I'd scaled the Needle. "I'm so sorry. I had no idea. Did I wake you up?"

"No. I was awake." He added without urgency, "You've been out too long. You need to head home."

I knew this lack of urgency was due to his assumption that I was calling from a dark alley or the city woods below our street on Queen Anne Hill. These were the places I *should* have been calling from, the places I had agreed to stick to when working off excess energy in the middle of the night. Suddenly I regretted making this phone call.

"I'll head home in a minute," I said, and then asked because I was really curious, "Why are you up so late?"

"I've been Skyping with my dad."

My stomach twisted. "Is he still on?" I whispered, positioning my finger to hang up the phone. Emery's dad scared the beejeebus out of me.

It had been a fine day when Mr. Phillips returned to his "accounting" job in "China" a week after they moved in. I put quotation marks around "accounting" and "China" because who really knows what the man's real profession is or where he really is in the world? Serena might know, but if she does she isn't enlightening Emery or me. Emery just sort of accepts the mystery surrounding his dad, where I un-accept it. My one hope is that Mr. Phillips' "clients" will keep him tied up in "China" for a long, long time.

"We hung up when my phone rang," Emery told me.

"Oh," I said, relaxing. "So how is he?"

"He seems fine. Cassidy, where—"

"Okay, come clean," I interrupted, attempting to delay the inevitable. "Are you volunteering at SnOOZe because you think I'll race the cheetah?"

"I hadn't thought of a cheetah," Emery teased. "Though I admit I have had images of you arm-wrestling a gorilla."

This was as close to a confession as I was going to get.

"Arm-wrestling a gorilla…" I echoed, noticing a loose thread on the cuff of my windbreaker. I pinched it and pulled. "Huh."

"Where are you?"

I didn't answer at first. This time it wasn't avoidance. It was the stupid thread. I couldn't get it to come out. When I did speak, I didn't answer his question. "Do you think I would?"

"Would what?"

"Arm-wrestle a gorilla."

"No. Where are you?"

"Jus' a sec." I caught the thread between my teeth and yanked. The thread disengaged, and I released a relieved sigh.

"Sorry," I said with a laugh. "I just had one of those short-circuit, OCD mutant moments. You know, when I get all focused like a cat. Formula 10X must have been heavy on the feline. Which reminds me, is your mom having any luck recreating the formula? She never mentions how it's going. I bet it's hard starting from scratch like that. Bummer King's henchman destroyed all her data. I mean, if she had it, I might be cured by now, just plain old, one hundred percent human—"

"Cassidy," Emery interrupted.

"Yes?"

"I'm hanging up now," he told me calmly. "I'll find your location on GPS."

Dang GPS! "Okay, I'll tell you! Just *don't* freak." An ironic request on my part, because Emery never freaks. "I'm at Seattle Center."

Silence, and then, "Why are you in the most lit-up part of Seattle?"

"You know, all the festive decorations and lights. I was just in the holiday spirit."

More silence. "Where at Seattle Center?"

Oh, boy. "The Needle."

"Where *on* the Needle?"

"Under the tree."

Emery barked an incredulous laugh. "You're on the top? Unbelievable." He laughed again, and a swishing sound led me to believe he shook his head, too. "I'm astonished. I don't know what to say, except: Get down now."

"All right, all right," I said. Wanting to sound responsible, I added, "I need to make sure the coast is clear first."

As I crawled to the roof's edge, I could hear Emery's stocking feet padding against his wood floor.

"Are you pacing?" I asked.

"Yes."

"Emery, there is nothing to worry—" Peeking over the edge, I cut myself short. To my dismay, Emery wasn't the only one pacing. Agitated, Joe walked back and forth in front of Moses.

"Um, Joe is down there. I'll have to wait until he goes back to bed."

Emery stopped pacing. "Joe?"

"Yeah. Old Joe. He lives in Moses. He shouldn't be much longer."

"Joe is a homeless man," Emery deduced instantly. By his calculating tone, I knew he was devising an escape plan, which was good because I really needed one. "Is he inebriated?"

"Huh?"

12

"Has he been drinking?"

"No, he's sober. I don't think Joe is a drunk or anything. Just down and out." I knew where Emery was going with this. "He'll know what he's seeing if I go down now."

Joe looked up abruptly. I pulled back from the edge and thought, *Crud. Joe already knows what he's seen. The crafty old guy was faking sleep.*

"He'll go back to bed soon," I reassured Emery, crossing my fingers. "I'll wait him out."

"Cassidy." The way Emery said my name, I pictured him slipping off his black-framed glasses and pinching the ridge of his nose—hard. "Please tell me you have your mask on."

Setting the phone down, I yanked the ski mask from my pocket and tugged it over my head. After tucking in hair, I swiped up the phone and said brightly, "No worries, it's on."

Emery was pacing, again. "All I can think about are telephoto lenses. Are you facing Queen Anne?"

"No, the bay. Now stop stressing. No one can see me, and who's up at two in the morning, anyway?" *Besides you, me, and Joe.*

As if a celestial power were answering my question, my senses suddenly sharpened, and I detected male voices below. Popping my head over the edge, I saw four men circling Joe. Their loudness, slurred words, and swaying movements suggested they had just finished up an evening of bar-hopping and now had decided to top it off with tormenting a defenseless homeless man.

I don't think so, I thought, hot blood pumping through my veins. A mental alarm went off in my head, warning me to take a deep breath and not act rashly. I slapped down that mental alarm as if it were the snooze button on my alarm clock. If these punks hurt Joe in any way, shape, or form, they were going to pay—dearly.

"I'll call you back," I told Emery, slow and lethal, watching the scene below through narrowed eyes. "I've got something to do."

13

I couldn't decipher Emery's response; my attention was fixed on the man who had just stepped too close to Joe for my liking. Words were still spilling from the iPhone speaker when I disconnected the call. I was dimly aware of slipping the phone into my pocket.

The punk jabbed Joe's shoulder with an open hand, and I saw red. The next thing I saw was my black Nike planting square on the guy's chest. The air left his body as he flew backwards, slamming into Moses with a ringing thud. My right fist swung around and up, clipping another bad seed in the jaw. His head snapped back, and the rest of him followed. He collapsed to the ground.

The other two men fled in terror, and a powerful urge to chase them overcame me. Running down fleeing objects was a compulsion of mine. Serena called this impulse prey-drive, in which a carnivore instinctively pursues prey. Believing the virus birthed this instinct in me, she viewed the compulsion as "remarkable"; I viewed it as another short circuit. Much to my disgrace, I gave in to instinct.

In a beat, I was at the closest hoodlum's heels, reaching for his collar, preparing to take him down, when a voice broke through my adrenaline-induced insanity.

"Green eyes! Control the rage!" Joe shouted, his voice resonating. "Don't be like I was! Control the rage!"

I stopped dead in my tracks. The men kept running for their lives.

As I gulped in air, the haze cleared from my head like fog burning off the coast, giving way to clear skies. In this clarity, a tsunami of shame crashed over me, and I felt the tempered beast crawl back into the recesses of my mind, where it would lie in wait for the next time Cassidy lost control.

And I've been so good, I thought, devastated.

The punks were at the street by now, glancing back at me in terror. Peripherally, I saw the other men I assaulted unsteadily scrambling away. King's henchmen hadn't been

14

so lucky. About ten yards behind me, I heard Joe's uneven intake of air and smelled the nervous sweat beading on his skin.

Did they hurt him? I wondered anxiously, whipping around. My quick movement caused him to jump.

"Joe, I won't h-hurt you." My voice faltered from excess adrenaline.

At the sound of my voice, his jaw slackened and his eyes bulged. This time there was no scolding in them.

"Don't b-be afraid," I said, putting my hands in the air, slowly closing the space between us. Rooted to the ground, he watched me approach. The wary look on his face caused me to believe he viewed me as a wild animal that someone had the crazy notion of trying to domesticate. If these were his thoughts, he wouldn't have been too far off.

When I drew close enough for him to make out my eyes, he kept his pinned to them. I supposed he was gauging me, looking for signs of danger. At this point, I shook all over from dropping adrenaline. My adrenaline crashes totally bite.

Hands in the air, I stopped a couple yards away.

"Put them hands down," he demanded, his face fierce. "Ain't nobody goin' to the clink."

"Clink" must mean jail, I thought wearily, lowering my trembling hands. I so wanted to be home and in bed.

Joe regarded me soberly. His face displayed no fear, only a world of regret. *Regret for what?* I wondered.

Unable to hold still, I began moving around restlessly. Joe watched me, the sad expression still on his face. Confused, I craned my neck to the saucer. I was bleary about how I had gotten down.

"I don't r-remember coming down," I admitted, glancing at him.

His grim mouth curved into a sudden grin; the sadness melted from his face. "You moved down that beam like an eel," he told me, motioning to the Needle's northern leg. He gave a hearty laugh—a wonderful laugh. "And you went up

15

like a house spider runnin' up a wall." His smile widened, revealing big, square teeth. A few were missing. "I fooled ya, Green Eyes."

I had to laugh, too. "You did. I t-totally fell for it." A heaviness weighed in my chest suddenly. Next would be depression, then a flood of tears. That was how these crashes usually went. "Joe, don't t-tell anyone about me, okay?"

He placed his left hand on the Seahawks logo, which happened to be over his heart.

Tears stung my eyes. "Thank you," I choked out.

"Come back and see Ol' Joe," he requested, the sadness back in his eyes.

His loneliness caused more tears. "I will," I promised, sniffling. "Gotta go."

Turning on my heels, I shot off like a blazing arrow.

Two

Donuts And Death

I was back on top of the Space Needle, having no idea how I'd gotten up there. And worse yet, the sun blazed brightly overhead.

"Oh, no," I gasped and touched my face, feeling skin. "It's daytime." Panicked, I took in the rest of me. My feet were bare, and I wore a puffy pink dress covered in big purple polka dots. It was hideous!

"Emery is going to kill me." I inhaled a frustrated breath. The air was stagnant, heavy, and felt like lead in my lungs. "I've got to get down before someone sees me." Casting my vision below, I noticed the streets were empty. There was no traffic, no people, not a living thing in sight.

"Where is everyone?" I wondered, glancing at the bay. Though the sun shined, the water appeared as it does at night, a smooth sheet of black glass. It was ominous, eerie, and I suddenly felt very afraid.

Jumping to my feet, I cupped my hands around my mouth and yelled, "Where did you all go?" The only thing I heard was my echoing voice.

"Where are they?" Overwhelmed with loneliness, I sank down. "Why am I alone?"

"I'm here, Cassy."

Startled, I jerked my head left. Jared Wells sat next to me, staring down at the desolate streets.

Oh, my gosh! The dress! *I thought, glancing at myself. To my relief, I was no longer in the heinous pink puff of polka dots, but my favorite jeans and the Roxy T-shirt that I had regrettably passed on purchasing last summer.*

Turning back to Jared, I studied his thoughtful profile. "You're so beautiful," I told him, and strangely didn't feel embarrassed.

Keeping his gaze fixed below, he let the corners of his lips curl in the way that I loved.

Smiling, I brushed his dirty blond bangs away from his brown eyes. They were beautiful, too, luminous and soulful. Everything about Jared was beautiful. "I love you, Jared."

He looked at me, and for a second I thought I would drown in those limpid chocolate pools, fringed with thick black lashes. All at once, his face dissolved into sadness. "Then why did you do it, Cassy?"

He was referring to my public rejection of him 203 days ago, the last time we talked. Regret rolled through me like a river. "I'm not completely sure," I admitted. "I was embarrassed, and confused, I guess. Honestly, I thought it was a mean joke or something. Not that I'm disgusting or anything. I'm just not Jessica Blanchette or Robin Newton."

My throat tightened when I said Robin's name, and I pictured the piece of crooked cartilage that made her nose not so perfect anymore. I had broken it when misjudging my strength during a dodgeball game, and Robin hadn't been exactly forgiving about it.

"It's awful being all guilt-ridden over someone as horrible as Robin," I confessed. "Someone bent on making my life miserable. She's just so nasty and vindictive, starting rumors about Emery and me all the time. We're just friends, you know?"

Glancing away, I felt my cheeks flush. I hated the popular notion that Emery and I were more than friends. A moment later, I looked back at Jared. His expression hadn't changed.

"But I should've known better than to have thrown that ball," I said quickly, "all jealous like I was, and dangerous." I realized this last part wouldn't make sense to him. "I can't tell you why I'm dangerous. It's a secret, but I can tell you why I was jealous. I eavesdropped on Bobby Neigh and Ahmid Mazur in the cafeteria. They said Robin liked you. But the feeling isn't mutual, right? It doesn't seem like you're into Ro—"

18

"This isn't about Robin," Jared reminded me softly.

"You're right. This is about me apologizing to you." I shook my head regretfully and asked myself, *"Why haven't I ever apologized?"*

"Pride," Jared offered.

"Yes, stupid pride," I agreed. *"And the fact that I'm just a big chicken."*

Jared laughed, sending a chill up my spine. His laughter was strangely musical, unearthly, like chimes being blown by the wind.

"I liked you, too," I pressed on, though disturbed by this ethereal Jared. *"I just didn't realize it at the time. I miss you so much—miss hanging out with you, talking to you, looking you in the eye. I can count on my fingers the number of times we've made eye contact since what happened...what I caused to happen."* I took a deep breath of stagnant air and did what I should have done after class that day, two hundred and three days ago. *"I'm sorry for everything. I hope you'll forgive me. I hope we can be friends again."*

Sadness seeped into Jared's face. *"You've waited a long time to say you're sorry,"* he pointed out in a heavy voice. *"Why did you have to wait until it's only the two of us?"*

I became aware of the surrounding silence again. *"Where are they, Jared?"*

His gaze slowly moved up.

I lifted my eyes to see birds peppering the cerulean sky. There were so many, it surprised me they hadn't blotted out the sun.

Shielding his eyes, Jared pointed to the sky. *"There's my mom,"* he said, his finger bouncing around. *"My grandpa...Aunt Jolene...oh, and there's your dad."*

"My dad?" I shielded my eyes and squinted, seeing that the birds weren't birds at all, but people with shimmering brown wings. *"There's Nate!"* I cried, then called to my twin. *"Nate!"* Hovering high, he didn't appear to hear me. I noticed my mom and called to her. She didn't respond, either. With each face I recognized, I shouted names, waved my arms, but no ears perked or eyes glanced my way. It was as if I didn't exist.

19

A sick feeling slid through my stomach, and I was afraid again. My eyes moved to Jared. "Am I dead?"

"You can't die," he told me, looking mournfully up. The sun grew brighter in the sky. "I'm sorry, Cassy."

"No!" I jumped to my feet and shielded my eyes, screaming to my loved ones somewhere in the glare, "Help me! I want to be with you! I don't want to live forever! Please, help meeee!"

I woke with a start. Instantly, my eyes adjusted, and I looked around in a panic at my bedroom, bathed in morning light. I had neglected to lower the blinds after returning to my room in the wee hours of the morning.

Pressing a hand to my speeding heart, I whispered, "A dream. It was only a dream." Still, it felt like more.

"It doesn't take a psychologist to figure that one out," I mumbled. My mind had mingled two distresses: my lost friendship with Jared and my fear of immortality. Both seemed grievously hopeless. I couldn't change Jared's clear dislike for me any more than I could force a body able to regenerate itself to die. Not that I had great plans of doing such a thing, but who knew how I would feel a few centuries from now?

On the bright side, I've grown a quarter of an inch, I reminded myself, meaning I wasn't immortally fourteen. *Thank goodness*. Tears had welled in my eyes when Serena reported I had grown during my exam last Monday in her makeshift basement lab. Under the pretense that I was doing housework for her Monday, Wednesday, and Friday afternoons, Serena ran me through a menagerie of tests and had Emery draw my blood Mondays and Fridays, which I absolutely dreaded having done. Not that Emery wasn't good at it; needles just make my skin crawl.

Serena guessed that I would continue aging until my growth plates closed, around age eighteen. Fingers crossed, she'd develop a vaccine before then, and my immune system would finally recognize the retrovirus as an enemy and not a friend, and no one other than the three of us would ever know that I had been anything more than human for a while. Unfortunately, since viruses mutate rapidly, success wasn't likely—unless you consider the odds of finding a needle in a haystack good.

20

On that cheery note, my alarm clock went off, blasting "Jingle Bell Rock."

Letting the music play, I pulled myself out of bed to get ready for a weekend of hyper kids, tons of fun, and no worries. Carli's dad planned to swing by in forty-five minutes to collect Emery, Miriam, Bren, and me so we could help with the SnOOZe setup, as we girls had done for the past three years. We usually helped Mrs. Westing, the zoo's neighbor and biggest supporter, prepare crafts and organize activity centers in the auditorium, where we'd roll out sleeping bags that evening to watch animal shows and then go to sleep. Hopefully, we would help her this year, too, because I liked Mrs. Westing a lot.

While stuffing extra clothes and toiletry doodads into my backpack, I began experiencing trepidation about volunteering, again. What happened at the Space Needle had shaken my confidence in my ability to control myself. When I expressed this concern to Emery, after he had intercepted me on my way home, he had called my chasing down a man for the thrill of it "a lapse in otherwise good judgment" and said he had absolute confidence that I would conduct myself properly this weekend. My opinion then, and still is now: Emery is gracious to a fault.

Maybe after sleeping on it, he's thought better of me going, I thought, slipping a colorful zip hoodie over the sage volunteer shirt Carli had given us at school yesterday. Snapping up my backpack and sleeping bag, I flung my bedroom door open, sending scents of home and family wafting up my nose. I was instantly flooded with guilt. I hated deceiving them, though deception was for the best. If my parents were to learn what had happened to me two months ago and about all the lies since then, they would be terrified for me and furious with Serena. And who could blame them? No longer able to trust her, they would undoubtedly seek outside help, and then it would be all over—for all of us. According to Serena, there were "depraved individuals" who would stop at nothing to get their hands on me if made aware of my changes. This included hurting those I love. One of these individuals was Arthur King Senior, Junior's dad. The world believed he was dead; Serena said otherwise.

I'm sorry, I mentally sent my family. *Hope you never know.* My mind suddenly zeroed in on a delectable scent—evaporating guilt.

"Donuts," I squealed, and had to remind myself to descend the stairs at human speed. Heightened senses included heightened taste buds, and nothing tasted better than deep-fried, yeasty dough covered with sugar. Dropping my things on the foyer floor at the bottom of the stairs, I rounded the banister to the hall and walked rapidly to the kitchen, entering with a beaming smile. Assembled around the table, my family read sections of the newspaper over coffee and hot chocolate, a pastry box centering the table with a glazed old-fashioned calling my name. I'd been having a fetish for old-fashioneds lately.

"I love you, Dad!" I declared, plopping down into my customary chair next to Mom. With a sweet tooth second to mine in our family, Dad must have made the donut run that morning.

Looking up from the paper, he smiled at me. "Is it me you love, or the donuts?"

"Both." I reached for the old-fashioned. Nate snagged it.

"Do you want to live?" I growled across the table at him.

Clutching my donut, my twin glanced up innocently from the comics spread in front of him and Chazz. "That would be nice."

"Then…" I flipped my palm out.

"That's her favorite," Chazz told him, truly innocent.

"Since when?"

"Since *forever*!" I grabbed for the donut. Nate dodged my meager attempt, meager because if I really wanted the dang donut, a dozen samurais couldn't stop me.

"Oh, for heaven's sake. Give your sister the donut," Mom ordered.

Smiling, Dad sipped his coffee.

Nate slapped the donut in my hand. "Happy?" he asked, his mouth turning up impishly.

"Almost," I said, then proceeded to brush the donut's bottom with my fingertips. This was for Chazz's benefit, and he watched me with great interest. "I'm cleaning off Nate's cooties," I explained, glancing at his cute round face, chocolate frosting and sprinkles smeared around his mouth. My adorable little brother had a knack for wearing his food.

"Only girls have cooties," Nate stated, also for Chazz's benefit.

"No, these are definitely yours crawling all over my donut." I blew over the top, and Chazz squinted at the void in front of me, searching for the alleged cooties.

"Maybe they're yours, Cassy," he suggested. "'Cause only girls have cooties."

Nate's grin expanded at his success. Everything out of his mouth became law to our brother.

"Oh, my gosh, Chazzy!" I exclaimed in mock horror. "You've been indoctri-*nate*-d!"

Mom and Dad chuckled. Nodding, Nate complimented, "Nice," where Chazz didn't respond to my joke or ask for interpreting help. Thoughtfully puckering his lips, he added to his previous statement, "'Cept for Mommy. She doesn't got them."

Mom smiled at him warmly. "Thank you, sweetheart, though there are worse things than cooties in this world." Looking down at the paper, her mouth dipped into a frown.

"What are you reading, Mom?" I asked while breaking my donut into sections.

"Rory Michaels' obituary. He died from a heart attack." She said this like I should know who Rory Michaels was.

"Did you know him?"

"No, only of him." She glanced up from the paper. "Don't you remember when your father interviewed him?"

Nate and I exchanged blank looks. I wasn't the only one who had no idea what she was talking about.

Dad smiled at our blankness. "I interviewed Rory Michaels for the debut of "In The Spotlight," he explained.

"Ah," I said, because here lay the problem. Though we kids were proud of our dad's news broadcasting success, we rarely watched "In The Spotlight," the human-interest segment he hosted for Channel Five News. Our lack of interest had nothing

23

to do with his interviewing skills, because Dad was the best in the business. It's just that he tended to interview nerdy geneticists like Serena, and not very often anyone appealing to someone my age, such as the lead singer in a local band or a professional sports star. Ten to one, Rory Michaels had been a yawn producer, too.

Guilt followed this thought. Boring or not, Rory Michaels was dead. Out of respect for the deceased, I inquired, "Who was he, Dad?"

"A fascinating man," Dad said, explaining, "Rory Michaels' life was a classic rags-to-riches story. He was the son of a struggling corn farmer in Indiana, and one of twelve children. At fifteen, he dropped out of school and joined the Army under the false pretense that he was eighteen, which wasn't uncommon during World War II. Many young men passed themselves off as older in order to enlist, driven by the motivation to serve their country or to better their circumstances after the Great Depression. According to Mr. Michaels, both were his motivations.

"After the war in Europe ended, Mr. Michaels and a member of his Army regiment, Ernest Suttner, left the armed forces and relocated here, where they founded Material Dynamics, which is one of today's leaders in metal alloys."

"Did he have any family?" I asked. This man's personal life held more interest for me than his business life. Who cared if he knew how to make aluminum or not?

"His wife and son died a number of years ago."

"Yes, it mentions that here," Mom said, scanning the paper. "How sad. His son was killed in a car accident at seventeen."

"So sad," I agreed somberly. "Did Mr. Michaels have anyone else?" I couldn't stand the thought of someone dying alone.

"He and the Suttner family were very close," Dad recalled. "I'm sure they were involved with him."

The doorbell rang just then, and I jumped up from the table, announcing, "That's Emery! See you at three-thirty, Chazzy."

Gulping hot chocolate, my little brother nodded, causing milk to stream down his chin and splatter the comics. Only Chazz could make that cute.

"Dude," Nate complained at him, salvaging the comics.

I scooped up the remainder of my donut, bid goodbye, and popped the donut in my mouth as I jogged to the front door. Swiping up my things from the foyer floor, I opened the door to the perfect representative of tall, dark, and handsome. With black eyes and hair, a milky complexion, and a smile that made your toes want to curl, Emery was six feet of gorgeous.

I swallowed the donut, keeping my eyes somewhere between his face and the SnOOZe shirt. "That color looks fantastic on you."

"Thank you," Emery said, glancing down at the shirt then up at me. After a quick study, he reciprocated with: "That color makes your eyes look very green."

"Very *green*?" I teased. "Man, I feel sorry for the girl you try to woo someday." As I stepped onto the porch, the smile fell off my face, and I quickly turned to the door, pulling it shut. My ears picked up the lock clicking into place.

Moving closer, Emery surmised in a hushed tone, "You're still concerned about going today."

"How could I not be?" I exclaimed. "More surprisingly, how can *you* not be concerned?"

"Voice," he reminded.

I rolled my eyes. "I know you think I 'mastered my impulse,'" I said quietly, imitating quotation marks with my fingers. This is what Emery had told me after I cried my eyes out for acting like a crazy person. "But I didn't stop on my own. Joe stopped me."

"*Could* Joe have stopped you if you had chosen not to?" Emery challenged. We both knew a tank couldn't stop me if I were so determined.

"That's not my point, and you know it. Okay, what you said last night about wanting me to enjoy life as I normally would was super sweet, and yes, I enjoy going to SnOOZe with my friends. It's our tradition, and I really like being with them. It makes me feel, you know, normal. But the zoo is really far away, and after what I did…You know how scent can affect me. What if there's an animal smell or something that triggers…" I shook my head. "Nope! Not going."

I turned around and aimed my finger at the doorbell.

Emery slid his hand over the button. "What about Chazz?"

"He'll be disappointed about not going, but better disappointed than terrified when his sister does something shocking."

"That's conjecture," Emery argued, rushing on before I could counter his counter. "Last night you granted me final say on the matter. Are you breaching our agreement?"

"Can I?" I asked, hopeful.

He smiled. "No."

"Darn it, Emery!" I shook my fist in frustration. "*Fine!* I'll go. Far be it from me to be an agreement breacher. But if I lose it, don't say I didn't warn you." The perfect tease popped into my head. "There's a factor that you haven't calculated into this weekend."

"I doubt it," Emery said, leaning casually against the doorframe. "But shoot, anyway."

"How do you plan to keep an eye on me with all the fending off you'll be doing?"

Emery grinned. Like any boy, he always appreciated a good harassing. "You're referring to our neighbor?"

"Who else? I really wish you'd stop playing hard to get." After his family had moved in to the neighborhood, it had taken me a solid week to convince Miriam that Emery and I were strictly friends and he was free game. She'd been a little obsessed with him since he had "rescued" her from Dixon Pilchowski's fist plowing into her mouth. Miriam's mouth often had that effect on people.

"I'm not playing anything," Emery insisted. "And I have no intention of getting caught. Let me put it this way. When I think of your BFF, I picture an anglerfish, and FYI, I have no desire of being lured into *that* set of teeth."

I smiled at the acronyms Emery peppered his speech with from time to time. He sometimes muddled his perfect diction for those who were unaware that he was a brainiac with a

Molecular Biology degree—which was everyone I knew, except for my family and Dad's cameraman, Ben Johnson. They were privy to Emery's accomplishments, just not his true motivation for going to high school; they were under the impression he posed as a regular kid so he could be one for once.

Without the audience, the acronym usage was purely for my entertainment. Emery knew I could hardly keep a straight face when he talked his age.

Grinning from ear to ear, I swatted his arm. "That is so mean! And this"—I whacked him again—"is for the slang, *and* that's why I'm smiling, not because you compared my BFF to a hideous fish."

Emery busted up, and received another swat.

"*FYI*, you ungrateful boy, there are tons of guys who would jump at the chance of being devoured by Miriam."

Emery exaggerated a shudder. "Remind me to never hire you as a publicist."

"I'm just stating a fact."

With perfect timing, I heard Miriam's front door open two houses over. She and Bren, who had spent the night at the Cohens', yammered a mile a minute in the foyer as they prepared to come over and wait for Mr. Cooper with us.

"Another fact," I said. "The more you run, the more Miriam will chase. So do yourself a favor and give in. You'll have the opportunity to do that in about twenty seconds."

Emery slid his eyes toward Miriam's house. "Thanks for the heads-up," he said, pushing off the doorframe. He patted my head. "We make an excellent team." He started down the steps before the "anglerfish" could corner him on my front porch.

Miriam and Bren sauntered onto her porch.

"Hey!" I called to them.

The girls' heads snapped to me. Unable to see Emery over the tall hedge, Miriam called back unabashedly, "Where is he?" She furrowed her brow, placing a hand on her hip. "He didn't woosy out, did he?"

Continuing down the walk, Emery muttered something I didn't catch.

Responding to Miriam, I pointed at Emery, and she burst into giggles. We scampered down our porch steps.

"Good thinking," I whispered mercilessly to Emery when I caught up with him. "She can't corner you on the sidewalk."

"I have no idea what you're talking about," he replied, and stepped confidently onto the sidewalk.

Darting through her front gate, Miriam's black curls bounced as she skidded to a stop. Her cobalt-blue eyes twinkled like seawater on a sunny day. The twinkle usually meant mischief.

"*Please, please, please*, Emery," she pleaded, a naughty look on her face, "don't be angry with me."

He gave her his easy grin. "For dissin' me?" he called back, shifting into teenager jargon for my friends.

"Never!" Miriam shouted dramatically. "It is physically impossible for me to dis you." She quickened her pace, forcing Bren, who was half a head shorter, to practically run to keep up. Miriam winked at Emery, as if she had conspired to make Bren book it.

The girls stopped in front of us, and Bren shot Miriam an exasperated look. "A little eager, don't ya think?" she said, shoving a chunk of her straightened black hair off her face. Her eyes and skin were the color of richly brewed coffee.

"Very," Miriam agreed, staring up boldly at Emery. "You eager, too, Emery?"

Loud hooting behind us saved Emery from dignifying Miriam's flirting with a response. I spun around to see Carli leaning from the passenger-side window of her minivan, blond hair blowing behind her, long arms waving wildly. We girls let out shrill screams in return; Emery let out a long breath that hissed through his teeth. Before the minivan came to a complete stop, Carli jumped out and tackled us girls.

"I'm so excited," our perpetually happy friend squealed, pulling us into a group hug. "This will be the best SnOOZe *ever*!"

And in that moment, huddling with the girls that I knew like the back of my hand, I couldn't have agreed with Carli more.

Three

SnOOZe

S everal miles up Catamount Mountain outside Seattle, Mr. Cooper turned off the curvy, two-lane road and into Catamount Mountain Zoo's parking lot. Pulling myself away from girl chatter that had flowed nonstop for the last thirty minutes, I pressed my cheek against the shoulder of the passenger seat and gazed up at Mrs. Westing's sprawling mansion overlooking the zoo. An English Tudor like our house, hers probably fell more into the Tudor Castle category, with four steeply pitched gables, six chimneys, and a rounded turret encased in blocky stone.

"It's beautiful here," Emery remarked from the passenger seat.

"Yes, it is," I said with a sigh, glancing around the headrest at his thoughtful profile. His eyes skimmed over the tall trees lining the parking lot.

There were tall fir trees as far as the eye could see, and Mrs. Westing owned almost all of them. The miles of forest surrounding the zoo were hers. Her home and the zoo were the only interruptions in the thick green blanket covering the mountain on the left side of Catamount Mountain Road.

Mr. Cooper pulled up to the main gate. As Carli yanked open her door, a wall of exotic animal smells slammed into me, kicking in a primal instinct: the urge to hunt. Not hunt as in chase down and kill—thank heavens for that—but hunt, as in tracking down and searching out.

As the laughing girls tumbled out Carli's door, I slid mine open. Emery was already stationed outside it. "Everything all right?" he asked, assessing me.

I smiled. "Shiny."

Gathering my backpack and sleeping bag, I stepped onto the asphalt, inhaling deeply. The scents were intriguing, but intriguing was the sum of it. My smile stretched wider. I felt confident that what I feared wouldn't come to pass, after all. No unknown trigger in the zoo would flip the switch in my head to *feral*. I wouldn't lose control. This, I felt sure of.

Looks like only rain is in the forecast, I thought, smiling up at the gray sky. *Not screw-ups*.

"Nothing like fresh mountain air," I remarked to Emery, moving my smiling gaze to him. He smiled back, amused.

"Fresh mountain air is totally epic," he agreed, dumbing himself down more than usual, his way of letting me know that he knew I enjoyed more than "fresh mountain" in the air.

I rolled my eyes, redirecting them to Mr. Cooper. "Thanks for the ride, Mr. Cooper," I called to him.

"My pleasure, Cassidy. Have fun."

"Thank you. I will." I pulled the door shut and drew in another breath of fragrant air. This would indeed be fun.

~~~

When we reached the auditorium near the center of the seventy-acre zoo, the double doors flew open, and Mrs. Cooper came barreling out. All arms and legs like her daughter, she walked briskly toward us.

"My faithful girls!" she cried, hugging each of us. Turning to Emery, she offered her hand. "Brenda Cooper. You must be Emery. Welcome, and thanks for volunteering."

He shook her hand. "Nice to meet you, Mrs. Cooper, and I'm glad to help." Just then, his phone vibrated in his jeans pocket. "Excuse me," he said, releasing Mrs. Cooper's hand.

He retrieved the Droid, and I watched him carefully as he glanced at the Caller ID. Miriam grew quiet, too. Aware of his audience, Emery kept his expression blank.

"Hello," he answered the call, eyes on me.

I lifted my gaze heavenward.

The caller said something, and Emery replied, "Not at the moment." Shifting the phone from his mouth, he told us, "I need to take this call. Be right back." As he walked away, I fine-tuned my hearing.

"I can talk now," Emery said in a low voice, ambling toward the cafeteria on the other side of the courtyard.

My ears strained to hear the caller. "Where—"

Miriam blurted in my ear, "Is it a girl?" Startled, I lost concentration and the caller's voice.

"I don't know," I lied, because the caller most definitely was a girl—an *older* girl. *Riley*, I guessed. *It has to be Riley*.

I'd never met Emery's former college mate, but what I knew about her made me uneasy. Emery had once described her past as "colorful," which I interpreted as "shady." Other than this, I didn't know a thing about her, since Emery had opted out of sharing more, claiming that he preferred to keep his "worlds" separate. My teeth clenched. I didn't like Emery having a "world" that didn't include me.

"Better *not* be a girl," Miriam grumbled, eyes narrowed on Emery.

Not a girl, I thought, eyeing him. *But very much a woman*. The other thing that bothered me about Riley was how I envisioned her: a blond-haired, blue-eyed, Robin Newton-caliber beauty.

"My, he's a striking young man," Mrs. Cooper remarked.

Glancing at her, I saw she was watching Emery, too, as were Bren and Carli. Deciding this wouldn't do, I turned my back to him and kept my ears to myself. Just because I didn't approve of his "friendship" with a sketchy temptress, didn't mean that he didn't deserve some privacy.

"Oh, he so is!" Miriam agreed in a pained voice. "I just wish he wasn't so hot. Then there wouldn't be all this competition. You should see the way girls scope him out at school, especially Samantha Collins. I hate her!"

"No worries," I teased, resting an arm over her shoulders. "You scope him way better than Samantha does."

Miriam yanked my hair. "I want to be you," she whined. "*I* want to be his family friend; be his locker buddy; have him shadow *me* all day long—"

Taken aback, my arm slid off her shoulders. Miriam had no clue how much she did *not* want to be me.

"Okay, Miriam," Bren cautioned, exchanging a concerned look with Carli.

My insides tightened with resentment. The general consensus at Queen Anne High was that Emery and I had a "thing" for one another, but I trusted that my friends believed me when I insisted this *so* wasn't the case. Apparently I had been wrong.

Reckless Miriam ignored the warning, and began ticking "wants" off on her fingers. "*I* want to work for his mom, get paid to mop his floors, do his dishes, fold his clothes—"

"I have *never* folded his clothes," I interrupted, which was true. So we weren't being total liars, after Emery drew my blood and Serena completed prodding and poking, we would usually do some household or lab chores together, which consisted mainly of cleaning up after his messy mother. Whenever there was laundry to be folded, Emery whisked his stuff away before I could get a look—not that I tried to get a look or anything.

"You haven't?" Miriam questioned with surprise. A mischievous sparkle came into her eyes. "Well, you should!" she advised excitedly.

I laughed. It was impossible to stay angry with Miriam for long.

Carli and Bren visibly relaxed.

"Seriously, Cass, listen." Miriam smiled conspiringly. "Next time you're at his house, I'll pay you ten bucks to sneak into his room and snag his—"

"Socks," Mrs. Cooper finished for her, assuming, as we all had, that socks were not what Miriam had in mind.

We girls busted up.

Grinning and shaking her head, Mrs. Cooper amended her parental blunder. "Don't snag *anything* for her," she ordered, wagging a finger at me. "And don't *ever* tell Emery *or* his mother that I suggested you take his socks. What was I thinking? Okay, I'm outta here. I have to check on SnOOZe food prep and get back to duties. Mrs. Westing is waiting for you in the auditorium. Thanks, girls, and be good, especially you, Miss Cohen."

Miriam saluted her.

Mrs. Cooper took long strides toward the cafeteria, waving at Emery along the way. Right before following Carli into the auditorium, I glanced over my shoulder at him. Still talking on the phone, he met my gaze with a suspicious one. I smiled smugly. For once, Emery was wrong. His conversation remained private between his "friend" and him.

~~~

"Hello, ladies," Mrs. Westing greeted us as we entered the auditorium. High windows edged the vaulted ceiling in the large, open space, and a stage claimed the right wall, where Mrs. Westing sat at the foot of at a table stacked with craft supplies.

"Hi, Mrs. Westing!" we returned happily, dropping our things against the wall. As we approached, she rose regally to her feet, smiling. The smile didn't reach her eyes, however. They looked sad.

With her wavy gray hair stylishly pinned up, Mrs. Westing wore a tweed suit with a paisley silk scarf tucked neatly into the neckline of a cream dress shirt. Not exactly zoo attire, but casual for Mrs. Westing. She offered each of us her jeweled, manicured hand, and said, "How wonderful to see all of you." The words rolled off her tongue elegantly.

Shaking her hand, we returned the sentiment.

"As you can see, there is much to do." She gestured to the stack of paper. "Please, ladies, take a seat." After giving general directions for the task at hand, she added with a smile, "I'm looking forward to hearing what you ladies have been up to since our last chat."

And I believed her, because Mrs. Westing definitely seemed in need of distraction. *From what?* I wondered.

As we collected materials, I peeked up at her, discovering that she had been watching me. My throat constricted with dread. *Why is she looking at me like that?* I asked myself, on the edge of panic. *What is she seeing?* I quickly returned my gaze to the scissors piled on the tabletop, snatching up a pair as I self-consciously rubbed my nose. The light spray of freckles had vanished from it the morning after I had been infected in Serena's lab, due to my quick healing ability. Luckily, the freckles had been so light that no one had noticed they were gone—until now, maybe.

"Cassidy," Mrs. Westing said.

Gulping, I looked up.

"I apologize that my staring has made you uncomfortable." She smiled. "I wonder if you realize how radiant you are?"

I shook my head and shot back, "Thanks." Never could handle a compliment well.

"Women pay thousands for a complexion like yours," Mrs. Westing continued. "Your skin is flawless."

My "flawless" cheeks blushed, flawless because rapid cell regeneration meant having an awesome complexion. Feeling my friend's eyes crawling over my mutant anomaly, I willed, *Emery, get off the phone already!*

"You're a picture of health, Cassidy. Treasure it." Mrs. Westing's face dropped.

Her despair caused me to forget my own concerns, and I thanked her again, asking, "Mrs. Westing, are you feeling all right?"

"Apparently I shouldn't play high-stakes poker." She let out a humorless laugh then explained somberly, "A close friend of mine passed away."

We quickly gave our condolences.

"Thank you, ladies," Mrs. Westing replied, pressing her index fingers under her blue eyes, as if expecting them to suddenly overflow. They remained dry, but I could feel sympathy tears forming in mine.

The auditorium door opened, and Emery's scent rushed in. As Mrs. Westing shifted her gaze beyond me to the door, a look of recognition sprung onto her face. Alarmed, I whipped around in my chair and anxiously watched Emery placing his things with ours, unaware of the catastrophe that could be headed our way. *What if she knows him—knows who he really is, and blurts the truth out in front of the girls?*

Emery looked up. His eyes sharpened in scrutiny on Mrs. Westing, but it was clear he didn't know her.

"Mrs. Westing, this is our friend, Emery," Carli introduced him brightly as he approached us.

He stopped next to my chair and shot his hand to her. "Nice to meet you, Mrs. Westing," he said in a good-natured, boyish way.

Rising to her feet, Mrs. Westing took his hand. "It's a pleasure, Emery. Phillips, isn't it?"

Emery rearranged his features into confusion. He was really good at this stuff. "Have we met before?"

"Forgive me, Emery," Mrs. Westing said, smiling sheepishly. "I'm slightly off-kilter today. No, we have not met before. I recognized you from the news, when that horrible Arthur King kidnapped your mother and Cassidy's father."

The story of Emery bravely holding Junior's henchman at gunpoint had given him instant cool-guy celebrity status when he started school, much to his chagrin. His goal had been to stay under the radar, which I had never thought possible in the first place. How could he avoid drawing attention when greatness oozed from his pores?

The way Mrs. Westing had said King's name made it sound as if she knew King, too. Emery noticed this also.

"Do you know King?" Emery asked.

In my head, I added, *that lunatic*. Mental illness had been Junior's defense, which I seriously doubt anyone witnessing the trial had disagreed with. King had conducted himself the only way he knew how: crazy. Even though it was clear the guy was shy a full deck, his insanity defense hadn't flown with the jury, and he was now a resident of Washington State Penitentiary, enjoying that orange jumpsuit, I'd wager. Junior had a thing for bright colors.

"Unfortunately, I do," Mrs. Westing confirmed with a look of distaste. "My husband had business dealings with King. Other than that, I have no association with the man."

As Emery settled into the chair next to me, I played with the idea of asking her if she knew Junior's dad, too, since Serena refused to elaborate on how he was a threat to me. *But maybe Mrs. Westing knows more about him,* I schemed, *and will divulge inf—*

Emery jabbed a finger in my ribs. Startled, I shot him a frown. He looked back at me, relaxed, and gave his head an almost imperceptible shake. I wasn't sure what for, but his timing was too spot-on not to creep me. This wasn't the first time it felt like Emery had crawled into my head.

~~~~

An hour later while we wrapped up preparations, the auditorium door flew open and a human scent laced with a lilac-scented perfume swooshed in. Looking up, Mrs. Westing's face abruptly hardened.

"Yoo-whoo," a cheery voice sang out behind me. I twisted around to take a look at the person Mrs. Westing had reacted so strongly to.

A petite woman stood in the doorway, holding a tray piled with sandwiches, bags of chips, and juice boxes. She wore a teal-colored dress and pumps, and her features were delicate, precise, and pale. "Pale" is an understatement. It was as if a faucet had been turned on, draining all the color from her except for the deep blue of her eyes, gleaming like polished sapphires. The silky ringlets framing her pretty face were a shade darker than ivory, and "pearly" best described her complexion. She looked more like a china doll on a shelf than a living person with warm blood flowing through her veins.

The atmosphere in the room darkened. The darkness came from Mrs. Westing, whose eyes narrowed on the dainty woman. Meeting her gaze, the woman's face lifted in delight.

"Hi, Lily," Carli enthusiastically greeted the woman.

"Hello, Carli, kids, Margad," Lily returned in a soft, singsong voice. "Brenda asked me to bring in your lunch," she explained, gliding toward us. The lithe way she moved was mesmerizing, like a well-practiced dance. As she flitted toward us, I heard things being shuffled on the table. Turning around, I watched Mrs. Westing grimly clear a spot for the tray, glaring down at the papers she stacked.

Ignoring Mrs. Westing's iciness, Lily smiled sweetly at us. "Look at all you've done!" she exclaimed, gently setting the tray in the spot Mrs. Westing had cleared. "Brenda will be so pleased." As her hands moved from under the tray, a huge diamond caught the light.

Miriam's eyes widened. "Your ring is so beautiful!"

"Thank you," Lily sang, smiling at her ring. "I think so, too. My fiancé has excellent taste." Her gaze moved expectantly to Mrs. Westing, who gave her a chilling look.

Glancing uncomfortably between the women, Carli gnawed a fingernail, clearly in the midst of a mental debate. Nodding her head, she resolved her deliberation and spoke up brightly, "Lily, these are my friends." After quickly introducing us, she presented Lily. "And, guys, this is Lily White."

My eyebrows shot up at her name. "Lily White" was way too contrived to be a fluke. *Her parents must have named her after she was born*, I decided. Thankfully, Lily was looking at Bren and missed my reaction to her name.

"Lily and Mrs. Westing's son just got engaged," Carli informed us excitedly. She avoided looking at Mrs. Westing. "The way Mr. Westing proposed is so cool, super romantic." She hooked a chair with her foot and pulled it next to her. "Here, Lily. Sit down and tell them."

"That's sweet of you, Carli," Lily said gratefully. "But I shouldn't take up everyone's time—"

"Please, Lily," Miriam urged. "I love romantic stories."

Smiling, Lily sat down. "Well, our story is that, last Saturday, William and I—"

"Thank you, children," Mrs. Westing cut her off, her voice slicing the air like a knife. "I can finish up here. Please, enjoy your lunch in the cafeteria." She smiled uncivilly at Lily. "I've appreciated spending time with such quality young people."

Lily's eyes hardened on Mrs. Westing, softening into hurt almost instantly. For some reason, that glimpse of her rage caused my heart to quicken. Why it would bother me, I don't know. If I were Lily, I'd be furious, too.

Emery pushed his chair from the table and stood up. "It was nice meeting you both," he said to the women in a neutral tone, picking up the tray. Before they had a chance to respond, he turned on his heels and headed for the door. Mumbling goodbyes, we girls jumped to our feet and scrambled after him.

Four

It's All Happening At The Zoo

In the cafeteria, we sat at a table looking out at the courtyard, directly across from the auditorium.

"Carli, what the heck is Mrs. Westing's problem?" Bren asked, grabbing a sandwich off the tray. Her fiery eyes slashed sideways toward the auditorium.

Opening a chip bag, I waited for Carli to reply, unsure what to make of either woman.

Carli lifted her lip like she had a bad taste in her mouth. "Well, I like Mrs. Westing and all. She's been real good to the zoo, but basically what it comes down to is that she's a total snob." She leaned towards us confidentially. We girls responded in turn. Emery, slumped back in his chair, worked on a bite of sandwich as if he were counting chews. "Lily's brother, Ian, is one of our zookeepers. You guys haven't met him yet. He's like one of the funniest guys I know—"

And cute, too, I gathered, plopping a potato chip in my mouth.

"You'll see tonight when he does the reptile show. Anyway, Li—"

My hand flew up. "*Whoa*!" I said, inhaling the chip. It caught in my throat.

"Cass!" The girls gasped. Carli pounded my back, while I hacked, clutching my throat. Emery calmly slammed a straw into a juice box and handed it to me. Sucking down juice, I frowned around the straw, as I noticed a smile twitch at his mouth. The stinker had already figured out my almost choking to death had to do with my fear of reptiles—

especially squirmy, legless ones with unhitching jaws. Just thinking about snakes makes me lightheaded.

Slower on the take, my concerned friends watched me gulp down juice, until I yanked the straw from my mouth and wheezed out, "Reptile show? As in *snakes*?"

All three grinned like Cheshire Cats.

"As in snakes," Carli confirmed. "As in *Pythie the Python*."

Staring at her in horror, I crushed the emptied juice box.

"Oh, my sweet Pythie!" Bren squealed, clapping her hands.

"Sweet?" I spat. "That thing is like thirteen feet of pure evil!" Emery chuckled, and I pegged his arm, declaring, "It could swallow a small child whole!"

Carli's lips stretched over pink-banded braces in a big grin. "Good point, Cass," she said. "I'll remind Ian to feed Pythie a goat before bringing him on the stage."

"Eeewww!" Miriam squealed.

I blurted over her, "He's taking it out of the *terrarium*?"

Carli gave me an exasperated look. "Of course, he's taking Pythie out of the terrarium. That's part of the show."

I whimpered.

"*Anyway*, like I was saying, Lily moved in with Ian right after my mom hired him. She and William met here, at the zoo. It was one of those 'love at first sight' things. They fell for each other hard and fast, and Mrs. Westing has been totally miffed about it. Ian says she threw a temper-tantrum when Lily and William got engaged last weekend."

This explains Mrs. Westing's hostility towards Lily, I thought, glancing at Emery for his reaction. Appearing oblivious, he dug through a chip bag. I nudged his leg with mine. He ignored me and kept eating chips.

"Why would Mrs. Westing be angry?" Miriam asked Carli. "Lily is so nice, and obviously in love." She glanced wistfully at Emery, who took no notice—or seemed not to, anyway. I knocked his leg again.

"Super nice. She and William are head over heels in love! You should see William when they're together. He can't take his eyes off her! But, like I said, Mrs. Westing is a snob. She doesn't think Lily is good enough. Ian says she wants William to marry money."

Aiming a finger at her mouth, Bren made a gagging noise. We girls nodded agreement. Sipping juice, Emery glanced around the room.

"I bet Ian's ticked," I remarked.

"Well, yeah. He doesn't like his sister being treated like dirt! But he's being super cool about it. He just looks at it like this is how Mrs. Westing was raised, you know, money being more important than character."

"I don't know," Miriam said, looking doubtful. "It's not like she looks down her nose at us."

"Maybe that's because we're not engaged to her son," Bren bit out.

The auditorium door flew open, and Lily rushed out, tears streaming down her face. She paused to wipe them before walking away.

"Oooo!" Bren balled her hands and shook them. "Mean old bully! I'm going over there and telling Mrs. Westing what I think of her!"

Carli looked at her with alarm. "If you do, Bren, my mom will kill me! She's trying to stay out of this as it is. She doesn't want Mrs. Westing going sour on the zoo." Her mouth turned up into a cheery smile, and she added with her usual optimism, "Mrs. Westing will get over herself and come around. Lily and William are just so *cute* together. It's hard not to love Lily."

~~~

With time to kill after lunch, we decided to show Emery around the zoo. His mood was difficult to read. He was quiet, seemed lost in thought—or maybe he was just bored.

41

I, on the other hand, had a grand old time playing a private scent game that I called "What Belongs to This Stench?" The premise was to sniff out a scent and maneuver my friends toward the critter emitting it. As I cataloged dozens of new scents to memory, I realized my little game could be useful, because who knew if I would need to track a warthog or an Eastern wallaroo someday?

In pursuit of a scent drifting from the south end of the zoo, I unwittingly steered my friends to the Reptile House. Once there, Bren announced, "We're going in! I gotta see my sweet Pythie."

"And I bet sweet Pythie wants to give you a big hug," Miriam teased, tightening her arms around herself and bulging her eyes.

"Pythie wouldn't hurt me! He loves me!"

Grinning, Carli pulled the door open, unsealing the putrid odor inside. The stench pouring out smelled like greasy fried chicken that had been sitting out in the hot sun all day. Gagging a little, I held my breath. What had been a disgusting smell was now utterly intolerable.

"Get in there," Bren ordered Miriam, pushing her through the doorway.

"Ugh!" Miriam howled from inside. "It stinks!"

"Quiet in the Reptile House," Carli called to her.

Bren grinned at me evilly, and I gave her a *not even* look. Not a chance would I step into that snake pit.

"So we're doing this the hard way," she teased, preparing to tackle and pull me in.

Emery spoke up. "Cassidy, show me where the restrooms are?" He turned to the other girls. "Don't wait for us. We'll catch up. Which way, Cassidy?"

Tipping my head left, I kept smiling at Bren.

Bren stuck out her tongue.

"Ick!" Miriam yelled from inside. "This snake's swallowing a mouse!"

I swung away and started walking. Emery caught up with me.

"Chicken!" Bren called after me.

Continuing to walk, I hooked my thumbs under my armpits and flapped my arms like wings.

"What's Pythie eating?" Bren asked as Miriam and Carli joined her. When I heard the door click shut, I stopped walking and released my breath.

"Gross! I can taste them!" I complained, spitting.

"Impressive," Emery remarked, looking at his watch. "You held your breath 117 seconds. Any lightheadedness?"

"You timed me?" I asked, grinning. "Way too weird."

Emery shrugged. "If you can make up games to entertain yourself, so can I."

The grin froze on my face. "What are you talking about?"

"You've been tracking scents since we've left the cafeteria."

I stared at him, horrified. *What if the girls noticed? I would die!*

"You're subtle," he reassured me in his eerie way. "You're only obvious to me since I know how scent affects you. It's been fascinating watching you track."

"Watching me? You've been zoning out all day."

"I always pay attention," he insisted, fiddling with his watch. "We're tracking the next scent together." He looked up and smiled. "Time to hunt."

"Emery!" I complained, looking around to make sure no one was within earshot. No one was, of course. Emery wouldn't have spoken so freely if there had been. "Do you have to say it like that? Couldn't *you* be a little more subtle and say something like, 'So, Cassidy, is there a habitat you'd like to visit?'"

He grinned. "So, Cassidy, is there a habitat you'd like to visit?"

43

"As a matter of fact, there is. It's over there." I pointed straight ahead. Skewing my head to the right, I gauged the scent. "And then somewhere right. South."

"The Siberian tiger," Emery deduced, staring in the same direction.

"Yeah. I'm pretty sure. His name is Roga, but how did you know the habitat is there?"

"I looked at the map at the zoo's entrance."

I nodded, requiring no further explanation. One quick study was all Emery would need to memorize the zoo's layout. I suspected he had a photographic memory. This, like so many others, was a question of mine waiting for an answer.

"Let's confirm our theory," he suggested.

"You mean now?"

"Yes, now. I told Bren and Carli we'd catch up."

"But they think you're using the restroom," I protested. "Going off on our own would be ditching them."

"If we don't delay this any longer, we'll be back before they realize they've been ditched." Emery flashed a smile. "Come on. That scent will drive you mad if you don't follow this through."

"True." I looked longingly south. "You win. We'll hunt."

~~~

As we walked briskly in the direction the scent drifted from, Emery asked, "What do you know about Mrs. Westing?"

"I thought you said you weren't zoning."

"I'm not interested in her personal drama, which, by the way, I'd rather experience Chinese water torture before listening to again."

"Noted."

"I want to know who she *is*, or more specifically, who her husband is, since he has business ties with King. Anyone involved with King interests me greatly."

"You're not the only one. Mrs. Westing knowing King. Small world, huh?"

"For the most part. Do you know what her husband does for a living?"

"*Did* do for a living. He died six or seven years ago. Mrs. Westing told us last SnOOZe that he used to run her dad's company. Now William does."

Coming to the path leading to the tiger's habitat, we slowed to a stop.

Emery looked at me questioningly. "Well?"

"Mystery solved. Roga is the perpetrator. Ready to go back?"

"No," he replied, and started down the path. With a sigh, I caught up.

"Did Mrs. Westing mention the name of her father's company?" Emery asked.

I thought a moment. "No, I don't think so, or I forgot. I do know some details about William, though."

He motioned with his hand for me to continue talking.

"Well, he's an only child, played rugby in college, and has piercing blue eyes like a wolf's—according to his mom, that is. I've haven't actually seen them myself."

Looking ahead, Emery grinned. "You certainly have a thing for eyes," he observed with amusement.

"They *are* the windows to the soul," I pointed out. A middle-aged couple observing the tiger's habitat shifted their gaze our way. I lowered my voice so they couldn't hear. "Especially with my vision. You wouldn't believe what I see in eyes."

"Capillaries and cataracts?" Emery joked, pulling himself against the handrail that stretched across the front of Roga's habitat.

"Those, too." I pulled in next to him, whispering, "Except in your eyes. The black is really hard to penetrate, which really isn't pure black like everyone thinks. The color is a deep, dark brown outlined in black."

"So in other words, my eyes don't tell you much about my soul," Emery replied in a normal tone. The couple looked at me, and I could feel my cheeks redden.

"Well, come on," Emery urged mercilessly. "We're all waiting for an answer."

The couple quickly walked away, leaving us alone at the habitat. I shoved Emery, and he laughed.

"That was so rude," I scolded.

"*I'm* rude? I wasn't eavesdropping. Now answer the question."

"I don't need to see your soul. You prove it to me every day." Having said this, I quickly turned to the habitat. Mentally berating myself for saying something so stupid, I gazed at the hulking orange- and black-striped Siberian tiger lounging on the pavilion. It was hard to believe that this beautiful and terrifying five-hundred-pound cat was the same scrawny cub with huge paws I had helped bottle-feed three years ago.

Emery broke the silence. "Was it the tiger you were tracking, or his spray?" he said, crinkling his nose.

"Him. Once you get past the spray odor, he smells really good." I leaned on the rail next to Emery and stared at Roga, musing aloud, "I wonder if Roga memorizes scents, too? Huh…I wonder if I smell good to him?"

"Of course you do." Emery nudged my elbow with his. "You smell like food."

I laughed. "Well, I'm glad we don't have *that* in common."

A lanky zookeeper appeared at the back of the habitat. Whistling, he lightly banged a metal bucket on the bars. Suddenly alert, the tiger lifted his head, looked at the zookeeper, and launched off the pavilion toward him.

"I suppose I have some explaining to do," Emery said.

I glanced at his profile. "For what?"

"My phone call earlier."

"Why? What did Riley say?"

Surprised, he turned to me. After quick scrutiny, he deduced smugly, "You listened long enough to know Riley was the caller, but then something caused you to lose concentration. Miriam, is my guess."

I could feel annoyance on my face. Seeing it too, Emery's expression grew smugger. "*Or* maybe I was being polite and minding my own business," I fired back. "I don't always abuse this little ability of mine, you know."

Emery grinned. "How did she distract you?"

"*What* did Riley want?"

He looked into the habitat. "Not much."

"*Yes* much, or you wouldn't have brought it up. Now spit it out! What did she say?"

"Point taken," he said, suddenly distracted. "I hadn't thought this through. I should have let you broach the subject." His voice trailed off, and his gaze sharpened on the tiger and zookeeper.

"What didn't you think through?"

"Nothing," Emery evaded, staring into the habitat.

I sucked in an angry breath. "Why do you stay in touch with her?"

"Riley doesn't know about you," he explained without explaining anything.

"What about Mickey?" I demanded, bringing up Emery's other friend. I had spied the rough-looking man the night Emery snuck off with him to stake out the apartment of Junior's right-hand "man," Selma Heart. "Do you keep in touch with him, too?"

"Yes."

"Oh."

His response took me by surprise. I had presumed he only kept in touch with hottie Riley. Visualizing Mickey's red spiked hair, dragon tattoo, and the scar slashing across his right cheek, thin as if made by a knife blade, uneasiness set in my gut. Emery had met Mickey through Riley. Where had she meet Mickey?

"Who are they, Emery?"

"Not who you're assuming." He straightened up. "Listen in on the zookeeper and tell me what he's saying to the tiger."

"Who are they?" I demanded.

He smiled. "Not who you're assuming."

"You have no idea what I'm assuming! Why can't you give me a straight answer?"

"Because it would lead to other questions that I don't feel like answering at the moment," he replied calmly, still looking at the blasted tiger and zookeeper.

I gripped the rail and blew out a furious breath through my nose.

"Cassidy, I know I exasperate you."

I glared daggers at the ground, letting my angry silence confirm that he did, indeed, exasperate me.

"I'm sorry." Emery touched my forearm. "Please, Cassidy. Listen for me."

"Well, who can resist 'please' coming out of your mouth?" I said with sarcasm, but relented. What was the use of holding out when Emery wasn't going to tell me squat? I looked up, and instantly understood why his interest had been piqued. Lips puckered in a coo, the zookeeper handfed Roga chunks of raw meat through the thick bars. "Is he insane?"

"Why? What is he saying to the tiger?"

"It's not what he's saying, it's what he's doing. He's going to lose his hand." I pulled the zookeeper into my enhanced vision, observing three deep scars disfiguring his face. Obviously this wasn't the first big, dangerous kitty he had gotten too close to. "You should see the scars on his face."

"Tune him in."

"Patience. One thing at a time." I focused on the zookeeper's mouth until I could hear the words spilling from it, not that I understood any of them. "He has some kind of an accent or speech impediment. I can hardly understand a word he's saying."

"Don't worry about translating for me. Just listen."

Nodding, I concentrated on the zookeeper's garbled voice.

"Ah, nowa thars ah good Raga," he was saying. "Sush a magnificet criture shadant be lockt up een ah halval. Tiz crimineel! I ees goin ta spring yee, my friend. Count on dat." With a doting smile, the zookeeper fed Roga a final piece of meat before turning away and ambling out of sight.

"Well?"

Frowning, I watched Roga stare after the zookeeper, tail twitching back and forth. "It's difficult to say, but I think they're planning a prison break."

~~~

After we found the girls and endured some harassing for ditching them, Emery casually mentioned to Carli, "The Siberian tiger is really cool."

We had decided to craftily elicit information about the odd zookeeper, since we couldn't share what I had heard. It was not humanly possible that I could have heard him from that distance.

"Roga *is* cool," Carli agreed proudly. "And soon we'll have two Siberian tigers. We're getting Roga a mate when the new habitat is finished."

"Will the habitat be where the forklift is?" Emery asked.

I looked at him with surprise. "What forklift?"

"It was parked on the hill next to the tiger's habitat," he explained, smiling at my frown. Even with all my enhanced senses, I could be incredibly unobservant.

"Yep," Carli confirmed. "Now all we need is a million dollars to finish it." She grinned at our stunned faces. "Guys, it's more than just throwing up a fence. It cost big bucks to get a habitat up to code. Otherwise, we'll have a Siberian tiger running loose."

A feeling of calamity suddenly stirred in me. I piped up, unable to cover my worry, "Carli, there was this zookeeper hand-feeding Roga meat."

Emery shot me a warning look. I ignored it.

"Oh, that's James Flynn. He's a little…" Carli whistled and twirled a finger at her temple. "*And* a huge pain in the rear. He's obsessed with Roga and thinks the zoo is doing a sucky job taking care of him, and he *knows* that Roga will get a bigger habitat when we get funded." Glancing around, she lowered her voice. "Don't tell anyone, but my mom is firing James tomorrow."

"Does he know?" Emery asked quickly.

"No way! My mom has to blindside him because he'll probably go ballistic. In fact, Ian is going to be with her just in case James loses it."

"Do you think he would set Roga loose?" I blurted.

Emery cleared his throat. I ignored this warning, too.

"What?" Carli said, her lips stretching over her braces. "That would be like *murder*. James is whacko, but he's not a psychopath. You'd have to be a psychopath to set a tiger loose."

Emery caught my eyes with his. Frowning, he slightly shook his head.

Heeding the caution this time, I clamped my mouth shut. Emery was right. I couldn't say more without saying too much.

Five

Squeeze Me

"Cassidy!"

"Chazz! There you are!" My excited brother leapt into my arms. I had been waiting for him outside the auditorium, where Emery and the girls were settling in with their campers. With a significant number of parents volunteering so their children weren't alone overnight, there were enough "big buddies" to be responsible for only one "camper."

"Hello, sweetheart," Dad greeted me, wearing jeans, a fleece jacket, and his Huskies baseball cap. No one around us took notice of him. Almost as if covering his head had magical powers, Dad was rarely recognized when wearing a hat, but if he were to flip it off, revealing his golden-blond hair, people would start tripping over themselves, as though he had suddenly appeared from thin air. Funny how that worked.

"I always enjoy coming out to this zoo," he shared, glancing around. "Too bad it'll start raining soon." We both looked up at the sky, which had deepened to a foreboding gray over the last hour.

"It's okay if it does. Everything's inside until tomorrow."

"There's always a chance the weather will clear by then. This *is* Washington." Dad wrapped an arm around Chazz and me. "Have fun with Cassidy," he wished Chazz, kissing his head. "I'll miss you both tonight."

I caught the worry in Dad's voice. Allowing Chazz to spend the night at the zoo was a huge deal for my parents. When I was young, Mom had insisted on staying with me.

51

Knowing their protectiveness made their willingness to entrust my little brother to me that much more touching. "Don't worry, Dad. I'll take good care of him."

Dad kissed my cheek. "I know you will."

I put Chazz down, and relieved Dad of my brother's backpack and sleeping bag. Bending over, he hugged and kissed Chazz again. "See you tomorrow at eleven."

"Okay, Daddy," Chazz said with a sniff. "I love you."

"I love you, too." Dad straightened up, looking conflicted. For a moment, I thought he was going to change his mind about leaving Chazz. Then he instructed, "Call if he decides all night is too much."

"I will," I promised. "Bye, Dad."

"Love you both," he said again, then turned away.

"I love you, Daddy!" Chazz cried after him tragically, tears pooling in his big round eyes. I tightened my grip on his hand.

Smiling sadly, Dad blew him a kiss and disappeared into the crowd. There wasn't a chance I would let anything bad happen to my little brother.

~~~

Chazz overcame his sorrow the second he met Emery's camper, Ethan, who introduced himself as "Sabertooth." In turn, Chazz introduced himself as "Wolverine," and then the two little superhero fanatics just grinned at one another. I couldn't have ordered a better SnOOZe buddy for my brother.

The boys never broke character. Sabertooth and Wolverine made crafts together, played games, had fierce growling battles, and lapped up juice like dogs during dinner. According to Sabertooth and Wolverine, they didn't know how to suck through straws or eat chocolate pudding with anything other than their "claws," and they certainly had never mastered the art of cleaning with napkins, favoring their tongues instead.

Bren and I put our foot down when it came to the tongues.

When their tongues shot out of their mouths, we pinned the boys to the cafeteria floor and properly cleaned their faces and hands with napkins. Bren and I were alone in our effort. From the table, Emery, Miriam, and Carli howled with laughter, while the three little girls, who were the girls' campers, stared in wide-eyed horror at the two scary big buddies forcing good hygiene on the struggling boys. By the time the dinner hour commenced, the boys, though resentful, were adequately clean. They forgot their resentment once we left the cafeteria and stepped into the rain, which was pelting the cement like BBs. Lifting their chins, they howled at the seeping sky as we ran across the courtyard to the auditorium.

Almost every child cheered and danced on the foam covering the floor, which volunteers rolled out during dinner. Sabertooth and Wolverine went to battle, locked in one another's arms, rolling around the padded floor, snarling. The little girls looked on with a mixture of fascination and distaste. It was really cute. In the meantime, we big buddies arranged sleeping bags about twenty feet from the stage. Bren set up on my left while Emery set up on my right. Miriam staked her claim on his other side, and Carli rolled out next to her. Arranging Chazz's sleeping bag at the foot of mine, I felt as giddy as the kids around me. Their excitement was contagious.

While Mrs. Cooper requested that everyone sit down on their sleeping bag for the animal shows and refreshed memories about the rules, zookeepers scattered electric lanterns around the room to be turned on for a goodnight story later. A lantern was placed between Chazz and Ethan, which Emery promptly relocated behind him. A wise move, I would say. Then zoo staff and visitors who had come to watch the animal shows filed in, taking seats in the metal chairs lining the walls. I picked out Lily's lilac-laced scent entering the enclosed space immediately.

Twisting around on my sleeping bag, I found her settling in a chair at the back of the auditorium. Carli's high opinion of her had chipped away the uneasy feeling I had after glimpsing her rage. Lily had been angry. So what? Who wouldn't be if they knew their future mother-in-law looked down on them? A man sat in the chair next to her. *Obviously William*, I thought, resisting a sigh when his arms roped around his fiancée. His blue eyes were every bit as brilliant as his mother had raved, but what she hadn't described was their kindness. If eyes are indeed the windows to the soul, then William Westing had an exceptional one.

"Awww. He looks like such a nice guy," Bren said, echoing my thoughts.

"So nice," I agreed. "He has the most pleasant face."

Bren giggled. "That's not how I'd put it, but okay."

Glancing over his shoulder, Emery followed our wistful gazes. Making a quick assessment of his own, he turned forward again, just missing William softly pressing his lips to Lily's head.

"*Awww*," Bren and I simultaneously sighed. Emery's shoulders shook with quiet laughter. Snapping my hand against his back, I smiled at what had to be the happiest couple in the world.

~~~

Ian presented the macaw show first, and Carli was right. He was totally funny.

A couple shades darker than his sister, Ian had mischievous blue eyes, a charming cock-eyed smile, and a mop of flaxen curls. I could only imagine the handful he had been as a kid. His quick wit had the audience in stitches, especially Miriam, who howled with abandonment. I noticed Emery watched her more than the show.

After the macaw show, I caught a whiff of "spoiled fried chicken" and felt the blood drain from my face. Reptiles were being transported inside through the emergency exit behind the stage. Keeping my breathing shallow, I grew very still while watching zookeepers remove the macaws from the stage and carry out small terrariums and various sized boxes containing who-knew-what inside.

Emery flattened his hand between my shoulder blades. Leaning toward my ear, he whispered, "Are you all right?"

I sucked in a quick breath, taking advantage of his close proximity. The concentrated dose of his scent masked the odor the *things* in the boxes gave off like toxic gas. "I'm fine," I assured in a tight voice, stealing another breath of him.

"We could go outside for this show."

I glanced at my beaming brother clapping his hands and insisted, "I'm fine."

"Let me know when you're not," Emery whispered back. As he started shifting away, I sucked in a final breath of him and decided to see how long I could hold it.

The breath rushed out, however, when Roger wheeled a huge box onto the stage. *Pythie*, I guessed, rubbing the goose bumps cropping up on my arms. I couldn't believe they had *it* in a cardboard box. I couldn't believe they were going to take *it* out of the cardboard box.

Emery returned to my ear. "Cassidy?"

"Fine," I snapped, watching Roger and Ian lower the box to the floor. To prove how fine I was, I drew in a long breath of snake-saturated air. My stomach churned, and I thought for a moment I would hurl. It was ridiculous how crazy scent made me.

"Mind over matter," Emery encouraged.

"Whatever," I grumbled, my mood as foul as the air. Feeling bad for the snide response, I added, "Sorry about that. Good advice, though. Mind over matter. I'll do that."

"I'd like you all to meet my friend, Tango," Ian said into the microphone. "Tango is a Scarlet snake, and she is non-venomous. We'll get to the venomous ones later—"

My eyes rounded like saucers.

"*Or* we could go outside," Emery suggested again.

"Or I can just suck it up." Determined, I looked forward. However, I didn't look at Tango. I didn't want to *see* Tango. It was bad enough that I had to *smell* Tango. Instead, I focused on a tattoo that a male volunteer brandished on his bicep. It was a triangular shape made up of intricate interlacing knots, similar to the one I had glimpsed on Mickey's arm. Smell faded and noise muted as I pulled the tattoo into my enhanced vision, scrupulously studying the stained pinholes where inked needles had punctured skin. There were thousands of these punctures.

I can barely handle one needle prick, I mused, readjusting my vision until the pinpricks melded together, forming the interlacing knots again. *Mickey's knotwork tat was a circle. The dragon blasted it with fire. Wonder what that means, if anything?*

"Are you in shock?" Bren's teasing voice broke my concentration. As the tattoo visually receded to actual distance, stimuli overwhelmed my senses. Smells, laughter, talking, and applause crashed in on me, reeling me for a second. Sometimes when I focused too intensely on something, vision took dominance, eclipsing other senses. This was yet another short circuit of mine.

"I was *trying* to go into shock," I replied after recovering from stimuli-overload. "Thanks for messing it up. Now I have to start all over."

"Better get going, because Roger is opening Pythie's box."

"Already?" I jerked my head to the stage, and sure enough, Roger was bent over the box, stroking the killer inside. "What about the other snakes?"

Emery leaned to my ear and whispered, "You effectively 'zoned' for almost half an hour."

"No way."

"Yes way. Handy skill you have, though I'd advise against employing it in hostile situations."

I stared at Emery in disbelief. *Thirty minutes? How is that possible?* It was as if I had lost a chunk of time, skipped it completely.

"I hoped you'd keep your mind occupied until after the grand finale," Emery added.

"Pythie," I said, whipping my head to the stage.

Emery scooted closer.

"Now, who would like to meet a thirteen-foot python?" Ian asked the audience. Hands and hoots filled the air. Laughing, he asked, "Now, who would like to help me pick up my reptilian friend we here at Catamount Mountain Zoo fondly call Pythie? He is *really* heavy."

To my horror, Chazz's arms flew into the air. "Me! Me!" he pleaded, wiggling his fingers. Horror turned to panic when Ian looked straight at him and pointed. "The eager red-headed lad." His finger bounced to the next victim.

Chazz shot to his feet before I could get command over my lips to form the word *No*.

"I'm so jealous, Chazzy!" Bren shouted after him.

My mouth still held the silent protest as Chazz skidded onto the stage, joining the other hapless volunteers.

"Pythons are harmless," Emery reassured me.

"To an elephant," I snapped, running slick palms down my jeans.

Beaming, Chazz gave us a thumbs-up.

"Look how excited he is," Emery urged, grinning and returning the thumbs-up.

"I'm looking," I said, but my eyes were latched onto Pythie being hefted out of the box by Ian and Roger. Emery placed his hand on my back as the men stretched the hideous thing across the stage.

"Everyone, spread out and choose a section," Ian instructed, pinning its head to the floor.

Chazz ran for the head.

"Not the head, Chazz!" I yelled, pointing at the snake's center. "The middle! The middle!"

Hearing my voice but not the command, my smiling brother waved and parked himself next to Ian and the thing's head.

Emery's hand moved to my shoulder. "Chazz is safe, Cassidy."

"I know," I said, covering my eyes. "Tell me when it's over."

"All right, everyone. Get a good grip. On the count of three—"

As if *red alert* suddenly flashed in my head, my senses sharpened. *What's wrong?* I asked myself, opening my eyes. *Something is wrong.*

"Three—"

Instinctively, I shifted into a low crouch, eyes darting around the room. I inhaled deeply.

"Two—"

"What is it?" Emery whispered anxiously. He gripped my shoulder.

My mind zeroed in on a new scent, one just entering the premises. I had smelled it earlier today. *Where?* I shut my eyes to think. *When we were walking around, in the Night-and-Day Exhibit—*

"Heave-*ho*!"

My eyes popped open. "Bats," I gasped.

Emery grabbed me.

The lights went out.

In the midst of startled voices, I could hear the bats' wings flapping. Looking up, my eyes cut through the dark, and I quickly pinpointed them, counting seven. Only seconds had passed since the lights went out.

Eyes around me began adjusting to the dark. A woman screamed, "Over us! What is it?" Other screams followed as dim light from the high windows revealed the frantic silhouettes of the bats in flight. The bats chirped their fear, inaudible to human ears.

Chazz.

I shot my eyes to the stage. Covering his ears, Chazz sobbed my name. As I poised to spring for him, Emery's arms tightened around me. "Don't panic," he ordered.

"I'm not panicking." My voice was calm, my mind focused. "Let go. I need to get Chazz."

Hesitantly, Emery released me.

"Don't turn on the lantern until I call your name," I instructed, glimpsing the surprise on his face as I sprung. He had forgotten about the lanterns.

Leading with my arms, I soared toward the stage. Thankfully, no one between the stage and me stood up; otherwise I would have clipped a few heads. Grabbing the edge of the stage, I flipped over and up onto my feet.

"The doors are locked!" a man yelled as I zipped to Chazz. The information created a new wave of hysteria. A body slammed against the doors, rattling them.

"Chazz, I'm here," I said in his ear, gathering him up.

"I can't see," he wept, clinging to my neck.

"You're safe," I reassured, and shouted at the top of my lungs, "EMERY!"

"The emergency door is locked, too!" someone else yelled. More screaming.

A lantern lit like a beacon. From the stage, I glimpsed Emery in the mayhem squatted next to the lantern, holding Ethan. Other lanterns flicked on as I carried Chazz from the stage, swiftly maneuvering through the confusion. Panic began to ebb with the soft glow filling the room. Huddled on the floor, my friends had their arms protectively around their campers and other children, fearfully watching for bats. I was proud of the girls for keeping their heads.

"What a nightmare," I said a little too loudly, causing Emery to jolt. As he turned to me, I spotted the python weaving toward us from a dozen feet away. "Take Chazz!" I shoved my brother onto Emery's free hip. Ethan occupied the other.

Emery blinked at me as if I were out of focus. Since he hadn't taken hold of Chazz, I grabbed his arm and threw it around my brother. Finally his gaze lowered to Chazz.

"Cassidy!" Chazz screamed, wide-eyed, comprehending that he was no longer in my arms.

Darting away, I straddled the python, pressing its head hard to the floor. The python thrashed. I pressed the head down more firmly, and felt its tail graze my cheek. I shuddered violently at the touch, and my skin seemed to shudder, too. A rippling sensation shot down my body to my feet, leaving behind skin that felt tight and numb, as if stretched over bones and muscle.

The snake stopped thrashing. Its body lifted in a controlled, purposeful way and began rapidly looping around me. Scales skimmed my neck, which confusingly felt like the light brush of a feather.

My mind must have dulled my nerve endings, causing me to lose the sense of touch, I deduced as the snake continued coiling. I couldn't figure out if this was a bad thing or a good thing, but decided it was a good thing a second later when the snake's body constricted.

Feeling the strength of the squeeze, I marveled that I had not been crushed like a soda can.

"Cassidy!" Emery shouted. Wrapped in the python, I watched him jet over. "Don't kill it," he ordered anxiously, skidding on his knees to me.

"Don't kill it?" As I exhaled my words, the coils tightened. "*It's* trying to kill *me*. Get it off before I lose it and the python goes flying everywhere." I had resisted breaking free because I didn't want to traumatize all these poor little kids any more than they already were.

Miriam released a piercing shriek. "No!" She ran towards me, fear and fury blazing on her face. Launching at the python, she punched it. The snake constricted more.

"No, Miriam!" Emery grabbed her fist. "Help me unwrap the body."

Wide-eyed, she nodded, grasping the python above Emery's hold.

"Where's Chazz?" I asked.

Emery pried off the tail. "With Bren and Carli."

Ian appeared. "My, oh my. What do we have here?" he said, taking hold of the snake. He tried to sound carefree, but his expression gave him away. "Pythie is only giving you a hug," he reassured me as he, Emery, and Miriam worked off another loop. People behind me collected the body from their hands. "If this python wanted to hurt you, you and I wouldn't be talking."

I laughed, and Ian looked at me with surprise. He had no idea how much this snake wanted to hurt me.

"That's the spirit!" he encouraged, uncoiling. He took a closer look at me. "Hey, you're a pretty little thing." He handed off more python. "If you were a few years older, there'd be some trouble." He winked, and silly me blushed. Even wrapped in a python, I couldn't take a compliment.

Seconds later, I was free. While others behind me held the snake's body down, I kept its head pinned to the floor.

"It's all right to let go now," Ian soothed.

"No. It's angry. It'll hurt someone." Proving me right, the python savagely jerked its head. I held it down more firmly.

Ian chuckled. "You've got quite a hold on that python. Now, look." He motioned to the people behind me holding down the body. "Pythie is the only one in danger here. He isn't an aggressive snake. Before you attacked him, he was just minding his own business, trying to find a good place to hide." Ian touched the top of my hands. A bewildered expression crossed his face, and I wondered if my skin felt weird to the touch, too. His confused expression gave way to his charming, cock-eyed smile. "Now, please let this poor snake go," he coaxed, patting my hands.

I exhaled a yielding breath. What did I know about snakes, anyway? "You're the expert," I said, and released the python. Instantly, the tension left its body, and it lay perfectly still, exhausted from the struggle.

"See how happy you've made him?" Ian cooed, stroking the snake's head.

Roger appeared with the box. His face puckered with irritation. "*You*—off," he commanded me.

"Rog, don't be harsh," Ian scolded good-naturedly. "She was only playing hero."

I smiled at Ian. He smiled back. "Thank you," I said.

"Sure thing, and I hope I never get into a tangle with you. You're a scary girl," he teased.

You have no idea, I thought, rising to my feet and stepping away from the snake.

Chazz threw his arms around my waist. "I thought you were dead," he wept.

Lifting him into my arms, I told him, "No, buddy. I'd never do that to you." Upon saying this, I thought it a mighty strange thing to say.

Chazz's reply was even stranger. "I know you wouldn't." He snuggled his nose into the crook of my neck and whispered, "Because you're going to live forever."

~~~

The police arrived on the scene fifteen minutes into the ordeal. Someone in the auditorium had called 911 on a cell phone when the doors were discovered locked. While the police broke the lock, one name nagged my mind: James Flynn.

Campers whose parents were present were escorted in a group to the parking lot by two armed police officers, while other police officers searched the zoo with flashlights for the perpetrator. Two stayed in the auditorium with kids waiting for their parents to collect them, as more manned the main gate, keeping frantic parents from rushing the zoo.

While we waited for Dad and Mr. Cohen to pick us up, I was relieved to discover that no one had seen me pounce Pythie. In fact, my friends were surprised to learn that I had left them to rescue Chazz, believing I had been with them until Miriam noticed me coiled in the snake. When the girls' conversation moved to the bats, now nesting in the high rafters, Emery explained in a whisper that I had appeared and disappeared before him like an apparition. He said the instant he comprehended I was there, shoving Chazz into his arms, I was suddenly gone again. Then he glanced around and spotted me wrapped in the python. He said he actually rubbed his eyes to make sure that he wasn't hallucinating.

Eventually it was our turn to be escorted out. After we girls hugged Carli goodbye, the five of us huddled under the police officer's huge umbrella while the other officer in rain gear walked alongside us, his hand on his holstered gun. Emery offered to carry Chazz, but my brother only wanted me. He clung to me as if for dear life.

The rain pounded as we progressed toward the main gate, each of us on the alert and wary—no one more so than I. A couple hundred yards from the auditorium, my ears picked up a disturbance. Stopping dead in my tracks, I concentrated.

"On your feet!" I heard a man yell from somewhere in the zoo. Focusing on his voice, I was dimly aware of the police officer with the gun inquiring why I had stopped walking.

"He can't get on his feet. He's intoxicated," a woman replied. Her words were softer and more difficult to make out. Her next words, however, were very loud and very urgent. "The gate to the habitat! It's open! Schuler, is the tiger—"

"No!" I gasped.

Hands gripped me. Jerking my chin up, I looked into the face of the police officer with the gun.

He jostled me. "Are you all right?" he demanded, as a dispatch came over his portable radio.

"All units, the tiger has escaped. I repeat, the tiger has escaped."

Six

The Man With The Plan

Mr. Cohen sat in the passenger seat of our minivan. Bren and Carli sat behind him and Dad. Too miserable for words, I dragged Chazz and his booster seat to the very back with me. Emery sat next to me. Once we had all clambered into the car, Dad hopped on his cell phone, drawing information from his police contacts. He learned what I already knew. James Flynn, discovered intoxicated at Roga's habitat, was the prime suspect in both crimes occurring this evening.

Yammering a mile a minute, Miriam and Bren gave the dads the lowdown, while Emery and I participated when a question was directed our way, but otherwise remained silent in our guilt. Lives would not be at risk if we had reported what I overheard to Mrs. Cooper, and if any were lost, that would be our fault, too. We had made our choice, and now others might pay the price for that choice.

My eyes misted at this thought. *I couldn't live with myself if Roga hurt anyone*, I told myself, stroking my sleeping brother's hair. *What if Roga kills a little boy like Chazz?* A slow, warm tear rolled down my cheek.

"Cassidy, this is my fault, not yours," Emery said so softly that only my ears could hear him—not that anyone else could have, with Miriam and Bren talking over one another.

Turning my head from Chazz's peaceful face, I looked into Emery's bleak one. Seeing my tears, he seemed to grow angrier with himself. Emery had a bad habit of shouldering blame, taking responsibility that wasn't his. Giving up

Stanford to play watchdog to me was a prime example of this noble flaw of his.

"You can't take all the blame," I whispered. "I decided to keep my mouth shut. *I* did. At the time, it seemed like the wisest thing to do. Hindsight is always twenty/twenty."

Dad's worried eyes caught mine in the rearview mirror. He couldn't hear me, but could see the distress on my face. I managed a smile for him, and he managed one for me before shifting his gaze back to the freeway.

"We made a mistake," I continued, watching Dad frown at the road. "Now we need to fix it."

"Yes, we do."

I looked at Emery and knew by his expression that he had a plan. I had a pretty good idea what it entailed.

"How far are you willing to go?" Emery asked.

"I'm willing to hunt a tiger."

He smiled. "That makes two of us."

~~~

After dropping our passengers off, Dad pulled into our driveway. Our front door flew open immediately, and Mom ran out. Nate and Bobby Neigh followed her.

"No," I groaned. "I can't handle Bobby tonight." What can I say? Bobby was a Bobby, the epitome of a fifteen-year-old male driven by hormones.

Gangly and cute in a dopey sort of way, Bobby had a mess of brown curls, a quick grin, and a new girlfriend like every five minutes. His whirlwind romances were notorious, and always ended badly, the latest of which was with Ashley Butcher. After a couple weeks of finger-down-your-throat displays of affection in the school hallways, Bobby had decided to call it quits in a text message that he'd sent from science class. When Ashley received the text in our Spanish class, she'd let out a blood-curdling scream that caused Mr. Sanchez to throw himself against the smart board in shock, hugging his heart. Ashley had become quite inconsolable after this. Mr. Sanchez had excused her to the restroom, sending Paris Townsend along for moral support, where the girls had defaced the walls—with all sorts of things I would have preferred to have never known about Bobby Neigh—in purple sharpie pen. This was about a week ago. I figure "Boshley" would be back on again by the end of next week. Bobby was all about the drama.

He had asked me out once when we were in seventh grade, and thanks to my parents' rule about no dating until we could legally drive, I was able to let him down easy. His reaction had been to shrug and go back to mercilessly harassing me.

"Bobby will be relentless when he finds out about the python," I whined to Emery as Dad climbed out of the car. The boys intercepted Dad while Mom made her way to our door.

"Yes, he will," agreed Emery—unsympathetically, I might add. "Call me when you go out tonight."

I scowled at Bobby, who was waving his arms exuberantly at me through the front windshield, as if trying to halt traffic. This was going to be a long night.

The door slid open, and Mom stared crazed at us. When stressed, she can be slightly intense. "Oh, dear," she said in a pained voice. Emery quickly stepped out of the van so she could duck in. Her hand made contact with my hoodie, and she exclaimed in horror, "You're drenched!" Her hand shot to Chazz's chest. Out like a light, he snored. "You're both drenched!"

"It was raining pretty hard when we ran for the car," I explained as she leaned over me, frantically unbuckling my brother. The downpour had abruptly ceased when we reached Seattle's city limits.

After scooping Chazz out of the van and complaining about how we were all soaked to the bone, she scooted me toward the house and told Emery to go home and change his clothes, as if he wouldn't have thought of this on his own. Then she paused, took a deep breath, and composed herself. Exhaling, her face relaxed. I could almost read her thoughts: *My children are safe. All is well again.*

Sedate, she smiled at Emery. "Why don't you join us for breakfast around nine tomorrow? And please invite your mother for me. I would love to see her."

"Thank you, Mrs. Jones. I will." He hoisted his backpack onto his shoulder. "Good night. See you all in the morning." After everyone wished him a goodnight, too, he walked down the driveway, reminding me under his breath, "Don't forget to call."

As if I could, I replied silently. We had much to discuss, such as what I would do with Roga once I found him.

~~~

While Mom got Chazz ready for bed in his room, Nate and Bobby hung out with Dad in our parents' room, peppering him with questions while he changed his clothes. From my bedroom, I listened with dismay as Dad answered *all* of their questions. *The boys will never let me live this down*, I thought, tugging on sweats. *Bobby will blab to everyone.* I fantasized briefly that it was Jared spending the night instead of Bobby, like he used to almost every weekend before I screwed everything up. Then I remembered what Dad had shared and was really glad my fantasy was only wishful thinking. Facing Bobby would be bad enough.

While I pulled on socks, Dad and the boys headed downstairs to watch the news. Seconds later, I heard Chazz's door close quietly. Then Mom knocked on mine.

"Cass, join us downstairs," she said softly.

"I will," I replied tightly.

Getting up from my bed, I walked over to my dresser and took a look in the mirror. My hair was a disaster! Swiping up a brush, I began detangling the wet, red mess while mentally preparing witty responses for every tease I could conjure up Nate and Bobby unleashing on me.

Of course, the first thing to come from my twin's mouth when I entered the family room was a rib I hadn't anticipated.

"So, Cass, was the python, like, this long?" Nate held his index finger and thumb two inches apart. Sitting next to him on the sectional, Bobby gave me a harassing grin. I rolled my eyes and headed for a spot between Nate and Mom, who cuddled with Dad as he flipped through channels. Dad's channel surfing meant Channel Five News was on a commercial break. He always channel surfs during commercials.

"About two hundred times that," I answered my brother, and began edging past Bobby's knees and the ottoman. His feet trapped mine, and Nate swung his leg onto the ottoman to block my progress.

"I'm not doing the math," he informed me.

"Like you could."

"Burn!" Bobby mocked Nate.

I slid my foot from his "trap" and ground my heel into it.

"Dude!" he laughed, extracting his foot. "You're brutal!"

"*Dude*, you have no idea." Shoving Nate's leg off the ottoman, I plopped down next to Mom. She gave me a look for the violence.

"He started it," I mumbled, then answered Nate. "Thirteen feet. We'll do more Q&A, like, *never*." No way was I giving Bobby Neigh more ammunition than he already had.

"Man, you're cranky," Nate remarked.

Bobby snickered like an imbecile.

Dad flipped back to Channel Five News. The broadcast had already returned. Dad's colleague and head anchor, Dale Daniels, somberly reported, "Local law enforcement is advising residents and their pets to stay indoors—"

My heart plummeted. "They haven't found Roga," I dismally stated the obvious.

"Roga's the tiger?" Nate asked, putting his feet back on the ottoman.

"Yeah," I breathed.

"Tracking experts are being flown to Seattle this evening to help locate the Siberian tiger. Among these experts is *Big Game* host, Leroy Rays—"

Bobby sprung up. "Leroy Rays! Kick butt!" he declared, pumping his fist.

"Is *Big Game*, like, a hunting show?" I guessed.

"Yep," said Nate. "It's on cable." His mouth turned up impishly. "Right after *Reptile Rescue*."

Bobby laughed at my expense. I kicked my oh-so-clever brother's feet off the ottoman.

"Nate, behave yourself," Dad warned. Thinking the warning sounded a little half-hearted, I looked over at him. The slight grin turning up his mouth confirmed my suspicion. Having once been a tormenting brother himself, everything Nate said and did entertained him.

"Psst, Cassidy," Bobby whispered.

I looked at him and thought, *Bring it on, Neigh*.

"Why aren't you...?" He mashed his palms together, sliding them in a crushing motion. This was his way of asking why I wasn't dead.

"Obviously because I have superhuman strength." I smiled at my personal joke, then squinted at Bobby, reminding him, "Didn't I say something about no Q&A?"

Ignoring the question, he pressed on as if we were having the conversation I so wasn't going to have with him. "You and a python." He shook his head, attempting to look baffled. "I can't picture it."

"Don't try too hard. You might hurt yourself."

"Cassidy," Mom scolded me for my rudeness. She didn't understand Bobby thrived on rudeness.

Thriving, a goofy expression came on his face, as if a light bulb suddenly turned on in his pubescent brain. "Dude!" he said to me. "I totally see it now—the picture—and it's *hilarious*!"

"Thank heavens, I can't see it. Anything in your head—" I cut myself short, making a *brrr* sound and shaking all over.

Mom gave my forearm a little swat as half-hearted as Dad's warning to Nate had been.

"Now, stick Miriam in your picture," Nate suggested devilishly to his friend. "Beatin' on that mean ol' python." Bobby doubled over with laughter, slapping my brother a congratulatory high-five. I gave my brother a congratulatory whack in the face with a throw pillow.

"Settle down," Dad ordered. "I want to be able to hear this interview coming up."

The broadcast switched to a live interview with a bartender at a place called Finnigan's Irish Pub. I remembered seeing this bar next to a restaurant called Jerry's near the I-90 freeway entrance by Catamount Mountain Road.

The bartender, Eric Schmidt, claimed to have served James Flynn a few drinks earlier this evening, before Flynn became belligerent, rambling on and on about the tiger. When Schmidt asked him to leave, Flynn refused, forcing the bartender "to show him the door." That's what Schmidt said, "Show him the door." I believed he meant it literally, because there was no question in my mind that when Eric Schmidt, a burly German man with hard blue eyes and shoulder-length blond hair, told someone to skedaddle, they would be wise to do just that.

~~~

Dressed in black, I lay on top of my colorful bed quilt in the dark, reading *Wuthering Heights*. Just at the part when Heathcliff learns Cathy accepted Edgar Linton's marriage proposal, my alarm clock glowed *12:00*. Reluctantly, I placed my bookmark on the page I had been reading. I really wanted to find out what happened next, but duty called. I had two responsibilities to fulfill tonight. Well, three, if I counted working off excess energy as one.

Swinging my legs over the side of the bed and sitting up, I yanked open the nightstand drawer and dug out my ski mask and iPhone. Standing, I pulled on the mask, tucked in my ponytail, slipped the phone into my sweatpants pocket, and swiped up the twenty-dollar bill for Joe. Thanks to Serena, I had cash to burn.

When Emery devised the housecleaning cover, I had refused to take Serena's money until she pointed out that I couldn't very well "work" for free. So to justify accepting the twenty-dollar bill that she handed me on Fridays, I viewed it as payment for household *and* lab services. My diseased blood had to be worth something.

After tucking the bill into my windbreaker pocket, I did a back flip to the window, landing on my feet as silent as a cat. Opening the window, my heart quickened with excitement as it does every night when I go out. Nighttime was the only time of day I was free to be what I had become.

Crouching on the windowsill, I sprang. My feet planted solidly on the grass in our side yard. Straightening up, I shot my eyes to Emery's house. His bedroom light was on and the curtains were open. Obviously he was up, waiting for my phone call. As I slipped my hand in my pocket for the phone, an idea cropped up in my head.

We should hammer out details in person, I decided, and without giving the impulse a second thought, I darted across the street and leapt onto the overhang that covered Emery's front porch. It only occurred to me after looking into his bedroom window, glimpsing him stretched out on his bed, plucking away at his laptop, that I should have texted before dropping in like this, in case he was indecent or anything.

Fortunately for us both, Emery was fully clothed in basketball shorts and a graphic T.

Focused on the laptop, Emery didn't notice me at the window. When I tapped on the glass, he startled, but not enough to send the laptop flying.

"Cassidy," he sighed to himself, without looking at the window.

Under the mask, a grin spread across my face. Emery's reaction was so Emery, so "nerves of steel."

Calmly, he struck a few more keys before closing the laptop. Setting it on the bed, he finally turned to the window. I waved at him exuberantly. With an eye roll, he pushed himself up and walked over leisurely and slid the window open. "Please tell me you don't make a habit of this," he said, scanning the street beyond me.

"Didn't you know I check up on you every night?" I teased.

Emery stared at me with uncertainty.

I managed not to smile. I couldn't believe he'd fallen for it. How sweet to have the upper hand for a change. "Well, aren't you going to ask me in?"

Stepping back, Emery made a formal *come in* gesture. "Please. Be my guest."

"You're inviting in a mutant, not a vampire." I hopped into his room. "I haven't bitten anything—yet."

Emery closed the window and drew the curtains. Keeping my back to him, I rolled the mask up my grinning face. "I'd like to say you sleep like an angel, but I can't," I told him.

He didn't respond.

"Not that you don't look like an angel when you're asleep, because you *so* do." I tossed the mask on his dresser. "It's just all that snoring—"

Emery chuckled, and I swung around to him. Smiling appreciatively, he wagged a finger. "You had me for a second," he confessed.

I caught his finger. "Is it impossible to believe that *you* snore?"

"Yes." He wiggled his finger free. "Would you mind explaining why you were lurking outside my window?"

"You wanted to talk, remember?" I said, glancing around his too-neat room. Everything was either brown or black, except for the walls. They were stark white and empty, unlike mine, which were plastered with posters, pictures of family and friends, and each painted a different color from my bed quilt.

"Your room is depressing!" I declared, motioning to the blank walls. "You need to hang something up, like a poster of the Periodic Table or Einstein or something. And *where* are the piles of dirty clothes? You are a teenager, you know. What teenager doesn't have clothes thrown everywhere?"

"I have something called a hamper," Emery quipped. "You should really try using one sometime. And this may surprise you, but I find Madame Curie much more appealing to look at than Albert."

"Yes, she was quite the looker," I conceded, snatching a hoodie from the hook on the back of his door. "A poster of Madame Curie. I'm on it." Stretching my arm high, I dropped the hoodie. Emery caught it before it hit the floor.

Returning the hoodie to the hook, he said, "Are you here only to annoy me, or would you like to discuss tomorrow night's endeavor, if Roga isn't captured by then?"

"Tomorrow night's endeavor. I can annoy you later."

"I've no doubt of that." He swung the chair around from his desk and motioned for me to sit, which I did. Parking himself opposite me on the bed, Emery got down to business. "Will you be able to recognize Roga's scent?"

"Definitely. I'll have no problem picking up his trail. Question: What do I do with him when I find him?"

"You won't do anything. I'll take care of Roga."

I didn't like the sound of this. "What do you mean you'll 'take care' of Roga?"

"I'm capturing him chemically," Emery explained. "I'm acquiring a tranquilizer rifle and darts tomorrow."

I eyed him. "What exactly do you mean by *acquiring*?"

"What I mean is, I don't presently have a tranquilizer rifle in my possession, but will by tomorrow evening." He flashed a smile.

"I wasn't asking for a definition!" I snapped.

His expression grew more amused.

"Oh, my gosh, Emery! What the heck are you up to now? *Please* tell me nothing illegal—again!"

"Relax." He waved a dismissive hand.

A muscle jerked in my jaw. I hated being pacified. Anyone who knows Emery—*really* knows Emery—knows concern is completely warranted. When he's in mission mode, boundaries can get a little blurry for him, along with the law.

Emery assured me, "My hunting license is current, so it is *legal* for me to have a rifle in my possession. Granted, I'm not supposed to use a firearm without adult supervision, and we won't have any of *that*. Perhaps I won't need to break the law if Roga—"

"Why do you have a hunting license? You don't hunt!"

"True, but nevertheless, I have one."

"You *hacked* into some computer to get it!" I said, pointing an accusing finger at him. Computer network hacking is one of Emery's many specialties. He is also very handy with lock picks. My eyes darted to the laptop. "What were you doing on the laptop?"

Twisting around, Emery retrieved the laptop nonchalantly. Turning back to me, he opened the screen with a smile. Paused on the screen was the online role-playing game *Gods and Kings*.

I smirked. "Yeah, right. *You* were playing *Gods and Kings*."

He angled the laptop so he could see the screen, too. "It's a lot more difficult than you would think," he insisted, his expression oh-so-innocent. "Highly strategic, and collecting 'jewels' is—"

"Pull up the page under that stupid game," I challenged smugly. I figured *Gods and Kings* was a decoy, hiding some guns and ammo website he had found a way to order a tranquilizer rifle from. A rifle and darts were probably being FedExed to his house at this very moment.

Emery didn't pull up the window. He just stared at me and asked, "Do you trust me, Cassidy?"

His question threw me off.

"With my life," I assured without hesitation. My protector, my guardian, my friend deserved no less than my absolute trust.

Emery's eyes softened. "Thank you, and likewise." His tone, the look on his face made me feel all mushy inside. Emery could be so sweet at times.

"Now that we've squared that away," he announced abruptly, slapping his knees, "you should go." Before I knew what was going on, Emery was on his feet, pulling me to mine and toward the window.

"You're trying to get rid of me," I complained as he plucked up my mask, dragging me along.

"Don't be silly." He yanked the mask over my head—backwards. "If Roga isn't captured by tomorrow evening, we'll meet at your fence line eleven sharp," he instructed, opening the curtains and window while I wrestled the mask around with gritted teeth. "I know we'll be taking a chance leaving earlier than you normally go out, but Catamount Mountain is a fair distance away, and I don't know how long we'll be there."

"How are we getting there?" I asked, peering at him through the eyeholes I had just situated. "Bus lines don't run that far."

Emery scanned the street. "Transportation is a particular you'll have to trust me on." He glanced over his shoulder at me and frowned. "Your hair, Cassidy," he said with exasperation, grabbing my ponytail. "Always hide it. The color is too memorable."

He pulled the back of the mask off my neck and began shoving the ponytail up into it. I was so irked with myself for agreeing to trust him blindly that I let him.

"Makes sense to keep me in the dark," I grumbled, arms crossed, as Emery tucked loose pieces of hair into the mask like a mother hen. "I am just brainless muscle."

"Hardly brainless," he corrected, amused. "But definitely muscle."

I scowled.

"Oh, all right," he said as if relenting.

I deepened my frown to let him know I knew he was full of it. He wasn't going to tell me squat.

"One clue: You won't like our means of transportation."

As I said, *squat*.

"Well, that's reassuring," I retorted, shouldering past him to the window. Sometimes Emery could be a real pain in the rear.

"Is your phone on?" he had the nerve to ask.

I laughed at the irony. "So you can track me?" I held up the phone and placed my thumb over the power-down button. "Trust is a two-way street, dude." I pressed the button. "See you at breakfast."

I dove through the window and disappeared into the night.

Seven

Ben's Life-Altering Experience

The delicious aroma of bacon roused me out of sleep in the morning. Sizzling fat wasn't such a bad thing to wake up to.

Yawning, I tuned into the kitchen, hearing jovial voices, the clicking of pots and pans, and other breakfast preparation noises. Emery's voice was among the happy chatter, but not Serena's, which was no surprise. The surprise would have been if she had come. Serena rarely emerged from her basement during daylight hours, obsessed as she was with studying my mutant-virus and recreating Formula 10X.

Fine-tuning my hearing, I listened with a scowl to Bobby and Nate badger Emery for a rundown of the python "attack," which Emery slickly evaded giving—thank heavens. When he managed to move the subject to yesterday's Seahawks game, I switched frequencies to Mom, who was talking with Grandma Jean on the phone. They discussed the zoo, of course. Being sick of the topic, I severed the connection and thought instead about my visit with Joe the night before, which had basically circulated around the topic I was sick of. That was my fault, though, since the first thing out of my mouth after startling him out of sleep was: "Joe, did you hear about the tiger that a deranged zookeeper set free?"

After recovering from his initial shock that I had come back, Joe had climbed out of Moses and asked, looking around nervously, "Did you say somethin' about a tiger runnin' loose?"

I realized then that I had neglected to clarify which zoo Roga had escaped from. "Oh, the tiger didn't escape from Woodland Park Zoo. He escaped from Catamount Mountain Zoo, which is miles and miles away."

Joe had never heard of Catamount Mountain Zoo and confessed that he didn't know much about the outlying areas of Seattle.

This led to my next obvious question: "Where are you from?"

"Oh, from here and there," he answered vaguely, obviously not wanting to talk about himself. "Tell me more about the tiger."

I presented each incident as if I had heard about them and not experienced them. I didn't fool Old Joe, though. I could see in his eyes that he knew I hadn't only been one of the 140 people trapped in the auditorium—I was the person who had pinned the python.

He didn't come out and admit this, though. In fact, he didn't ask any personal questions, except one: "Were you born this way?"

To which I replied: "No, it was an accident. Sort of like what happened to Peter Parker. You know, being bit by a radioactive spider."

Joe just nodded, while looking off at something only he could see.

When it was time for me to go, I took out the twenty-dollar bill and instantly regretted doing so. My cheeks burned under the mask as Joe stared at the folded bill in my hand, looking conflicted. He needed the money, but didn't want to take it from me.

He ended the awkward moment by smiling and saying, "Now that's real thoughtful, but you keep your money. I'll tell you what, though. I've had a hankerin' for home-baked oatmeal raisin cookies."

Joe had no idea how much I'd rather he just take the money.

"Well, okay," I replied brightly, cringing inside. I had never baked cookies in my life. Like Serena, I avoided kitchens. "Homemade oatmeal raisin cookies, it is! See you soon, Joe."

"I hope so," he said sadly. The look on his face broke my heart.

"No need to hope, because you will." I stuck out my hand for him to shake, because it seemed the right thing to do.

Sadness melting from his face, he took my hand. "Thank you, Green Eyes." He shook firmly. "I look forward to it." I had a feeling it had been a long time since Joe had shaken hands with anyone.

"Me, too," I said, and shot off.

Behind me, I heard Joe say to himself, "Oh, lordy, lordy, lordy, lordy."

My gut told me then, as it told me now, that somehow he would play an important role in my life. What that role would be I wasn't sure, though I suspected it would be that of a friend, a friend who accepted me for what I am, which really is no small thing when you think about it.

"A homeless man and a mutant destined to be friends—who would have thought?" I said to myself, stretching. "Now all I have to do is figure out how to make cookies." Rising from bed, I dressed and went downstairs.

~~~

At the island, Emery caught my eyes with his before I entered the kitchen from the hall. Without appearing to do so, he had been waiting for me as he poured orange juice into glasses, shooting the breeze with Bobby, who buttered toast. At the range behind them, Nate transferred bacon onto a platter while Dad scrambled eggs. Chazz stood at Dad's side, watching him push raw eggs around a large frying pan with a spatula.

The brief glance Emery gave me spoke volumes. Even without the advantage of GPS, he knew who I had visited last night and wasn't happy about it. If I had to put the look into words, it would have been something like: *You put yourself in danger, Cassidy. I won't allow you to take a risk like that again. However, this is not the time, nor the place to discuss this matter, while I'm in the midst of performing duo acts, the just-trying-to-fit-in-teenage-genius for your family and the-just-an-average-teenager for Neigh.*

If we were telepathic, he would hear me reply: *Yes, Emery, I took a risk and I plan to take it again. Joe needs a friend and somehow I need Joe. But agreed. We'll hash this out later when neither of us has to put on a show.*

Though he couldn't hear my thoughts, Emery seemed to get the gist. With a slight concurring nod, his mouth curved into a smile that said, *Showtime*.

Tossing on a smile myself, I walked into the kitchen as if nothing had transpired between Emery and me seconds beforehand. "So what's the status on Roga?" I asked.

Dad looked over his shoulder and smiled. "Good morning, sweetheart! Unfortunately, the status hasn't changed. The tiger hasn't been sighted yet." He glanced down at Chazz. "Would you let Mommy know breakfast is ready?"

"Okey-dokey, Artichokey," Chazz replied and spun around. Beaming, he threw his arms around my waist. "I love you so much!" he declared, squeezing me, then darted away, my "love you, too" trailing after him.

"Good of you to join us," Nate harassed, sauntering by with the platter of bacon. I snagged a piece.

"I was tired, okay?" I snapped, and nibbled the bacon. My eyes rolled in ecstasy. Enhanced taste buds were the bomb. I parked myself next to Emery, and Bobby yowled like a cat for some reason.

Setting the bacon on the table, Nate slapped his forehead. "Silly ol' me. I almost forgot." He turned around, grinning. "You need extra beauty sleep."

I crossed my eyes and stuck out my tongue.

"I think you needed a few more minutes, Sunshine," Bobby told me, and reached for my face. His fingers were poised to pinch. Once they entered a twelve-inch radius of me, however, they'd find themselves in a nasty finger lock.

"Not wise," Emery warned him, smoothly placing a juice glass in Bobby's outstretched hand. "Make yourself useful," he said, then lowered his voice so my dad couldn't hear, "In my opinion, she's had plenty."

My jaw dropped. How in any realm of the imagination did a remark like that suggest "strictly friends"?

"You *dawg*!" Bobby laughed, and snapped up another glass to take to the table.

"At least *someone* has some decorum around here," I sent after him. Bobby looked back at me and puckered his lips. I pointed at my mouth in a *puke* gesture.

"Dude, how can you handle all her fancy words?" Nate teased Emery.

Emery and Bobby busted up for different reasons. Emery understood Nate's covert rib about all of his "fancy" words, where Bobby, unaware Emery knew any beyond three syllables, presumed Nate was giving me a bad time.

"I guess I'm just a fancy guy," Emery replied when he finished laughing.

"A fancy guy who doesn't like braggin' about his girlfriend," Bobby added.

Dad glanced over his shoulder at us, and I felt my face flush. It was bad enough I got this at school, but not in my own home. Not in front of my dad!

"Dude, if my girlfriend took down a py—"

I delivered a sharp jab to Bobby's arm. Wincing, he grabbed it, as Emery shot me a warning look, but I didn't care. Bobby wasn't getting away with needling me.

"Geez." He massaged the spot I had hit. "So violent." He shook his head. "Man, I feel for that python."

"You should, since you're a direct descendant. And for your information, I am *nobody's* girlfriend!"

Bobby picked up a juice glass. "Here, Nobody." He handed the glass to Emery. "Make yourself useful."

Emery and Nate sputtered into laughter, while it was all I could do to keep from tackling Bobby to the floor.

"Cassidy," Dad called, "please take the hash browns to the table."

Throwing Bobby a dagger-glare, I turned away and stomped to the range. Dad held out a platter of hash browns. "Boys will be boys," he commiserated while the boys continued harassing one another.

"I hate boys," I growled, taking the platter.

Dad grinned. "Music to my ears."

~~~

We had just served up breakfast when the doorbell rang. Our third guest had arrived: Ben Johnson, Dad's cameraman, our honorary family member, and one of my most favorite people in the world.

"Chazz, would you please let Ben in?" asked Mom, seated at the end of the table between Bobby and me. From the other side of Emery, Chazz shot out of his chair and into the hall. After breakfast, Dad and Ben were heading up to Catamount Mountain, where Dad had an interview scheduled with Leroy Rays. Bobby just about had a heart attack when Dad shared this.

After an exuberant greeting with Chazz, Ben strolled into the kitchen with my little brother on his back and a sunny smile on his face. Tall and lanky and twenty-three, he had skin the color of a café mocha, happy amber eyes, and wild corkscrew hair that was currently held back with a red bandana. Though we were on the threshold of winter, Ben dressed like it was summer, in faded jeans, flip-flops, and a mustard-colored T-shirt advertising a surf shop in Costa Rica.

"Hi, all," he greeted, plopping Chazz in the chair next to Dad. He patted Dad's shoulders and sat down. "How's it goin', boys?" he asked, lightly thumping Nate's chest with the back of his hand. "Keepin' up with the soccer?"

"Keepin' up," Bobby responded with a mouthful of food.

"Whenever my mom lets me out of the house." Nate flashed her a smile.

"I know how tough she is, dude," Ben commiserated, winking at Mom. "Betcha never get out." He rustled Nate's hair and picked up the egg platter. "What about you, Emery?" he asked, heaping eggs onto his plate. His interest was understandable, since he had taught Emery how to play soccer.

"I play a couple times a week," Emery answered.

Ben's hand paused over the bacon plate. He looked at Emery. "Why only a couple?"

"Well, you know, all the homework," Emery said, teasing. Ben knew high school work for Emery was equivalent to him doing dot-to-dots.

"Bet you're struggling to keep up," Ben teased back. His hovering hand nabbed six strips of bacon. "But, not getting out to the field?" He shook his head and scraped hash browns onto his plate. "It's a shameful waste of athletic prowess." He thumped Nate's chest again. "And what kind of friend lets his bud waste his God-given talent like that?"

"Like Em said" —Nate grinned impishly at the strip of bacon he was about to eat— "he has a lot of homework."

Bobby snickered, and I narrowed my eyes on my twin. These boys didn't know when to let up. Cutting my glare sidelong to Emery, I saw that he thoroughly appreciated the harassment. *Flabbergasting!*

"So, Ben, were you able to reschedule your meeting?" asked Dad, his voice holding a teasing note. I looked at him, curious to see what he would dish out.

"Lucky for you, I was," Ben responded sportingly. He flipped his hand to the small mountain of food on his plate. "And it's a good thing you're feeding me so well, because I'm bummed about cancelling."

Oh, I thought, knowing what meeting Ben referred to, but why he would challenge my dad to rib him about it, I hadn't a clue. I was beginning to feel like Jane Goodall observing the strange ways apes interacted.

"Pity you had to reschedule," Dad apologized, tongue-in-cheek. "I would have felt terrible if the NWSA's *other* member wasn't flexible about putting lattes on hold."

"Oh, Drake," Mom said, rolling her eyes. Ben's grin stretched the width of his face. I grinned, too. What can I say? Dad's joke was funny.

Ben held up two fingers. "The other *two* members, Drake. And may I ask what is so wrong about assembling over an exceptional cup of latte to discuss highly charged, ground-breaking information? And Lyuba makes those little leaf designs in the foam, and her ristretto—" He kissed his fingertips. "And *she* isn't so bad to look at, either."

Mom rolled her eyes again. Pinching the ridge of his nose, Dad chuckled. Ben shoved hash browns in his mouth. We kids eagerly looked on, waiting for more bantering.

Swallowing, Ben challenged, "I would think a news guy like you would be a little more interested in what we do."

"A news guy like me needs confirmable facts."

"The NWSA *has* facts. *You* just need to be open-minded."

"What's the NWSA?" Bobby piped up, looking confused. I would have been, too, if I hadn't had prior knowledge of the event that Ben claimed had awakened him to the possibility of extraterrestrial life forms, the existence of mythical creatures, and the government's desire to keep the public ignorant of these "truths." Why the government wanted to do this, Ben had never really clarified.

"You *had* to ask," Dad said, throwing his hands up in mock defeat.

"Of course he did." Ben reached around Nate to grip Bobby's shoulder. "Bobby here is an inquisitive guy. A *young* mind opened to different points of view."

Dad grinned at the "young" slam.

"You know it, dude!" Bobby said, slapping Ben a high-five.

I exchanged amused glances with Nate and Emery. We would see how open-minded Bobby was after Ben's story.

Ben began, "My two best buds, Howie and Tom, and me established the NWSA after a life-altering experience we had together. Before I tell you about the NWSA, you need to understand the experience.

"When we were kids, my dad took us boys on a fishing trip near Stevens Pass every summer. When we were thirteen, we hiked deeper into the wilderness than ever before, setting up camp near the river. During the day, everything was normal, expected, until the sun went down. Then things changed. Now, dude, you know I'm an avid camper and hiker. I've camped in some gnarly places, but what we experienced those five nights on this particular trip, well, I've never experienced since." Ben dropped his voice. "Around midnight, the woods became real still, not a cricket chirping, a frog croaking, or a mosquito buzzing, only the sound of the river's current."

While Ben's voice lowered, Bobby instinctively leaned in closer. Nate had pushed himself back in his chair so Bobby could do this. Staring at his plate, Nate wrestled a grin. I fought one, too, until it naturally dissipated. At "the woods," Chazz slid off his chair and ran straight to me. As he climbed into my lap, an alarm rang in my head, triggering a vision of him fingering a tear in the blood-splattered ninja costume I had thoughtlessly left on my bedroom floor. At the time, I was sure he had figured out that I was the purple-faced ninja who had saved our dad, but since that night, he had never given any indication of knowing—until his odd remark about me living forever.

Wishful thinking, I thought, dismissing the fear. *What little boy wouldn't hope that his sister would live forever, after believing a python almost crushed her?* I kissed his red head and sucked in air, preparing for some sweet revenge on Bobby. Cringing, Mom covered her ears.

Ben's voice was just above a whisper. "Then, out of the blue, we heard—" He and we Jones kids let out blood-curdling screams. Bobby threw himself back in the chair, and jerked around as if being riddled with bullets. When we did the same thing to Emery, he had barely blinked an eye.

"What the—" Bobby gasped, hand over his heart, watching us laugh. "Dudes! That's cruel. You could kill a guy screamin' like that!"

"Need to change your pants, Bobby?" Nate inquired, laughing.

"You wish!" Bobby put him in a headlock. Nate grabbed Bobby's midsection, pulling him to the floor, tipping the chairs on top of them. I laughed so hard that I thought *I* might wet my pants.

"Enough, boys. Come back to the table," Mom ordered. With a laugh, she indicated to dad that her ears were ringing.

Cupping his ear, Dad said, "What's that, dear? I can't hear you above the ringing."

Once the boys were seated again, Ben picked up where he had left off. "The first night we heard the shriek, Howie and Tom and I thought a woman was being murdered. It was *that* intense. Now, my dad, who always needs to come up with some comforting explanation, convinced himself that a bird was making all that noise. A bird? Crazy! He wasn't inclined to break down camp for a bird, but don't get me wrong. We boys weren't, either. That shriek was thrilling, and we were itching all day for nightfall to hear it again, especially when we realized each night it came closer to our campsite.

"Now, I have to agree with my dad in one respect. The shriek was by no means human. It was primitive, untamed, wild. On the fifth night, the sky was clear, and there was a full moon. The campfire was burning low, and the moonlight cast strange shadows. That dead silence fell all around us. We boys hunkered down in our sleeping bags, all wide-eyed and waiting.

"*Suddenly*, there was a loud cracking sound like a limb being ripped off a tree, and something real heavy-footed ran at us. Our pounding hearts were in our throats, and we could scarcely breathe as it came closer and closer. And then, letting out a wail like a banshee, was the most amazing creature I have ever seen.

"The shriek had been totally misleading, because the creature standing before us wasn't aggressive, just curious. Observing us with intelligent eyes, it walked upright like a man, but was covered head to toe in brown fur and stood over seven feet tall. After checking us out, the creature ran back into the w—"

"Wait a second," Bobby cut in, eyeing Ben suspiciously. "Are you talking about Bigfoot?"

"The Northwest Sasquatch Association—i.e. the NWSA—refers to the creature by its Native American name: Sasquatch."

Bobby stared at him in disbelief for a moment before busting up. "Dude, you had me going!" He laughed.

"No, it's true, Bobby," Chazz insisted. "Ben saw a real live Sasquatch, and it shrieked like a banshee. Right, Ben?"

"That's right, buddy," Ben confirmed, giving Chazz a warm smile. He wagged a finger at Bobby. "I ain't yankin' your chain, dude, and you can laugh when you've looked a Sasquatch in the eye. Believe me, it isn't an experience you'd soon forget."

"Now, Ben," Dad piped up, a glint in his eyes. "To present this experience fairly, shouldn't you give *all* eyewitness accounts?"

"Three to one! The odds are in the Sasquatch's favor."

"But according to Arlin, what you boys saw was a very large brown bear standing on its hind legs."

"Dad's in denial. What *bear* just strolls around on its hind legs?" Ben smiled and shook his head at the ludicrous idea.

I sputtered into laughter. Ben was simply the best!

His infectious smile turned to me. "Any girl who gets herself tangled up in a python has no room to laugh."

Well, I couldn't argue with that.

Eight

Grudgingly Resigned

Since the boys had made breakfast, according to Mom it was up to the girls to do the dishes. Oh, joy. So while the boys skateboarded out front, Mom and I cleaned up the breakfast mess, which wouldn't have been half as bad if we had similar definitions of "clean."

The phone rang while I was in the midst of scrubbing the disgusting frying pan Dad had made hash browns in and Mom scrupulously degreased the range. Letting the pan sink into the greasy, soapy water, I ran for the phone at the end of the counter. The caller was Bobby's mom. She needed to talk to him.

"I'm taking the handset to Bobby," I told Mom, eagerly exiting. With any luck, she would finish the pan while I was gone. She does things like that.

Opening the front door, I looked out. On the street, Nate helped Chazz balance on his skateboard while Bobby practiced kick flips on his. Emery wasn't with them, but I could smell him. I figured he was skateboarding somewhere down the street.

"Bobby! Your mom!" I called, holding up the handset. Trotting over, he dropped his skateboard on the grass and jetted up the porch steps. "Where's Emery?" I asked, handing him the phone.

"Talking to your neighbor," he told me, then said into the phone, "Whassup, Ma?"

"Neighbor?" Edging past him, I spotted Emery talking with Jason Crenshaw, the twenty-five-year-old bum son of our neighbors two doors over on our right. In a khaki trooper's jacket and ripped jeans, Jason leaned nonchalantly against his Jetta, smoking. I rarely saw the guy without a cigarette hanging out of his mouth.

Whassup, Emery? I thought, concentrating on his profile. Weeding through surrounding noise, I located his voice.

"Do we have a deal?" he asked Jason.

Jason blew a stream of smoke. "If you're good for it," he replied apathetically, though his hazel eyes revealed more, regarding Emery with troubling interest.

The handset suddenly blocked my view and broke my concentration, causing me to lose Emery and Jason's frequency.

"Earth to Cassidy," Bobby said, waving the phone in my face. I snatched it from him and looked back at Emery. To my frustration, the conversation had ended, and Emery was rolling away on his skateboard. I clenched my jaw, suspecting that he had spotted me and was now avoiding me.

"Em keeps some sketchy company," Bobby remarked, while we watched Jason comb a hand into his sandy-blond hair, a pleased smile forming around his cigarette. I ground my teeth, knowing why he smiled. Emery was so dead.

~~~~

Back in the kitchen, I cruised my memory bank for Jason Crenshaw facts while rushing through my remaining tasks. Intel was sparse, most of which had been gathered throughout the years from Mrs. DeAngelo, the neighborhood gossip, whose Dutch Colonial sat between our English Tudor and the Crenshaws' Victorian. According to Mrs. DeAngelo, Jason had been "the cat's meow" in high school, football player, swooning cheerleaders, the whole bit, but hadn't been the stellar student, due to lack of motivation, not intelligence. After graduation, she claimed Jason decided "he'd had enough with growing up" and planted himself on his parents' couch, where he remained to this day, playing "those darned computer games." I had a pretty good idea what one of those games was.

Emery, have you lost your mind?

"Mom," Nate said, coming into the kitchen, "Chazz is watching TV. Can Bobby and me go to the field?"

"Yes, unless you both would like to go Christmas shopping."

"No, thanks. See ya later." Nate started to leave.

"Nate," I said, sponging the island. He looked back at me. "Is Emery going with you?"

"Yep," he answered, and went on his way.

I slammed the sponge against the marble. Soapy water splattered my shirt. *Very clever, Emery*, I grumbled silently, savagely swiping up excess water and suds. *If you think I won't go to the sports field because of Jared, you've got another think coming!* I hadn't told Emery—or anyone else, for that matter—my feelings for Jared. The brainiac figured them out for himself, and was apparently now trying to use them against me!

"You are *so* dead," I growled, slamming the sponge against the counter.

"The sponge is our friend, Cassidy," Mom said. She placed Windex and a cloth rag in front of me. "Please go over the top with Windex once you've wiped up the suds." Frowning at the limestone tiles, she added, "Then sweep the floor, please."

Gritting my teeth, I did what she asked. When finished, I announced as calmly as I could, "Mom, I'm going down to the field."

She glanced up from the table that she was meticulously polishing. "Don't you want to go Christmas shopping?"

"Yes. I just have to ask Emery something real quick." I felt my eyes flash when I said his name.

Mom went back to polishing. "All right. But stay away from those woods. They're dangerous. All sorts of unsavory characters in them."

93

You're telling me, I thought. Mom would croak if she knew I spent many a night leaping and swinging around in those woods, and knew all of the unsavory characters by sight and scent. And quite honestly, I was the most dangerous of the lot.

"Be back soon," I told her, and then headed out to the field with every intention of upsetting Emery's apple cart. Not upset—I was going to flip the dang thing over!

~~~

Quarter way down the stone stairs leading from our street to the playground below that we neighborhood kids called "Spinning Park," I caught a whiff of Robin Newton.

"Fantastic," I muttered. "This'll be a *blast*!" Around Miriam's house, I had distinguished Jared's scent, much to my chagrin. I'd hoped he was spending the weekend at his dad's. But no such luck. "Not only do I have to feel all weird around him," I whined to myself, "but I'll have to deal with that witch! But what's the worst Robin can do? Glare, sneer, talk trash about me, start rumors—basically what she does at school? Thanks, Emery! Thanks *so* much!" At the bottom of the stairs, I glanced longingly at the woods before swinging a purposeful left toward the sports field. Emery wasn't the only one who was mission-oriented.

Approaching the sidelines, I pinned a glare on Emery. Flushed and sweaty, he glanced casually at me from the position he played, and had the nerve to smile. I made a slashing motion across my throat. He smiled more and went back to playing the game.

Parking my backside heavily on an aluminum bench, my glare followed him as he pursued Sam Mulrooney, who had the ball. I pretended not to notice Robin and her remoras, Mindy Ames and Jessica Blanchette, who sat in the bleachers right of me. I figured Jessica was here for her stuck-up boyfriend, Chad Dunham, and the other two, who were presently unattached, were scouting out new victims to wrap their tentacles around.

"What is *she* doing here?" Mindy whispered snidely to her friends. She hated me, too, as did all remoras. *By the decree of their crooked-nosed queen*, I thought wryly, staring daggers at Emery and giving no indication that I could hear Mindy, not that she would care, anyway.

"Following Emery around like the pathetic loser she is," Robin hissed.

I couldn't help but smile, because they were here, too.

"Maybe they're fighting," Jessica suggested wistfully.

My eyes took a break from glaring to roll. *So it's not true love with Chad, after all, Jessica. And to think I liked you once, before you became a Robin minion. And* I'm *the pathetic loser?*

"You're right," Mindy agreed. "She looks super pissed."

Darn tootin'! I increased my glare voltage on Emery.

He passed the ball to Zach Guzman. From out of nowhere, Jared swept in and stole it. My heart crashed into my ribs, having him suddenly appear in my line of sight like that. Though my eyes ached to chase him as he swept the ball to the opposing team's goal, I forced them to stay on Emery.

He and Ahmid paused, staring in disbelief at Jared. From the corner of my eye, I watched the ball fly into the goal net.

Ahmid cussed and told Emery, "Go talk to your woman. Her bad vibe is messin' with us."

I smirked, happy that Ahmid thought I was sending bad mojo their way.

Emery returned the smirk. "I don't think talking is what she has in mind," he replied.

Ahmid slapped him a high-five. "I feel for you, dude," he said with a laugh, then jogged to center circle for kickoff.

As Emery moseyed my way, I tried to keep at bay the girls' whispers that had kicked up like dirt devils. Listening in was tempting, but I was mad enough. My hard stare only wavered from Emery when Bobby caught my attention at center circle. Watching me, he said something to Jared. The possibilities of what he could be sharing compelled me to lower my auditory guard and track down his frequency, not that I ever resisted a conversation involving Jared, anyway.

"Man, that chick has a bad temper," Bobby said, looking at me.

"Always has," Jared replied, without so much as glancing my way. He dropped the ball to the ground, preparing for kickoff.

My face reddened with embarrassment and offense. *What does Jared mean that I have "always" had a bad temper? That is so not true!*

Emery plopped down next to me. "For a girl who hates attention, you're certainly good at drawing it."

I was too furious to pay his comment any heed.

"Do you know what they said about me?" I demanded, snapping a hand in Jared's direction.

"A dozen possible exchanges come to mind," Emery replied in a muffled voice.

I whipped my head to him. Glasses off, he pressed his sweaty face into the bottom of his T-shirt. Beyond him, the three girls ogled his exposed midsection. I grabbed the shirt from his hands and yanked it down. Surprised, Emery jerked his face to me, and I stared back at him, momentarily stunned, as I always am when I see him without glasses. Let's just say that lack of glasses brings up the *wow* factor several notches.

Recovering, I told him, "Bobby said I have a bad temper, and Jared said that I always have."

Emery feigned shock. "Imagine that."

Now I was really mad. "It's not my fault the virus that *your mother* infected me with has messed up my body chemistry, making me all agro."

Emery smiled thinly and brought his face close to mine. I fought the natural instinct to draw back. No way would I let him cow me down.

He said, "Number one: my mother did not infect you. And number two: the operative word in Jared's statement is 'always,' which means well before nine weeks ago."

I hated it when he spoke to me all parental-like, but pointing this out would have opened me up to a comment I'd rather avoid.

Emery's smile widened. "Now that we've established that your temper has *always* matched your hair color, would you get on with breaking up with me so our audience can get back to the game?"

Now that he mentioned it, things were awfully quiet, and this sort of did resemble a break-up scene.

"Are they all watching?" I whispered in dismay.

"What else would they be doing? Minding their own business?"

I could feel my cheeks turn crimson.

"You're beautiful the color of lobster," Emery teased.

"I'm such an idiot!"

"No, just a fool in love." Emery smiled slyly. "Why don't we give them something to really talk about?" he suggested, wiggling his eyebrows. He made a move like he was coming in for a kiss. My hand shot up, blocking his face. He laughed into it.

"Yeah, real funny," I said, dropping my hand to reveal his big grin. "If I even thought you were serious, you'd be knocked flat on the ground right now."

"I should hope so," Emery agreed, slipping on his glasses. Grabbing my arm, he pulled me to my feet. "Come along, compañera. We're going to do something unusual for us and iron out our differences calmly, rationally, and—though it won't be as much fun—privately." He flashed Robin and her remoras a cheesy smile.

97

"I'll chew you out on our swing," I consented, looking at the playground so I wouldn't have to look at anyone around us. Luckily, Spinning Park was empty.

"*Our* swing?" Emery teased.

"Don't even! You've embarrassed me enough—or I've embarrassed myself enough. Okay, I promise 'calm and rational' until the swing, then I'm lighting into you about 'transportation' and...you're right! I don't like it! I don't like it at all!"

I kept my cool until Emery and I were seated on the old-fashioned wooden swing, facing one another as we had on the day I brought him into my confidence. Then I ripped into him. "Jason Crenshaw? Have you lost your mind? Asking *Jason Crenshaw* to drive us? Stop smiling! This isn't funny! Don't you get it? Jason will tell my parents. He probably already has. I am in so much trouble! Thanks, Emery! Thanks *so much*!"

Legs stretched around my feet planted tensely against the slats, Emery leaned back and nonchalantly waved a hand. "Relax. Crenshaw doesn't know you'll be with me tonight, not that it would matter if he did. He'll keep his mouth shut."

"How can you possibly know that?"

"Because I know an opportunist when I see one," he replied. "A couple weeks ago, Jason's mom and Mrs. DeAngelo were talking at their fence while Nate and I tossed a football on the street. I overheard Mrs. Crenshaw complain that Jason spends his days playing online video games instead of looking for gainful employment. As luck would have it, she happened to mention the game he's most partial to."

"Let me guess. *Gods and Kings*."

"Bingo," Emery confirmed, pointing at me. "Deducing which avatar is his wasn't difficult, since it's basically a glorified version of himself. His username is Sera, Ares spelled backwards, and Sera has dominion over all the game's territories. In other words, Crenshaw is top dog, and after I played him the other night, he proved to be what I always suspected—"

"Despicable," I offered dryly.

"Essentially. He's corrupt, self-serving, and extremely innovative, just the sort of individual we need to help us. And, as I said, an opportunist, and I plan to provide him tremendous opportunity."

I was almost afraid to ask. "How?"

Emery rubbed his thumb over his fingertips, making the gesture for *money*.

"You're going to *pay* him?"

"Well, I doubt he'd chauffeur us out of the goodness of his heart."

I stared at him, astounded. "So what you're saying is you've hired yourself a henchman?"

Emery peeled into laughter.

"I'm being serious," I insisted, but Emery was laughing so hard that I couldn't help laughing, too. "I am!" I clamped my hand over his kneecap and shook his leg. "Tell me how much. What does a henchman run nowadays?"

Catching his breath, he said much more seriously than I had been able to pull off, "I'm new at this diabolical stuff, but I believe I've gotten a fairly good deal on my henchman. His rates seem reasonable. Thirty dollars an hour, plus gas and entertainment, which I'm assuming will be a couple packs of Marlboros. He didn't specify when we discussed terms."

I was shocked. "You're joking, right?"

Emery forced a solemn expression on his face. "Do I look like I'm joking?"

"Thirty dollars an *hour*? Where are you getting that kind of money?"

"From myself. There's something I haven't told you."

"There's, like, a million things you haven't told me!" I protested. "But, okay. What?"

Emery leaned forward confidentially. I leaned toward him, too.

"I have a part-time job," he confessed in a hushed tone.

"You do not."

"Do, too."

"When? Where? But you don't—" I paused, putting pieces together. Emery's late nights; the Sports Authority bag stuffed with brand-new black sweat clothes he had given me; treating Miriam, Nate, and me to café mochas on the way to school; never being at a loss for ready cash; plucking away on his laptop...Emery wasn't a night owl; he was working!

"Okay, I get it," I said. "You have some kind of online job. What is it?"

"I'm doing research, for the most part, which is what I was doing when you dropped by last night—research, and playing Crenshaw."

Recalling his refusal to let me see the pages behind *Gods And Kings*, I suddenly had a real bad feeling about his job. "What were you hiding on the laptop?"

"Highly sensitive material," he said, examining his cuticles.

"That you *hacked*?"

He sighed. "Such an ugly word."

"*Who* do you work for?"

"We'll discuss my employment in detail after we've captured Roga. View it as your reward." He grinned.

"My *reward*?" I challenged him, all fired up, but then abruptly lost the gumption to fight. What was the use? I wouldn't get anywhere, anyway.

Emery's expression turned pleased. "I didn't expect you to throw in the towel so easily."

"Why waste my breath?"

Now he looked downright amused. "My thoughts exactly. However, knowing how active your imagination is, I'll tell you this much for now. I am not employed by anyone running numbers, laundering money, trafficking arms, or named Massino or Gotti. I was not required to take the La Nostra Code of Silence, and I do not run a high risk of being sentenced to federal prison or being tossed into Lake Washington in cement boots."

"Huh?"

"In other words, I'm not doing anything illegal. Moving on, do you have questions pertaining to the matter at hand?"

"Yes. Why not get Mickey to take us tonight?"

"For several reasons, the most prevalent being that Mickey wouldn't leave me alone in the woods where a tiger is on the loose. He'd insist on coming along and would flatly refuse to take you altogether. Crenshaw, on the other hand, will have no problem with anything I want him to do—for a price, that is. Which brings us back to your original concern: Jason's silence. He gains nothing from turning us into your parents, where he gains much working for me, as will be confirmed this afternoon when he drives me to my friend's condo to pick up his tranquilizer rifle I'm borrowing. Before you ask, you don't know him."

"Which of your shady friends *do* I know?"

"Good point." He grinned. "When I peel a few bills from an impressive wad of cash to reimburse my friend for the darts, Crenshaw will know that I am, indeed, a deep well and will not do anything to jeopardize his opportunity to bleed me dry."

"Seems like you've got him all figured out," I observed sourly.

"I'm not arrogant enough to say completely, but pretty much. I'll figure out the rest of what makes him tick as we go along. Are you comfortable with transportation?"

"More like resigned."

"Resigned works for me." Emery stood up, offering me a hand. I took it. "I'll have Jason wait for us around the corner tonight," he said, as he helped me off the swing. Totally unnecessary, but sweet anyway. "I don't want to chance him

101

seeing you jump from your window. Don't forget your phone and earpiece. Now, if you don't mind, I'd like to get back to the game. Soccer is cathartic for me."

"I guess you deserve a mental break, with all the scheming that goes on there." I patted his head. "I need to go home, anyway. My mom's waiting for me to go Christmas shopping."

"I'll walk you to the steps," Emery offered, smiling warmly.

Smiling back, I realized I wasn't ready to part ways quite yet. "I have a few minutes. How about I watch you play for a while? I want to see if you're as good as Ben says you are."

"Didn't you notice the five minutes you glared at me?" Emery teased.

"No. I was too busy trying to bend you to my will. Obviously I wasn't very successful."

~~~

Curious stares latched onto us as we returned to the field, tempting me to do an about-face and go home. Figuring that would look super lame, I pretended not to notice instead. The only player I made eye contact with was Nate. He gave me a questioning shrug, which I returned, because what else was I supposed to do?

We stopped at the bench I had previously occupied, and Emery placed a hand on my shoulder. "Have fun shopping," he said, glancing beyond me at Robin and her remoras. He frowned and looked back at me. "Don't listen in on them," he instructed. "You won't hear anything edifying."

"The shocker would be if I did, but no worries. I won't."

"Good." Emery squeezed my shoulder affectionately. "See you at eleven."

As he rejoined his team, I settled on the bench, determined to ignore the existence of the mean girls right of me. Almost immediately, Emery gained possession of the ball and made a goal. Beaming, I clapped my hands lightly, bursting with pride. Then I watched Nate for a minute or so, beaming proudly at him, too. After that, I kept my eye on the ball as it was passed from player to player. The set of feet possessing it the most was Jared's. After a while, I realized that I was no longer watching the ball, but watching him, and I wasn't the only one who had noticed.

Less than a second after I had clued in that I was ogling, Jared passed the ball to a teammate, turned to me, and boldly stared back. My jaw slackened in mortification. If it were possible, I would have died on the spot. The corners of his mouth began to curve in a slow smile, and before thinking better of it, I answered his fraction of a smile with a huge one. Confusion washed over his face, and he quickly looked away and darted after David Hsu, who had the ball.

What just happened? I asked myself, grinning like a fool. This was perhaps the happiest moment of my life. Jared almost smiled at me!

"Did you see that?" someone said. It was Mindy's voice. Her overjoyed tone made it impossible not to listen in.

"And here she's going out with Emery," Jessica whispered, her fake outrage doing a crummy job masking her excitement. "We should tell him she's scamming on Jared."

My mouth went dry. *Oh, crud. They saw.*

"Well, you know what they say about girls like *her*," Robin insinuated, and then proceeded to describe what people say about girls like *her*.

Robin's lies ignited my anger, and I could feel the dormant beast stir inside. *Time to go*, I announced to myself, just as Robin said, "She's a hooch in more ways than one." Her remoras snickered, while my hands clenched in response, as if making fists was a natural reflex to being called "a hooch."

I shot her a dirty look.

"Did she hear?" Jessica asked her friends anxiously.

103

Staring back at me, Robin smiled meanly, her nose crinkling into a crooked line. Usually the zigzag piece of cartilage that made her nose slightly favor the left side of her face triggered guilt, but guilt wasn't close to what I felt at the moment.

Get out while the getting's good, I advised myself. Jumping to my feet, I made a hasty retreat.

The girls burst into laughter, and my fingernails dug into my palms, tearing flesh open. Those little witches had no idea how fortunate they were that I kept walking.

Nine

Could Things Get Any Stranger?

"At least Jason makes himself easy to find," I remarked to Emery as we neared the end of our street. Jason waited around the corner. "Just follow the smoke."

Emery pulled off his ski mask and sniffed the night air. He grinned. "It's like a trail of breadcrumbs."

"Pretty much," I agreed, discretely admiring him. Loved it when he wore contacts.

I took off my mask, too, giving my coat pocket a little pat when I stuffed it inside. Mom had bought the coat for me earlier this afternoon. It was the most feminine thing I'd owned since I was, like, seven, made of black faux fur, soft as a kitten.

"Remember, no chit-chatting," Emery reminded me. Jason was on a need-to-know basis, and as far as Emery was concerned, he needed to know *nada*. He had no idea where he was taking us this evening or that there was an "us," for that matter. Emery hadn't told him I was coming along, too.

When we rounded the corner, the first thing I noticed was Jason's hand draped from the window, with a cigarette trapped between his fingers. Ashes burning off the tip resembled a flurry of dirty snowflakes floating to the asphalt. Through the back windshield, I observed him in the rearview mirror, slumped down in the seat, hazel eyes staring impassively ahead at nothing in particular.

"Are you sure you know what you're doing?" I whispered to Emery, feeling anxious.

"Always," he replied, and opened the back door for me. The cab light came on, and Jason kept staring forward. "In," Emery prodded me.

Shyness struck me, as it often does when in the company of someone I don't know well. Nervous, I quickly slid into the back seat. Emery shut the door, and I peeked up, meeting Jason's gaze in the rearview mirror. Surprise flickered on his face, fading to blasé, and his eyes drifted to the front windshield again. I watched him take a deep drag off the cigarette as Emery climbed into the front seat. I couldn't believe he hadn't at least said hi.

Jason exhaled smoke and asked Emery, "Where to?"

"I-90 East."

"Groovy." Jason snubbed out the cigarette and started the car.

I couldn't take it anymore.

"Hi, Jason," I spoke up, brightly and very loudly. "Thanks for driving us!" I glimpsed Emery's jaw tighten as he buckled up. But what could showing a little common courtesy hurt?

Jason regarded me in the mirror. A small crinkle appeared between his eyebrows on his otherwise deadpan face. With some surprise, I realized he was trying to remember my name.

"Cassidy," I assisted him, forcing a smile. *How can he not know my name? I've only been his neighbor my entire life.* "My name is Cassidy."

"Thought it was something like that," he replied, sounding bored.

The smile fell off my face.

Jason rolled up his window, trapping us in the gaggy cigarette odor absorbed into every soft surface of the car. It was like shrinking to thumb size and diving into an ashtray.

"Uh, Jason," I said as politely as I could. Polite was becoming more difficult by the millisecond. "Do you mind if I roll down the window?"

He pulled onto the street. "Whatever floats your boat, sugar."

Sugar? You've got to be kidding me.

Sensing Emery grinning, I reached between the seats and pinched his arm, then proceeded to roll down my window roughly. The car stank, the company stank, and I *so* did not want to be here. With crossed arms, I glared at the city passing by. As far as I was concerned, that was the last bit of pleasantries Jason Crenshaw would ever get from me again.

~~~

Since Jason wasn't much of a conversationalist and Emery wanted to limit it, the car ride was the quietest one I'd ever had. Fifteen minutes into it, I decided to take advantage of the silence and lose myself in thoughts of Jared. After a really sweet fantasy where we rode horseback across a meadow blooming with orange poppies, my arms wrapped around his waist, the sun playing over the golden strands of his hair, I shifted back into reality and chewed on what happened at the sports field. Did Jared smile because he caught me staring at him? Or did he want to bury the hatchet, so to speak, make peace, and be friends again? *Please, please, please let it be 'bury the hatchet'!*

Emery broke the silence. "Take the next exit and veer right."

Shifting my gaze from the side window to the rearview mirror, I watched Jason's eyes slide toward the exit sign for Catamount Mountain Road. His expression became alarmingly smug. "Been a lot of news about that mountain lately," he commented.

Freaked, I straightened up.

"Something about an escaped tiger, I think," Emery replied casually.

Jason smirked. "Something like that." He swung onto the exit, veering right.

~~~

As we weaved our way up the mountain road, I contemplated this phenomenon called Jason Crenshaw. *He has the morals of a toad*, I mused, as shadowy woods periodically dotted with porch lights zipped by. *No, that's unfair to toads, because they don't eat their young, and I wouldn't put eating his young past Jason.* Rounding a bend, the last porch light gave way to utter darkness and wilderness. *I can't believe he's going to leave us up here, two kids alone in the forest, in the middle of the night, with a tiger on the loose! He's an adult, for crying out loud! How can he be okay with this?*

We passed a parked truck sporting monster wheels and a gun rack. *Tiger hunters*, I surmised, trying to make out if the gun rack was empty or not. I couldn't tell. We drove by another parked vehicle, and then another, and another. All hunters, I was sure. Slipping my hand inside my coat, I touched the bulletproof vest. Emery had insisted we wear them. Until now, they had seemed overkill.

"Pull over to the left, near that sign," Emery ordered.

The sign warned of winding roads ahead. I took this as a bad omen.

Making a U-turn, Jason pulled over and shifted into park, leaving the engine idling.

"Near the freeway entrance, there's a diner called Jerry's," Emery informed his henchman as he fiddled with something in front of him. "It's open twenty-four hours and has WiFi for your laptop," Leaning forward, I peeked around the seat to see him fingering through his wallet. My eyes rounded as his finger flipped past hundred-dollar bill after hundred-dollar bill. "Coffee and smokes are on me," he said pleasantly, pinching up a twenty and offering it to Jason. "Expect a call in a couple hours."

Jason plucked the bill from Emery's hand. "See you in a couple hours," he agreed, and popped the trunk.

Emery climbed out of the car, while I hung behind, staring at Jason in disbelief. Ignoring me, he tapped a cigarette from his pack, clamping it between his lips.

"So, you're going to leave us?" I questioned him.

"Don't want me to, sweetheart?" he asked around the cigarette while rooting in his jeans pocket. He pulled out a lighter.

"My name is not '*sweetheart*.' And, of course, I want you to leave us."

He lit the cigarette. Exhaling, he said, "So what's the problem?"

What is the problem? I asked myself. Was I trying to persuade Jason to have a moral dilemma? Was I crazy?

"No problem," I said hastily, scooting to the door. Emery opened it, and my eyes widened on him, taking in the rifle case slung over his black field jacket, and the dart holster cinched at the waist. He looked like a Special Forces sniper preparing for deployment. After quickly running my eyes down his black cargo pants to his combat boots, I glanced at Jason, who mildly watched the smoke rings he was puffing toward the ceiling.

"Do you know how to get back here?" I asked, floored that he wasn't demanding "GI Joe" get back in the car so he could take us stupid kids home.

"Follow the road?" He took another drag.

Deplorable! Absolutely deplorable!

"Whatever," I spat, and flung myself out of the car, almost knocking into Emery. He shut the door and grinned at me.

"What are you smiling at?" I snapped, stomping onto the road's shoulder.

Emery followed, chuckling. We had just cleared the Jetta when it shot down the road, leaving us with only the light of the moon and a tranquilizer rifle.

"You've got yourself one heck of a henchman, Junior Rambo," I remarked, watching the car retreat with disgust.

"Don't I?" Emery agreed, imitating Arnold Schwarzenegger.

I laughed at his ludicrousness, at the ludicrousness of the situation. "What are we doing out here?" I waved my arms at the dark expanse. This was insane!

"Hunting a tiger," Emery answered matter-of-factly. "Speaking of which, do you have a bead on Roga yet?"

"One sec." I inhaled deeply, analyzing smells. The tiger's scent was not among them. "No Roga. But there are hunters that way." I pointed west.

"Then we'll go east," Emery said with zest, clarifying, "After we've put on earpieces and masks, in case we get separated or should run into hunters."

"Which will not happen." Not a chance would I lose Emery on the Westings' property or let a hunter come within half a mile of him—or a tiger, for that matter.

After plugging in my earpiece and pulling on the ski mask, I added another element to my ensemble: fuzzy black angora gloves that my mom had bought to go with the coat.

~~~

Once we entered the woods, an obstacle presented itself. The canopy of dense branches obstructed the moonlight, making the woods pitch black. I could see fine, but Emery not so much. Our progress diminished to a painfully slow pace, with me leading the way.

"Turn on the flashlight," I encouraged him. He had one clipped to the dart holster.

"No, I don't want to attract attention." Just then, his foot caught on a tree root. Sensing him falling forward, I spun around and caught his chest with my palms. Standing back up, Emery frowned with disappointment in himself, as if he had failed because he didn't have night vision, too. "Change of plans," he announced. "You're going alone."

"Not a chance! We stick together. You're way too vulnerable."

Emery grinned and tugged the arm strap of the rifle case. "I have a rifle."

"Have you forgotten *why* you have a rifle? There's a tiger somewhere out here that you can't smell. You won't know Roga's around until he's feasting on you."

"You won't be able to find Roga with me slowing you down," he pointed out, and I knew by his tone that the only way he would go with me was if I tossed him over my shoulder and forced him to. Emery pulled off his mask and squinted at the shadowy branches overhead. "Find a sturdy limb for me to wait in," he ordered.

"What good will that do? Roga will just climb up and get you."

"Tigers don't climb by nature."

"Oh." This was news to me. I thought all cats could climb. Scanning the high branches, I decided this wasn't a half bad idea. Emery would be high off the ground, safe from Roga, and not wandering around where he might get shot. Plus, he really was slowing me down.

"Found one," I told him, and led him beneath it. "It's high, about twelve feet up. I'll give you a boost." Squatting down, I entwined my fingers, scooped up his foot, and lifted him until he could reach the branch. Grabbing the limb, Emery pulled himself up, hitched his leg onto the branch, and flipped onto it.

"Looks like I'm not the only muscle," I complimented him.

A smile snuck onto his face. What boy wouldn't like being told he's strong?

While Emery situated himself in the tree, I slipped off my coat and the bulletproof vest. The vest was binding, and I would be able to move more comfortably without it. Setting it on the ground, I had just zipped on my coat when my

111

phone vibrated in my pocket. Retrieving it, I answered the call. "Yep."

"Are you happy with this setup?" Emery asked, his voice flowing through the earpiece.

"As long as you stay up in the tree. Take out the rifle and load it. Just don't trank me."

"You have a vest on," he reminded me. I considered telling him I had taken it off, but decided against it. Emery would insist that I put it back on, and I would refuse, and we'd go round and round, waste a bunch of time, and I still wouldn't put it back on.

"We'll keep this connection, but I won't distract you with conversation," Emery said. "When you locate Roga, we'll decide how to proceed from there."

"Sounds good," I agreed, and was off.

~~~

Half an hour later, I leapt up into a tree near the center of the forest. True to his word, Emery hadn't spoken the entire time I zipped around the miles of woods, skirting the handful of hunters I happened upon. He was due an update, which I summed up in one sentence: "I've covered most of the woods and haven't found a trace of Roga."

Through the earpiece, I heard a rustling sound that led me to believe I had startled him. If the sudden sound of my voice had taken him by surprise, the steadiness of his voice didn't betray him. "I know. I've been tracking you on GPS, and trying to make sense of why you haven't picked up his scent."

"Weird, huh? Do you think the rain washed it away?"

"No. It hasn't rained since yesterday evening. Puzzling. Roga's scent should be all over the Westings' property, unless he escaped from the front of the zoo, crossing the parking lot to the other side of the road. If that were the case,

I would think he would have been spotted by now. It's fairly well populated on that side of the mountain."

A faint human scent wafted up my nose—a familiar human scent, but not so familiar that a face connected to it came to mind. *Must belong to a hunter I crossed paths with*, I concluded, and told Emery, "I've got a hunter headed my way."

"Then we should stop talking."

"No, it's okay. He's not that close." I caught another whiff and realized I had been wrong. The guy was a lot closer than I had thought, but not so close that he could hear me if I whispered. "Another possibility is Roga escaped from the south side of the zoo and just kept going south, into the mountains."

"Wouldn't you have picked up his scent from the road then?"

"You'd think, but it's sort of windy tonight. Maybe—" I interrupted myself, catching the hunter's scent again. Its potency suggested that he was closing in. My senses sharpened, and I instinctively shifted into a crouch.

"Cassidy, is something wrong?"

"Shhh!" I could hear feet pounding against the ground, and they were moving fast. "Faster than a human!"

"What is it?"

I scrambled down a few branches, and peripherally saw a flash, the sort of flash a fishing lure reflects in sunlight. Heart galloping, I whipped my head toward the flash, spotting a clearing soaked in moonlight through the trees. Running across it at exorbitant speed was a man, and not just any man—a man made of metal—a *naked* man made of metal. The only item he wore was an insulated bag strapped across his shoulder, bouncing off his shiny exterior like a beach ball.

"A metal man!" I gasped out, tracking him with my eyes, so excited that I could barely form a thought. "A naked, metal man—like *Silver Surfer*! Gotta catch him!"

113

"No, Ca—" was all I heard before my mind reduced Emery's voice to a hum. Call it prey-drive, primordial instinct, or just plain mutant madness, but every fiber of my being had to capture that man. Springing from the tree, my feet hit the ground running.

Metal Man was fast, but I was faster. Within seconds, I caught up with him. About twelve yards behind, I slowed my pace to his, slinking low to the ground, careful not to alert him of my presence. The reasonable part of my mind justified stalking him, pointing out that it would be smart to see what he was up to. Truth was, the greater part of me just wanted to catch him.

On closer inspection, I discovered Metal Man wasn't actually naked, nor was he made of metal. He wore some type of metallic suit which molded to his body like a second skin. Then I realized his scent was familiar from some place other than the woods, but I still couldn't put a face to his smell. *Who are you?* I eyed the edge of his hood clinging to the base of his neck. *I'll unmask you and find out.*

Metal Man came to an abrupt halt—as did I—and brought the bag in front of him. I crept forward, wanting to see what he was doing. A branch cracked under my foot. His head snapped to the side. Holding my breath, I deepened my crouch. Clearly, he was listening.

Slowly, he turned around. The metallic hood had openings for his mouth and nostrils, and a sleek visor embedded over the eyes. The design was sort of gothic, very menacing. Behind the visor, I could make out blue eyes warily scanning the shadows. They settled on me, narrowing. Obviously, Metal Man didn't have night vision.

In a swift movement, he snatched up a stick and shook it in the air. "*Arrrrr*," he yelled.

This tickled me, and I had to compress my lips to keep from giggling. *He thinks I'm an animal, probably thinks I'm Roga, but if I were, come on! What good would a stick do?*

114

Coming back to my senses a bit, I decided to let him know that he wasn't in danger.

I came out of the crouch slowly, raising my hands to show him that I meant no harm. Just as I opened my mouth to tell him everything was cool, he threw the stick at me. It flew at me with unbelievable velocity. I dropped to the ground, narrowly avoiding getting pegged. The stick whistled over me, and I yanked my head to follow its progression. It struck a tree trunk like a knife, the tip piercing several inches into the bark. *Okay. Metal Man strong, very strong.* I heard swift movement and swung my head forward. He had another stick in his hand.

"*Arrrrr*," he yelled again, wielding the stick and running at me. Springing up, I closed the space between us, hooked his shoulders with my hands, and flipped over him. Landing on my feet, I scuttled into the shadows. Metal Man spun around.

"What?" he gasped, squinting in my direction.

My breath caught, hearing his voice. I knew it, but like his scent, I couldn't conjure a face to go with it.

Metal Man flung the stick. As I dove from its path, he pivoted and bolted. I launched to my feet after him. He glanced over his shoulder, which proved dire when he ran straight into a tree clocking about thirty miles per hour. Bouncing off it, he fell flat on his back. His head rolled to the side, and his breath came out in short bursts. A human wouldn't have survived such a collision.

What we have here is no mere human, I deduced, leaning over him. His eyes were shut. *You knocked yourself out, silly Metal Man. Let's give you a name. Your scent tells me that we know one another.* I reached for the edge of the hood.

Metal Man's eyes popped open, and his hand shot up, gripping my arm like a steel clamp. Before I could recover from the surprise, he flung me sideways. Arms and legs flailing, I soared toward a pool of mud that seemed to have come from nowhere.

115

Not even, I thought prior to plummeting into it. Thick mud enveloped me, and I took an unfortunate breath, inhaling goo. Never had anything so foul entered my mouth before. Jumping to my feet, I hunched over and choked up mud, puking on top of that. Furious, I swiped my mouth with my hand, getting more of the foul stuff in it, and then savagely yanked off my left glove and scooped away the mud packed over my nose and eyes, which stung and watered like all get out. I blew my nose and mud sprayed out, then I looked around for that stinkin' Metal Man, discovering that he was long gone.

"AHHHH!" I screamed, shaking my fists with rage. Trudging through the disgusting cesspool of mud and rot, I howled again, so enraged that I could hardly see straight. On solid ground, I shook from head to toe like a dog, but the mud stuck to me stubbornly, saturating clear through to my skin. "So gross!" I hissed through mud-coated teeth. Spitting violently, I revamped my mission. Roga would have to wait. Top priority was treating Metal Man to a mud bath.

"Cassidy." The incessant hum in my ear became anxious commands. "Talk to me. What is going on?"

"Metal Man threw me in mud," I growled, scanning the woods. "Now he's going to pay."

"He *threw* you? Do *not* engage him. You don't know what you're up against."

"Correction! *He* doesn't know what *he's* up against!" I caught his scent, and Emery's voice droned again as I ran full-throttle in the direction of his scent.

Moments into the pursuit, I barreled into another moonlit clearing. A wind kicked up, and I momentarily lost Metal Man's scent. Hastily coming to a halt, I took a deep breath, evaluated, and had just noted other human scents in the near vicinity when something bit into my thigh. My head clouded, and my skin tightened around the pain. A rippling sensation ran over my body, the same sensation as when the python's tail grazed my cheek. Something struck my chest with a dull thump. Woozy, I managed to move my blurred vision downward, making out a tranquilizer dart dangling loosely from my coat. I felt another pelt, this one on my shoulder. Sinking to my knees, my eyes fell to the dart lodged in my thigh. Then I fell forward into blackness.

"Ya sure ya hit it?" asked a man, his voice resonating as if we were in a tunnel.

"It's down," another man's voice echoed.

"Can ya see what it is?" the first man asked.

He sounds nervous. What is he scared of? I wondered dreamily.

Twigs crunched under a set of feet. "Don't know for sure," said the second man. I sensed him hovering over me.

What is he doing? I asked myself then realized I was facedown in dirt. I attempted to move, but couldn't.

"Looks like some kind of an ape."

"An ape? Movin' that fast?"

The second man's knees popped as he squatted. "Hand me the flashlight."

"I left it back in the blind."

The blind? All at once the fog cleared from my head, and I remembered Metal Man, the mud, the clearing, the tranquilizer dart in my thigh. *I'm drugged! These men are hunters, and they have a flashlight in their hunter's blind. I can't let them get a look at me!* I tried to move, but my muscles were still paralyzed from the sedative. I was helpless. Completely helpless.

"This musta been what was screamin'." The second hunter's hand prodded my back. "Its fur is coated with mud."

In a second he'll know the fur is a coat, I thought desperately, willing myself to move. My muscles twitched as I overcame the sedative.

The hunter squatting next to me shouted, "It's reviving, Jerry! Trank it!"

Flipping over and up, I pressed my palms to his burly chest and pushed. He flew backwards, crashing into a tree. Gasping for air, he clutched his side and stared at me in terror. I returned his gaze with an astonished one. Shaved head, blond mustache growing down the sides of his mouth, *Big Game* host Leroy Rays looked just like his picture.

A dart whizzed past my ear.

Whipping around, I faced Jerry. The rifle shook in his hands as he fumbled another dart into the chamber. Springing at him, I tore the rifle from his hands. His eyes crossed, and his mouth formed into a silent scream. His expression would have made total sense if a bee sat on the tip of his nose. Worried that his eyes would stick that way, I reached up and gave his face a little slap. My glove left a muddy handprint on his stubbly cheek. Eyes uncrossing, his scream let loose in a deafening high-pitch, trailing after him as he frantically ran for the trees. I watched him run, amazed. I had no idea a grown man could scream like that.

Dropping the rifle, I turned to Leroy. He hadn't moved an inch. Still clutching his side, he stared back at me with eyes full of wonder as if he had just witnessed a miracle. I turned away and took a running leap into the trees.

Behind me, Leroy Rays gasped a prayer.

Ten

As If I Wasn't Freakish Enough

When I finally made it to Emery, covered in mud and trembling from dropping adrenaline, cold, and stress, he was the sweetest. I had already given him a weepy lowdown over the phone, so he was completely prepared for me. Before I knew it, he had my mud-soaked coat off and was pulling his jacket on me, while giving a sympathetic ear to all my whining and fretting. When I asked who he thought Metal Man could be, and how he could be so strong and fast, Emery simply replied, "We'll discuss it later. My only thought at the moment is getting you home." Then he gathered our things, including the bulletproof vest that he had considerately opted out of scolding me for, and lugged everything out of the woods to the road.

The sympathy ended with Emery.

When I climbed into the back seat of the Jetta, Jason glanced back at me. I was so cold by then my teeth chattered like a wind-up toy. His eyes slightly widened, and he slowly turned forward, taking a long drag off a cigarette.

Having deposited our things in the trunk, Emery got into the front seat. "Start the engine," he ordered Jason.

Jason tossed the cigarette on the road. "The car's going to have to be cleaned," he stated matter-of-factly.

"I'll give you enough for detailing," Emery said as he fiddled with the heater dial.

Jason's face became smug. "Just so we're clear." He started the car, and cold air blasted me from the overhead vent. Gasping in response, I hugged Emery's jacket closer to me.

"It'll heat up in a moment," Emery reassured, watching me regretfully. Jason accelerated onto the road, with his window down, and I had to wonder if there were two more different males in the world.

~~~

Jason parked around the corner from our street. After cutting the engine, he popped the trunk and turned to Emery expectantly.

"Wait five minutes before going home," Emery instructed and held out some cash. "Plan on meeting us at eleven tonight, unless you hear otherwise from me."

"I'll pencil you in," Jason replied, snatching his earnings. To me, he added with a smirk, "After catching up on some z's, I'll see what I can do about that back seat for you."

"You're all heart," I retorted. Ten to one the muddy imprint of my backside would still be plastered on the upholstery tonight.

"So they tell me," Jason responded, counting cash.

We climbed out of the car. At the trunk, I whispered to Emery, "Would a henchman with a little compassion be too much to ask for?"

Emery grinned. "The two don't usually go hand in hand," he pointed out, and slung the rifle over his shoulder. I reached for my filthy coat, but he grabbed it first. "I've got it," he told me then collected my vest, too.

After I closed the trunk, we walked briskly to our street. When my house came into view, Emery observed, "All is quiet, which means you weren't discovered missing. Let's cross here to my house."

"Why your house? Shouldn't I go home?"

"You're covered head to toe in incriminating evidence. You won't get away with showering at your house at one-thirty in the morning."

"Well, won't your mom find it strange if I shower at your house at one-thirty in the morning?"

"My mom?" Emery laughed.

I could see his point.

~~~

Leaving our shoes on the front porch, we walked into the Phillipses' foyer. The stairwell lights came on. My heart popped up to my mouth.

"Emery?" Serena called down.

"Yes." Unconcerned, he pulled the rifle strap over his head.

"Busted," I whispered nervously. Emery smiled like I had cracked a good joke.

Serena appeared at the top of the stairs, wrapped in a lavender terry-cloth robe. Her doe-like eyes rounded on me then darted to Emery. "What happened?"

Observing no admonishment on her face, I blew out a relieved breath. Of course Serena would be cool. This wasn't my mom. This was Serena, who was unlike any mother I knew, or any person, for that matter.

"It's a long story," Emery told her, feeling no compulsion to explain. He propped the rifle against the foyer wall. With my vest and coat in hand, he ambled past the stairs toward the kitchen, as Serena came down, looking like a sweet little pixie, wild brown hair tumbling over her slender shoulders and big brown eyes full of curiosity. Her knitted brows meant that she was in "concerned mother" mode, which was good, because the other option was "mad scientist," which can be a little unnerving.

"Cassidy, you poor dear," Serena cooed, stopping in front of me. She pulled away a clump of hair that had stuck to my mud-coated face, clucking her tongue. "You certainly get yourself into some interesting fixes," she stated, oddly taking no notice of the rifle next to her.

I almost pointed out that my interesting fixes had usually involved her, but decided to give her the lowdown of this particular fix instead. Obviously Emery hadn't filled her in on tonight's mission, which really came as no surprise since the Phillips family motto was, *Mind your own dang business*.

Midway through my report, Emery strolled into the foyer with a garbage bag. He leaned against the stair's banister and watched me amusedly, chuckling when chunks of mud flew off my hands. I tend to flop them around when talking. His mom, on the other hand, seemed to hang onto my every word, though she displayed no surprise whatsoever at anything I said. Even Metal Man didn't get so much as an eye blink. In fact, it wasn't until I mentioned being shot with a tranquilizer dart that her expression changed. All at once, she regarded me with as much warmth as she would something squirming around a Petri dish. Recognizing that "mad scientist" was now in the driver's seat, I stopped talking.

"Keep going," Serena encouraged in her clinical tone. "Spare no detail."

"Well, uh. The guy had blue eyes—"

"This 'Metal Man,' nor his eye color, is of any consequence," she replied. "What happened when you were tranquilized?"

"Oh! I forgot to tell you! Leroy Rays shot me. He's like this famous hunter and stars in a hunt—"

"Of no importance," Serena interrupted again. Emery grinned. "What happened when you were shot?"

"Well, the first dart hit my—"

This time Emery interrupted me. Losing the grin, he cut in, "The first dart? You told me that you pulled out one."

I winced at the memory. Even jacked up on adrenaline, yanking a two-inch needle from your thigh is no easy thing to do. "Only one dart got lodged. The other two sort of got caught on my coat."

"They struck the vest," Serena surmised, unimpressed.

"She wasn't wearing a vest," Emery said, staring at me.

Serena didn't look so unimpressed anymore.

"Are you sure you were shot three times?" Emery asked me.

I nodded, not liking how puzzled he looked. Puzzlement did not suit him. "I pulled the other two off my coat," I began explaining, when the cause of their confusion suddenly dawned on me, confusing me, too. "Those darts were going, like, one hundred miles per hour. My coat wouldn't have stopped them, no way." I glanced at Serena, regretting doing so. Her eyes had that spooky glow they get when she is intrigued. Bouncing my gaze back to Emery, I added, "I don't know what to say. The first dart hit my thigh, my skin got tight—"

"Define 'tight,'" Serena interrupted.

"You know, tight, stiff. I don't know...hard, I guess. I think it was like a muscle reaction or something. The same thing happened with the python."

"Cassidy, you've never mentioned this," Emery protested.

"I didn't think about it until now."

Scrutinizing me, Serena asked Emery, "How long did it take her to overcome the sedative?"

I had an urge to scratch my head. I had no idea where she was going with the question.

"Seventy seconds, perhaps. I can't be precise. It was difficult to tell exactly when she was struck."

My mouth dropped open. "You were timing me—*again*?"

"The scientist in me was, but your friend was extremely worried for you."

"Thanks, I think." Sometimes I didn't know what to make of Emery.

His expression became his relaxed, inscrutable one, which meant he was masking something that he didn't want me to see. Looking at his mom, he asked, "Do you mind if Cassidy showers in your bathroom?"

Serena smiled pleasantly. "Of course not."

I eyed them suspiciously. They were definitely hiding something. "So the conversation is over, just like that? Don't you have any more questions? Well, I have one: Is the guy in the silver suit a mutant like me?"

"My dear, there is no one else like you," Serena said elusively. Wrapping an arm around my waist, she escorted me to the stairs. "The towels are clean. Emery will lend you clothes to go home in." Emery offered me the garbage bag, his mask in place. Scowling, I snatched the bag from him. All the while, Serena kept talking, "I'll bring them in to you. Please don't eavesdrop. I have private matters to discuss with my son." She glanced purposefully at the rifle.

Somehow I doubted the rifle would be their topic of conversation.

"Give me your word you won't listen," Serena pressed.

"Whatever," I agreed, feeling resentful. As I stomped up the stairs, I felt like a child being sent away so the grown-ups could discuss grown-up things, or in this case, so the "grown-ups" could discuss their mutant.

~~~

After showering, I dressed in the clothes Serena had brought in, pulled on Emery's tube socks, and then rinsed mud from the shower and wiped up chunks from the tile floor with the towel I had used. Finishing clean-up, I tossed the towel in the garbage bag with my dirty clothes, opened the bathroom door, and almost jumped out of my skin. Emery sat on his mom's bed.

"I should have warned you I was out here," he apologized, surveying me in his clothes. "I didn't realize you were so small."

I glanced down at the Seattle Sounders jersey hanging mid-thigh and the sweatpant legs bunched around my ankles. "I'm not small. You're just tall." I held up the garbage bag. "Where do you want these?"

"We'll take them to the basement with us," Emery said, standing up. "I'll run them through the washer."

"Thanks. Hopefully my coat isn't ruined. And just so you know, my ears were burning the whole time I was in the shower."

Emery grinned. "We did discuss other things, too."

"Ah-ha! So you were talking about me."

"Of course," he teased, taking the garbage bag. "You are our favorite subject." His expression became serious. "I've been mulling over your encounter. I'll run my thoughts by you on our way to the basement." As we exited into the hall, he said, "To my knowledge, there isn't a pliable metal compound that can reinforce the human body in the way you described."

"Translate, please."

"I don't know how the suit made that man so strong."

"Why do you think the suit made him strong?" I paused at the top of the stairs. "Maybe he's like me."

"There is no one like you," Emery reminded me, prodding my back. We started down the stairs. "The connection between the suit and tiger has me stumped."

I stopped descending and looked back at him. "Why do you think there's a connection?"

"This man being in the same woods Roga escaped into doesn't feel like a coincidence."

"Agreed," I said, descending again. "It's too bizarre to be a fluke." I halted abruptly, as the "on our way to the basement" suddenly stood out in my mind like a neon sign. There was only one reason we would both be required in the basement.

"No," I groaned, grabbing the stair rail and clunking my forehead against it. "Why does she want blood *now*?"

"She's inspired," Emery explained, a smile in his voice. He gripped my shoulders and tried to pry me off the rail. "Oh, come on, Cassidy. You were shot with a dart earlier. What is one more hypodermic needle?"

"It's one more hypodermic needle." I pushed off the rail and threw my hands up in surrender. "Whatever. Serena can have her blood."

"You'll make her so happy," Emery joked.

"Yeah, I'm sure she'll do cartwheels." *I so do not want to do this.*

~~~

I so, so, so don't want to do this, I whined to myself, flipping my legs onto the medical exam table in Serena's "laboratory." Lying back on the headrest, I stared at the exposed beamed ceiling, gnawing my lip. *This'll be my seventeenth blood draw in seven weeks. You'd think needles would be no big deal by now. Man, I'm a wuss.*

I rolled my head and looked beyond Emery, who was preparing a syringe, to Serena. Peering into a microscope, she had pulled her hair back into a messy ponytail and switched the robe for a wrinkly white lab coat. Scattered around her were slides, Petri dishes, various lab equipment, stacks of food-encrusted dishes, and a few dirty mugs. Emery called her messy habits "organized chaos." I called them just plain sloppy.

"Serena, what do you think you'll find in my blood?" I asked.

Emery swiveled around on the stool and began tying on a tourniquet above my elbow.

"I haven't a clue," she replied, staring into the microscope. "The microbes are always full of surprises."

"Relax," Emery urged me, swiveling back to the stainless steel cart displaying neatly arranged torture devices. "You're so tense."

"Yeah, I wonder why?" I retorted. "Serena, is this really necessary right this minute? Hasn't my night been bad enough?"

"Would I have asked if it were not?" She jotted something in her "Mutant Girl" journal.

"You're beginning to make me nervous," Emery teased, grinning at the cotton ball he doused with rubbing alcohol.

"Great! The guy who's going to jam a needle in my arm is nervous."

"I don't *jam* the needle," he corrected, swiveling back. "I insert the needle into your cubital vein in a smooth, skilled motion." He dabbed my inner elbow joint with cold rubbing alcohol. I shivered involuntary.

You're psyching yourself out, I told myself. "Why bother cleaning the skin?" I asked peevishly. "It's not like I can get an infection."

"Old habits die hard," Emery replied airily. He studied my face. "Look at the ceiling and think happy thoughts?" he suggested.

"Happy thoughts," I echoed, shifting my eyes to the beams. "How's this? We are sixty seconds from now, you have a syringe full of my blood, and I don't have a needle stuck in my arm."

"In sixty seconds, the slight incision I'm preparing to make will be healed, and you'll be on your way home. Hm…You'll need to make a fist this time."

"Can't find the old cubital vein, huh?" I said heartily, whimpering inside. Shutting my eyes, I clenched my hand so tightly that the muscles in my arm contracted. *Happy thoughts, happy thoughts*, I commanded, waiting for the needle prick. Every inch of me now felt as if I had been tied to one of those medieval racks and stretched.

"Mom, come here."

My eyes popped open and jumped to Emery. His face matched the bewilderment in his voice as he held the syringe.

"What is it?" Serena appeared at his side.

Staring at me, Emery explained to her, "I can't get the needle through Cassidy's skin."

"But you didn't even try!" I said.

"I did, Cassidy. Several times. You didn't feel the needle?"

"No." I hadn't felt a thing.

Serena grabbed my arm and rubbed her fingers over the joint. "Epidermis appears normal," she reported. "I don't detect anything unusual in the tissue. Give me the syringe."

Oh, crud. I held my breath and squeezed my eyelids shut. I had already experienced Serena's syringe skills before, and let's just say she lacks her son's skill.

Seconds later, Serena requested in her clinical tone, "Cassidy, describe how your skin feels."

I opened my eyes, meeting her dispassionate gaze. Serena was in full "mad scientist" mode now. "My skin? I don't know." I shook my arm. "It feels okay now, but it did feel tight."

Emery released a long breath.

"Interesting," Serena said, feeling my skin again. "Please sit up."

What are you up to, Mr. Hyde? I sang nervously in my head, flipping up into a sitting position.

Serena grabbed my wrist and stretched out my arm. Her fingers curled around the syringe.

Oh, this cannot be good, I thought, and looked at Emery desperately. He attempted a reassuring smile, but failed.

"Cassidy, this will not work properly if you look to Emery for solace."

Blushing, I cut my eyes to her. She had embarrassed me so much that I forgot to ask what wouldn't work.

"Listen carefully. Your natural instinct will be to stop me, but you are not to do that. Do you understand?"

Gulping, I nodded. No matter how scary Serena could be, in my heart of hearts I knew her desire was to help me. However, as she raised the syringe needle above my arm, aiming dead center for the inside of my elbow, I questioned how this would help me.

"Remember." Her eyes narrowed on her target. "Do not stop me. Do not move. Only watch this needle." With that, she plunged the syringe rapidly at my arm.

129

I fought every natural instinct I had, almost giving into those instincts, when Emery gasped, "That's too high," and reached for her hand. But before he had gotten all the words out, I witnessed something astounding. My skin literally rippled and grew taut, taking on a slight leather-like appearance.

As if the needle struck granite, the syringe ricocheted off my arm. Amazingly, all I felt was a faint tap. The sensation reminded me of how a dental tool feels poking into gums numbed with novocaine.

For a moment, we all stared at my arm, stunned. During that moment, my skin relaxed, becoming normal again.

"Incredible," Serena whispered in awe, handing Emery the syringe. She massaged her hand as if she had hurt it. I wanted to ask her if she was all right, but I was having trouble forming words.

Emery held up the syringe and examined the needle. "The needle is bent," he observed in disbelief.

"How?" I croaked out.

"It appears your body has developed a new defense mechanism," Serena explained in a pleased tone, catching loose strands of hair that had fallen over her eyes. "Look at this as a type of armor," she suggested, tucking the hair behind an ear. "When your mind senses danger, your body will encase itself in this armor to protect you." She smiled smugly. "Obviously it's difficult to penetrate."

"Great," I muttered. "Just great." As if I wasn't freakish enough, now I had armor.

"This is a good thing, Cassidy," Emery urged. "This could save your life."

I stared at him bleakly. "Have you forgotten that I *can't* die?"

"No." He grinned, remembering. "That's a difficult image to forget."

I knew he didn't find nunchucks cracking my skull funny. Smiling about my death was his attempt to nip in the bud the pity party I was preparing to throw myself. Wanting to wallow, I scowled resistance, but Emery wasn't easily defeated. Widening his grin, he rearranged his features into something ridiculously juvenile. "Dude, your armor is sick," he said. "It's all that and a bag of chips."

Despite myself, I laughed. "I swear I'll kill you if you ever say 'all that and a bag of chips' again! Who even says that?"

"I do," Serena called from her desk, where she was already fervently recording today's thrilling findings in her "Mutant Girl" journal. "I think your armor is a bag of chips, too. Emery, draw her blood."

His expression became incredulous. He swiveled to her. "And *how* am I supposed to do that?"

Serena waved her pen at him like he was a pesky fly. "Get her to relax."

He spun back to me. "Thanks, Mom," he said, rolling his eyes. "I wouldn't have thought of that."

"So, how are you going to get me to relax?" I asked, smiling. Wiggling his eyebrows, he picked up a new syringe. I stretched my arm to him challengingly.

"Little sister," he said, eyeballing my elbow joint, "prepare yourself for some smokin' hot slanguage." Then, one after another he spouted the most ludicrous, gut-wrenchingly funny combination of slang words and phrases, some I had heard before— most I hadn't. I swear he had memorized the entire Urban Dictionary! He had me laughing so hard that tears rolled down my face, and I could hardly sit up.

In the midst of one snorting laugh, Emery jammed the needle in my arm. My skin hardened around it.

"You stinker!" I laughed, glancing between him and the syringe filling with blood, smiling at his cleverness. "I'll never fall for that again!"

"Yeah, right," he said, and yanked the needle from my granite-like skin.

Eleven

Myth Of The Third Reich

After his blood-draw success, Emery escorted me to the front door. In the foyer, he pulled my cell phone from his pocket. The hot pink exterior shined.

"Oh, you cleaned it!" I said. "Thank you."

"I'll get the earpiece back to you tomorrow." Yawning, he glanced at my phone. "Three-twenty-two. What a night," he remarked, handing it to me.

"Quite a night—and morning. Bummer we have to get up for school soon."

"Sleep in. We're taking the day off."

"Playing hooky, huh?" I grinned sleepily. These past few hours had burned through my energy reserves. All I wanted to do was climb into bed, pull the covers over my head, and pretend this night had never happened.

"I have research to do," he explained as he turned off the foyer and stairwell lights. "Plus, I would like to see how your encounter with Rays unfolds."

"Oh, I already know. He thinks a rabid orangutan attacked him."

"And threw him into a tree?" Emery questioned with a knowing look. He opened the door and peered out. "Still quiet at your house. Text me when you wake up."

"I will." I stepped onto the porch. "Night."

"Sleep well." He bent over and picked up my filthy tennis shoes just outside the door. "I'll throw these in the wash," he offered, glancing at my feet and frowning. "I'm sorry you have to go home barefoot."

"I'm not barefoot." I lifted a foot, modeling his tube sock. "I've got socks on." With that, I jetted off and was taking a running leap to my bedroom window before Emery had the chance to shut the door.

Mortals are so slow, I told myself, mid-leap, and dove through the window. My palms touched carpet, and I rolled into a somersault, bouncing up onto my feet.

A startled scream shot up my throat, which I managed to smother by covering my mouth. Thankfully, the strangled sound didn't wake up Chazz.

Staring at my brother sleeping peacefully in my bed, I mouthed a word that would have prompted Grandma Kay to ram a bar of soap in my mouth.

Okay, don't panic. Think! I urged my brain. *I might not be as dead as I expect. If Chazz noticed I wasn't in bed, he would've gone running to Mom and Dad, and no one would be sleeping right now.* Chazz mumbled something in his sleep about a kitten, flipped over, and snuggled the pillows I had placed under the blankets to look like me. Relief swept through me. My brother had fallen for my decoy.

Tiptoeing to the window, I carefully pulled it shut, cringing at the squeaks the hinges made coming down. Chazz snored. Tiptoeing to the bed, I slipped under the cover and gingerly lifted his limp arm off the decoy. He smelled like strawberry jam.

Chazz stirred. "Don't scratch, kitty," he ordered in his sleep.

Snagging the pillow, I lowered his arm to the mattress. *Enough close calls for one night*, I thought, situating the pillow under my head. Closing my eyes, I fell asleep instantly.

~~~

Help meeeeee!

"I'll help you, Cassidy!" Chazz screeched in my ear.

134

Sticky palms rapidly drummed my cheeks, and I smelled strawberries. My eyes sprung open to Chazz's worried face. Dried jam on the sides of his mouth dipped into a deep frown. I smiled groggily. What was it with my little brother and food? I glimpsed the alarm clock. *6:33*.

"No," I groaned, dropping my forearm over my eyes. What a dream my brain had concocted! That there was someone as strong and fast as me out there, that Leroy Rays had tranked me, that I had armor!

What next?

Chazz shook me. "Was it a clown getting you?"

I smiled. Chazz couldn't imagine anything more terrifying than a clown. "Yeah." I cracked an eye open to him. "A tall one with a frizzy orange hair and feet as long as sailboats."

Chazz looked significantly disturbed. "I hate those big feet."

"Oh, my gosh! You are so cute!" I squealed. Grabbing his face, I smooched his round, sticky, strawberry-flavored cheek.

"Yuck!" Chazz spat, wiggling free. Scowling at me, he used his pajama sleeve, also encrusted with jam, to wipe where I had contaminated him.

"I'm not toxic," I told him, grinning, and then remembered that I wasn't supposed to be feeling so well. Dropping the smile, I asked him pitifully, "Can you get Mom? I don't feel so good." Which was true. I really was tired.

"Are you gonna barf?" he inquired eagerly.

"Yeah, all over you if you don't get going."

My brother shot out of my bed like trolls were chasing him.

"Hey, Chazz," I called to him.

He looked at me from the doorway.

"Why did you come into my bed last night?"

"I had a bad dream, too," he explained, adding, "I won't tell anyone you love Jared."

I stared at him, shocked. "Why would you think that?"

"You said so in your sleep. But I'm really good at secrets." He flashed a big smile and darted away.

~~~

Taking one look at me, Mom told me to go back to sleep, which I gratefully did. I was dreaming about animals walking on hind legs, doing the cha-cha, when Ben's elated voice suddenly broke up the party, rousing me out of sleep. Stretching, I glanced at the clock. 10:12. I had slept for over two and a half hours.

"I'd be in World History right now, listening to Mr. Koster drone," I mumbled drowsily. Shutting my eyes, I curled into a ball and listened in on the conversation in Dad's office downstairs.

"What did I tell you, Drake?" Ben exclaimed excitedly. "What did I tell you?"

"Now, Ben, don't jump in feet-first. I'm sure there's a logical explanation."

"I agree! One hundred percent! Rays has a *very* logical explanation. Oh, come on, dude! You interviewed the guy. You know he's the real deal and not one of these tinfoil hats that you're so opposed to. If Leroy Rays is calling it a Sasquatch, then it's a Sasquatch."

I sprung straight up and bit my hand to keep from screaming.

"Think about it. The creature leapt, like, twenty feet. What five-foot-tall bipedal animal can leap twenty feet?"

I sprung from my bed and landed in front of my dresser. Opening the top drawer, I snapped up pajama bottoms.

"And what wild animal can throw a two-hundred-fifty-pound man into a tree, hard enough to crack ribs?"

Cracked ribs? Clenching the pajama bottoms between my teeth, I yanked Emery's sweats down, tangling my feet in the legs and tumbling to the floor.

"Did you hear that?" Dad asked Ben.

I wiggled on the pajama bottoms.

"Nope. And don't forget, Rays wasn't the only eyewitness. There's that other hunter, Jerry Buckles. The dude was so freaked that he had to be admitted into the psych ward."

Oh, poor, poor Jerry! I grabbed my robe and ran into the hall, smacking into the wall. *This is bad, bad, bad, bad,* I told myself over and over, skipping steps on the stairs.

"Them, Drake, are the facts. Face it, there's a Sasquatch on Catamount Mountain."

I flung into the office, startling Dad and Ben. Dad jolted at his desk, where he sat looking at a file, and Ben sprung upright on the leather sofa, sending the Nerf ball he had been tossing between his hands across the room. Hand over his heart, he barked a laugh, and said as he lowered his head back to the sofa arm, "Cassy girl, you sure know how to make an entrance."

I smiled awkwardly and glanced down. My eyes widened on Emery's jersey. He wore it at least once a week. Quickly closing my robe, I looked at Dad. Rubbing his chin, he studied me.

"How are you feeling, sweetheart?" he asked. I couldn't tell if he had recognized the shirt or not.

"Better," I said, clearing my throat. I glanced at Ben. "Uh, I thought I heard something about a Sasquatch?"

Ben's face lit up. "You haven't heard?" he asked excitedly, sitting up. "There was a sighting last night, on Catamount Mountain."

"Alleged sighting," Dad clarified, flipping through the folder.

Jerking his thumb toward Dad, Ben grinned at me. "Right, Drake." He rolled his eyes. "An *alleged* sighting."

Scooting over, he patted the cushion next to him, urging me, "Sit down, and hear the good news."

I took him up on the offer and worked real hard to appear astonished by the details that he exuberantly shared about Leroy Rays tranking me. His third-hand version was surprisingly accurate—except for the part about me being a five-foot-five Sasquatch, that is. The entire time he talked, I scrambled for a way to lead him off this rabbit trail. I knew it wouldn't be easy. Ben lived for this kind of stuff.

"I thought you said Sasquatches were tall," I challenged him.

"Usually they are. This one may be young."

Dang! Can't refute "young."

As my brain fumbled for a new tactic, Ben watched Dad contemplatively. "Hey, Drake," he piped up. "I want to run something by you."

Dad's eyes sprung up from the folder. "Not now," he said, presuming, as I had, that Ben was about to ask for time off so he could go Sasquatch hunting. "I need you with this tiger fiasco."

"I won't leave you high and dry," Ben assured him, "but you gotta understand the importance of this sighting. The NWSA has to take this opportunity by the horns. It's a once-in-a-lifetime! The woman who owns the woods gave us Sasquatch enthusiasts permission to camp out."

"You can't!" I blurted. "There's a tiger in those woods!" *Not to mention Metal Man!*

Taken aback, Dad and Ben stared at me.

"I appreciate the concern, Cassy girl," Ben said, patting my hand. "But there's no need to worry. The tiger isn't in the woods anymore."

My heart leapt for joy. "Roga was captured!"

"Unfortunately not," Dad said. "Evidence was found early this morning that indicated Roga has migrated south into the mountain range."

I nodded, thinking this made sense. Roga had escaped from the south side of the zoo and continued south, just as I had suggested as a possibility to Emery. "What's the evidence?"

"Hair, dung, paw prints, stuff like that," Ben answered. "So the hunters have gone south, and the Sasquatch enthusiasts are moving in! What do ya say, Drake?"

"That I have a headache," Dad teased, closing the folder. "I need to know you won't be dragging during the day, and that I can get a hold of you."

"You know my endurance, and—" Ben held up his cell phone, grinning. "It'll be powered up day and night."

"Before you set up camp," Dad said, "we have a couple interviews to do."

Ben slapped his leg in triumph, while Dad pushed away from the desk, stood up, and stuffed the file into his attaché. Glowing, Ben collected his gear. I slumped miserably on the sofa. How was I going to keep Ben out of those woods?

I'll just have to find Metal Man, I decided, rising to my feet. "Good luck, Ben," I said, with every intention of checking up on him while we both hunted tonight. I hugged Dad.

"Mom will be home in an hour or so, after picking up Chazz from school," he told me, pulling back to look at me. He frowned. "Get some rest, sweetheart. You look peakish."

"I feel peakish," I admitted, and scooted off.

~~~

In my bedroom, I texted Emery: *Have you seen the news?*

He texted back: *Yes. Come over when your dad leaves. We have much to discuss.*

"No kidding," I muttered, and sent back a reply.

While I dressed, Dad and Ben ambled out of the office. "Bye, Cass," Dad called up the stairs.

"Bye," I called back, running a brush through my hair. It was always such a mess.

Seconds after they pulled out of the driveway, I hightailed it to Emery's. At the front door, I could hear the news broadcasting from the television. When I knocked, the sound muted.

The door opened, and Emery stood there, grinning. "Well, if it isn't my neighbor the Sas—"

I clamped my hand over his mouth. His grin expanded against my palm. Shoving him into the foyer, I closed the door with my foot, released his mouth, and scolded, "This isn't funny. Ben is camping out in those woods. Mrs. Westing gave the NWSA permission."

Emery computed the information. "Interesting," he said a moment later.

"What's so interesting about Ben endangering his life?" I demanded to know.

"Ben will be fine," Emery assured. "The tiger is miles away from Catamount Mountain, and I doubt the man you encountered poses a direct threat to anyone on the Westings' property."

"Why's that?"

"He didn't attack you. *You* attacked him," Emery reminded me. "He defended himself, and then ran away. Obviously his goal was to be stealthy, which he would have been if he hadn't had the misfortune of crossing paths with you. He avoided the hunters, and will most likely avoid the Sasquatch enthusiasts, too. You should watch the interviews with these enthusiasts. They're very passionate people." He glanced over my head into the living room. His eyes sparkled. "Well, look who it is! Your assailant." He pulled me into the living room. "You're going to appreciate this," he claimed, plopping down on the couch and yanking me beside him. "Leroy is very entertaining."

I narrowed my eyes on the television. All energy and muscle, Leroy Rays towered over Paula Kimble, a reporter from my dad's news station, and Paula wasn't exactly short.

"He's huge," I remarked, watching Leroy animatedly talk. "And so hyper. He's like one of those big-time wrestlers."

Emery grinned at Leroy. "I think of a Viking warrior. Picture him in chain mail, animal skins, and wielding a battle ax."

"Totally," I agreed.

Emery picked up the remote control and turned on the sound.

"Well, Paula," Leroy's voice boomed from the television. "The Sasquatch has a primate face with a real high forehead, long, brownish hair growing from its cheeks and chin, big ol' buck teeth—"

"He didn't even see my face!" I exclaimed, offended. "How would he know if I looked apish or not?"

"And it had this real strange way of walkin'. Leadin' with its right shoulder like this." Hunching over, Leroy shuffled around like Dr. Frankenstein's Igor.

"I don't walk like that!"

Emery busted up. I punched his arm.

"Well, I don't!" I snapped, glowering at the big fat liar on the TV.

"Of course you don't," Emery concurred, massaging where I had hit him. He pretended to study my face while I glared at Leroy. "Rays is wrong about the hair, you know. And you don't have an overbite…not a significant one, anyway."

A smile crept onto my face, and I gave him a little shove.

Tapping his chin, he contemplated my forehead. "About three inches. Within normal range, I would think. Grab my laptop, and we'll Google—"

I shoved him again, this time hard enough that he fell to his side, laughing. "All right!" I socked his arm again. "You made your point." Turning back to Leroy, my smile flipped. "So is he making this all up for the publicity?"

Clearing the laughter from his throat, Emery sat up and looked at Leroy, too. "That was my initial impression. He's obviously not adverse to publicity or attention, but he doesn't display liar's tells, and the consistency of his story suggests that he genuinely believes his claim. As far as his physical description of you is concerned, it was dark, and a traumatized mind will see what it wants to."

"Well, that's crazy! How can he think a real Sasquatch attacked him?"

Emery shrugged. "Why not? You overcame a sedative within seconds that would knock an elephant out for hours, threw Rays hard enough to crack ribs, and then leapt into a tree."

"But *Bigfoot*? How lame is that?" At that moment, Leroy pulled up his camo shirt, revealing impressive abs and a tightly bound rib cage. Instantly, I was swimming in guilt. "Leroy can believe what he wants," I amended. "I can't believe I hurt him. I mean, the guy's humongous." I shook my head remorsefully. "I feel awful. He must be in so much pain."

Babbling away, Leroy grabbed Paula's hand and guided her fingers over his broken ribs. Surprised, Paula lost her professional face and actually giggled. I was so embarrassed for her.

"He does appear to be suffering," Emery agreed facetiously, and glanced at my miserable face. "Enough entertainment," he announced. "We have much to discuss." He turned off the television and collected his laptop from the coffee table. When he opened the screen, a website titled "Myths of the Third Reich" came up.

"The Third Reich? Nazis? What does Hitler have to do with any of this?"

"I'll show you." Emery placed the laptop in my lap. "Normally I wouldn't give a site like this much credence. Scroll down to the seventh myth, and you'll see why I have."

I scrolled to the seventh myth, titled: *Dr. Josef Richter's Supernatural Suit of Armor.*

I looked at Emery. "Seriously?"

"Read."

I looked back to the computer screen. The myth said Dr. Josef Richter had been a Nazi scientist who claimed Vulcan, the Roman god of fire and metalwork, came to him in a dream and gave him a gift: the process used to forge the magical armor of the gods. With this gift, Vulcan promised Richter he would fulfill his superior destiny by creating an army of undefeatable soldiers for Fuhrer Adolf Hitler, thus guaranteeing world domination for the Third Reich. Supposedly, after giving audience to Richter, Hitler became a believer and set up Richter in a secret laboratory rumored to have been in Salzburg, where he could create a prototype, which, according to a fellow scientist, Hilda Osborn, he did. Osborn claimed the armor had mystical powers, making the wearer invincible. She professed that individuals wearing the suit outran jeeps, flipped tanks with bare hands, and withstood being sprayed by bullets from an MP18 machine gun. Osborn was never able to prove her story, nor was there evidence to date that Richter had developed a successful prototype. So there it stood, a myth.

The site went on to say that Hitler had planned a trip to Salzburg to view the prototype when Soviet forces stormed Berlin. Germany surrendered to the Allies two weeks later, and Dr. Richter and his gift from Vulcan disappeared soon after. He was never heard from again.

There was an image prompt underneath the story. I clicked on it and gasped. It was a sketch of the suit Osborn had described. "It's him! Metal Man! That's the suit!"

Solemnly, Emery nodded. "Now I'll share my theory of how a man wearing what appears to be Richter's prototype came to be in the Westings' woods last night. Have you heard of a company called Material Dynamics?"

"Yes! The guy who started it, Rory Michaels, just died."

"He and a member of his Army infantry, Ernest Suttner, founded the company together."

"I know. My dad told me. He interviewed Rory Michaels once."

"And I know that. Your dad's interview is what helped me connect the dots."

"You watched that interview, and remember it from two years ago?" I asked, incredulous.

"Yes, and yes. When your dad queried Michaels about his war experience in Europe, Michaels mentioned that he and Suttner were members of the Third United States Army Infantry Division. I researched the troop's movement in France and Germany this morning and discovered the Third Infantry had been in the vicinity of Salzburg when the war in Europe ended."

I connected the dots now. "So you think Rory Michaels and Ernest Suttner took the suit?"

"And much more. Obviously, they also obtained metal alloy solutions, which explains how two relatively uneducated men without backgrounds in metallurgy founded an alloy company three years after returning from Europe."

"That myth said Dr. Richter wasn't heard from again," I pointed out, with a sick feeling. "What do you think happened to him?"

Emery shrugged. "That mystery may have gone to the grave with Michaels and Suttner."

"So you think they murdered him?" I certainly did.

"That, or Richter, being a war criminal, escaped Germany and went into hiding, forming a new life under a new name."

I chewed on this momentarily. "Okay, so this explains why the suit is in Seattle, but you said specifically the Westings' woods. Why?"

"Because Mrs. Westing's maiden name is Suttner."

Twelve

Broken Heart

It took me a few seconds to process this news. "*Mrs. Westing* is the daughter of the man who stole Dr. Richter's suit?"

"The daughter of the man whom we are *presuming* stole Dr. Richter's suit," Emery corrected. "One of the men, at least. We can only assume how it came into Michaels' and Suttner's possession. Let's review what we do know." He held up his index finger. "William Westing is acting CEO of Material Dynamics, the company his maternal grandfather and Rory Michaels founded. I've verified this." He brought up his middle finger. "William Westing lives with his mother in their family home adjacent to the zoo. Also verified."

"Okay, then." I held up three fingers. "William Westing is Metal Man."

Emery tapped my ring finger. "This is theory, not fact. William Westing is our most likely suspect, but we don't have conclusive evidence to prove the man you encountered was him."

"What about the fact that his grandfather stole the suit, that he has blue eyes and the same build as the guy in the woods, his family owns the woods, and I recognized the guy's voice and scent?"

"Compelling arguments," Emery granted, "except for 'voice' and 'scent,' since you can't identify the owner of either."

"I will!" I said, unreasonably irked. It bothered me that this family I thought was so nice could have a very *not nice* secret—like murder. "Just as soon as I hear and smell him again."

"Which you may have the chance of doing tonight."

"I was hoping you'd say that," I admitted. "I wasn't sure if you'd still want to go, with Roga out of our jurisdiction."

"'Our jurisdiction,'" Emery echoed. "I like that. And, yes, I plan to go tonight, and every other night that it takes to uncover the motivations regarding this suit. It's also important that you monitor the woods when possible, in case Roga does circle back into our jurisdiction."

I frowned. "Worrisome." It wasn't as if Ben—or likely any of the other Sasquatch enthusiasts—were seasoned hunters like Leroy Rays. With this thought, something occurred to me. "Maybe William was searching for Roga? Since he had the suit, maybe he thought he would try a hand at capturing him, too." I was digging in my heels about William Westing being Metal Man.

"Did it seem like the man in the suit was hunting?" Emery asked, digging in his heels, too.

I mulled this over. "No. It was more like he was running in a marathon, a race against the clock sort of thing. Just had a thought. What if the suit is only a secret to the general public? What if Material Dynamics made another prototype for the military, and what I saw wasn't Dr. Richter's prototype, but a new suit William brought home to test out?"

"Inventive, but there's a hole in your theory. A top-secret weapons project would be heavily guarded at a secure government facility. Westing couldn't just check it out like a library book and bring it home."

"He might be able to. He *is* the CEO," I argued, picturing William's kind face and how he had cuddled Lily so lovingly. I just couldn't believe that he had been up to anything sinister. "Why do you think the suit is a secret, then?"

"I lean towards two possibilities. One is nefarious, the other is noble. The first is the concern you've expressed already, that Michaels and Suttner kept the prototype a secret because their acquisition of it involved foul play. The second, the virtuous one, is that they believed making the prototypes' existence public or turning it over to the government was too risky, so they sacrificed a vast fortune to protect humanity as a whole. Imagine what would have happened if Richter had accomplished his goal."

"We'd be speaking German."

"Likely. This is why we must follow this through. We have to ensure this suit is not being used for evil gains."

I nodded. "Do you still think there's a connection between the suit and James Flynn letting Roga go?"

"Yes, though I haven't a clue how. Perhaps we'll uncover evidence backing up my hunch tonight." Emery glanced at the time on his laptop and announced, "Meeting adjourned. Your mom and Chazz will be home soon."

"How do you know? I never told you when they're coming home."

"It's my job to know," he simply answered, and stood up.

~~~

I spent the afternoon doing research on the desktop in our family room and didn't come across anything new about Richter or his "mystical suit of armor," but did find much about the Michaelses, the Suttners, and the Westings. What I discovered made me wish really hard for Emery's "virtuous" theory. Both men were said to have been excellent fathers, husbands, sons, grandfathers, employers, and friends. They were hard workers, honorable businessmen, upright citizens, and dedicated humanitarians. I couldn't find one black mark against either gentleman, nor could I find any against William, who continued his grandfather's legacy of good works. I found a picture of him passing out boxed lunches for Operation Night Watch, an organization with the mission of helping Seattle's homeless. In the picture, he shook hands with an elderly man that many would have been afraid to touch. Studying his face, I saw no squeamishness on it, only kindness and compassion.

"You're a good person, William," I told the picture. "I can tell."

"Who's he?" Chazz's voice came from behind me.

"No one," I answered, chiding myself for having spoken out loud. I had been so preoccupied with research that I had forgotten Chazz was curled up on the sectional, drawing in his sketchbook.

I maneuvered the arrow to the top left corner of the screen, but wasn't quick enough to close the page before my little brother popped up at my side.

He squinted at the homeless man. "That guy's got no teeth. Why doesn't he got teeth?"

"He forgot to brush," I teased.

Chazz's eyes rounded. "Be right back," he said, and dashed out of the room.

"You are so mean, Cassidy," I scolded myself, grinning, and looked back at William. The front door opened, and I caught a whiff of Nate.

"Where's the fire?" he asked Chazz, who was stumbling up the stairs.

I clicked the mouse, and William vanished.

"Gotta brush my teeth," Chazz called to him, and his little feet pattered down the upstairs hall. Giggling at his cuteness, I got up from the computer and flopped down on the sectional.

"And here I've been worried sick about you all day," Nate said, entering the room.

Flipping over, I grinned and whispered, "Don't tell anyone, but I played hooky today."

"You and Em both." Nate plunked down next to me. "He must've caught what you have," he added devilishly. "Huh. Wonder how that happened?"

I snapped up Chazz's sketchbook and whacked him with it. "You are so obnoxious!" I whacked him again. "Why does everyone have to give us such a bad time?" Laughing, Nate blocked my assault as I brought down the sketchbook repeatedly, proclaiming, "Emery and I are just friends! Friends, friends, friends, friends, friends!"

Getting hold of the sketchbook, Nate hugged it to his stomach. "I'd be a little more convinced if you guys weren't all lovey-dovey all the time."

I stared at him, stunned. "We are not."

"You're like magnets." Nate tossed the sketchbook onto the ottoman. "Or you're the magnet, and he's getting pulled into your force field. The dude is *schmuck*-mitten over you."

"It's not like that." I dearly wished I could explain what it was like.

"He gave up Stanford for you," Nate pointed out, and he was right. He just didn't understand the *why*.

"Emery didn't give up anything for me," I insisted, averting my eyes. I hated lying to Nate. Absolutely hated it. "And Stanford is only on hold, just until Emery gets his fill of being a normal kid. Remember, that's what Mr. Phillips told Dad—"

"Whatever," Nate cut me off. Irritated, he swiped up the remote and turned on the television. I watched him guiltily, assuming he sensed that I was being deceitful.

As he flipped through channels, I felt the distance between us, like a chasm as wide as the Grand Canyon. *This is what secrets do,* I thought, overwhelmed with a sudden loneliness. *They're wedges, driving people apart. And my secret has driven Nate away—my twin, the person I'm*

149

closest to in the whole wide world...or used to be. "I miss you, Nate," I heard myself say.

His head jerked to me. "What?"

"I miss you." Sadness clenched my throat. "We don't talk anymore. We used to be best friends."

"Yeah, when we were, like, three," he teased, but his eyes regarded me with questioning concern.

"No, we were until—" *I became a mutant and a liar!* Tears welled. I pulled my knees up and pressed my face into them. "We don't talk anymore," I wept into my jeans.

My brother wrapped his arms around me, and it occurred to me that the last time Nate hugged me, we actually were three. This thought made me cry even harder.

Nate pressed his cheek to my hair. "So talk," he encouraged gently.

"I love you," I sobbed.

"Okay, now you're just scaring me," he said, and I could hear in his voice that I truly was. I also detected an edge of anger. "Spit it out, Cass." He tightened his arms around me, as if protecting me from a dark force surrounding us. "My imagination is running wild here."

Not even your imagination is this wild, Nate, I opened my mouth to speak, then snapped it shut, as I realized with some surprise that I was about to spill the beans.

"Come on, Cass." Nate kissed my head. "You know you can trust me."

Crying, I nodded. How I ached to tell my brother the truth, that I was a mutant, and maybe an immortal one, if Serena couldn't cure me, and that Emery didn't love me, he was responsible for me, because I was a little unpredictable and dangerous, dangerous and in danger. *As we all will be if I don't keep my mouth shut*, I reminded myself.

So I did the next best thing: I confessed my second biggest secret. "I-I'm in love with J-Jared."

The room fell excruciatingly silent. I squeezed my eyelid tight against my jeans, waiting for Nate to say something. When he did, it was hardly what I expected.

"You've gotta be kidding me." He barked a laugh.

Instantly offended, I lifted my head to give him a dirty look. Sunk in the cushions, my brother appeared as if he had been steamrolled. My tear ducts dried up, and I wiped the remaining moisture from my glaring eyes. Nate could be so insensitive.

"That's it?" he asked, grinning, and mimicked wringing my neck. "I thought—Forget what I thought! You'd kill me if you knew what I thought." He sank further into the cushions, evaluating me. "You sure that's all?"

"That's all? That's huge! What is *wrong* with you? I have never told anyone how I felt about Jared before! *Anyone!* Well, not directly, anyway. Chazz says I said something in my sleep, and Emery figured it out on his own. Otherwise—"

"Whoa! Back up. Emery knows you like Jared?"

"Yeah, so?"

"*So*—that's just plain cruel."

"You drive me crazy!" I pressed his cheeks between my hands. "Read my lips. Emery and I are just friends. F-R-I-E-N-D-S. Friends. That's it. Nothing more. Friends."

"Are you trying to tell me that you and Em are just friends?" he asked through fish lips.

"You're incorrigible!" I pushed his face away.

"I try," Nate returned, then asked, "So, does Em know you two are just friends?"

"Of course he does! I'm like his sister."

Nate made a face. "Twisted, but okay. And just so you know, I already knew about Jared. No big surprises there."

I stared at him, stunned. "How?"

"You're my sister, and not all that complicated. I just figured you'd moved on."

"I tried to. I really did." I slumped miserably. "I am *so* hopelessly in love—and I know it's hopeless because Jared totally hates me." My eyes misted, and I grabbed a throw pillow and hid my face against it. "Every time I see him my stomach knots up, and I can't stop thinking about him. I even dream about him. Why, Nate, why? Why'd I have to mess up so bad? Why am I such a *stupid* jerk?"

"Crap."

I lifted the pillow off my face and looked at him. Nate looked like he would rather be sitting on a beehive than next to me at this moment. "What?" I straightened up, alarmed.

"Uh, Em is a really good guy," Nate fumbled.

My heart plunged. I knew my brother, and knew when he was attempting to soften a coming blow.

"Maybe you should give him a chan—"

"Just tell me," I cut in, wanting to know and not wanting to know. I had a feeling, a terrible, awful feeling.

Nate contemplated me a moment, then blew out a breath and said, "I don't know how else to say this, except to say it, and you need to know so you're not blindsided at school tomorrow. Jared and Rob—"

I let out a scream that rivaled a dozen banshees.

~~~

The scream brought Mom running into the family room. At the sight of her, tears gushed, and before I knew it I had confessed my second biggest secret to her, too. In the midst of all my blubbering and confiding, Dad came home, and I had to start all over again, which I didn't mind doing at all. The tears and confessing were purging, and my family's consolation nourished me like food for the soul. I hadn't realized how hungry I was. However, by the time I met Emery at eleven, I had been so emptied and filled back up with good things that I had no desire to empty myself again. In other words, I decided not to share with him that Jared had a girlfriend. It would only cause him worry, especially when he found out that my nemesis, Robin Newton, was Jared's girlfriend.

But it won't be a problem, I promised myself as we rounded our street corner to the Jetta. *I will control myself. I won't lose it when I see them together.*

"What's bothering you?" Emery asked.

"Nothing," I said with an evasive smile.

After quick scrutiny, he concluded, "You'll tell me when you're ready."

~~~

When we reached the turnoff for Catamount Mountain Road, Jason veered into the center turn lane, pulling up behind three cars waiting for the stoplight to change. The vehicle in front of us was an old Volkswagen bus, painted canary yellow and covered with Sasquatch bumper stickers. My favorite was: "I Don't Count as a Bigfoot Sighting."

"Evidently the party is this way," Jason remarked as he followed the cars streaming up the mountain road when the signal changed. Two cars followed us.

About a quarter mile past the Westings' driveway, Emery asked Jason to pull over, giving him the same basic instructions as last night's and another twenty bucks to boot.

153

After we collected Emery's gear from the trunk, Jason took off down the mountain. A few cars cruised by us while Emery equipped himself. They rounded the bend, and darkness closed in.

"Too much cloud cover," Emery grumbled, unclipping the flashlight from the dart harness. "Obviously I'm not the only one who needs a flashlight tonight." Across the road on the Westings' property, a flashlight beam shone between the trees. Emery's frown deepened when the beam angled toward the treetops. "Be careful," he cautioned me needlessly.

My ears picked up enthusiasts carrying on a conversation somewhere in the woods. "They're so loud," I remarked. "If there was a Sasquatch, they would have scared it away by now."

"At least I'll hear them coming, too." Emery turned on the flashlight and motioned for us to get moving. Half a dozen yards into the Westings' property, he switched it off. "I'll wait here for you. Once you've verified Roga isn't nearby, we'll stakeout the Westings'."

"Sounds good." And it really did. I had always wanted to do a stakeout. "But you're waiting in a tree."

Emery sighed. "As you wish." He turned on the flashlight and selected a blue spruce that he could climb without my assistance.

After he was settled and we had established a phone connection, I zipped off. Several minutes later and miles away from Emery, I came across the NWSA's campsite. High in a tree, I watched the men around a campfire doing activities that perfectly reflected their personalities. Ben fiddled with his camera; Tom thumbed through a *Sports Illustrated*; and Howie played a muted game on his Nintendo DS. An owl hooted, and all three snapped their heads in its direction. I imagined their eager expressions were similar to the ones they wore when they were thirteen waiting for the

154

shriek. To give them a little excitement, I shook a couple of branches before resuming my task.

Finding no signs of Roga or Metal Man, I doubled back to Emery, and we set out for the Westings' residence. When we could see the twinkling of white Christmas lights through the overgrowth, Emery turned off the flashlight and had me lead him over the dark terrain. We stopped at the edge of a lush lawn rolling down to the Tudor mansion, magnificently outlined in strings of light. There were brilliant red poinsettias in gold urns on each of the seven wide stone steps leading up to a massive stone front porch. Christmas trees trimmed in gold and red ribbon and big shiny bulbs stood on either side of the blocky stone arch that framed mahogany doors, each sporting a huge wreath. This was the first time I had ever seen Christmas trees on the *outside* of a house. Showcased on the lawn with spotlights was a life-size replica of the Nativity. It was really cool and looked like our Nativity decoration, except ours fit on the coffee table.

"My oh my, the rich have fancy decorations," I whispered to Emery. "None of those blow-up Santas for them. How long do you think it took them to hang all of those lights?"

"'Them' would probably be a crew of men who professionally hang Christmas lights, and I can't imagine how long it would take to string lights on a twenty-thousand-square-foot house. Since your eyes are already there, check for security cameras? Look along the eaves."

I spotted four, one at the bottom of each gable. Emery frowned when I told him this. "We'll have to stay back in the trees," he said. "Let's explore the perimeter of the lawn, and see if there's a place where the woods cut in closer to the house."

The only place we found was at the far end of the mansion. Even still, there was around seven yards of lawn exposure between the woods and an entertainment patio, which featured an outdoor kitchen, bar, a fireplace made of river rock, and cushioned rattan furniture arranged around the fireplace like a living room. There was even an area rug.

"I could live on that patio," I whispered.

"Have you picked up his scent yet?" Emery asked, referring to Metal Man.

"Nope, but that doesn't mean he's not William," I replied. "Maybe William hasn't been outside since last night. Believe me, scent doesn't stick around forever."

"Do you smell other humans?"

"Mrs. Westing. Lily. I don't recognize the others."

The Christmas lights turned off then, engulfing the mansion in darkness. I glanced at Emery. He was staring at a soft glow illuminating the far end of the house. "Let's see who's still up," he suggested.

We hunkered down behind a rhododendron bush bordering the lawn. About fifteen yards before us, dim light shone from a bank of windows on the second floor.

"Judging by the apparent size of the room and location," Emery said, "I would guess we're looking at the master suite."

"That looks like light from a lamp," I remarked. "Mrs. Westing must be reading in bed. What do we do now?"

"We wait." Emery shifted onto his backside for the long haul.

About ten minutes later, I started getting a little antsy. "Hey, did you notice there's a balcony off the master bedroom, around the corner?" I asked, thinking I should leap onto it and make sure that it was Mrs. Westing in the room.

"Security cameras," Emery reminded me. "Your idea won't work."

"At least let me tell you my idea, *mind reader*. It would be nice to have a chance to say what I'm thinking before you blurt it out."

Emery sighed. "If only I could read minds, then I wouldn't be racking mine trying to figure out why you're upset."

"I'm not upset. Now shhhh, before someone hears us."

Half an hour after that, the lamp turned off. I had been counting rhododendron leaves to pass the time. When the light went out, I had counted four hundred and six. "What now?" I asked, desperate for something to do other than just sit behind a bush.

"We wait," Emery said again.

Twenty minutes later, I had counted all the leaves on the backside of the bush and had moved to counting heartbeats via the pulse in my wrist. Thirty beats per minute, better than an ultimate athlete's, and about the same as someone ready to keel over. An ultra-healthy heart meant a heart that didn't have to work so hard. After a few rounds of counting, I became bored with the activity. "When are we going to do something?" I snapped off a leaf. "Has anyone ever died from boredom?"

"You're like the kid in the back seat of a car, asking, 'Are we there yet?'"

"Well, are we?" I snapped off another leaf. "So, this is all a stakeout is? Just sitting around, doing nothing?"

"Basically."

"Well, then, stakeouts bite."

"For the most part. Sometimes there's a payoff, but apparently tonight is not one of those times." Emery got to his feet, and I sprung to mine. "Maybe we'll have better luck tomorrow night."

"Yeah, maybe William will put on the suit, and I can chase him down again."

"That isn't what I had in mind by 'luck.'" Emery gripped my shoulder. "Lead the way, Kemo Sabe."

I rolled my eyes. He could say the dorkiest things at times.

Thirteen

Lethal

By lunch period the next day, after not spying Jared and Robin together, I felt confident that the latest rumored couple was just that: an ugly rumor.

Someday I'll see him with a girl, I told myself as Emery caught the cafeteria door. *But someday is thankfully not today.* Upon entering the cavernous room teeming with bodies, noise, and odor, someone bumped into me, causing me to stumble forward. Annoyingly, my skin reacted, prickling and tightening. This armor would take some getting used to.

"Oh, excuse me, Snake Charmer," Bobby apologized, grinning at his perceived cleverness. Trailing him, Ahmid twanged the Snake Charmer song.

"Your mouth needs to be duct-taped shut, *Bobby*," I snarled after him, knowing he had furnished the nickname I had been tormented with all day. To Emery, I complained, "He doesn't know when to stop."

"Why should he, when you reward him so irresistibly?" Emery posed, pinching my cheek. I snapped my teeth at his hand, drawing a huge smile. "See?" he said. "Irresistible. Neigh isn't the only one with a flapping jaw, you know. Which girl do you think blabbed?"

"All of them," I growled. "You better get in line before all that's left are Sloppy Joes."

Weeks ago, I had banned Emery from eating at our girl table for two reasons: One, because I knew inwardly he laughed at our conversations, though outwardly he was careful not to show signs of amusement. Sensing this made

159

participating in our silly conversations difficult for me to do. Two, my friends were so highly aware of his presence that they hardly acted like themselves. I figured this made Emery as uncomfortable as it did me, so in my mercy—and selfishness—I excused him from lunch duties, which, I might add, he didn't object to. Now he ate with the other freshman guys and conversed about sports, video games, and hot girls. I knew this because every so often I'd listen in on him, and let's just say that Emery could keep up with the best of the adolescent minds.

"I'll see you after lunch," he said, and headed for the end of the lunch line.

"Say hi to Nate," I called after him, and continued on to the table my friends occupied, receiving a few Snake Charmer cracks along the way, which fouled my mood even more. By the time I reached the girls, I was practically foaming at the mouth.

I plopped my lunch bag next to Carli and gave Miriam a look across the table as I sat down. She sipped her juice and stared back at me innocently.

"Hey, Snake Charmer," giggled our friend, Livia, who sat on the other side of Bren.

Miriam smiled around the straw.

In response to Livia, I hissed to be playful, only it didn't come across so playful. Hooking Carli's back with an arm, I pulled her forward with me and motioned to Miriam and Bren with a finger to come closer. Grinning, they did.

"Remind me to never wrestle a python in your presence again," I whispered. "So who has the big mouth?"

"Who do ya think?" Bren whispered back.

Our eyes cut to Miriam. She couldn't keep a secret if her life depended on it.

"Not cool," I scolded her.

"What isn't?" Grace nosed in from the other side of Carli.

"The python," Miriam explained. She flashed me a smile. "Come on, Cass. It's funny. Why would you want to keep something so hysterical to ourselves?"

"Because you and me making complete idiots of ourselves is why it's hysterical,"

"Agreed," Cheyenne chimed in support. I motioned a *See?* gesture to Miriam.

"Since when is bravery idiotic?" Miriam challenged us.

I groaned and rubbed my temples.

"Bummer no one videotaped us," she went on—loudly. "We'd be like YouTube superstars! Yahoo would have totally featured our video!"

"I can see it now," Bren said, adding in a monster truck announcer voice. "*The Adventures of Snake Charmer and the Snake-a-natorrrrrr.*"

We all busted up. I wasn't the only one granted a new nickname.

"Snake-a-nator!" Miriam snorted a laugh and said to me, "See, this is fun, and every guy in this room thinks we're awesome!"

"You're delusional! They think we're jokes."

"Yep, they think you're jokes," Bren concurred.

"No, they think they're awesome," Carli countered, looking at Bren.

"Oh, who cares what they think?" I said.

"I don't," Bren admitted, and switched the topic to the five seconds of airtime we had when a news cameraman filmed us exiting the zoo with our armed escorts.

While the girls excitedly bragged about our fifteen minutes of fame, I emancipated my PB&J from plastic wrap and slid it in my mouth. My teeth sank into the soft bread and froze in place. At the next table, Robin sat down with a lunch tray and her new boyfriend.

No, no, no, no, no, I chanted in my head, watching her open a chocolate milk carton. I couldn't even look at Jared.

"Cass, are you choking again?" Carli gasped.

If only I were so lucky.

"I'm fine," I said around the sandwich. Ripping off the bite with my teeth, I chewed ferociously in an effort to fend back tears. No way would I cry and make an idiot of myself. *How can he go out with her? Of all people! Why her? Why Robin?*

Through the internal storm whipping up inside me, I barely heard Carli cheerfully respond, "Shoo. Had me worried there for a sec. Hey, I forgot to tell you guys—" From this point, I tuned out her voice, along with the rest of the clamor in the room, focusing my attention on the witch at the next table.

Robin took a swig of milk and turned to Jared. Chocolate milk lined her upper lip. Jared smiled at her and said something, indicating on his exquisite lip where the milk was on her foul one. Giggling, Robin wiped her mouth, missing the milk. *A calculated move*, I was sure. I dropped my gaze to the sandwich so I wouldn't have to witness Jared wipe her mouth for her. That's where Robin was taking this, *the little—*

Bridle your emotions, Cassidy, I ordered myself and forced another bite of sandwich. *I will not go Hulk on Robin. I will accept this. They're together now. Maybe if I weren't such a screw up*—I swallowed hard. Getting that bit of food down my grief-constricted throat was like swallowing a watermelon. Who knows what would have happened if I hadn't been such a jerk all those months ago…

Robin let out a shriek of laughter. My eyes bounced up, meeting her flat blue mocking ones. Triumph gleamed on her snobby, horrid face, and I understood what she was celebrating—much to her detriment.

She went for Jared on purpose, to get back at me. My fingers ploughed through the sandwich. *She's wreaking her revenge, and wreaking it well!*

Robin smirked, her damaged nose curving slightly to the left. The smidgen of reason I still held lost ground, as I contemplated her crooked nose, deciding it better favored her right side.

With a lethal calm, I placed the twisted mess of bread, peanut butter, and blackberry jam on the plastic wrap. *You chose the wrong weapon, Robin,* I mentally sent her, sucking peanut butter off my fingers and regarding her coldly. Watching me with anticipation, she munched on a fry and mouthed *loser*. My anger climbed to "homicidal." The girl had no idea who she was egging on.

I pressed my palms to the edge of the table, preparing to rise. My backside lifted off the bench. *Robin, experience what you've unleashed.*

"Cassidy, no!" Emery thundered.

The command startled me back into lucidity. My bottom dropped to the bench, and my hands reflexively grabbed it as I realized with appropriate horror, *Holy crap! I was about to ruin her face—again!* An obstacle suddenly filled the space between Robin and me. I blinked up at Emery.

"Miriam," he said casually, looking at her. Startled, she jerked her chin up to him. He smiled. "Mind if I sit?"

Miriam's mouth slackened, and for an unprecedented moment, Miriam Cohen was rendered speechless. A split-second later, she found her wits and her tongue.

"Make my day," she said in her usual brazen way, shoving Bren over to make room.

As this went on, I dug my fingernails into the plywood underside of the bench, taking deep breaths in an effort to subdue the anger. Underlying the rage, other emotions swirled: remorse, guilt, humiliation, relief, and, yes, disappointment that I couldn't take Robin down.

In this twister of conflicted feelings, it occurred to me that something else was wrong. Conversation around the room continued as if Emery hadn't yelled at me.

Why didn't they react? I wondered, glancing down the table and around me, confused that no one was watching us. I massaged my forehead, forcing myself to think. *Emery whispered my name,* I realized. *Only freakish me heard the whisper as shouting. No one else heard a thing.*

Emery placed his lunch tray directly across from me, blocking my view. Assuming he was acting as a human shield for Robin, I stared unseeingly at my mangled sandwich. A new wave of emotions washed over me: regret, gratitude, resentment, shame—so much shame that I thought I would drown in it. Disgraced, I wondered how I could ever look at Emery again. He knew what I was about to do. He knew what I was. *I shouldn't be here, wandering freely among all these helpless human beings. I need to be locked up, in a cage!*

"Cassidy," Emery summoned.

Hesitant, I looked up.

His face displayed no hint of condemnation, only warmth. He raised his hand. Ketchup smeared his fingertips.

"Do you have a napkin?" he asked, his voice not betraying that anything was amiss. Robin shrieked another laugh. Emery's gaze secured mine, and I found I didn't care about Robin anymore.

I smiled at him gratefully. He smiled back. "Yeah," I answered as I retrieved a napkin from my lunch bag. I handed it to him, and wasn't even tempted to look beyond him. Emery made a very good shield.

"Thank you," he said, and I knew he was thanking me for more than the napkin. Cleaning his fingers, he looked at Carli. "So what part of the fence do they think Roga went over?"

Surprised, I turned my head to her. What had I missed while feeling murderous and sorry for myself?

"The petting zoo," Carli answered.

Emery and I exchanged a look that said, *Impossible*. The petting zoo occupied the northeast corner of the zoo. For sure I would have picked up Roga's scent on Sunday night if he had escaped that way.

"Why do they think that?" I asked Carli. "And who are 'they?'"

"Zoo staff." She puckered her lips. "Were you spacing again?"

"Sort of." It was hard to believe my internal war hadn't been obvious. "So, why do they think Roga escaped from the petting zoo?"

"Ian found tiger tracks under the goat's portico. We figured the rest got washed away in the rain."

"Are any other animals missing?" Emery asked, which was a really good question. What tiger would pass on a petting zoo smorgasbord?

It took Carli a second to compute why he had asked. When she got it, her face broke out into a huge grin, exposing her hot pink bands. "Yep, all legs of lamb are accounted for," she joked, laughing.

I forced a chuckle, while Emery narrowed his eyes on my lunch bag in thought. None of what Carli had just shared made any sense.

~~~

"Should we leave?" Emery asked me as we walked to our locker after lunch, which we shared because there weren't any available when he registered for school. Since he was only here for me, it was only right to ask him to be my locker mate.

"Why would we leave?"

"I thought you might like to avoid P.E.," he explained, exchanging pleasant smiles with Annie Slater.

"Oh," I said, embarrassed all over again. P.E. was the only class I had with Jared and Robin, making the last period of the day a hot spot. That, and the fact that when my adrenaline spikes, things can get a little precarious.

Emery looked from Annie to me. "What do you mean by 'oh'?"

"'Oh' means I'm fine, so let's drop it."

"Unfortunately, I can't do that." Emery seized my arm. "Let's step out of the cattle corral, shall we?"

He steered me into the entryway of a locked classroom. Flipping me to the wall, he demanded to know, "Why didn't you warn me about Jared last night?"

"Because it's my problem, not yours." I glanced at the hall, making eye contact with some boy who was still growing into his ears.

Emery brought his arm up and pressed his palm to the wall, obstructing my view of the hall. "I beg to differ on that. Don't forget why I'm here."

"Uh-huh." I rose up on my toes to peek over his arm. He moved it up, defeating the effort. "People are going to talk," I protested.

"And what will they say that they haven't said already?" he said impatiently, being rhetorical again.

I could only shrug, because he was right. Gossips had already said the worst.

"Their opinions are of no significance to us," he reiterated for the hundredth time in the last seven weeks. I only wished I could share the opinion. "What is significant is your hiding information from me that could ruin everything."

"I wasn't hiding anything! And if you don't mind my saying, this is really none of your business. And don't you think ruining *everything* is a wee bit melodramatic?"

"So you were only getting up from the table to stretch your legs?" he challenged.

I stared at him, at a loss for words. What could I say? We both knew I had been about to ruin everything.

"Keep in mind everything that affects you *is* my business," he went on, "even subject matters that you and I would rather not broach. Having said that, point-blank, will seeing Jared with Robin in P.E. be too much for you?"

"In other words, will I lose it and hurt her?"

"Yes, and understand if you are not completely committed to controlling your impulses, we are leaving *now*."

Someone walking by in the hall made loud kissing noises. Emery kept his eyes latched on mine. I chomped down on my lip, resentful. I was so sick of being harassed.

"Of no significance, Cassidy," he reminded. "Are you committed?"

"Yes."

Emery looked doubtful.

"Yes," I repeated with more conviction, then raised my hand in a pledge. "I solemnly swear to control myself and not toss Robin instead of a ball, no matter how much she tempts me to do so."

Our faces broke out into grins.

Lowering my hand, I continued in earnest, "You said you want me to live life like I normally would. Normally, if the guy I like hooks up with the girl I despise, I would just have to suck up and deal with it. So that's what I'm going to do: suck up and deal with it."

"How do you plan to *deal* with it?"

"You know that saying, 'If the kitchen is too hot, get out?'"

Emery smiled. "Yes, though I'm wondering where you've heard it."

"From my Grandpa Alton. He says it all the time."

"So in applying this adage to our situation, your strategy is to hightail it out of the gym if Robin tempts you to toss her instead of a ball?"

I nodded. "I'll run like the wind."

Letting out a laugh, Emery plunked his forehead against mine. "*That* is a terrible strategy," he teased.

"Oh, you know what I mean. They just took me off guard earlier, but now I'm prepared."

"We'll test your resolve in P.E. under one condition: you let me help you."

"Deal, and thanks."

"That's why I'm here," Emery replied, looking at his wristwatch. "Two minutes, twenty-one seconds before final bell. We'd better hoof it."

~~~

I had almost convinced myself that keeping my emotions in check would be a piece of cake until I walked into the girls' locker room after sixth period and got a whiff of Robin. My blood went instantly hot.

Down, girl, I told myself, taking care not to look in her direction as I quickly crossed the room to my friends and my locker. "Hey, guys," I greeted the girls, my voice pitched higher than usual.

"Hi," Nicki, Katie, and Josie returned.

Josie asked, "Were you sick yesterday?"

"No, just tired." I opened my locker.

"Was Emery tired, too?" Nicki inquired suggestively. Nicki was in the Cassidy-is-in-denial-about-her-feelings-for-Emery camp.

"Ha ha." I pulled off my shirt. "So what did I miss yesterday?"

"Aerobics," Katie answered.

"Aerobics? Has Mr. Saunders lost his mind?"

167

"No, just his gallbladder," Josie said. The other girls laughed. "He's having his gallbladder removed, so we'll have subs for, like, two weeks. The one yesterday was this aerobics fanatic."

"It's not her today," Katie informed us. "It's some guy. He's like twenty-five, but not cute or anything."

This disappointed all of us. Cute male subs were always a perk.

As I pulled the maroon gym shirt over my head, Robin declared on the other side of the room loudly, "Jared is so hot!"

My spine stiffened, and I popped my head through the shirt's opening and looked at my friends. They were grinning at one another, eager for Robin to continue.

"And those lips! They were made for kissing."

"Tell all," Mindy encouraged, just as loud.

Please, Nicki mouthed to us, clasping her hands together. Josie and Katie giggled, shifting wistful eyes in Robin's direction. I decided to get out while the getting was good.

"Yesterday, after school—"

"See you guys in the gym," I blurted. My friends waved for me to keep quiet.

"—his house."

I did an emergency *lala* thing in my head, grabbed my shorts and made haste to the restroom. Slamming the door behind me, I pressed my back against it and flipped up the light switch. Florescent lights buzzed on, and the fan rumbled to life, covering the noise in the adjoining locker room. After congratulating myself for not pulling Robin's flapping lips over her head, I slid to my bottom and grieved. Minutes passed while I rode a roller coaster of emotions, punctuated by putting my fist through the wall. *Better the wall than Robin*, I told myself, as I watched my red knuckles swelling up. The pain suggested that I had broken a bone or two. After healing, I pulled the trash can in front of the busted wall and finished dressing. With a splash of cold water on my face, I was ready for another round.

I entered the gym and faced a challenge of monumental proportions. Standing next to Amber before our classmates, Jared looked directly at me, "Cassidy," he said

I froze in mid-step.

The sub turned around to look at me. "Jones?"

I stared at him blankly. "Yeah."

Frowning, he marked the roll book.

"Cassidy," Jared said again.

I cut my eyes to him. He stared back at me expectantly.

"Huh?" I lamely replied.

Jared looked at a loss.

Snickers projected me out of the stupor, and I made a split-second deduction. *Jared and Amber are team captains. I'm Jared's first pick. Why?* But there was no time to ponder *why* if I didn't want to look even more moronic. Fixing my eyes on a spot behind Jared, I walked toward it.

"Emery," Amber sang out.

Emery's sneakers plodded behind me. Reaching the spot, I pivoted around, parking my gaze on the silver tips of my Pumas, cringing inside. I figured Jared would call Robin next. Being sandwiched between them seemed the way this torture would go.

"Bobby."

Bobby? I bit my tongue to keep from blurting, *What's the deal, Jared? Why Bobby and not her? Why me and not her? Why me, period?* With the exception of Emery, no one in the gym knew I had any athletic ability. I wasn't a star player. I had never been picked for a team first before. I didn't get it!

"Rock n' roll, Snake Charmer," Bobby teased, walking up.

Jared chuckled.

My eyes flew up to witness Bobby elbow him. Then I got it. *I'm the butt of a joke!*

"Hey, now!" Bobby put his hands up as if to fend me off. "No going loco on Neigh."

"Grow up," I said through my teeth and swung around before he could learn just how loco I was. Fixing my burning eyes on the drinking fountain in the short hall between the gyms, my singular goal became getting to the dang fountain. From there I would work out what to do next, pounding Bobby Neigh to a pulp not being one of the options.

I bent over the fountain, turned on the water, and pretended to drink. Glaring at the arched water stream striking the drain, I smelled Emery approaching.

"You're not really drinking from that, are you?"

"Do you think I'm crazy? Who knows what's on this spigot?" I straightened up and turned around to him. Relief flooded his face.

"This is much better than I expected," he confessed, dropping his face close to mine and peering into my eyes. "Minimal pupil constriction, which means you're upset, but not alarmingly so."

"Thanks for the report. FYI, your breath smells like beef tacos."

"Does it bother you?"

"No," I admitted. My face fell. I was too weird for words.

"Test over," Emery announced. "Time to go."

"I've told you a million times," I said, releasing my frustration on him, "this is *not* college. We are *not* adults. We can't just leave. There are rules."

"They're not our rules," he replied calmly. "We have our own set."

I responded with the first thing that popped into my head. "Having our own rules is dangerous."

"Frankly, what's dangerous is your staying in an emotionally charged situation. Before you dig your heels in any deeper, you need to know what this substitute teacher has unwittingly decided we play today."

My stomach plunged. "Dodgeball?"

"Dodgeball."

I was the butt of a joke. A cosmic joke.

"Well, there you go." I threw my hands up in defeat. "The writing is on the wall. I'm killing Robin today."

"And that's our exit line." Emery attempted to secure my arm, which I easily evaded. He stared at me sternly. "I am not allowing you to step foot on that gym floor if you believe that you're the puppet of a conspiring universe, doomed to repeat history."

"I don't believe that! Well, okay. I do. But it doesn't matter, because I have to see this through. I *need* to see this through. Understand?"

Emery scrutinized me quietly, and then did something totally unexpected. He relented. "Your goal is the same as any other day: control your strength when your adrenaline spikes, and keep movements within bounds. Of course, today there is the added challenge of keeping emotions in check. Shove them down."

"Way down," I promised, happy as a clam. I loved winning.

Emery analyzed my eyes again. "Pupils are normal. We're good to go."

"Back by the fountain," the sub shouted. "Join your teams."

Emery gave him the *okay* sign, whispering to me, "If it becomes too much, let me get you out."

"No way! You'll have to do that all on your own." *Just how pathetic does he think I am?*

His eyes sparkled. "I like a challenge."

"So do I. Too bad I won't have one." I popped his chest with the back of my hand, and took off to join my team.

"Everything cool?" Josie asked when I pulled up alongside her.

"Absolutely," I assured her, looking at the sub setting up balls. My mouth dropped open when I spied Robin beyond him, on the opposing team.

"Robin's on *that* team?" I said before thinking better of it.

Josie smirked. "Yep. Gotta love it."

"Go figure." Jared not snagging his girlfriend had me dumbfounded. If he was the god of sports in our freshman class, then Robin was the goddess. I turned my shaking head back to Robin and was surprised to see that she had been watching me. The look on her face was downright murderous.

Oh, this'll be fun, I thought sardonically, positioning to run for a ball.

Having set up balls, the sub swiped up the emptied ball net and walked off the gym floor, blowing the whistle. As bodies rushed forward, I hung back as usual. Every move I made had to be calculated, carefully thought through. Not doing so could end in tragedy. My vision adjusted to the movements of the advancing teams, slowing the players down. A split second after the whistle blew, I lurched forward, keenly aware of the pace of those around me and the adrenaline already dumping into my veins. I took care not to exceed it. I watched two balls coming at me, which appeared to move through Jell-O. Stepping right, I evaded the first ball, since Emery had thrown it, and had to wonder if he really thought he could get me out. The second ball, I caught, getting Ruben Schelper out. His name reminded me of a meaty sandwich, which pretty much described him. Miffed, he stomped off the floor to the bleachers.

My eyes sought Emery. I had no desire to get him out, but I would make him work real hard to stay in. When I cocked my arm to throw the ball, Trevor Young, on the opposing team, covered his nose and shouted, "Cassidy has a ball!"

Everyone stopped and looked at him.

Infuriated, Robin whipped around and pelted him with her ball. Trevor went into hysterics, slapping a high-five with Zach Guzman. Watching the boys laugh, a smile tugged at my mouth. Noticing my struggle, Robin sneered at me.

"She's gonna kill ya, Snake Charmer," Bobby predicted from my left, as balls started flying again.

A laugh escaped. "Well, she can always try," I said, glancing sideways at where his voice had come from. To my utter shock, I met Jared's gaze instead. Bobby was long gone. Being taken off-guard sent my mind reeling. My lungs felt immobilized. Usually I was so aware of where Jared was in a room. The one time I wasn't, he was standing right next to me.

Looking away, Jared cut in front of me and caught a ball. My breath rushed out in a gust as he continued forward. Shaking off the shock, I dashed left, captured a bouncing ball, and launched it several degrees to Emery's right. Grinning, the clever boy didn't move a muscle, having predicted that I wouldn't actually target him. The ball swooshed by him and nailed poor Katie, which I felt totally bad about. Game or not, I never target my friends. Sighing, she trotted to the bleachers and joined the other "out" players.

Emery, you're too smart for your own good, I told him silently as we seized balls. Backing up from the centerline, I palmed an incoming with my free hand, snapping it to my chest. Emery frowned. I nodded agreement. The move had been a wee bit suspicious.

"You're out of hands, Cassidy," Jared's voice came from behind me. My heart skipped a beat. "Start throwing," he advised.

Mechanically, I targeted two players and threw the balls simultaneously, pegging both players.

"What?" Jared said in astonishment, and I wanted to kick myself hard for stupidity. I didn't dare look at Emery.

"When did you learn to throw like that?" Jared asked, appearing on my left, armed with a ball. "And when did you become ambidextrous?"

"I've been practicing," was all I could think to say.

His mouth curled at the corners in the way that I loved. My heart flip-flopped in response.

"So you got over your ball fear?" he asked, pitching his ball.

"Yeah, I guess," I said, swaying to avoid a Robin launch. I couldn't believe he was trying to carry on a conversation in the middle of a dodgeball game, much less trying to carry on a conversation with me.

The curl pulled up into a perfect smile. "And I hear you're also over your snake fear."

Jared's remark triggered a memory, and in my mind's eye, I saw Nate pass a garter snake to him in our back yard. I watched from the deck, refusing to come down. Nate teased me, but Jared released the snake under the fence, then smiled at me and said, "It's safe now…"

I caught a ball to the gut. "Why did you choose me, Jared?"

Palming a ball, he didn't answer. I glanced at him and saw that he was pondering. I knew his "thinking" expression well, and I understood what confused him. My question could be taken in more than one way.

"Why did you choose me first to be on your team?" I clarified.

"Last time I played this game, you got me out," he answered, stepping toward me to skirt a ball.

This I grasped. "So it was strategy."

Surprised, he looked at me, and our eyes locked in a familiar way. At that same moment, I saw Robin hurl a ball with all her might from the corner of my eye. It flew over the centerline, en route to Jared. Tearing my gaze from his, I instinctively threw myself in front of him, a fraction of a second too late to catch the ball, only to act like a shield. I could hear his quick intake of breath when I moved in front of him at mind-boggling speed. Emery would not be pleased. My armor came up, just as the ball struck my chest, making a sharp smacking noise.

Robin hooted in victory.

"Cassy, are you hurt?" Jared gasped in my ear. I saw his fingertips brush my arm, but couldn't feel the touch with my hardened skin. Alarmed, I lurched forward, anguishing that he might have noticed my skin. The possibility overwhelmed me.

"Obviously I'm not the only one she has it in for," I said, the words flying out of my mouth before I could stop them.

Appalled with myself, I ran away, maneuvering around players and not looking back. I climbed the bleachers, gave my friends a tight smile as I passed them, and continued to the top where I could be alone. Dropping down on the bench, I pressed my elbows to my knees, raked my hands into my hair, glanced up, and ruefully watched Jared throw a ball, his face fierce. The ball hit the floor and bounced into Emery's waiting hands.

I closed my eyes and imagined Jared saying my name again. *Cassy.* He had called me "Cassy" when we were friends.

I can't think about this anymore, I decided, and forced my thoughts to something productive: the mystery. Eyes shut, I slouched against the cinderblock wall and broke down Saturday night's events. *James Flynn unlocks Roga's habitat. Roga escapes, walks across the zoo, resists feasting along the way, and climbs over the petting zoo's fence into the Westings' woods, leaving no scent behind.* I shook my head. No scent made no sense. Every creature leaves behind scent.

Okay, lack of scent doesn't compute, but there is the physical evidence: hair, dung, and paw prints. My mind stumbled, and I swung my thoughts back around, as if looking back at a rock I had tripped over on the road. *Hair and dung: scents. Why didn't I pick them up Sunday night?* I revisited Sunday evening. Against my eyelids, William ran across the clearing, moonlight bouncing off the metallic suit, bag bouncing on his hip—

My eyes popped open, and I sat up, having solved a piece of the puzzle. Beyond excited, I looked down at Emery. He was already watching me, and because he was watching me and not paying attention to the game, he didn't see the ball coming straight at him, compliments of Jared.

"Ball," I gasped, wincing as it plowed into his stomach. That had to have hurt.

Displaying no signs of pain, Emery jogged off the floor without delay. I motioned for him to hurry up the bleachers. Flush face dripping with sweat, he slid next to me and deduced, a little out of breath, "You've had an epiphany."

"If that means I figured something out, yeah, I had an epiphany!"

He brought his fingers to his lips, reminding me to keep my voice down.

Hardly able to contain myself, I rushed on, "There's something I forgot about that night, and it totally breaks my heart telling you this, because, okay, I admit, I was crushing on William a little. He just seemed so nice and kind, but he isn't! Not at all! He had a bag—"

"He planted a false tiger trail," Emery jumped ahead.

"Exactly! He must have had a stamp in the bag, you know, to make tiger prints. The rest he probably collected from Roga's habitat."

Emery ruminated. Watching him think, I sensed he had ideas other than mine.

"What are you thinking about?" I asked.

"Our next step. Here's what we'll do. Tonight, we stakeout the Westings' as planned, then tomorrow after school, we'll look for clues in the zoo."

"Perfect! We'll have all afternoon." Wednesdays were our modified school day. We were dismissed at 12:30.

"Tell your mom that you're helping me run errands before cleaning house," Emery schemed. When I frowned, he quickly added, "It isn't a complete lie."

"Every lie is a complete lie," I grumbled. I could see a way around being deceitful, but not if I wanted to check out the zoo, too. "I'll just add this to my 'Ask-Forgiveness-For' list."

Alarm crossed Emery's face. "This isn't an actual list, is it?" he inquired quickly.

"Only up here." I tapped my temple. "And it's getting longer by the day. As far as the zoo goes, remember Carli told us it's closed for now?"

Emery shrugged, unconcerned.

Sighing, I tapped my temple again. "'Trespassing on zoo property' added in advance."

Emery smiled slyly. "Thank heavens, I don't feel compelled to keep a list," he said.

"Yeah, let's not go there," I teased.

Hoots and hollers let loose around us. We both looked at the gym floor. Panting, Hudson Cox walked toward the bleachers as his remaining teammate, Zach Guzman, scooped up a ball. Before he could straighten up, my remaining team member and captain pegged his back. Sweaty and exhausted, Zach dropped to his knees, leaving Jared the Last Man Standing.

Robin jumped up and ran toward him. I quickly looked back at Emery. His attention was already on me. I offered him my fist.

"Here's to the end of another fun-filled day of high school," I said.

"Hear, hear," he agreed, and we bumped fists.

Fourteen

Monkey Wrench

After school on Wednesday, Jason dropped us off near the zoo's parking lot. The plan was to follow the zoo's perimeter to the petting zoo, where we would then climb the fence, trespassing the same way Roga had presumably escaped. Fingers crossed that this undertaking would bear better results than last night's stakeout. We needed a break, and we needed it fast. Our guts told us that somehow time was running out.

Cutting through the woods, we walked along the fence enclosing the zoo. Three feet of weedy ground separated it from high habitat walls until we reached the open corrals of the petting zoo. At the end of the last wall, Emery peeked into the alpaca pen. "No one in the near vicinity," he reported. "What about the not-so-near vicinity?"

I did a broader scan, evaluated scents and sound, and concluded, "Nothing in the not-so-near vicinity that will do anything other than bite or spit on us."

Emery lifted his eyebrows. "Spit?"

"Yeah, the alpacas," I explained, motioning to the pen. A chocolate-brown alpaca with severely protruding teeth stared at me, awkwardly chewing hay. "They spit."

Emery grinned. "They do not."

"Yes, they do," I insisted, having no idea if alpacas spit or not. "Just like camels."

"Well, I guess there's only one way to find out," Emery said, grabbing the chain link high. "I'll race you over."

Unsurprisingly, I made it over first. As we crossed the pen, the alpacas kept their distance—thank goodness. The last thing I wanted was to be right in this instance.

After checking out the goat portico, we made our way to the tiger's habitat. Behind the Reptile House, we took a path marked "Zoo Staff Only," assuming it led to the backside of Roga's habitat. Several yards down the restricted path, I caught William's scent.

"It's William," I whispered, pointing ahead. "Coming this way."

Emery motioned to a pump house off the path. Sprinting for it, we hunkered down behind it. By then I had distinguished another human scent drifting from the direction of William's. This scent was vaguely familiar, too.

"He's with someone," I whispered.

"Listen in," Emery whispered back.

I concentrated, coasting the airwaves until I heard a man's voice. I recognized it immediately. "He's with Ian, and there's also a woman. Ian called her Deb. I think she's another zookeeper."

Emery nodded, and I kept listening. Ian and Deb carried on a conversation consisting of bantering and flirting. It didn't surprise me Ian was a flirt. As I waited for William to contribute to the conversation, I tried to distinguish a third human scent but couldn't. It dawned on me at this point that William hadn't talked because he wasn't with Ian and Deb. I had made a mistake. It had been Ian in the suit.

"Ian wore the suit, not William," I whispered quickly.

"Keep listening," Emery urged. "I'll nod when I can hear them, too."

I got the nod right as Ian and Deb's conversation switched to the Sasquatch enthusiasts.

"These crazies are driving me crazy," Ian complained. "Do you know I caught a couple of these nutcases wandering around here this morning?"

"'Nutcases' is a little harsh, though I will admit they are a little unusual."

"*Unusual*? Look at what they're doing. Combing these woods every night, looking for a hairy humanoid."

"So is Leroy Rays. Are you also calling him a nutcase?" Deb challenged.

"Well, not to his face. I like my pretty one too much to do *that*. But, yes, my opinion of the mighty hunter has diminished. I doubt I'll be able to stomach his hack, third-rate cable show again."

Deb giggled. "You're terrible."

"Yes. Yes, I am. But I'm honest. Take away all the muscle and bravado, and Rays is off his rocker like the rest of his Bigfoot cohorts. Mark my words, Bigfoot isn't the scariest thing roaming around here these days." Ian's voice took on a serious edge. "I had a talk with Margad this morning about running these people off her property."

"What did she say?"

"She's sold out to this nonsense. Deb, you should talk to her. I'm encouraging all the staff to."

"I don't know. What harm are they really doing?"

"Aside from extreme annoyance, none—*yet*. It's only a matter of time before one of these loonies goes off the deep end. This really is a safety issue, you know. Are you comfortable alone here at night knowing what's out there?"

"Now you're just being dramatic, and you know I won't be alone. Speaking of cub duty, you do realize you're scheduled Thursday and Friday?"

"Thanks, Mom. What would I do without you? Hey, just had a thought. How about I keep you company tonight? Help you with that last bottle feeding?"

Deb laughed. "I'd be safer with the Sasquatch."

"Oh, break my heart, Deb! Don't you want a Herculean trained in the art of Twon-Jun-Doe something-or-other to escort you to your car after the shift? Midnight is the witching hour, when all these mythical creatures come out of hiding and terrorize us mere mortals, you know?"

"I'll take my chances, and you had better watch yourself, too. I can't imagine a Sasquatch resisting such a *pretty* face."

When they ambled further up the path, Emery signaled for us to move. Resuming our quest, he quickened his pace with added intensity. I could see by his expression that he believed he had solved another piece of the puzzle and was now eager to confirm his theory. At the backside of Roga's habitat, he eyed the gate, stating without stopping, "It's wide enough."

"Wide enough for what?" I asked at his heels.

He walked up to a tall gate with strips of thin wood woven through the chain link and pulled it open, revealing the tiger's future habitat, which was currently a hundred yards of excavated land with a couple dozen erected steel bars edging a mound of dirt.

"Wide enough for that." Emery pointed at a forklift parked on the dirt mound. "Come through, so I can close the gate." While shutting the gate, he explained, "You couldn't pick up Roga's scent in the woods because he was never in them. Roga didn't escape. He was stolen."

"Stolen?" My mind quickly organized a scenario. "They—whoever they are—drugged him, drove that forklift into the habitat, loaded him up, then drove him out here." I indicated the ground.

"Where they transferred him to another vehicle and escaped that way," Emery finished, and pointed to a wide chain link gate on the south side of the fence that gave access to a dirt road. "That road feeds into Catamount Mountain Road," he explained. "We drove by it the first night we came up."

"Should we walk along it and look for clues?"

"No. Running surveillance on Ian will turn up more." While fishing his phone from his pocket, he gave me the game plan. "After we take you home, Jason and I will come back and wait for Ian to get off work." Before I could protest, he pushed speed dial and gestured for me to hold the argument that he knew was coming. Bringing the phone to his ear, his gaze drifted to the gate.

"Ready?" I heard Jason answer.

"We'll meet you in fifteen," Emery told him, and then disconnected the call. He looked at me. "I know the objections you're about to lambaste me with, but we don't have time for anything heated, so I'm appealing to you to be reasonable and hear me out."

I crossed my arms, offended but reasonable.

"I plan to tail Ian when he gets off work, which I'm presuming will be around five or six o'clock this evening. I have no idea where he will go, or how long we'll be out. What I do know is you are due home late afternoon and won't be able to leave your house again until your family has turned in for the night. So you see why your coming along with us is impossible."

I scowled, because Emery was right. There was no way for me to participate.

"Now that that's settled, let's address your obvious concern about my decision to involve Jason deeper. This will be a two-man operation. If Jason doesn't drive, I'll have to borrow my mom's car—"

"I didn't know you knew how to drive," I interrupted with surprise.

"Huh?" Emery said, without elaborating, and went on, "Needless to say, borrowing my mom's car would be chancy, driving at such a distance. If I were pulled over, that would end tonight's undertaking. Also, with so many unknown variables, it's wise to have someone watching my back, which Jason will do, if I pay him, of course."

"Or he'll stab it," I warned.

"Always a possibility, but don't worry. I have more than enough to cover his imminent blackmail."

"Blackmail? You think he's going to blackmail you?"

"It would go against his character not to. Presently he believes that we're just a couple of thrill-seeking kids, but once I have him tail Ian, that changes."

I didn't like this. I didn't like it one bit. "You said Jason is smart. What if he figures this all out?"

"Well, it would be nice if someone did," Emery joked.

"I'm being serious!" I clamped my hands to my chest, ready to hyperventilate. "It feels like the world is closing in, like everything is teetering on the edge, ready to fall down around us."

Emery placed his hands on my shoulders. "I would never let that happen," he said, looking into my eyes. "Everything will be all right, and rest assured that I do know how to play this all off with Crenshaw. Between tailing, surveillance, and the misleading hints I'll drop like breadcrumbs, he'll conclude that I'm doing P.I. work, illegally, of course, since I'm too young to be licensed."

"That's your plan?" I said, questioning his sanity. "That is the lamest thing I've ever heard! Why would Jason believe something so ridiculous?"

"Why not? It's more plausible than the truth."

After thinking this over, I had to admit that a fifteen-year-old private eye was more conceivable than a savant and his mutant friend trying to solve a mystery revolving around a supernatural suit of armor—which was a gift from a mythical Roman god, no less.

"All right. I'll trust that you can handle Jason, and I acquiesce to your plan." I had looked up *acquiesce* after Captain Jack Sparrow used it in *Pirates of the Caribbean*. It meant "to reluctantly agree," which was what I was doing.

Emery grinned. "How long have you been sitting on 'acquiesce'?"

"A long time, and leave it to you to give me an opportunity to use it. Well, let's go meet your new partner so you two can dump me off at home."

"I only have one partner," Emery said, flashing a big smile.

"Whatever," I replied, but inside I smiled real big, too.

~~~

Lost in our separate thoughts, we walked silently until we veered from the zoo's perimeter fence and into the woods. It was then that I ended the silence.

"Okay, this is what I've figured out. James Flynn has nothing to do with this. William set him up. He also had Ian put on the suit and create a fake tiger trail. What I can't figure out is why. What would William want with Roga? And why did he want the tiger hunters out of these woods?"

"Not to belabor the point, but we still don't know if Westing is directly involved. In regards to Flynn, I agree with you. He is definitely someone's dupe, and whoever it is knew that he was about to be fired."

"Like Ian?"

"Like Ian," Emery confirmed. "Carli said her mom asked Ian to be present when she fired Flynn, giving him prior knowledge. This would explain why Roga was stolen on a night that was hardly ideal, with a hundred plus potential witnesses in the zoo. The perpetrators had no choice but to act then. Their fall guy would have lost staff access the next day."

Chewing on this, I mused, "William and Ian were trapped with us. I wonder who their accomplices are?"

"Exactly, accomplices. It would take a minimum of three people to pull off everything that night."

"At least, and I suppose they set the bats loose and cut the lights so we would all freak and cover up any noise they were making."

"The rain worked to their advantage, too, creating noise and washing away tire tracks. Being trapped in the auditorium also provided an airtight alibi for Ian and William, *if* he is involved."

"Of course he is. Man, you're *so* stubborn."

"Isn't that the kettle calling the pot black?" Emery teased.

"I never understood that saying, but *don't* explain. Okay, so how does Roga fit in? Why steal him? Why try so hard to make it look like he had escaped? And why send the hunters on a wild goose chase?" The hair on the back of my neck prickled, and I glanced around quickly. *Something bad is going to happen in these woods*, I thought. I felt it in my bones. *What, though?*

"And why is Ian trying to persuade Mrs. Westing to revoke permission to the Sasquatch enthusiasts to be on her property?" Emery added. His eyes narrowed, drifting up to the canopy of branches. "What are they up to?"

"Do you think they're bringing Roga back here, to the woods?"

"Perhaps." A sudden grin split Emery's face, and his sparkling eyes dropped to me. "But whatever their scheme is, we've thrown a monkey wrench in it," he said, giving my hair a jovial yank. "Haven't we, Sasquatch?"

~~~

Reclining on my bed and outfitted in my nighttime clothes, I glanced at the alarm clock for the hundredth time. *11:56* glowed in the dark.

"Most excruciating night *ever,*" I grumbled, shifting my eyes back to the cell phone. It had been almost two hours since Emery's last text. At that point, he was sitting in the Jetta parked outside Finnigan's, where Ian made a beeline after work. Emery sent Jason inside to pose as a patron and run surveillance on Ian, who "caroused with a gaggle of bimbos"—Jason's words, not Emery's. To pass the time, Emery texted other "Jasonisms." Sad that his henchman's sarcasm had been the highlight of my evening thus far,

"Please be home, Joe," I mumbled, getting to my feet. "I need someone to talk to, other than myself." After pulling on my windbreaker and ski mask, I swiped up the box of Oreos from my dresser and took off. Oreos weren't homemade cookies, but I figured they were better than nothing.

I was thrilled to pick up Joe's scent when entering Seattle Center, though I had already decided if he had moved on that I would track him down. Hearing his snores echo inside Moses' belly brought a smile to my face. I just couldn't wait to see him.

"Knock, knock," I whispered, lightly tapping my knuckles on the sculpture's steel. Joe's snore caught. "You awake, Joe?"

There was silence, and then a tentative, "That you, Green Eyes?"

"Yep. Hope you don't mind me stopping by."

He poked his head out of Moses and stared at me briefly before smiling. "Not at all," he said. "I've been wonderin' how you're doing. Gimme a minute." As he crawled out, I glanced at the Oreos and felt a little guilty. I had promised homemade oatmeal raisin; I should have brought homemade oatmeal raisin.

"Sorry about the cookies," I apologized when Joe was out. "These were all we had at home. It's been a little crazy, so I haven't had time to make the oatmeal raisin, but I will, just as soon as I get a chance."

Joe stared the box, a grateful look on his sad face. "Thank you. That's real thoughtful of you." He gestured to Moses. "Why don't we take a seat?"

We sat next to one another on the wood chips, our backs against the cold steel. I opened the box and offered an Oreo to Joe. With a toothy grin, he scooped one out with his index finger. "Thank you kindly," he said, twisting the top off like a kid.

I twisted mine off, too, and scraped the cream filling off with my teeth.

"I hear there's a Bigfoot on that mountain now," Joe remarked conversationally.

I smashed my cookie halves together and stuffed them in my BIG mouth. I had shared too much our last visit.

Joe plopped the cookie bottom in his mouth. Chewing, he studied me thoughtfully. "You can't talk about what's goin' on up there," he ventured.

I nodded.

"Well, all right then. You just talk about what you can."

"Thanks," I said, showing my relief. "You're one of three people who even know about me. One of the other two, uh, Mendel…" I gave myself a quick mental palm to the head for using Emery's middle name as a pseudonym. My stupidity was endless. "Uh, anyway, Mendel would be upset with me if I shared more than I already have. He's worried you'll tell someone about me."

"Well, you tell Mendel a herd of wild horses couldn't drag your secret out of me," Joe said passionately.

I searched his aged face for signs of betrayal, finding none.

"You start the conversation," he suggested, "so I don't tread on forbidden ground."

Joe munched another cookie, waiting for me to come up with a safe topic. I decided there wouldn't be any harm in telling him about Jared, or in this instance, "Edgar." I gave him a brief rundown of Edgar's history, telling him how Edgar had a dad who floated in and out of his life and a mom who worked so hard to make ends meet that Edgar hardly saw her, and for these reasons he had been drawn like a magnet to my family, which he almost seemed part of until I blew everything up. I was too embarrassed to tell Joe how I had ruined it. From there, I moved onto Edgar's character, sharing that he was the kindest, toughest boy I knew, smart, a deep thinker, an avid reader like me, and could throw a baseball ninety miles per hour. This impressed Joe a lot. Then came "Jezebel," who for some mysterious reason

Edgar was going out with now. Well, maybe not so mysterious, when you factored in that Jezebel was tall, blond, and beautiful. This praise of Jezebel triggered so much irritation that I switched the topic back to Mendel, explaining how he had put me on "eavesdropping restriction" at school so I wouldn't overhear any gory "Edgbel" details.

Joe chuckled at "Edgbel." However, one look in my eyes and his laughter ceased. "Mendel sounds like a real good friend," he remarked gently.

"The best," I confirmed. "He watches out for me, and that's why he's doesn't want me eavesdropping on the gossip. My emotions can get a little crazy, because of what's *wrong* with me, but you already know that. You saw me go after that guy." Fidgeting, I thought about how to phrase my next statement. "When I get angry, it's not like regular anger. I have in me what I call 'the beast.'"

Joe stared grimly at the cookie that he rolled back and forth between his fingers. "We all got our beast to control," he said, his voice hollow and pained. "A long time ago, I allowed my beast to kill a man."

A shocked gasp escaped before I could catch it. Lost in remorse, Joe appeared not to notice.

"I say 'a man,'" he continued, watching the cookie, "but Theo was just a boy. We was eighteen, angry at each other, and we fought." Tears pooled in his haunted eyes. Sympathetic tears moistened mine. I had never witnessed sorrow to this depth before.

"I paid my debt to society, but never will to myself. Not a day goes by that I don't think about my friend, Theo."

"Theo was your friend?" I whispered.

"Since we was babies." Joe wiped his eyes, then looked at me fiercely. "Don't ever let that beast get the best of you."

"I won't," I promised him, promised myself. Then I hugged Joe, a convicted murderer and my friend. "I swear I won't."

"I know you won't." Joe patted my back. "What happened to you was meant to be. You have a destiny like no other."

I pulled away and stared at him. Word for word, I had thought this very thing before, a still voice in the back of my mind comforting me when I was in my deepest despair. Before I could tell Joe this, my phone vibrated in my pocket.

"That's Mendel," I told him, retrieving my phone. Clearing the hoarseness from my voice, I answered, "Hey, Mendel."

"Mendel?" Emery repeated, then blew out a frustrated breath. "You're with the homeless man, Joe," he deduced, and added, angry with himself, "I neglected to discuss your last visit with him."

"You've had a lot on your mind," I pointed out. "But no worries. Everything's cool."

Joe put his hand over his heart, reminding me.

I smiled at him and passed along to Emery, "Joe wants me to tell you that wild horses couldn't drag my secret out of him."

"Well, that's reassuring," Emery replied dryly. An unhappy silence followed, which he ended in a much-improved tone, "I'm trusting that you're being wise, Cassidy, and not giving Joe critical information."

"That's right. I'm not."

"Of course you're not. You're a bright girl. We'll discuss this later. Jason will be back anytime. He went to 7-Eleven to stock up on snacks and cigarettes for the night."

"For the night? Em—Mendel, where are you?"

"Leaning against a tree about ten yards from Ian White's driveway. He lives a little over a mile up the road from the zoo. Jason and I are going to stake out his house tonight. Tomorrow when he leaves, I'll let myself in."

My throat tightened, and I clasped it, trying to compute all the horrifying information I had received in those few sentences. *Emery is alone in the dark on Catamount*

Mountain Road, only yards from Ian's driveway. He's waiting for Jason to return so they can spy on Ian, a bad guy, and maybe dangerous. They'll be in the Jetta, all night, in the cold. When Ian leaves his house, Emery will put his lock picks to work and break in. I don't think so!

"I'm coming up!"

As if they were in cahoots, Joe frowned at me and shook his head as Emery stated firmly, "You are not coming up."

"I most certainly am!"

"Cassidy, think this through. Your alarm clock goes off at 6:45 a.m., and if you are not there to turn it off, the next phone call leaving your house will be to 911. Face it. You don't have my autonomy."

"You might not have as much freedom as you think! Did you tell your mom your plans?" I was too flustered to come up with a pseudonym for Serena.

"Yes, she's aware of where I will be tonight. I want you to stay home from school today."

"Well, I want you to come home!"

"Cassidy."

"I can't, okay? I just missed yesterday. I'll fall behind. I'm not you."

Emery grew quiet. I guessed he was debating what to do. "Will it be too much for you to go solo?"

Apprehension rippled through me. I wasn't worried about what I might do at school without Emery to keep an eye on me. I just couldn't imagine a day without him. *Don't be pathetic,* I scolded myself, and stated with remarkable confidence, "No problem."

"Be honest. Is it too much?"

"Stop asking me that! I'll be fine. I can take care of myself. Be careful, okay?"

"How can I not be with Jason watching my back?" he teased.

"I thought you said you didn't want me to come up there."

"You're right," Emery amended. "I don't. I'll be fine, too."

"I know." I squeezed my eyes shut. "You can take care of yourself, too. Still, be careful."

"I'll text you in the morning. Head home soon."

"Okay. Night, Mendel."

"You, too." Emery disconnected.

Opening my eyes, I put on a brave face for Joe. "Sorry you had to sit through that. Mendel had a lot to say."

"You and Mendel are real close," he remarked, looking at me with concern.

"Like two peas in a pod! Uh, I need to go. If I don't get some exercise, I won't be able to sleep tonight." We got to our feet, and I handed him the Oreo box. "Next time, I'll bring homemade cookies, but that probably won't be for a couple days." *No way am I letting Emery go up to Catamount Mountain without me again. No way!*

"Thank you, Green Eyes," Joe said, studying me. "Take care of yourself, and listen to Mendel."

"He gives me no choice," I replied, deciding not to address the fact that I could take care of myself again. I was really tired of people worrying about me. I was the last person anyone should worry about. "You take care, too. See you soon." With that, I shot away at top speed. I had much fretting to work off.

Fifteen

A Star Wars Encounter Of The Worst Kind

Those hours before lunch period the next day crawled by. I was so worried about Emery that I couldn't concentrate on anything or anyone around me. I would clue in seconds after being spoken to, meeting the questioning look of the speaker with a questioning one of my own. After the speaker repeated the comment a couple of times, and I failed to listen again, the questioning look became an annoyed look, and they would give up altogether—not that I cared. I didn't want to talk to anyone. I just wanted Emery back safe and sound.

Needless to say, when I picked up his scent on the way to the cafeteria, my heart leapt for joy. Scanning the crowded hall, I spotted Emery lingering along the edge of the entryway to a custodial closet, his eyes searching the tide of bodies for me. When our eyes met, a smile exploded on my face. Answering with a smile, he crooked his finger for me to come over, then moved into the doorway. Going against the flow, I maneuvered to where he had disappeared. The entryway was empty, but the closet door was cracked open a few inches. I laughed a little, because this closet was usually locked. Obviously Emery's lock picks were getting some action today.

I slipped into the dark closet and pulled the door shut behind me. "Are you a sight for sore eyes," I declared as I threw my arms around Emery's neck.

"I'd like to say the same about you," he said, reaching around me to feel for the light switch. I released him so he could search better.

"Am I at least close?" Emery asked.

"A little to the left," I instructed, enjoying watching him fumble around. "That's it. No, too high."

"I don't suppose you could turn them on?"

"You suppose right. Come down, just a tad."

Emery found the switch. "Are you all right?" he asked, blinking his eyes to adjust them to the light.

"I am now that my best friend is here. So how much in harm's way did you put yourself?"

"Hardly any, but I'll let you be the judge. When Ian left this morning, I let myself in—"

"Only you? Not Jason?"

"Only me. Jason kept a lookout from Ian's neighbor's driveway. They're conveniently out of town. That's where we spent the night, in the Jetta."

"Were you cold?" I had fretted most of the night about him being cold.

"No, Jason's stimulating conversation kept me toasty inside," he joked. "As it happens, Lily is also out of town."

"Oh, that's right. She lives with Ian."

"Yes, she does." Emery's face became uneasy. "When I listened to his phone messages, one was from Lily. She accompanied William on a business trip to San Francisco. They're due back Friday evening. After not finding anything incriminating in Ian's messages or on his desktop, I searched his bedroom, uncovering nothing suspicious there, either. Then I went into Lily's room."

"What did you find?"

"It wasn't so much what I found, but what I felt. Her room was disturbingly immaculate."

"That is disturbing," I teased, this coming from Mr. Clean himself.

"Cassidy, it was excessive. Every item appeared to have a precise place, as if Lily laid them out in such a way that she would know if they'd been tampered with. Needless to say, I was extremely careful. This photo was taped dead center on her dresser mirror." He took his phone from his jacket

192

pocket. On the screen was a picture of Lily and William in formal wear, arms around one another, looking very happy. William had his other arm around his mother, while Lily locked arms with another familiar figure.

"That's Rory Michaels," I told Emery.

"I know." He studied the picture. "It's obvious that he was close with Lily."

"Makes sense. He and the Westings were like family, and Lily is almost a Westing."

"Yes, she is." Emery frowned at the screen. "Something about this picture doesn't sit right with me. Something about Lily doesn't sit right with me."

"Well, she shouldn't. She *is* William's fiancée, and her brother planted a tiger trail while wearing her fiancée's suit," I pointed out. "Whatever is going on, she's in on it, too."

"No, it's something more." Emery studied the picture a moment more before shaking his head and returning the phone to his pocket. "This next part you won't like, though it's the break I was hoping for—once we use it to our advantage. Right after I snapped a picture of the photo, Jason called to let me know Ian had driven by him. Luckily, Ian's driveway is very long, so I had plenty of time to get out. By the time he pulled up, I was already hidden behind bushes near the front porch. This is when things got interesting." His eyes sparkled. "Ian parked, cut the engine, and did a 360 scan out the car windows. When he worked up enough courage to get out of the car, he did another scan. With his back to me, I chucked a rock at a pine tree on the other side of him. You should have seen the look on his face." Emery grinned at the memory. "He ran full-throttle to the front porch, literally quivering with fear, and could barely unlock the door."

"What was he afraid of?" I asked, confused.

"You."

I pointed at my chest. "Me?"

"Yes, you! You wonderful Sasquatch," he confirmed jovially, gripping my shoulders and shaking me. "Ian White is terrified, and we'll use his terror to our advantage."

This was a lot to soak in. "How?"

"I'll explain when you come over after school. Right now, you need to go before the cafeteria stops serving lunch. Lack of lunch bag tells me you're purchasing today. Pizza?"

"Belgian waffles."

Emery grinned. "That was my second guess."

"So, I suppose this means you're not staying," I said, bummed.

"No, I have to track down a costume."

This soaked in real fast. "No," I groaned, slapping my forehead. "Please, please, please tell me you're not thinking what I think you're thinking."

"Smart girl." He tapped my nose. "You've already figured it out." Wrenching the doorknob, he added with a smile, "By the way, you're my best friend, too."

Before I could answer, he slipped away. To the door, I whined, "But, Emery, I don't want to be a Sasquatch!"

~~~

After the longest school day ever, I practically ran home. Flinging my backpack into the foyer and yelling to Mom that I was going over to the Phillipses', I sprinted across the street and knocked impatiently on Emery's front door. He had much to explain, such as how scaring the beejeebus out of Ian would accomplish anything.

Emery answered after the second knock. "How did P.E. go?"

"Great. I ignored them. They ignored me." I pushed past him into the house.

"Have you actually seen Jared and Robin together yet?"

I sniffed the air, detecting an earthy odor. "I don't look," I replied, glancing around. "Why?"

"They just don't appear all that enthralled."

"Oh, they are, all right. You should hear how *enthralled* they are. Robin won't shut up about it in the girl's locker room."

"You're not supposed to listen," Emery reminded me, raking his bangs back with his hand. My eyes locked on his hand. His fingernails were dirty and his skin was moist, like he had just washed his hands.

"I see you've been gardening," I said, knowing full well what he had been doing, and it was not gardening.

Emery observed his filthy nails. "I assume by the sarcasm that you know I've been authenticating your costume."

"*Authenticating*? Oh, please! And you do realize that I haven't agreed to anything?"

"You will," he replied with the utmost confidence, and motioned for me to come along. "Follow me to my creation."

"Don't need to. I have a nose." I walked by him toward the kitchen where the earthy smell emanated from. The door to the enclosed porch was partially open. I flung it wide and had a *Star Wars* encounter of the worst kind.

"*That* is not a Sasquatch." I pointed at the muddied Chewbacca costume that lay sprawled over the cement like flattened road kill.

"A wookie was the best I could come up with on such short notice," Emery protested playfully.

"Poor Chewie," I said in commiseration, walking up to it and looking down into Chewbacca's mournful eyeholes. "Look at what this madman has done to you. But it's nothing compared to what he wants to do to Ian White." I flopped down on the chaise lounge and stared at Emery hard. "Why do you want me to give Ian a heart attack? And if you don't get that grin off your face, I'm out of here."

Emery forced his face solemn, and somehow kept it that way as he clarified, "I don't want you to kill him. I only want you to traumatize him."

"Thanks for clearing that up. See ya." I started to rise from the chaise. Emery pushed me back down.

"Do you want to find Roga?" he asked.

"Yes."

"Then you'll hear me out." He pulled up a folding chair and sat down. Beyond him, Serena appeared in the doorway with a red apple in her hand. *Good*, I thought. *She needs to hear what her own flesh and blood plans to do.*

"There is a method to my madness," Emery said. "The objective in ambushing Ian is to make him believe, for one reason or another, that the Sasquatch has become fixated on him as prey. With his animal knowledge, he should also conclude that it tracked his scent to his house."

Serena bit into the apple.

"How does Ian thinking a Sasquatch is after him help us find Roga?" I asked.

"I don't believe Ian has carte blanche with the suit, but he'll want it. He'll view it as his best means of protection from the creature that he believes is hunting him. The hope is he'll lead us to whoever does have possession of the suit, which could also lead us to Roga."

"What if Ian just skips town?" That was what I would do.

"He won't," Emery said, as if Ian had sworn to him that he wouldn't.

I looked at Serena. "What do you think about all this?"

"What Emery is proposing is highly speculative," she replied, not at all parental-like, but very Serena-like. "He's similar to his father in this way."

This bothered me. I didn't like Emery being similar to his dad in *any* way.

"I'm taking that as a compliment," Emery said to her over his shoulder.

"Take it as you wish. Show Cassidy what you have in the bag." She took another bite of apple.

For the first time, I noticed the paper grocery bag next to the bucket Emery had made mud in.

"This is the best part of the costume," he claimed enthusiastically. Pulling the bag to him, he reached inside and gingerly lifted out a pair of hand claws, three-inch steel blades that slipped over the wearer's fingers, and a leather strap to secure the weapons in place. They were perhaps the most terrifying things I had ever seen.

"And *what* do you expect me to do with those?"

"When you drop onto Ian's car as he's coming down his driveway, you're going to use these to destroy his custom paint job, which will be a shame, because his car is a 1968 Camaro in mint condition. But we'll make the sacrifice in order to leave its owner with undeniable evidence that he was indeed attacked by the mythical creature he mocked when hitting on his co-worker yesterday afternoon." While explaining this, Emery had slipped on a claw and now admired the blades with boyish fascination. He had never looked more adorable or more frightening.

Dumbfounded, I asked Serena, "Is his dad a juvenile delinquent, too?"

Serena shrugged. "More or less."

Emery cracked up, while I shook my head in amazement. The Phillipses had to be the strangest family on the planet.

"Emery, I'm assuming you'll have the young man from across the street tail Ian White after Cassidy assaults him," Serena said, picking apple pulp out of her teeth.

"I'm not assaulting him," I corrected quickly. "Only his car." After clarifying this, I had to wonder at what point I had agreed to assault anything.

"I'm planting a tracking device on Ian's car before he leaves the zoo," Emery explained to his mom, which was news to me, like almost everything else. "I didn't have time to plant one yesterday. After Cassidy assaults Ian,"—he paused to flash me a smile—"Jason will pick us up, and we'll track Ian on GPS."

"Did Mickey give you the tracking device?" I asked, since Mickey had provided the one Emery had planted on Selma Heart's car.

"Emery," Serena said, abruptly exasperated, "I hope you have not involved *them*."

Now this was very curious.

"So you know Mickey and Riley?" I asked, though it was obvious she certainly did know them. It was also obvious that she didn't care for them one bit.

"I know enough," Serena huffed, staring at Emery with disapproval. "People are not chess pieces," she warned him cryptically. "What happens if you make a wrong move?"

Emery smirked. "I suppose I'd be checkmated."

"Don't be cheeky," Serena scolded. "And I stand corrected. You are the very *embodiment* of your father."

"I think he's the very embodiment of you," I told her, having had enough of Emery being compared to his dad. "He inherited your brains," I pointed out.

Because his back was turned to her, Emery missed the odd fleeting look that crossed his mother's face. I had seen that particular expression once before: when I accused Serena of wanting to make me her lab rat. "That may be," she said to me, her features haughty again. "I wish he would make better use of his inheritance, however, and choose more suitable individuals to socialize with."

Emery rolled his eyes.

I started to ask why she didn't just tell him that he couldn't "socialize" with Mickey and Riley. She was the mother, after all. But Serena spoke right over me. "As far as this scheme of his is concerned," she said, reprimanding me now, "I suggest you trust Emery's opinion."

"Hey! When did I become the bad guy?" I asked. "I'm not the one with the sketchy friends."

Emery lifted a finger and joked, "With the exception of one, apparently."

"Nonsense," Serena said dismissively, turning to toss the apple core into the kitchen sink. "I haven't accused anyone of being 'sketchy.' My point is: Josef Richter's prototype must be recovered, and any malicious intent regarding it must be exposed for the greater good of all. Emery is the perfect candidate to accomplish both."

"Thanks for the vote of confidence, Mom," Emery said, "cheeky" again, and then inquired of me, "Do I have yours, too?"

"Guess I'd be an idiot not to give it to you," I retorted, and then amended, "You always have it. I want to do a dress rehearsal, though. I'd rather know sooner than later if I'm going to skewer an eyeball with those things." I motioned to the weapon strapped to his hand.

"When you're finished, come down to the lab," Serena said. "I need a blood sample." With that, she walked away.

"Geez, you'd think she'd at least be curious if I poke out an eyeball or not," I said.

"You'd think," he agreed, slyly watching the blades clicking together on his fingers. "You should know that she wants me to teach you to draw your own blood."

My jaw dropped. "You're kidding me, right?"

Click. "Doesn't that sound like something my mom would suggest?" he asked, that crafty look on his face.

It most certainly did sound like something Serena would say.

"Like I would stick a needle in my own arm!" I exclaimed, vexed, horrified.

"She thought it would help ease your anxiety." *Click.*

"Yeah, I'm feeling calm already!"

Click. "Of course, we can avoid all that unpleasantness if you can control your skin reaction." *Click.*

I glared, getting the game. They knew I would jump through hoops of fire before sticking myself with a needle. "You guys are such manipulators," I told him.

Emery smiled at the blades. "Only when we don't get our way." *Click.* "Shall we begin the dress rehearsal, Sasquatch?" *Click.*

Sixteen

Terror Time

"Safe to say they're still gone," Jason remarked as we three stared down Ian's neighbor's driveway. Clouds blocked the moon, making the driveway look like a black hole. Jason had doused his headlights, so Ian's porch light was the only source of light in a long stretch of darkness.

Lucky for us, potential witnesses are either asleep or not home, I thought, twisting my ponytail until it felt like hair would pluck from my scalp. "Safe to say," I agreed in a small voice, struggling to come to terms with the ugly thing I had consented to do—consented because this ugly thing might prevent an even uglier thing from happening. *Big picture,* I reminded myself. *Stay focused on the big picture*.

"Eleven-thirty-three," Emery reported. "Cassidy, we had better set up our equipment." He sent me a conspiratorial smile. Nervous, I stroked the backpack propped next to me, impregnated with "surveillance equipment."

Jason eased the Jetta into the driveway. Shifting into "park," he devilishly advised Emery, "Don't do anything I would do."

"Well, that doesn't leave much," Emery ribbed him.

Briefly setting aside panic, I contemplated the "one-eye-open" friendship Emery and Jason had developed since yesterday afternoon. I figured breaking a litany of laws brought people closer together.

"Park at that construction site a quarter mile down the road," Emery instructed Jason as I went back to fretting. "I'll call you if Ian doesn't head home." Emery had planted the tracking device on the Camaro's underbelly five minutes ago. His phone would alert us when it moved, and we'd be able to track it on the screen. "If that's the case, double back and meet us here. Then we'll catch up with him."

"Will do," Jason replied, seeming to pay more attention to the cigarette he tapped out of a carton than Emery. "You and cupcake better get on that *equipment*."

Emery let out an appreciative laugh while I glared at smug Jason. He knew surveillance equipment was a pantload and was rubbing our noses in it. Question was, what else did he know?

"If you even think about double-crossing us, I'll make you regret it," I warned him.

Jason stuck the cigarette between his smirking lips. "Got me shaking in my boots," he said around the cigarette while scrounging in his jeans pocket for a lighter. "Don't let the door hit you on the way out," he added.

I sensed Emery grinning, so I bopped the side of his head.

"My name is not *cupcake*," I returned acidly, roughly opening the door. Flinging out and yanking the backpack, I slammed the door and stalked toward the strip of woods dividing the two driveways. With each step, my anger dulled, dissipating into anxiety again. I dragged myself a few yards into the trees, sank to the damp, mossy ground, and pulled my burden onto my crossed legs, burying my face in it. The powerful smell of formaldehyde from the costume, intermixed with fertilizer from the mud, burned in my nasal cavity, making me feel like puking even more.

I can't do this. I simply can't.

I listened to the Jetta backing down the driveway and Emery's purposeful footfall coming my way. The beam from his flashlight filtered through the crack between the backpack and my face, illuminating the veins streaming through my eyelids like minuscule rivers.

"Cassidy," he said gently, his clothes rustling as he squatted next to me. "You do have a choice. I'll understand if you choose not to follow through with this."

"Do I have a choice?" I demanded into the backpack. "Do I really?"

"You *always* have a choice. Forgive me if I made you feel that you didn't. I know I can be forceful at times."

His apology made me smile. I lifted my face to his grim one and said, "Well, if that isn't the understatement of the century. You're, like, the bossiest person I know."

The grim line of his mouth turned up ruefully. "I deserve that. Thank you for being gracious, as you always are. What would you like to do?"

"Scare Ian into leading us to the prototype and Roga. Help me suit up?"

After slipping my feet into Chewbacca's rubber-soled feet and pulling on the rest of him, I let Emery zip me in. Tugging the furry gloves on, he strapped the hand claws over those, and then pulled the head over mine, safety-pinning it to the costume. Then we were ready to roll.

While walking to Ian's, Emery went over the plan. "After you drop on the Camaro's hood, give Ian a moment to comprehend what he's looking at. Before scraping the hood, make a bit of a show with the claws."

I glanced at the blades sheathing my fingers, feeling my resolve waver. *How am I going to do this?* "But they're steel, and they look like steel."

"He won't notice. Between shock, darkness, and the ominous way the headlights will illuminate behind your shadowy silhouette, Ian will only see what he has feared he'll see again these last few days."

We stepped onto Ian's driveway, and I stared down at his humble abode, a square log house with a covered porch running the length of it. Stomach acid blasted up my throat. "I'm going to be sick."

"Everything will be fine. Focus on the objective, and remember, no more than twenty seconds from the time you land on the Camaro to when you spring off. I should put on my mask. Hold the flashlight, will you?" After saying this, he glanced at the claws and thought better of the request, opting to clamp the flashlight between his knees instead. "About twenty yards down, there are several hefty limbs hanging over the driveway," he continued as he pulled on his mask. "Why don't you choose one to drop from?"

"Why don't I do that?" I nervously clicked the blades together. The sharp clang penetrated my mental numbness, giving me an idea. "How much time before Ian shows?"

Emery lit the face of his watch. "At least ten minutes."

"Plenty of time! I'm going to personalize the attack for him." I held up my claws. "I'm shredding his house."

"Brilliant! He'll think the Sasquatch is marking its territory."

"Exactly. Just like a tiger would. Poetic, huh?"

"And just desserts," Emery agreed. "Wreak havoc on his bedroom window. The first window on the right side of the house."

"With a vengeance." I smiled cruelly at the house. "By the time I'm done, there will be no question in Ian's mind that he is my chosen one. Hide, and I'll get to work."

Before Emery had stepped off the driveway, I was mangling the front door, red paint shavings sprinkling to the porch. Jumping the porch rail, I zoomed to the back door, giving it a similar treatment. Ian's window frame I inflicted the most damage to, splintering the bottom of the wood frame until it no longer qualified as a board. After that I sped back to the front and assaulted the pine tree that I assumed Emery had thrown the rock at. When finished, I viewed the damage and felt a pang of guilt for making an innocent tree suffer like that.

The next thing I make suffer won't be so innocent.

Don't think, just do. I sped down the driveway, kicking loose gravel behind me, and leapt onto a thick branch. Centering myself over the gravel and pulling my legs up, I emptied my mind, drumming the claws on the bark and fixing my gaze on a piece of obsidian amongst the dull gray gravel. The smooth triangular shape reminded me of an ice cream cone.

"Cassidy, everything will be all right," Emery encouraged from somewhere below. I scanned the trees but couldn't find him. In the distance, a car engine protested up the mountain road. Gulping, I shifted my eyes to the driveway's mouth.

"That isn't Ian," Emery spoke again. I glanced around, but couldn't find him. "I'll tell you when he leaves the zoo. Remember, twenty seconds and it's over."

"Twenty seconds and it's over," I repeated mechanically, and focused on the obsidian again.

A car careened down the mountain while another came up, and I began counting "Mississippis." On the one hundred seventy-seventh "Mississippi," Emery spoke. "Ian just left the zoo. He'll be here in less than a minute."

"Twenty seconds and it's over," I chanted, listening to an engine power up the mountain. "Twenty seconds and it's over. Get the heck off his car after twenty seconds."

Headlights swung into the driveway. The air wheezed from my lungs. "Don't think," I commanded myself. "Just do."

The Camaro crawled over the gravel. Painted marina blue, it had dual black racing stripes running down the hood, which my eyes traveled up to Ian's groggy face behind the windshield. He yawned, and I thought, *You'll be wide awake soon enough.* Feeling my nerves begin to fail, I forced my eyes from Ian to the end of the hood where the racing stripes ended, deciding, *When my toes line up with their edges, I drop.*

Focusing on my toes, I blocked out the crunching of gravel under tires, the smooth hum of the car's engine, the sound of my heart pounding in my ears, and my fear. The edge of the stripes hit the tips of my toes, and I pushed off, dropping like a cannon ball. My feet planted squarely on the hood, crushing it, and I fell into a squat. Ian cried out and slammed on the brakes. The jarring car caused me to lose balance, and I rolled onto my back like a turtle on its shell. Swinging my arms forward, I rolled up into a squat again and met Ian's stare. Gaping, he leaned on the steering wheel, blinking as if I were a mirage.

Terror time.

I lifted my claws and splayed my fingers. Light shimmered off the blades. Ian's eyes bulged, and he breathed a cuss word. Pressing the claws to the stripes, I pulled them down slowly, metal screaming against metal, the sort of grating sound that could drive somebody mad.

The engine let out a roar. Ian kicked the Camaro into reverse, sending me tumbling over the side. My armor came up as I plummeted, landing hard on my hip. Reeling wheels spewed gravel, and one piece struck my left eye. The pain was excruciating. Screaming, I jerked my face away from the onslaught of gravel and forced my eye open, only to discover I had lost vision in it.

He's blinded me! Panicked, I reached for my eye, but caught myself before the razor-sharp tips could fulfill my earlier fear and skewer an eyeball. Pain and shock ignited my anger, and I sprung to my feet, watching the retreating

Camaro through eyes narrowed to slits, gasping in furious breaths. My eye had already healed, but this hadn't lessened my fury raging like wildfire.

Sprinting for the Camaro, I dove for the hood, diving into pure animal instinct. Flying hard and fast, my shoulder slammed into the windshield, cracking the glass. The sound of fracturing glass triggered a memory: the way ice sounded breaking under Nate's weight when stepping on a pond assumed frozen through. The human memory faded, leaving something very inhuman behind. My mind sharpened, and yet was hazy at the same time.

The Camaro slowed to a roll, Ian's foot having slipped off the gas pedal. Chest heaving and heart pounding with excitement, I twisted around to the windshield and glared into his terrified eyes through the webbed glass. I smiled around clenched teeth, thrilled to see his fear, to hear his heart racing with mine. Flexing claws, I clamped onto the sides of the windshield, determined not to let him escape.

His foot found the pedal.

Accelerating in reverse, the Camaro shot backwards, rocketing onto Catamount Mountain Road. Ian cranked the steering wheel hard right, tossing me off. Airborne, my armor came up, encasing me just as I plowed into asphalt. Through the mental haze, I was dimly aware of pain. Rolling a couple of times, I ended up on my side, facing the Westings' property. The Camaro idled a few yards ahead, and I played dead, biding time for my body to recover. I wasn't finished with Ian yet.

Ian fell for my ploy, easing the Camaro back alongside me. Smiling to myself, I willed him to cut the engine and climb out to take a look at my dead carcass. When he didn't do this immediately, I lost patience, flipped over, and jumped to my feet. The look of sheer terror on his face gave me pause.

What am I doing?

He revved the engine, and the Camaro shot off. Watching it speed away, reason lost the small ground gained, and I ran after him, like a cheetah chasing down a gazelle. Approaching the car at inhuman speed, I launched at the back end, soaring over the trunk, and colliding into the back windshield. It broke, forming around me like a cocoon. Ian let out a choked scream, cranked the steering wheel, causing the car to fishtail. As we spun, the horror I had caused penetrated through my jacked-up adrenaline state.

Ian is going to kill himself! I've got to get off this car so he can get hold of himself before he crashes!

Extracting myself from the cocooned glass, I sprang off, not giving one iota where I landed. I smacked fifty miles per hour into a tree and learned my armor had limits. Crumpled in a heap on the road's shoulder, I experienced indescribable pain, and judged by location and my difficulty breathing that my rib cage had been crushed. *Ironic,* I thought, remembering Leroy Rays, the other man I had terrorized. *And just desserts.*

The Camaro raced down the mountain. Gasping for air, I listened for a crash, and thankfully didn't hear one. *He's calmed down. He'll be all right.* My ribs shifted, and I muttered a curse, not wanting to mend so quickly. I deserved pain.

Angry and disgusted with myself, I closed my eyes and listened to another car coming my way and a set of feet pounding the pavement. *Emery,* I knew by his scent. Almost healed by now, I had no gumption to move from the roadside. *Let them see me,* I thought, the car closing in. *Let the world learn my secret. I just don't care anymore.*

However, someone else did.

Umph! Emery landed on top me, knocking the wind out of me and re-cracking ribs. Locking me in his arms, he rolled us off the road and into a ditch.

"Yay!" I gasped out as headlights swept above the ditch. "More just desserts. You broke my ribs."

"The question is whether I've broken mine," he groaned, rolling off me.

"Serious?" I yanked up to my side.

Alarm shot over his face. "Cassidy, don't move," he pleaded, sitting up. Gently, he pushed my shoulder to the ground. "Stay still until you're healed," he ordered.

"Whatever." Tears pooled. "Obviously your ribs are okay. What about the rest of you?"

"I'll have a few bruises, but that's the extent of my injuries, thanks to you."

"*Thanks to me*? I think you have a concussion. What could you possibly be thanking me for?"

"For one, you kept your skin from reacting when I dove for you. If you hadn't it would have been like diving into a cement pool. Good thing you discovered you had that ability during the blood draw. Then there are the claws. I don't even want to tell you the image that popped into my head mid-air."

I winced. He didn't have to tell me. "If I had stabbed you, I would have rammed these stupid things into my heart! I'm evil, Emery! Totally evil."

"You're not evil," he countered, smiling, "just very thorough. Are you healed?"

"Yes," I bit out.

Without a word, Emery turned on the flashlight, picked up my right hand, and unbuckled the claw. By the time he moved to the other claw, I was trembling all over and bawling like a baby. He unpinned the head, took it off, and pulled me into his arms.

"Th-this is the m-mother of a-all crashes," I sobbed into his chest.

"You'll feel better soon," Emery soothed, smoothing my hair. "Then we'll catch up with Ian."

Seventeen

Crenshaw And Casanova

As Emery predicted, my crash wrapped up relatively quickly. After a couple minutes of blubbering in his arms, it was over, and I was amped to find Ian. That isn't to say I didn't feel awful for going feral on Ian. My behavior had been deplorable.

While I de-costumed, Emery called Jason to pick us up, then monitored Ian's movements on GPS. Just as Ian reached the mountain's base, Jason pulled up.

"Where to, Slick?" he asked Emery as we jumped into the Jetta.

"The I-90 frontage road. Ian turned west."

Looking over his shoulder, Jason peeled out of the driveway. "Must be looking for her," he commented, referring to the wife of Emery's fictitious client. The story that had evolved from Emery's "breadcrumbs" was that a suspicious husband had procured his private eye services to prove that his wife and Ian White were involved. Whether or not Jason had actually fallen for this pile of malarkey, who knew?

"Hopefully," Emery replied, playing along. "Did you see Ian drive by?"

"Got a glimpse, runnin' from the Devil like he was." Jason winked at me in the rearview mirror, sending a ripple of alarm up my back.

All the way down the mountain, that wink tormented me. *Was the "Devil" statement a figure of speech?* I mentally wrung my hands. *Or was Jason letting me in on the fact that he hadn't parked where Emery had told him to and witnessed me chasing down Ian?* The possibility of this choked me with fear, until I suddenly recalled that the Camaro wasn't the only car that had a tracking device attached to its underbelly. Emery knew exactly where Jason had parked.

So Jason was just playing with my head, I concluded, annoyed and relieved. *Wouldn't the creep just love to know he had me freakin' this whole time?*

At the frontage road intersection, Jason turned into Finnigan's parking lot, where we could easily tag onto Ian when he reached the intersection. We had watched him on GPS pass through the intersection three times already. He had gone about quarter mile beyond it and was now headed back. A dozen vehicles and a few hog motorcycles occupied the asphalt slab running up to Finnigan's brick, flat-front exterior. Pulling alongside a black double-cab GMC truck with tinted windows, Jason cut the engine and cranked his head left to the intersection, waiting for Ian. When the Camaro came into sight, he made a disgusted sound.

"That is just wrong," he stated, referring to the damage I had caused. I barely noticed the damage, however. My attention was on the haggard man peering through the unharmed band of his windshield as he came to a stop at the intersection. To say I felt bad was a gross understatement.

The signal changed, and Ian drove through the intersection, slowing down.

"He's pulling in," Jason predicted, and we sunk in our seats and peered over the dash. Ian didn't turn into the parking lot, though. He stared anxiously at the bar before picking up speed.

"He's looking for someone," I guessed as Jason started the car. "He thought they might be here, at Finnigan's."

"Well, he'd better find them before a cop pulls him over for that windshield," Jason remarked. He swung the Jetta onto the frontage road and got an eyeful of the Camaro's backside. "Oh, come on!" he complained. "The back windshield, too? *That* is a 1968 Camaro, kids."

"Why are you blaming us?" shot out of my mouth before I could stop it.

A condescending look came on Jason's face, and he advised me, "Sweetheart, you don't want to open that can of worms."

Now he had made me just plain mad. "Okay, I confess," I said, calling his bluff. "It was *me*. I did that to Ian's car."

I could feel Emery groan in his head.

"With what, Sweetie?" Jason baited. "Mean little thoughts?"

I had no idea how to respond. Jason was right. I did not want to open this can of worms.

"She dropped from a tree and went to town on his car," Emery explained, doing damage control with the truth. "I tried to stop her, but no one can when she gets like that."

Jason smirked at me in the mirror. "Yes, she is a killer," he teased. I forced a grin until he looked back to the road. "Got me, Slick," Jason told Emery. "Unfortunately for me, I can't come up with a better explanation than a sledgehammer, so I must fall prey to your insinuation that Casanova spotted your main squeeze back there, and like a dip-weed crashed his sweet ride into a tree. Now, Pumpkin,"—Jason looked at me again—"a 1982 Camaro I could easily forgive, but not a 1968."

"A 1982 Camaro, I would have helped her," Emery claimed.

Jason grinned appreciatively. "You're cagey, Slick," he said, wagging a finger at Emery, "real cagey, and not half as predictable as Casanova. He's going to make a U-turn in a moment, so I'm going to pull into this Chevron. He doesn't appear to be in the presence of mind to notice a tail, but it's always the seemingly unwitting ones who surprise you. Isn't that right, sweet thing?"

"I have no idea what you're talking about," I said, and meant it.

Ian made the U-turn Jason had predicted. Jason drove past the gas pumps and back on the frontage road, easing into the left lane behind the car following Ian. Ian crawled by Finnigan's again, then accelerated through the intersection. We got stuck at the red light.

"Does he know we're following him?" I wondered.

"No." Jason drummed the steering wheel. "He's just throwing a temper tantrum. Where is he, Slick?"

"Still on the frontage road."

The light turned green, and Jason caught up with Ian. Half a mile later, Jason urged him, "Come on, my flaxen-haired beauty. Find a place to land."

"You are *so* weird," I couldn't help but say.

"Matter of perspective, cutie pie, matter of perspective. Well, it's about time."

The Camaro slowed, and Ian turned into a motel called Utopia Inn.

"*Utopia* Inn? Somehow I doubt it," Jason said of the pink stucco atrocity. He drove past the driveway.

"What are you doing?" I asked, looking back at the motel.

"Trying not to tip Casanova off," Jason explained, and then turned the car around.

He pulled into Utopia Inn and parked where we had a good view of the motel but didn't stick out like a sore thumb. Ian had parked outside the office and was already inside, we presumed checking in for the night. Minutes later, he emerged, fiddling with a room key and glancing around nervously. He got into the Camaro, started the engine, drove five doors down from the office, and parked.

"Now that's just pathetic," Jason stated, disgusted. "Slick, your client must be seriously lacking in the virile department if this wuss appeals to his wife."

"His virility isn't my concern," Emery replied, unzipping something. Looking over the seat, I had to catch a laugh. He had a camera case in his lap. Emery Phillips P.I. had brought props.

Ian dashed to Room 5, fumbled the key into the lock, then threw himself inside and slammed the door behind him. In my mind's eye, I imagined him frantically setting every lock mechanism in place. The side table lamp came on, revealing a room through plated glass that didn't contradict the exterior of the Utopia Inn.

"What does this place offer in amenities?" Jason said. "Local cable and a complimentary athlete's foot infection?"

Emery and I laughed. What can I say? His henchman was funny.

"Turn the ignition so I can roll down the window," Emery ordered as he assembled the camera. He explained, "I want to be prepared to take pictures if she should show."

Of course, his true motivation was to open the airwaves for me so I would have a better chance of eavesdropping if Ian did have a visitor.

Ian appeared in the window. Pacing, he talked on a cell phone. Emery glanced back at me, signaling me to listen in. Nodding, I concentrated, searching for Ian's voice, to no avail. The motel was built sturdier than it looked.

If only I could read lips, I thought in frustration, as Ian's voice escalated. His face turned bright red as he listened with gritted teeth to the voice on the other end of the line. He yelled into the phone, threw it across the room, and then started kicking the heck out of the bed.

"What a schmuck," Jason commented, though I could understand Ian's losing his temper. He was frightened and obviously not getting help from whom I could only assume was William.

Exhausting himself, Ian stomped to the window, and yanked the blue plaid curtains over it, ending the show.

"Apparently he won't be entertaining tonight," Jason remarked with amusement, referring to the fake client's wife.

"Guess she isn't the consoling type," Emery agreed, genuinely disappointed. We both were. Ian hadn't led us to Roga or to the suit. "But let's not be hasty. She still may show."

Ian's lights went out fifteen minutes later. Seven minutes after that, Emery decided to call it a night, mumbling that he had to get me home.

"We'll pick Ian up on GPS in the morning," Emery said in consolation. "Jason, are you willing to be on call if he should leave during the night?"

"For a price," Jason replied, starting the car. "Always for a price."

Eighteen

Fight, Fight, Fight

I'd like to say crawling into bed was heaven after returning home, but I can't. With the covers pulled over my head, I ruminated over the evening, analyzing, speculating, scolding myself for my atrocious behavior. The only positive was that my thoughts took a detour from the usual worries, such as my fingerprints the police had lifted from King's henchmen's guns, which remained unidentified-—for now. Then there was the missing towel soaked with my blood—my DNA—and who knew who had that? I had my suspicions, as did Emery and Serena, though we never verbalized them. The towel had disappeared from Serena's lab after Raul Diaz, aka Silver Tooth, had set fire to it. Diaz worked for King Junior, making those dots not hard to connect.

When finally knocking off around three a.m., I fell into a deliciously dreamless sleep and awoke at 6:45 to "A Holly Jolly Christmas," feeling a little jolly myself. In the light of a new day, I could see the humor in what had happened with Ian. And why should I feel miserable about shaking him up? He was one of the bad guys, after all.

Providence seemed to shine upon Emery and me when Dad announced at the breakfast table that he had an interview scheduled late that afternoon with Mrs. Cooper and none other than Ian White.

"Can Emery and I go?" I asked, recognizing this as a golden opportunity. If Ian hadn't gone over the edge, Emery and I could give him a decent shove.

"I don't see why not. Meet me here right after school."

Hardly able to contain my excitement, I went up to my room to text Emery the exciting news.

He texted back: *Excellent. See you in a few.*

When he met Nate and me out front, conspiratorial grins exploded on our faces and neither of us could wipe them off the entire way to school. Even Nate's suspicious looks and Miriam's frowns didn't deter us. We were simply too pumped to care.

Between second and third period, Emery's phone alerted us that Ian was on the move. When the little dot on the screen showed the Camaro turning up Catamount Mountain Road, I predicted, "Ian's going home."

"Not without the suit," Emery disagreed. "My guess is the Westings."

This proved to be one of those rare instances where Emery was wrong. Ian did go home, but he didn't stay for long. Ten minutes into Spanish class, Emery, discretely monitoring his GPS, reported under his breath, "Ian is at the zoo."

I nodded with relief, having been concerned that Ian was packing his bags and skipping town. I relaxed a little, until calculating the hours between now and midnight. Fourteen. Way too long of a workday.

I scribbled in my notebook: *Why is he at work so early? Is he still working until midnight?* I angled the notebook to Emery, who glanced at the question and shrugged, which left me with a new set of frets.

On the way to algebra, Emery called the zoo and learned that Ian was working a double shift today. Everything was stacking in our favor.

"And when he gets off tonight, we'll be there waiting," I whispered as we took our seats. Brandon Graft and Sean Jaing walked in then, and I barked a surprised laugh seeing them. They wore identical graphic-T's featuring a caped

Bigfoot flying like Superman. The caption: *SUPER SASQUATCH RULES!*

"Talk about two worlds colliding," Emery remarked through smiling lips.

Dropping my face to the table, I smothered giggles with my hand. Even after class began, I had trouble controlling them. Mrs. Darcy would periodically cast a disapproving look my way from the smartboard, where she rambled on and on about formulas. When at last she'd had enough, she placed her hands on her hips and demanded, "Miss Jones, would you mind explaining what is so amusing about linear equations?"

Emery and I lost it. I had never laughed so hard in my life, or so unabashedly. Normally even the mere thought of being a public spectacle gave me heart palpitations, and here I was, a public spectacle and not giving a rip about it. A truly remarkable thing for a girl who was always worrying about what everyone thought about her.

~~~

In P.E., the current sub, clearly a free spirit, decided not to lock us into anything organized, so she gave the options of shooting hoops, handball, or participating in a casual game of volleyball in the second gym. Emery and I chose hoops.

We must have been putting out an exclusive vibe because friends who would normally hang with us kept their distance, which was okay by Emery and me. We had much to discuss.

"It shouldn't be too difficult to get Ben to impart his Sasquatch knowledge to Ian," Emery remarked as he aimed a basketball at our hoop.

"This is Ben we're talking about," I joked, dribbling my ball. "We won't be able to get him to stop imparting."

219

Emery threw his ball, making the basket.

"Good shot," I praised, adding, "We have to make sure 'The Boggy Creek Monster' comes up. That'll make Ian shake in his shoes."

"You doubt he's already shaking?" Emery asked, watching me dribble. "Are you going to shoot?"

Shrugging, I threw the ball half-heartedly. It whipped through the hoop with a vengeance.

Emery grinned. "At least try to make it look difficult," he challenged, passing me a ball.

"For you, I'll try. I really will." Lining up the ball with the rim, I closed my eyes and threw. Hearing the ball swish through the net, I opened my eyes to see Emery catch it.

"Shameless show-off," he teased, pitching the ball to me.

"Thanks, Slick," I said, as he retrieved his ball, too. "That reminds me. Why do you get the cool nickname and I get called every degrading pet name in the book?"

"Because I'm not as cute when riled," Emery replied, shooting. His ball hit the rim. Frowning at the hoop, he bent his fingers in a *give me* gesture. "Your ball. Quickly! Before I suffer machismo loss."

"Machismo loss!" I exclaimed in mock horror, passing him the ball. "Heaven forbid!"

Feigning stress, he shot. The ball hit the backboard and bounced into the basket. Emery exhaled in exaggerated relief. "Machismo still intact," he assured, flexing his biceps.

"So I see. Thank goodness you weren't reduced to a 'cupcake.' Now fetch me a ball so I can prove my machismo."

"Hate to tell you this, but machismo isn't possible for you. Now don't pout. There's no harm in trying." Emery swiped up a ball and passed it.

I was preparing to take the shot when another ball struck my back, so hard that I lost my breath. The blow stung like all get out before my skin rippled and hardened a millisecond later, numbing the pain. This stank of Robin— literally.

Emery gave Robin a dirty look. I kept my back to her. "She's trying to start something," he informed in a low voice.

"You think?" I said crossly, but quickly apologized, "Sorry. That just hurt. My skin reacted *after* the fact. Ignore her. I'm going to."

His glare sharpened.

"Emery, I don't care. Just turn around."

Reluctantly, he complied. "This will be a challenge for you," he warned.

"Finally. A challenge." I aimed the ball again. As I prepared to shoot, a ball clocked my head, and for the briefest moment I saw stars.

"Hey!" Emery shouted, whipping around.

Grabbing his arm, I told him, "I'm handling this."

His smoldering eyes cut to me. His arm muscles were tense. Shockingly, I believed that I would keep my head better in this instance than he could. "Seriously, I can handle her."

Emery gave a sharp, quick nod of consent.

It took a second to comprehend that he had chosen to trust me in this potentially volatile situation. Amazed, I rushed on, "Don't step in unless you absolutely have to. I need to confront her. Otherwise this won't stop."

A muscle jerked in his jaw, and he gave another sharp nod. I had never seen him so angry before.

"Thank you," I whispered, planning to make him proud. Releasing his arm, I clamped the ball to my side, pivoted around, and met Robin with a smile. "What?"

An audience had already assembled. They looked from me to her.

Flanked by four remoras, Robin sneered. "Oh, sorry. Didn't see you there."

There were some snickers and whispers. Ignoring them, I focused on Robin. For the moment, the little witch had my undivided attention.

"You need to get over this," I told her calmly.

She responded by calling me a crude name.

A few boys let out catcalls when I took a step toward her. As my other foot came forward, I tuned in to the second gym, and was glad to hear the sub cheering on the volleyball game. *Good*, I thought. *No intervention.*

Robin's fingers twitched at her sides. She was ready for a showdown, and so was our audience. Anticipation was thick in the air.

"If you need a nose for a nose," I said, stopping before her, "go for it." Busting my nose was the only way Robin could move on, and I really wanted her to move on. The sacrifice was worth it, and it would heal, anyway.

Whispers kicked up, and Robin glanced around with uncertainty. I understood she wanted to bash my face in, but didn't want to pay the consequences for doing so. She needed reassurance. I gave her some.

"I won't stop you," I told her, and to show my sincerity, I clamped the ball behind my back. "My hands stay where they are. This will be an accident."

"Are you like some kind of masochist?" she spat.

"Big word," I mocked.

Robin's eyes narrowed to slits.

"Fight, fight, fight," a few boys chanted low.

Robin's compressed lips relaxed into a vindictive smile, and she balled her hand into a tight fist, pulling back at the elbow, eyes locked on the target centering my face. Exhaling a slow breath, I concentrated on keeping my skin from reacting. The last thing I wanted was to be responsible for breaking her hand, too.

Suddenly my nose was buried into a maroon T-shirt. Startled, I sucked in a breath, receiving a potent dose of Jared. My head instantly swam.

"Back off, Robin," he commanded.

I took another breath, a long, voracious one.

"Chill, dude!" Robin said. "I don't touch trash."

This knocked me sober.

"You're calling *me* trash?" I said incredulously, and stepped out from behind Jared and saw that Robin's tough talk was a pile of hooey. She stared up at Jared like a puppy seeking approval. I was so disappointed in her.

"Robin," I snapped.

She looked from Jared to me.

I gave her a mocking smile. "Smash my face like I smashed yours," I challenged, offering her the ball.

Jared blew out a low, frustrated breath.

Nostrils flaring, Robin reached for the ball as I let it roll toward her hands. Jared snapped it up, and her eyes returned to him. Gritting my teeth, I looked up at him.

"Jared," I said through my teeth.

His fierce gaze jumped to me, taking mine hostage. Stunned, I stared into those mesmerizing chocolate pools for a moment before getting a hold of myself.

"Give her the ball," I said, ignoring the weak feeling in my knees. "She won't get in trouble. It'll be an accident."

Not looking away from me, Jared lightly tossed the ball over his shoulder. "Robin, leave," he commanded.

"Don't leave," I ordered her, staring him down.

"Bite me," Robin hissed, and then, much to my dismay, stomped off, remoras fluttering after her. Watching the girls retreat, I asked, "Did she mean you or me?"

Emery laughed behind me.

"Does it matter?" Jared said, on the verge of laughter himself. I didn't see what was so funny. Robin was his girlfriend, after all.

"Yes," I answered sharply. "If I were her, I'd dump you."

"What?" he said with surprise, flipping his palms up and squinting at me like I was speaking Chinese.

My irritation evaporated. What can I say? Confusion became him.

"All right. I get it." I smiled at his bewildered face. "You think I'm crazy."

His mouth curled at the corners, and he leaned toward me. I tried not to pay attention to the fact that he was closer.

"You offered your face on a silver platter," Jared whispered. The audience grew still, straining to hear him. "Yeah, I think you're crazy."

"Fair enough." I eased back, away from him. "Now, go make up with her. Robin and I will pick up where we left off later."

"Yeah!" Bobby cheered.

Fierce again, Jared said, "Not if I'm around."

"No problem. You won't be."

Jared flipped his palms up again, this time in frustration. Looking over my head, he gave Emery a disgusted look. "Dude, are you hearing this? What is *wrong* with you?"

Our heads turned to Emery. Casually leaning against the back wall, he held a ball loosely in front of him, shrugged his shoulders, and replied, "Cassidy said, 'Stay.'"

Everyone roared with laughter. I laughed, too, until I noticed Jared's eyes narrow dangerously on Emery. I knew the look. Within seconds, this bloodthirsty crowd would get what they wanted: a fight.

"Go talk to her," I urged Jared, giving him a push. "Go on. Go make up."

The fire left his eyes, and he scrutinized me like he was trying to solve a really challenging riddle.

"Go," I repeated, waving for him to leave.

"Whatever, Cassy," he said, and walked away. I watched him go, wishing sadly that he hadn't called me "Cassy."

Applause ended my grieving. Smirking at the boys egging me on, I spun around to Emery, who didn't even attempt to hide his amusement. Rolling my eyes, I sauntered his way. He pushed off the wall, and we met under our hoop.

"Happy to entertain you," I said, taking his ball.

"It was fascinating," he teased. "I felt like I was watching an episode of some low-budget teen television drama."

I pretended to throw the ball at his face. Grinning, he didn't flinch.

"You do realize by not allowing me to be chivalrous that you have single-handedly demolished my tough-guy rep?"

"And you seem so sad about that. No need to worry. With all that machismo, you'll bounce back."

"Undoubtedly. By the way, I like crazy."

"Why doesn't that surprise me?" I sighed and threw the ball.

As the ball soared for the hoop, I felt fingers weave into my hair. In a fluid movement, I grabbed Robin's wrist, turned, and twisted her arm behind her back. I couldn't believe that I had let her pull a sneak attack on me like that. If there were other mutants in the world, I would have just shamed them all.

Robin yelped. The audience gasped.

"I didn't give you permission this time," I admonished her.

Robin cussed at me. I responded by hiking her forearm up so she felt a nice tug in her triceps. In a pained voice, she called me a nasty name, and I eased her arm up another notch. Chest heaving, she compressed her lips, giving me the response I wanted.

"Now listen, Robin."

She turned her head to the side, glowering.

"This is ending. No more pitching balls at my back or bragging about your boyfriend in the locker room"—Robin cringed, which I found interesting—"or flaunting him in my face. I'm sorry about your nose. You have no idea how sorry. But it's time to move on." I looked beyond the outline of her profile at Jared, who had returned to the scene. His reaction puzzled me. Arms crossed, he stared daggers at Robin, making no attempt to intercede this time.

He must be mad at her for blabbing about their relationship, I guessed. *Jared hates gossip.* Sadness stung my heart. At least, the Jared I knew hated gossip. This one— Robin's boyfriend—I had no idea how he felt about it. Moving my mouth close to Robin's ear, I whispered, "Don't you get it? You won. You got him."

"Yeah, I get it," she hissed. "But it's not enough."

"Too bad." I hiked her arm a fraction of an inch more, then released her. She gasped, grasping her arm, and turned to look at me with surprise. I understood her surprise. If she had been in my position, her arm would have been dislocated.

226

I turned my back on her, on all of them. Smiling proudly, Emery dropped a ball in my hands.

"Why don't you stop *flaunting* your boyfriend, *Cassidy*?" Robin mocked behind me.

I smiled at Emery. "Jealous, Robin?"

The audience murmured and snickered.

"Jealous of a *loser* like *you*?"

I lined the ball up with the rim. "That's right. I'm a total lo—" I stopped talking to make the shot. The ball whisked neatly through the net.

"Nice," Emery praised, as if we were the only two people in the gym. He handed me another ball.

"Thank you," I said, suppressing a laugh. Eager tension built around us, everyone on the edge of their seats waiting for me to continue. I obliged them. "In fact, I'm such a loser that I'm really not worth your time…" I let my voice trail, pretending to concentrate on the shot. Predictably, I sunk the ball. "So, stop wasting it."

Robin spewed something rather unflattering about me, and then stomped off. This time I knew she had left for good because the crowd dispersed, going back to whatever they were doing before the show. Seconds later, Emery and I were pleasantly alone again.

"Your nose would have appeased her, you know. Robin *is* that petty," Emery remarked as he spun a basketball on his fingertips. "I wonder, though, if you fully understand your motivation in stirring up that little scene."

I snatched the ball from him. "Pray tell."

"You had a taste of it in algebra today."

"A taste of what?"

"Being comfortable in your own skin." His eyes roamed the room. "Your goal was to rise above all this."

My heart sped. "Did I, rise above it?"

"Do you care what they think about you?"

I thought a moment. "No."

He smiled. "Then, you did."

Nineteen

Unhinged

"That house on the hill is Mrs. Westing's," Ben told my dad while collecting his camera equipment from the Volvo's trunk.

I forced a neutral expression and zipped up my furry coat that Emery had returned. I didn't like Ben having anything to do with anyone named Westing.

"Her home is beautiful," Dad remarked, admiring the stately mansion. "It was good of her to let the NWSA camp out."

"Mrs. Westing is fantastic," Ben concurred, closing the trunk. Hoisting the camera to his shoulder, he smiled to himself. Aside from needing a shave, he showed no signs of having roughed it for the last few nights, and he was clearly having the time of his life sleeping on the cold, hard ground night after night, believing a Sasquatch encounter was just around the corner. Poor guy.

As we four walked to the zoo's main gate, Ben shared, "When we first approached Mrs. Westing about camping out, she was stressing about what happened to Leroy. She relaxed, though, when I pointed out that if the Sasquatch meant to harm him, well, Leroy would have had more than a couple cracked ribs."

I winced.

"How does Mrs. Westing feel about the Sasquatch now?" Emery asked.

"She's a believer! After educating herself on our website, Mrs. Westing knows the creature to be what we know it is: intelligent and generally nonthreatening."

I nodded, agreeing with the description of this particular Sasquatch.

"And speaking of our website, we've had almost three thousand hits since Monday!"

Stepping up onto the curb, I was about to ask Ben if any of the website visitors had become NWSA members, when the latest member that I knew of tore into the parking lot in a gunmetal-gray Hummer, "Sweet Home Alabama" blasting from the windows.

"Hey, it's Leroy," Ben said happily, saluting the SUV flying toward us at thirty miles per hour. "He's early."

"I'd say he's right on time," Emery said under his breath, smiling at the Hummer whipping into a parking slot.

I grinned agreement. We couldn't have set up Ian better. With Leroy present, a Sasquatch conversation would naturally ensue.

He bounded out of the Hummer, tossing his huge arms in the air. "Ben! Drake!" he boomed. "How are ya'll?"

Leroy was gigantic, and I had to resist the urge to back up as he barreled our way like a runaway freight train. It was unfathomable that I could budge this gargantuan, let alone propel him into a tree.

After slapping Ben's back and pumping Dad's arm, Leroy looked at me. "Now, *who* do we have here?" he inquired with a Texas twang and a Texas-sized smile. Shyness instantly struck me.

Smiling, Dad made introductions. "Leroy, I'd like you to meet my daughter, Cassidy, and our family friend, Emery Phillips."

Leroy shot his hand at me. Forcing myself to take it, I watched my hand disappear in his. "Pleased to meet you, little lady," he drawled.

"Nice to meet you, too, Mr. Rays."

Leroy gingerly moved my hand up and down, and I had to smile at the irony. With a purposeful squeeze, I could crush his whale of a hand.

He turned his head to Dad. "Drake, better keep your shotgun *loaded* and *ready* with this one," he advised.

Ridiculous me blushed.

Grinning at my pink cheeks, Leroy chucked my chin and then roughly grabbed Emery's hand, giving it a manly shake. "So you're little Cassidy's *friend*?" He winked at Emery.

I was mortified.

Emery kept up with the shake. "Yes, Mr. Rays. I'm Cassidy's friend."

"You're a better man than me, son," Leroy said solemnly. "I was never able to be a friend to a pretty lady." This time I got the wink.

Taken aback, I glanced at Dad and witnessed a disconcerting exchange between him and Emery. Dad lifted his eyebrows inquiringly at Emery, who in return gave my dad a reassuring look. Understanding the gist of their silent communiqué, the blush crawled up my forehead. My mom had had a heart-to-heart talk with me about Emery, making sure nothing inappropriate was going on. It hadn't occurred to me that my dad would have a similar discussion with Emery. This was beyond humiliating.

"If you'll excuse me, I'll let the office know we're here," Dad said to us. I couldn't even look at him.

Once he was out of earshot and I made certain Leroy and Ben were immersed in conversation, I whispered to Emery resentfully, "I see you and my dad have an understanding?"

He whispered back, "I'm a teenage boy, and he's a conscientious father. Of course he would want to know my intentions regarding his daughter and lay down ground rules."

"Ground rules? What ground rules?"

Emery gave me a sly smile. "Come, now. You know what ground rules."

I blushed more, if that were even possible.

I was about to whisper, "Point me to the nearest rock so I can crawl under it and die," when Leroy grabbed our attention.

"So what about that sightin' last night?" he said to Ben.

Emery and I whipped our heads toward him.

"A sighting? No way! How didn't I hear about this? Where?"

I chewed a fingernail, waiting for Leroy to say "Catamount Mountain Road." Obviously I was the sighting. *Ian must have reported the attack or someone witnessed it*, I deduced. *Either way, not good.*

"About ten miles south, in the mountains."

Surprised, I quickly looked at Emery. He shook his head, cautioning me to control my reaction.

"A hunter spotted the Sasquatch 'round four this mornin'. By description, sounds like *my* Sasquatch." Leroy rocked back on his heels, beaming like a proud papa. I fought the urge to laugh. It most certainly was not *his* Sasquatch sighted in the mountains, or any other Sasquatch, for that matter.

"Sweet!" Ben exclaimed. "My boys will be here at five. We can head out then."

"Not south!" I blurted. "Roga is south!"

Leroy gave me a quizzical look.

"No worries, Cassy Girl," Ben reassured. "We've got Leroy." To the big game hunter, he explained, "Roga is the tiger."

Leroy blew his lips and waved a hand, his way of saying, *Siberian tiger, no biggie.*

Dad and Mrs. Cooper walked out the main gate, chatting. Ian shuffled behind them, not looking so good. Unshaven, shoulders hunched, hands in pockets, he stared grimly at the pavement. When he glanced up and caught sight of Leroy, his bloodshot eyes widened. He looked like he hadn't slept for a month.

After a round of introductions, Ian smiled at me stiffly. "Tormented any pythons lately?" he teased.

232

It took me off-guard that he remembered me. The surprise quickly evolved into guilt. Ian had no clue that he was trying to make friendly small talk with "the creature."

"Not pythons," I answered without thought. Emery tensed, unsure where the response was going, which wasn't anywhere until inspiration struck me like a bolt of lightning. I knew exactly how to push Ian over the edge. "But I have been tormenting Sasquatches."

The artificial smile fell off his face. "W-what?"

"Just kidding." I grinned and rolled my eyes. "Sorry about the lame joke. It just sort of popped in my head with all this talk about *violent* Sasquatches."

Emery looked as if he wanted to grab my face and kiss cheeks.

"Cassy Girl, what are you talking about?" Ben questioned, lighting the fuse as I knew he would. "Sasquatches aren't violent."

And Ian went over the edge.

"*Not violent?*" he exploded, visibly trembling. "I'll show you how nonviolent these Sasquatches are!" Jerking around, he stalked into the parking lot, leaving Dad, Ben, Leroy, and Mrs. Cooper gaping.

"I think he wants us to follow," Emery prodded, and caught up with Ian. After exchanging confused looks, they caught up, too. I lagged behind, smiling smugly to myself.

At the back of the parking lot, Ian dramatically waved his arms over the thrashed Camaro. "Behold! The handiwork of the *gentle* Sasquatch."

Dented hood. Clawed paint. Broken glass. My handiwork was rather impressive.

Shielding his mouth with the back of his hand, Leroy said to Ben from the corner of his mouth, "I think we need stronger tranks."

Eyes wide, Ben nodded agreement.

"Ian, why didn't you say anything?" Mrs. Cooper asked, stunned. She lightly touched a claw mark and yanked her hand back as though she had been bitten.

Ian expelled a weary breath. "I didn't know *what* to say."

I nervously watched Dad examine the windshield. I didn't like him inspecting the damage so closely, like somehow he would see my name written all over it.

"I'm still trying to sort this all out," Ian went on. "You should see what this monster did to my house."

Dad's eyes sprung up. "What did it do?"

Ian opened his mouth to speak, then clamped it shut.

"Ian, what did it do?" Dad repeated.

Shaking his head, Ian pressed his lips together and looked as if he wanted to hit something. "*What the hey!*" he exclaimed, throwing his hands up in defeat. Glancing at Mrs. Cooper, he asked, "Do you mind if I take off for half an hour?"

"Of course not, Ian. Would you like to take the entire day off?"

Ian let out a frustrated laugh. "Where would I go, Brenda? Home?" He looked haughtily at Ben. "Would you like to see how your *nonviolent* Sasquatch marks its territory?"

~~~

Coming down Ian's driveway, Dad lifted his hand off the steering wheel and pointed at the tree I had gouged. "Ben, look at the tree," he said, astonished.

Disheartened, Ben shook his head. "This is so out of character for a Sasquatch."

Emery patted my thigh and gestured with his chin to a white Honda Civic parked in front of the house. Ian had a visitor.

Dad maneuvered the Volvo between the Civic and Leroy's Hummer. Ian climbed out of the Hummer and stared

234

apprehensively at his house. Whoever was inside clearly had him concerned.

Getting out of the car, I heard the front door open and caught a whiff of Lily's lilac-laced scent. I turned my head to look at her. Wearing a silk pink dress and a string of pearls, she stood on the front porch, surveying the situation with eyes that were both scorching and icy. On command, an amiable mask slipped over her white fury, that sweet smile curving her glossy lips. In that moment, I knew that Lily White was not the duped fiancée I had assumed. She was a ringleader.

In the next moment, I fumed at myself for not going with my gut feeling about Lily. Why hadn't I? Because Carli liked her? Because she looked harmless? I would have to examine why I had been so easily swayed later, because from here on out I wasn't missing a thing.

"Ian, what's all this?" she asked in a saccharine voice, motioning to us.

"You're back," he stated the obvious—loudly. "I wasn't expecting you until tonight."

"I caught an early flight home," she explained, gliding down the porch steps. "I've been worried sick since we talked last night."

This answered who was on the other end of Ian's phone conversation.

Lily threw her arms around her brother's neck. Hesitantly, he hugged her, wary as if embracing a viper. Her hands moved up his neck. Ian visibly stiffened, and I adjusted my vision to observe better, to see Lily's pink index fingernail press into the skin behind his ear. Through a plastered on smile, Ian winced, but took his punishment for bringing us to his home.

Like a good soldier, jumped into my head. Weird thought, but I wasn't disqualifying anything from now on.

"Thank heavens you weren't hurt!" Lily exclaimed, choking up. She dug her nail deeper into his flesh. Watching purple blood pool under his skin around her pink nail, I struggled with what I was witnessing. Lily wasn't only a ringleader. She was pure evil!

"Not a drop of blood was spilled," Ian hinted, laughing to cover the pain in his voice. Lily lifted her fingernail. Through smiling lips, Ian exhaled a ragged breath.

They're sick! I thought, feeling a little sick myself. *How can she hurt her brother like that? And why would he just take it?*

Because he's afraid of her, I concluded, while Lily received introductions wearing a gracious smile. When she came to Emery and me, she said in a very disturbingly genuine way, "It's so nice to see you two again."

"Thank you," I managed, adding in my head, *It will be nice to see you behind bars, Tiger Stealer, Brother Abuser, and whatever else you are!*

We went up on the porch to inspect the damage. The three men crowded around the front door. Ian and Lily stood behind them. Emery and I hung in the background, leaning against the porch rail where we could survey the scene. Lily's gaze riveted on the three men, while mine riveted on her profile. Not aware of being watched, she allowed the icicles to come back into her eyes. The blood running through her veins was probably just as cold.

"Leroy, you're the expert," Dad said, running a hand over the gouges. "What animal could make these marks?"

"Grizzly swipes are deep, but doesn't make sense these would be grizzly."

"Did the creature you encountered have claws?"

"None that I noticed, but they could be retractable. Ya know, just comin' out for the kill."

Color drained from Ian's face.

"Ben, are there accounts where the Sasquatch was reported having claws?"

"What we have is more physical evidence, such as trees marked like the one in front. There's also the Montana trapper from the 1800s, but before I tell you this, remember he is the *only* reported Sasquatch fatality. Anyway, the guy's neck had been snapped, and his body was covered in bite and claw marks."

Ian's complexion now matched his sister's.

"Had the body been eaten?" Leroy asked matter-of-factly.

Emery and I exchanged quick, pleased smiles. Their conversation was perfect, as if we had scripted it.

"No. The Sasquatch didn't kill for food. According to the surviving trapper, it had been stalking them for days before the attack. But understand this attack was very unusual. Sasquatches are generally peaceful. Tossing rocks into campsites is usually the extent of their aggression, but that's more their curious nature than anything else."

And Emery went in for "the kill."

"Ben, why do you think the Sasquatch attacked the trapper?" he asked.

"Somehow, he made the Sasquatch feel threatened. Maybe he stumbled into the creature's territory and the Sasquatch held a grudge about it."

Ian staggered forward. Lily caught him by the waist. The commotion caught the men's attention. Sheepish, they gave Ian an apologetic look for forgetting about the Sasquatch victim in our presence.

"Gentlemen, why don't we move on to the other damage," Lily suggested with a smile. She hooked her catatonic brother's arm.

After checking out the back door, we went to Ian's bedroom window. Examining the splintered wood, Leroy asked, "Whose room is this?"

A garbled noise came from Ian. It sounded like he had swallowed his tongue.

"Ian's," Lily answered for him.

The men traded looks that said they thought Ian was in deep doo-doo.

Clearing his throat, Leroy requested, "Ian, why don't you show us where you was attacked."

~~~

"What animal can jump that high?" Dad asked Leroy as we stared at the limb from which I had dropped down onto the Camaro. After finding no telltale markings that suggested something with claws had climbed the trunk, Leroy determined—correctly, I might add—that Ian's attacker had leapt up to the branch.

"We're talking bipedal—" Leroy began, but stopped talking when Ian started gurgling.

"Ian," Lily warned him.

Manic laughter exploded from his throat. Lily grabbed his arm, but he jerked free, and yelled at my dad, "Are you an idiot? Why don't you ask *Mr. Big Game Hunter* what bipedal animal can chase me down at fifty miles per hour? You—"

"Enough, Ian!" Lily cut him off. "These men are trying to help you."

Ian swore at her.

"Hey, now, Ian," Leroy protested, holding up a hand. "I know you're upset, but that is no way to talk to a lady."

"*A lady?*" Ian spat contemptuously.

Lily gave her brother a hurt look. The look Leroy gave him would have made a crocodile's mouth snap shut. Proving that he was at least as smart as a crocodile, Ian shut his.

An awkward silence followed Ian's outburst. My gracious father ended it by stating, "We need to contact the authorities."

Rage crossed Lily's face, which she dutifully chased away. "Drake, forgive me, but how would involving the authorities help this situation?" she maneuvered. "We all know a person didn't attack my brother, and I doubt he'll get police protection from Bigfoot. Involving the police will only bring unwanted attention. Now, I've seen these Bigfoot folks around town, and let's just say that they're not as respectable-looking as Leroy and Ben. I'd be terrified if what happened got around and these men started snooping around here while I'm alone."

Dad looked at her with alarm. "Lily, surely you don't intend to stay here."

Lily held her chin up. "I most certainly do. Someone has to. Ian will be staying with friends—"

Ian gulped.

"—and my fiancé will be otherwise engaged this evening, so it's up to me to look out for this place. I won't let anyone or anything chase me from my home."

"Lily, I'd feel the same way myself," Leroy admitted, staring at her with admiration. "I'd sure like to help you out somehow. Hey! How about the NWSA sets up here?" He looked at Ben. "Most likely the Sasquatch will come back this way."

"Without a doubt," Ben agreed eagerly.

"Ben, this could be dangerous," Dad cautioned.

"I appreciate the concern, but this is a once-in-a-lifetime. No way am I missing out. That is, Lily, if you're cool with us camping out." Ben gave her an imploring look that I would have had a hard time saying no to.

"Oh, look at how cute you are," Lily said, smiling. "Let me think for a moment." For several seconds she appeared to do just that, but I knew her game. Of course, she wouldn't want the NWSA on her property.

"Well, all right," she consented, totally throwing me for a loop. "I'd appreciate it, however, if your group didn't set up until early evening. I'll be out tonight. Hopefully you won't need anything from the house." As they assured her that they wouldn't, I settled on two possible motives that she could have in consenting: First, Lily was worried about the Sasquatch and wanted the NWSA around for protection;

second, Lily wanted to know exactly where the NWSA was. This last possibility concerned me greatly.

"Ben and Leroy, may I join you?" Emery asked, throwing me for another loop.

"Absolutely not," Dad said instantly, compelled to be a dad.

"Oh, I didn't mean tonight, Mr. Jones. I'd like to help search for Sasquatch evidence tomorrow."

More like destroy it, I thought.

"Dude, you are more than welcome to help out," Ben told him, pleased. "If your mom gives you permission, I'll come get you in the morning."

"Thanks, and she will." Emery glanced at Leroy. "My dad and I go to the shooting range a lot. I'm a good shot. I'll bring his tranquilizer rifle tomorrow."

His rifle? I studied his innocent expression. *Who you plannin' on shooting, Emery?*

"Boy after my own heart!" Leroy declared, giving Emery a manly pat on the back. "If your daddy gives you the a-okay, bring it along!"

"Emery," Dad said, frowning. "Be sure Serena is aware of *all* the details."

"I will. But really, my mom won't mind. She knows how well my dad has trained me."

Trained him? I wondered, looking at his face that told me nothing. *Trained him for what?*

Twenty

Evil Revealed

A fter Ian's late shift, we tailed him to an RV Park called Happy Trails, a few miles up I-90. Inside Happy Trails, Jason turned off the headlights and followed the Camaro's taillights at a discreet distance. The Camaro slowed to a roll toward the back of the park, turning left into a site about twenty yards ahead of us. Jason hung an immediate right, easing the Jetta next to a darkened motorhome with pop-out sides and a big satellite dish on top. He cut the engine.

"Cassidy, see who Ian is meeting with," Emery instructed.

Jason turned his head to him in surprise.

"Put on your earpiece," Emery added, clipping on his.

Jason twisted around to look at me in the dim light spilling into the car from streetlamps. Going about my business, I took great pains to appear calm. The last thing I wanted was Jason Crenshaw questioning my professionalism.

Once the earpiece was on, I took the initiative and dialed Emery's Droid. Answering the call, he said, "Don't report status until you've collected intel. If you need to communicate, text."

"Copy that, Big Kahuna," I replied, unable to help myself. He sounded so 007ish.

Jason raised an eyebrow at the code name.

"It fits," I told him, shrugging. "Are the cab lights off?"

"Affirmative," Jason teased, adding carefully, "It's snowing in Beirut, Little Red Riding Hood."

Emery chuckled.

"And the rain in Spain falls mainly in the plains," I returned, trying to remember where Beirut was. Maybe then I would get the joke. I pulled on the mask, tucked in my ponytail, and cracked open the door, bidding, "Later." As I slunk to the road, I heard Jason through the earpiece ask Emery, "Fun and games aside, what are you getting that little girl into?"

I frowned at his concern and at being called a "little girl." I really hoped Jason wouldn't disappoint me and have a heart after all.

"Nothing she can't handle," Emery said, completely confident of this.

My frown flipped into a smile. Without a doubt, I could handle a little spying, as long as no one tempted me by running away.

I hid behind a dumpster across the street from the Camaro and peeked out. Ian's and Lily's cars were parked behind two other vehicles alongside an RV that looked as if it had seen many years and many miles. The vehicle in front of Lily's was a black double-cab GMC, the same truck from Finnigan's. This I was sure of.

Engine and headlights off, Ian rested his head on the steering wheel, his back rising and falling heavily. After a handful of these agonized breaths, he looked out the driver's side window. The car door slowly opened, and he ducked out, frantically scanning the dark treetops overhead.

Looking for dropping Sasquatches, I presumed.

Muttering a tortured cuss word, he shot to his feet, slammed the car door, and ran to the RV like a man being pursued, flattening his back against it. He did another scan while flinging the aluminum door open. It clattered against the RV. Hurling himself inside, he yanked the door shut behind him. In the blink of an eye, I was hunkered down behind Lily's Civic, tuning in to the RV. A sharp slap hit my eardrums first.

"You idiot," Lily hissed.

"Crap, Lily!" Ian's words were muffled. I imagined him rubbing the cheek his sister had struck. "You saw what that thing did to my house, my car! It's stalking me, hunting me like an animal! Don't you see why? It's where we've hidden the tiger. We drove this thing from its hole, and now it's after me. That night, in the woods, it recognized my scent, tracked me to my house and—"

"What are you going on about?" a rough male voice cut in.

"Oh, didn't she tell you, Sam? No? What about you, Wyatt?"

"Careful now, Ian," warned a man with a German accent.

"Of course, *you're* privy, Axel, being her sugar-on-the-side.*"

Someone quickly stood up. There was a scuffling noise, then Axel spoke, low and lethally, "You have the courage of a worm."

"And you have the wit of one," Ian said in a choked voice. I pictured Axel's hand clutching his collar. "Lily, give me the suit! I have to protect myself from this monster!"

A tense silence followed. Then Lily spat, "I should have known letting you wear my suit would whet your insatiable appetite."

"Hey, sweetie, I'm not the power fiend here. My only interest in *your precious* is survival."

"Dear brother, just who are you trying to fool?"

"Give me the suit!"

There was a swift movement, a crack, a crash, and the RV shook as if something heavy had fallen. I had a sickening feeling that Ian's face wasn't so pretty anymore.

Rising up, I prepared to storm the RV and rescue Ian if things heated up. I couldn't sit still and let him get hurt. Ian moaned, as fingers hooked the blackout curtain that covered the RV's rectangular window. I crouched down again. There was no reason to expose my presence until necessary.

243

I glanced around the front bumper to see a powerfully built man with chiseled features, shoulder-length blond hair, and hard blue eyes peer from the slit he had created between the curtain panels. My mouth dropped open as I recognized him.

Oh my gosh! The bartender from the news, the one who threw James Flynn out of Finnigan's—Eric Schmidt! A couple puzzle pieces clicked together. *Axel, aka Eric Schmidt, drugged Flynn's drink and helped set him up to be the fall guy. The GMC is his truck. So why didn't Ian go inside Finnigan's to tell Axel about the attack?* Another second of observing the brutal face in the window answered this question. Out of desperation, Ian had planned to tell Axel, but decided against it. A wise choice, I would think.

"Raise your voice again, and you lose your tongue," Axel threatened, his cold eyes scouring the dark.

"And none of us will miss your tongue," Wyatt ridiculed. "But why not put it to good use for once and tell us about this monster."

Axel released the curtain. It fell back into place.

"My pleasure," Ian responded with difficulty, beginning his account. Several times he stopped talking to spit. *Blood*, I figured. Being punched by Axel would be like being struck with a battering ram.

When Ian finished describing the attack, Lily accused, "It's all lies! He's fabricated this Bigfoot to get my suit."

"Or perhaps Rory Michaels has been reincarnated as Bigfoot, and is avenging his murder," Wyatt suggested humorously.

"If that were the case, then my *angelic* little sister would be the hunted one."

The men laughed at Ian's joke, while I processed the horrific truth just revealed. *Rory Michaels didn't die of natural causes. Lily murdered him!* Joe flashed to mind— Joe, who lived in torment over the life he had cut short.

Somehow I doubted Lily suffered a guilty conscience. Her only regret would be getting caught.

"Bigfoot or no Bigfoot, we proceed tomorrow as planned," Lily announced with authority.

"I *proceed* nowhere without the suit," Ian fired back.

"If you don't step back in line," Lily said, "I will see to it that you never *proceed* anywhere again."

Axel chuckled cruelly.

"Let's get something clear, dear brother. Grandfather Josef left the suit to *me*, not you. It's *mine,* and it will *always* be mine."

Josef? Another puzzle piece snapped into place. *Dr. Josef Richter is Lily and Ian's grandfather!*

"Yes, Granddaddy recognized your 'ruling with an iron fist' capability when you were still crawling around in diapers," Ian said. "You were always his darling little heartless prodigy."

"No sour grapes, Ian," Lily admonished, obviously pleased by what she perceived as a compliment. "Grandfather just realized which of us could rectify the wrongs done to our family and which of us could not. It's nothing to be ashamed of."

The other men snickered.

"Enough, boys," Lily scolded. "A house divided against itself cannot stand. United, we gain much. We gain everything."

Her rallying words sent a shiver up my spine.

"Oh, don't look so glum, Ian. I promise you'll have a suit of your very own, once we take back what is rightfully ours. All of us will have our own suits, our own army, and the world at our feet!"

Her accomplices grunted approval. Richter's fruit hadn't fallen far from the vine. His granddaughter had proudly stepped into his sinister shoes.

"Remember, Ian. Those *diebe*, Michaels and Suttner, stole our destiny. Tomorrow, we reclaim it."

Lily ceased her insane rhetoric, and I heard the sound of a kiss.

"What was that, the kiss of death?" Ian asked, but his voice had lost its sarcasm. The brainwashing had moved him. He was as evil and greedy as the rest.

"That was the kiss of life, dear brother, 'life extraordinary,' which will be ours very soon, just as Grandfather intended." Lily's tender tone turned abruptly businesslike. "All right! I have to get back to Ian's and keep an eye on his new friends. Ian, what were you thinking bringing those Bigfoot lovers to the house? Dollars to doughnuts they'd heard Sam's rumor and would have followed all the other sheep to look for Bigfoot if you'd kept your trap shut. My goodness! As if I don't have enough on my plate!

"Axel, sweetheart, get the Glock 30, please. Oh, and a few clips while you're at it. I want something with a little *oomph* in case that thing does come back...Oh, thank you, Axel. This will work real nice. I want you all out of here and on your way by eleven sharp. We rendezvous at one o'clock and turn the tide. Sleep tight, boys."

The RV door swung open, and Lily appeared in the doorway, jamming a big black gun in her pink silk purse. I moved stealthily to the front end of Axel's truck and watched her amble to the Civic, her lilac-infused scent staining the air. Once in the car, she applied a fresh coat of lipstick, fluffed her curls, and then started the car, backing out and speeding away. The television came on in the RV, and Lily's "boys" grew silent now that their "Big Kahuna" was gone.

Texting Emery that I was coming back, I zipped to the Jetta, beating the text message and startling Emery and Jason when I opened the back door. They jumped inches off their seats.

"Sorry," I whispered, closing the car door carefully. I pulled off my ski mask and told Emery, "We need to talk."

"Would you mind taking a walk?" he said to Jason.

Jason swiped up a cigarette pack. "Gimme a buzz when you want me to head back," he said as he left.

Through the back windshield, I watched him saunter toward the road as I explained to Emery, "They're murderers, Emery. Lily killed Rory Michaels, poisoned him, would be my guess." I turned to look at him. His expression was thoughtful and calm. "Doesn't this surprise you?"

"Not especially."

"Well, this will. Dr. Richter is Lily and Ian's grandfather. From what I could figure out, he left Lily the suit when he died, which means Rory Michaels and Ernest Suttner never had it. Dr. Richter did all along. He also totally brainwashed Lily and Ian into believing they're destined to take over the world. You should have heard her talk! She's certifiable, believing she's like Hitler reincarnated or something, and she's planning to build an army."

"To build an army, she'll have to be able to build the suit," Emery pointed out. Nestling his chin in his fist, he thought a moment. "Michaels and Suttner stole the process from Richter, and Lily is after it. Tell me everything you overheard."

After doing so, I added, "Lily called Michaels and Suttner 'deebs.'"

"*Diebe*," Emery corrected, enunciating the word with an accent. "It's German for 'thieves.'"

I stared at him in surprise. "You speak German?"

"Not fluently."

I leaned forward. "How many languages do you know?"

"Including the Pig Latin you taught me, seven, but I'm only fluent in four. That's including Pig Latin." He grinned.

I couldn't believe my ears. "Why didn't you tell me this before?"

"It never came up."

"How many other things have never come up before?"

"Cassidy, veer back on track," he advised.

247

I crossed my arms and frowned.

Amused, he said, "I'll tell you what. When this is over, you can interrogate me to your heart's content."

"And you'll answer *all* of my questions?"

"Most likely."

I deepened the frown.

Emery grabbed my dangling ponytail and pulled it. "You didn't mention William Westing."

"That's because *they* never mentioned him. Not once! Do you know what this means? William is innocent!" A new scenario unfolded in my mind, and I exclaimed, "Yes, this makes sense! Okay, listen. Ian getting a job at the zoo and Lily volunteering there was all part of a master plan. The zoo put them in close proximity to the Westings, so Lily would have a chance to sink her meat hooks into William. Marrying into the Westing family is the best way for her to learn the whereabouts of her grandfather's process. She murdered Rory Michaels because he figured out who she really is and what she's up to. Oh, poor William! He loves that evil, albino murderess! What do you think?"

"I think Westing is guilty until proven otherwise," was Emery's unsatisfactory response.

"Now he's guilty?" I said, exasperated. "Make up your mind."

"I won't have to. The underbellies of this cast of characters are being exposed. Soon we'll know how everyone fits. Was Roga mentioned as part of their 'day of retribution'?"

I shook my head. "He never came up, either."

"Regardless, we'll err on the side of caution and assume he will be. Here's what we'll do: before Ben picks me up in the morning, I'll call your house for my mom and say that she'd like to hire you for the day, to help organize the lab."

I groaned. "More lies?"

Emery regarded me soberly. "Deceiving your parents creates a moral dilemma for me as well. I wish there was some other way around it, and I don't only mean tomorrow."

My throat tightened, and I nodded. "I know, and thanks for feeling guilty, too. It's good to know I'm not alone. Okay, I'm about to cry, so moving on: what's the plan for tomorrow?"

"You'll meet Jason at nine a.m. He'll drop you off near Ian's, where you'll suit up and follow Lily when she leaves to rendezvous with the others. In the meantime, Jason will come back here and tail Axel."

The Glock 30 suddenly leaped into my head. "I can't believe I forgot! Lily has a gun! She's at Ian's! The NWSA! Ben!"

Emery grabbed my face. "Deep breath," he commanded.

I sucked in air and held it.

He patted my cheeks. "Exhale."

I did.

He smiled and released my face. "Lily will not hurt Ben or the others. Hurting them would upset her agenda. And rest assured that I will not let Jason go into this blindly. He'll be aware that these men are armed and dangerous. Jason is very resourceful and has a strong sense of self-preservation. If he feels he's in danger, he won't be valiant. He'll abort. Does this ease your mind?"

I nodded, not feeling relieved at all. "Okay. So, I'm following Lily, and Jason is following Axel. Where are you?"

"Tromping around the woods with the NWSA. They could stumble into whatever it is that Lily has planned, which by all indications will take place on Westing property. Being caught unaware, they stand a chance of being hurt if I'm not with them. Remember, I'll be armed, and I really am a good shot. Between Leroy and myself, we'll be able to protect the others, if it comes down to that."

I wished his confidence would rub off on me. I couldn't shake this feeling of impending doom.

"I hate this, hate this, hate this!" I popped my fist into my palm. "This is too big for us. We need help. We need to call the police."

"And tell them what?" Emery challenged.

My shoulders hunched in defeat. "I don't know."

"Cassidy, this is the only way," he said, reiterating what I already knew. "My plan will work. Trust me."

"I always trust you," I reminded him.

He smiled. "Thank you. Your costume is in the trunk. Are you ready to reward Ben?"

"You *can't* be serious."

"Au contraire. I would never jest about a Sasquatch encounter, which Lily is very much in need of. Just stay out of her crosshairs."

"Great advice." I flung the ski mask at him. He caught it. "What language is 'au contraire'?"

"French."

"And you can speak French, too?"

Emery gave me a mysterious look. "Oh, the things you will learn, Cassidy Jones," he teased, and snapped the mask back at me.

~~~

Suited up, I waited in a tree for Ian's house lights to turn out. Ten minutes beforehand, Lily had swept across the yard to the NWSA's tent, wearing a flowing white robe, which made her glow in the moonlight like a ghost. Poking her head through the tent flap, she had cheerfully wished the men, "Nighty-night," before returning to the house.

The lights went out, and I made my move. Leaping from the tree, I landed softly on a bed of pine needles and began collecting pinecones, tucking ten in the crook of my arm.

Then I crept to the tent, grinning from ear to ear. I was going to give the NWSA the thrill of a lifetime.

One of the men was already snoring like a chainsaw. *Leroy*, I decided, grabbing a pinecone from my stash. *Definitely Leroy*. I chucked the pinecone at the tent flap.

"Did you hear that?" Howie whispered.

Tom responded, "The only thing I hear is Leroy."

Leroy's snore caught. "Wh-what, boys?"

"Shhh!"

Shaking with silent laughter, I pelted three pinecones.

"No way!" Ben exclaimed in an excited whisper. Bodies scrambled to their feet.

"Howie, hand me my rifle," Leroy said in his version of a whisper.

I hurled the remaining pinecones at the tent, and let out a shriek I hoped sounded unearthly.

The tent flap burst open, and the men tumbled out, piling on top of one another. I covered my mouth to smother a laugh. As if Lily and I had timed it, the porch light lit behind me. The tangled men froze, blinking at me with disbelief. Lifting my chin to the moon, I shrieked again. The shriek cracked at the end into cackling laughter.

The house door banged open, and I swung around to see a steely-eyed Lily rack the slide on her Glock. Before she could take proper aim, I took off down the driveway at a speed they could all keep up with.

Grinning to myself, I peeked over my shoulder at my pursuers. Tranquilizer rifle grasped in his hands, Leroy led the way with Ben at his heels, armed with a flashlight. Howie and Tom followed close behind, and Lily came up on the backside, clutching the Glock, white robe fluttering. At the end of the driveway, I took a flying leap, soaring across the road, and disappearing in the trees—the Westings' trees. Scrambling up a humongous blue spruce, I looked down at my pursuers. The men stopped dead in their tracks, gaping at the spot where I had disappeared. Ben swept the flashlight beam over the spot.

Pushing past the men, Lily planted her feet wide and shot rounds into the trees, targeting the flashlight beam. Bullets sprayed the branches below me, as casings littered the ground around her white fluffy slippers. The men gaped at her.

"Lily," Ben admonished when the magazine was empty, "you might have hurt the Sasquatch."

Pushing curls off her face with the gun handle, Lily glanced back at him, shrugged, and said, "A girl has to defend herself."

Twenty-One

The Killing Field

Sometimes things don't go according to plan. You can have all your ducks lined up in a row, everything worked out to a T, and then out of the blue a big, old monkey wrench is thrown smack dab in the middle of all that perfection. Emery and I were Lily's monkey wrench, and now we had one of our own.

Reaching over to the steering wheel, I slammed the horn for the umpteenth time in the last hour and a half.

"Knock it off," Jason growled, pushing my hand away.

"This is unacceptable," I stated, glaring at the miles of stopped traffic on I-90. I knew I was being agro, and possibly annoying, but there was a lot at stake here! "We *have* to get out of this."

"It's an accident," Jason reasoned, drumming the steering wheel with his index fingers. "Nothing we can do about it, so just sit back and relax."

"Relax?" I tapped the dashboard clock. "See that? Eleven-oh-three! Axel is gone! You can't tail him! We are so hosed. I have to get out of this!" I slammed the horn again, keeping it pressed down as if it possessed magical power to blow the vehicles off the road.

Jason gave my hand a quick slap.

"Hey!" I yelled, barely resisting the impulse to slap him back.

Turning to me, Jason looked me full in the face. "New rule." He jabbed his finger at the steering wheel. "You don't touch this."

"You can't make up rules. You're on the clock for *me*!"

"Hmmm," he said, rubbing his chin. "Sweet thing, I don't recall you handing me a wad of cash."

"You still can't make up rules."

"Another new rule. We only use inside voices in the car."

Frustrated beyond belief, all I could think to say was: "Don't *ever* call me 'sweet thing' again."

Jason smirked. "Why not, when you're so sweet?"

"Oh, shut up!" I curled up on my seat, digging my hands into my hair. Why, oh why was this happening? "Sorry I told you to shut up," I apologized miserably. "You just don't understand."

"I'm being paid not to understand," Jason replied, unmoved.

Gripping my hair, I twisted my head to look at him. Sunk comfortably in his seat, he lit a cigarette. "And that's it? Emery pays you not to care, so you just don't?"

He exhaled smoke. "Money is a powerful thing."

Stress abruptly took a toll on me, and I sunk down, too, deflated like a balloon. "I don't get you," I told him, listlessly fanning smoke. "FYI, your *gray death* makes me want to hurl."

"Would you like me to roll down the window, cupcake?"

"*Please.*"

"Please," Jason echoed approvingly. "See, you are sweet." While rolling down the window, he said, "Why don't you text that boy you have wrapped around your little finger and give old Jason's ears a break?"

"I don't have *any* boy wrapped around my little finger, but if you're referring to Emery, good idea. I should update him that our status still sucks."

First, I checked the NWSA's location on GPS. They were in the Westings' woods searching for Sasquatch evidence, moving east, just as Emery had predicted they would do.

Wish Jason and I were doing what Emery predicted we'd be doing by now, instead of just sitting here being useless in this stupid, stupid car on this stupid, stupid freeway, and letting the bad guys slip through our fingers! Emery can't handle Lily and her crew alone! I took a long breath to calm my rising panic, then texted Emery that our predicament hadn't changed.

He texted back: *Don't worry. There is still time.*

"Are you crazy, Emery?" I shouted at the phone. "There is no more time!" I went for the horn again. Jason caught my hand.

"Chill on your own, or I'll help you." He tilted the cigarette back and forth.

Getting his gist, I yanked my hand free. "If you even *try* to put that disgusting thing in my mouth, I'll shove it down your throat!"

Jason grinned. "You sure talk a big stick, little girl. Thanks for reminding me why I value bachelorhood."

I ground my fist into my palm, pretending it was his face. *Okay, get a grip, Cassidy. Keep it together. Think, think, think.* I pushed hair off my face and objectively looked at the cars packed together like sardines. The answer to this dilemma became so clear. "I'm walking," I announced, reaching for the door handle.

The locks on all four doors simultaneously snapped down. Jason had hit the power lock.

Slowly turning to him, I demanded through my teeth, "Unlock the door."

He blew a stream of smoke. "No."

"No? This is not a game! Unlock the door—*now!*"

"This will be a little unusual for you, sweetheart, but I'm going to talk to you like you're a reasonable adult. See those mountains out yonder?" He gestured at the windshield with the cigarette. "That's where I'm being paid to take you, and the only way you'll get there anytime soon is if you sprout wings and fly."

"Shhh—don't give me any ideas." I cracked up at my joke. I was totally losing it.

"So, I'm taking it that we're okay here," Jason said, waving the cigarette between us.

"Unlock the door," I demanded again, laughing.

Jason grinned and shook his head. "Crap, you're high maintenance. Next time you text Lover Boy, inform him my rates have gone up."

Peripherally, I caught movement. Looking forward, I blinked at a sight that I was sure I would never see again.

"Jason! Cars!" I patted his arm. "They're moving! Start the car! Start the car!"

Straightening up, he quickly snuffed out the cigarette and turned the ignition. The beautiful sound of firing-up engines rumbled the freeway. The coupe in front of us rolled forward. We rolled with it.

"Yes!" I cheered. "All is not lost! I love you, Jason Crenshaw!" Smiling ear-to-ear, I looked at him. He was smiling, too.

"If only I had a nickel for every time I heard 'I love you, Ja—'" His smile abruptly disappeared. He muttered a cuss word and pressed the breaks.

Whipping my head forward, I screamed. Cars as far as the eye could see were at a standstill again.

"I want wings!" I howled, thumping my forehead on the dashboard.

Wordlessly, Jason shifted into park, cut the engine, and snapped up his cigarette pack while I continued abusing my head, hoping that I would eventually knock myself out cold.

~~~

Over an hour later, Jason dropped me off below Ian's driveway, where I suited up behind bushes with a fair amount of difficulty. Foreseeing my challenges, Emery had nixed the hand claws from the ensemble and cut the fingertips off the gloves to make handling a cell phone and texting doable. He had also added a Velcro strip to the inside

256

of the costume's left sleeve to secure the phone to. Chewbacca didn't have pockets.

After pulling on gloves, I anxiously checked the time on my phone. 12:34. Only a minute later than the last time I had looked. *It's still early*, I reassured myself. *Lily is still there. She has to be*. I ran to Ian's, burst from the trees and onto the gravel driveway, where my fear became realized. Lily's car was gone. I was too late.

"No, no, no!" I anguished, and began pacing, willing myself to think. *Where could she have gone? Where, where, where?*

Of course! The Westings'!

I shot down the driveway, kicking up gravel behind me, and crossed the road to the Westings' property. Lily might be meeting William so they could rendezvous with the others together.

Within a minute, I stood at the edge of the Westings' lawn, where I fell to my knees and thanked "the big guy" up above. Lily's Civic was parked in the driveway, along with two other cars.

After everything, I have her, I thought, settling behind a tree. *Now all I have to do is wait for them to leave*.

I texted Emery the good news, then checked the NWSA's location on GPS. They were near Catamount Mountain Road, heading southwest. Emery was slyly maneuvering the men along the road, which he believed was the most strategic spot to be in, especially if whatever Lily and William plotted included Roga. The tiger would have to be transported in a fairly large vehicle.

Or maybe this is the most strategic spot, I mused, peeking out at the mansion. *This could be the rendezvous point. Maybe they're bringing Roga here*. I welcomed this possibility, preferring to handle come what may on my own. Emery and the others could be hurt, or even killed, where I couldn't be either—at least not for long.

I'm invincible, I thought, reattaching the phone inside my sleeve, *Indestructible Girl and happy to be such—for once.* A sudden uneasiness nudged at me, and I swung my head back around to the house. *What is going on in there?* I wondered, scanning the windows and observing no movement behind them. The bad feeling deepened. *What if William isn't in on all this? What if Lily is planning to do to him what she did to Rory Michaels? What if she already has?* I was on my feet before completing this last thought.

I made my way to the back patio. During our second stakeout, Emery had pointed out that the best chance of entering the premises unobserved would be from the woods to the backside of the outdoor fireplace, then to the kitchen door, which would likely be unlocked during daylight hours. If it wasn't, planting my foot into it would do the trick, too.

Once parallel to the fireplace, I dropped to my hands and knees and crawled over grass to the fireplace's backside, figuring if someone watched the security feed, they would mistake me for a stray dog or a brown bear, not anything to get too worked up over. From there, I took stock, and was relieved to hear no sounding alarms or any other noises that would indicate I had been spotted. I prepared to make a run for the kitchen door when it opened.

"Oh, look at that sky," a woman lamented, coming out onto the patio. "Bernard, help me shake this rug out before it starts raining, will you?"

"Certainly, Clarisse."

I chanced a quick peek from my hiding place to see a gray-haired man and stout woman holding separate ends of an oriental rug.

"Oh," said Clarisse, as if suddenly remembering something. "Add furniture polish to your shopping list. I used the last of it this morning. Here, let's give it a good shake. Oh, my! Look at that dust!" She let out a sigh. "I wonder how things are going with Mrs. Westing. Did you see how Mr. Westing had to practically drag her out of the

258

house? Poor Miss White! She was so embarrassed, such a shame. A mother should be more supportive of her son, and Mr. Westing is so good to her!" She clucked her tongue disapprovingly. "All of this conflict over someone as darling as Miss White, which reminds me, have you seen the darling meadow where they plan to build their home?"

"Not yet, but I hear it's a nice parcel, right off the road at the back of the property."

I recalled the meadow we had driven past the first night we went into the woods. It had to be the same meadow.

"Oh, it's a lovely spot! I just hope Mrs. Westing is making the proper 'oohs' and 'ahs.' Miss White was so eager to show her and explain floor plans and such. Oh! That wasn't a raindrop, was it? There's another! Hurry! Let's get the rug back inside. Chop, chop."

As the housekeepers toted the rug into the house, I pulled my knees to my chest and absorbed what I had heard. *Lily left with William and Mrs. Westing. Her car is here, so they must have taken another car.* I frowned at myself. How stupid to assume she was inside because her car was in the driveway. *I'd sure make a sucky detective*, I decided.

Now that that's established, back to the matter at hand. Lily and William drove to the meadow, which is also where Emery and the NWSA will end up on their present course. Oh, geez! What are they walking into? I pushed down panic. None of us could afford for me to lose my head. Plus, there was something important my mind was trying to formulate, something obvious that I hadn't identified yet. *All right. Clarisse said Lily was eager to show Mrs. Westing the spot where she and William are going to build their house, in the meadow, the meadow off Catamount Mountain Road, the meadow in the...woods.*

The remaining scattered puzzle pieces finally assembled, forming a horrifying picture. In my mind, blood-red velvet theatre curtains slowly drew back, revealing a large canvas on a brass easel. It said: *Today's Lunch Special: Mrs. Westing.*

"Oh, no!" I gasped, snapping my phone from my sleeve.

It will look like a terrible accident. My fingers fumbled over the keypad, plunking out a single word that explained why Roga had been stolen. *No one will suspect a thing. Mrs. Westing would have simply been in the wrong place at the wrong time.*

Having typed MURDER, I began to add where they planned to unleash the tiger on Mrs. Westing when I paused and asked myself, *Do I really want Emery to know? Definitely not.*

But he needs to know, I reasoned with myself, hitting keys again. The NWSA would be in the meadow in minutes. Emery would have to protect everyone until I could get there.

I pushed "send" and was on my feet to beat Emery to "the killing field."

~~~

The forest streaked by in a green blur as I ran south at record speed. Seconds into the rescue mission, my phone vibrated against my wrist. Knowing Emery would only text in case of an emergency, I slowed to a jog to read his message. As I retrieved the phone, wind shook the branches overhead. On it, I smelled Emery, Ben, Lily, Mrs. Westing, Ian, and Roga. The stage had been set.

"SHRIEK" popped up on the screen, and I screamed as if my life depended on it. *Maybe it's Emery's that does,* was my next anxious thought, and I released a second blood-curdling scream for good measure before continuing my plight.

As another gust brought the scents of those I loved and those I deplored in more distinctly, my ears detected voices in the distance. Not slowing down, I dialed them in,

"Lily, come back!" William shouted.

A car door slammed, and I strained to hear William's next words. "I hope you're happy, Mother. Are you trying to drive me away, too?"

"How can you say such a thing? I am trying to save you from that chameleon."

"You're calling the woman I love a *chameleon*?"

"Darling, she isn't what she appears to be. There is something she wants, something she thinks we have."

"This is ludicrous! We're finished here, Mother. I'm seeing to my fiancée now."

"Uncle Rory called me the day he died." Mrs. Westing's raised voice suggested that William was walking away from her. "He wanted to meet with me the next morning. An issue of great importance, he said. A family secret involving an individual we had come to trust. Don't you see? He was talking about her!"

Whispering voices buzzed in my ears. I switched the frequency to those.

"Now," Ian commanded in a whisper.

There was the sound of metal scraping metal, and the low, angry growl of a tiger.

Ahead, Mrs. Westing stood at the back of the meadow, cheerless as the dark gray sky over her. She watched William open the back door of a Lexus parked at the top of a slope, where Lily wept in the back seat. Because she was watching her son, Mrs. Westing didn't see the tiger slinking low through the foliage, eyes fixed on her.

I ran into the meadow.

Roga sprung at Mrs. Westing as I sprung at him. He soared through the air, muscular legs outstretched, claws out. A fraction of a second before those deadly claws made contact with his intended prey, I plowed full force into his side. We tumbled to the ground, instantly flipping up into defensive crouches. Our eyes locked.

I was dimly aware of screaming, shouting, a revving engine, as the tiger and I circled one another. As my humanness faded into the background, I deepened my crouch, breathing Roga in. Spray and excrement saturated his fur, and his breath smelled salty and stale, all of which indicated that he had been kept in cruel conditions and starved. His golden eyes were enraged, yet cautious. I understood why. He viewed me not as food, but as competition. I didn't smell human to him; I smelled like kin.

Roga stopped moving, and I followed suit. A low growl rumbled deep in his throat. Instinctively, I growled, too. It sounded strange to my ears, guttural. I couldn't recall ever having made such a sound before.

In response, Roga curled his upper lip, exposing long, sharp, yellowed canines. My armor came up. His hair bristled; his black-tipped ears slicked back, and the rumble broke into a mighty roar.

Leaping up onto his hind legs, he slashed at me with his front paws. Evading them, I dove forward and rammed my head into his abdomen, causing him to lose balance. He toppled backwards, catching himself by twisting up onto all fours. Crouching and positioning my arms, I prepared to grab him when he came at me again. My plan was to restrain him until Emery could tranquilize him.

The tiger launched at me, and I ran forward, getting hold of his neck and flipping onto his back. If I had learned anything today, it was that things didn't always go according to plan, and this proved quickly to be one of those situations. Roga threw himself to the ground, crushing me under his weight. His brute strength, and the speed at which he made this move, took me by surprise. Before I could react, his mouth clamped onto my throat like a vice. If his teeth broke through my hardened skin, I would be mortally wounded.

Sorry, Roga. I hooked his nose with one hand and wiggled the fingers of my other into his lower mouth. *Can't let you kill me.* I began to pry his "jaws-of-death" off my throat, when all at once his jaw slackened. As he sank on top of me, I wondered in confusion if he had passed out, until Ben shouted, "Is the Sasquatch hurt?"

Oh, crud.

Figuring Leroy already had me in his crosshairs, I quickly rolled Roga off me. A dart whizzed past my nose, plunging into the sedated tiger. Springing to my feet, I made a split-second assessment: Leroy reloaded; Ben snapped pictures; Howie and Tom gaped; and William held his hysterical mother. The Lexus was gone, and Emery was nowhere in sight.

I had a sinking feeling where he might be.

As Leroy took aim, I swung around and bolted into the woods in search of my detrimentally brave BFF. Through the trees, I spied the men Emery was pursuing—Ian, Wyatt, and Sam. Guns drawn, they scanned the treetops for me, unaware that their immediate danger was an armed fifteen-year-old boy. Leaning out from behind a canvas-covered truck with a large cage in back, Emery held the rifle to his eye and squeezed the trigger. The dart struck Ian between the shoulder blades. He yelped and collapsed. Wyatt and Sam turned to him.

"Ian," Wyatt gasped. I recognized his voice. A fraction of a second later, both men realized what had happened. By then, Emery already had a dart in the chamber. He fired at Wyatt, who crumpled to the ground.

Gritting his teeth, Sam trained his gun where Emery had ducked behind the truck and fired a round. He didn't get off a second one.

Facedown in the dirt, Sam gasped, having no idea what had taken him down or what was straddling his back. I decided to show him. Flipping him over, I grabbed his jacket collar and yanked his face up to my furry one. In his terrified eyes, I saw my reflection and realized that Sam saw what he wanted to see: an honest-to-goodness Sasquatch. His wide eyes glazed over, and his head rolled, falling back, as he joined the "just tranked" club.

"We're short a man," Emery remarked in an unbelievably calm voice as I lowered Sam to the ground. I turned to look at him. His face matched his voice—unbelievably calm.

"Axel isn't here," I confirmed, adding with concern, "Are you hurt?"

Closing in, Ben called frantically, "Emery!"

Leroy shouted over him, "Emery! Where are ya, boy?"

Emery brought a finger to his lips, gesturing for me to keep quiet. "I've contacted the police," he whispered quickly. "They're on their way. When William went to help his mother, Lily escaped in the Lexus. I gave a vehicle description, but the police may miss her on their way here. Go to Ian's in case she stops off for clothes and money. If she isn't there, check the Westings'. Go! I can see Leroy."

I leapt off Sam and sped away.

Twenty-Two

Showdown

Lily wasn't at her brother's house, so I cut through the woods to the Westings' and got lucky. The Lexus was parked in the driveway, as was Axel's truck.

From the woods, I spotted him standing watch on the front porch, armed with a mini Uzi. When his hard eyes rotated in my direction, I ducked behind a huge fern.

Lily must be inside with the housekeepers, I thought, then recalled seeing only one car parked next to the Civic, not two. Pushing fronds aside, I peered out and confirmed a car was indeed missing. *Bernard went to the store*, I guessed, remembering the conversation between the housekeepers. *Which means Clarisse is alone in the house, with a murderess. I have to help her!*

Heart in my throat, I prayed Clarisse was still alive and looked back at Axel. *I have to take him out first, so he can't hurt anyone coming down the driveway. I'll approach the house like I did earlier and sneak up on him.*

As I crawled across the grass to the outdoor fireplace, the dark clouds finally made good on their threat. By the time I reached the house, rain was falling in sheets. Hunching over, I crept below the windows to the front porch, only pausing to loop a flat garden hose over my shoulder. I figured it would make a good rope. Below the porch rail, I listened to Axel shuffling around on the other side. I had to lure him to my side. The Nativity scene gave me an idea.

Well, it worked for Emery, I thought, picking up a smooth decorative rock at my feet and hurling it at the stable housing Mary, Joseph, and Baby Jesus. It struck the wood loudly.

Axel ran my way. When his square chin appeared over the rail, I sprung up and pegged it. He wheeled around, smacking his face into a stone pillar. I flipped up onto the porch behind him. Bloodied and woozy, he managed to pull his face off the stone and turn around, meeting me. I reintroduced my fist to his jaw. His eyes rolled up into his head, and he went over the porch rail with his gun.

Jumping the rail, I landed in a squat next to the unconscious man and slid the hose off my shoulder. As I jerked him up into a sitting position, his head flopped pathetically forward, and bloodied rainwater ran off his face, splattering my furry forearms. I rapidly wrapped him in the hose and lowered him to the ground. Snapping up the Uzi, I sprinted up the porch steps and cracked the front door open.

Something heavy crashed upstairs. I pushed the door wide and walked into the most spectacular foyer I had ever seen.

The large open room had cedar floors and wood wainscoting that crawled up to elegant burgundy and gold wallpaper. Everything in the room was wood, burgundy, or gold, with the exception of a massive stone fireplace and a majestic Christmas tree that reached up to a balcony. On my left, a bank of windows led to the fireplace with fire crackling in a firebox tall enough to walk into. Arranged around the fireplace was a grouping of furniture with lion's heads carved into the arms, and paws carved into the feet. To my right, a staircase swooped up to the second floor. My gaze traveled up it, settling briefly on an antique harpoon mounted over a door before continuing to the painted domed ceiling, a mural of blue sky, puffy white clouds, and singing cherubim. It was absolutely breathtaking.

My eyes returned to the ground floor, and I noted the more disturbing aspects of the foyer and the library beyond it. Strewn oil paintings covered the floor that had been hastily ripped from the walls. In the library, toppled bookshelves littered the Persian rug with books, accessories, and smashed ceramics. It looked as if a cyclone had touched down in the room.

Not a cyclone, I thought in dread as another crash came from upstairs. My gaze lifted to the balcony again. *Lily has the suit on. This will not be easy.*

I placed the Uzi in an umbrella stand next to the front door and made my way up the stairs, listening to Lily bang around. I figured she was holding Clarisse hostage somewhere on the second floor. Reaching the top, I entered a long hall. The ruckus came from the room at the end, which I knew from our stakeouts was the master suite.

Obviously Lily hasn't had luck finding her grandfather's process, I thought, passing a bedroom suite that "Cyclone Lily" had struck. I guessed it to be William's room.

When I neared the end of the hall, Lily suddenly spoke. "Well, well, well," she said from inside Mrs. Westing's bedroom. I came to a dead stop. "What do we have here?" *Crash!*

Is she ripping down walls? I wondered, glancing into the room next to me. Gasping, my heart sank. Women's loafers on pudgy feet poked out from behind a canopy bed.

I ran into the room. Clarisse lay sprawled on the floor behind the bed, unconscious and pale. Dropping to my knees next to her, I touched her clammy forehead. She didn't respond to the touch. *Lily must have thrown her against the wall*, I surmised, bending close to her ear. "Hang in there, Clarisse," I whispered. "Help is on the way."

"Where is it, Margad?" Lily raged in the master suite. There was a sound like something being ripped from metal hinges, which proved an accurate deduction when the door from a home safe soared past the doorway and down the hall. A second later, glass shattered.

The stained-glass window over the front doors, I concluded, shocked that Lily could throw the steel door so hard. This most definitely would not be easy.

"Okay," I whispered, standing up. "Here we go."

I shot into the hall. Lily stood in the master suite's doorway.

"What the?" she said, startled.

Her appearance distracted me. Sunbursts brightening the room behind her gave the suit an iridescent quality, a spectrum of color glistening off her every curve. Lily looked magical, otherworldly, as if Vulcan himself had sculpted her.

"So, you're the Bigfoot everyone is all worked up about," she mocked.

I tore my gaze from her shimmer and looked into the icy blue eyes behind the visor.

"I recognize that costume," she said, sizing me up. "It's that big gorilla from Star Wars." When I kept silent, she demanded, her tone razor-sharp, "Who are you?"

Your worst nightmare, I thought, running forward.

I aimed a roundhouse kick at Lily's chest, sending her flying backwards into the master suite. She crashed into a mirror affixed to the wall, cracking the glass in a hundred different ways. *That'll bring some bad luck*, I predicted, watching her slide to the floor. She stared back at me in shock.

Lily rephrased her question. "*What* are you?"

I walked into the room.

As if strung on invisible strings, she rose to her feet in a sweeping motion. In a flash, she had a ceramic lamp in her hand and hurled it at me. I dropped to the floor. Nothing had ever come at me so fast before. The lamp swooshed over me, exploding against the doorframe. Lily lunged forward, and I flipped onto my back, bending my legs to block her. The plan was to give her a sharp snap kick to the face, but before I could do this, she had my calf, yanked me off the floor upside-down, and brought her knee into my gut. Air rushed from my lungs. Armor or no armor, Lily's knee was equivalent to being whacked with a wrecking ball. In the suit, the woman was crazy strong.

Before I could catch my breath, she grabbed my other leg, too, spun me in a circle, and released. The room rushing by, I twisted around and caught the wall with my fingertips and toes. Springing off it into a back flip, I landed onto my feet and spun around.

Lily bolted into the hall.

She had just sprinted past the bedroom where Clarisse lay unconscious when I tackled her to the floor. We tumbled down the hall, kicking, punching, head butting, leaving smashed drywall and Chewbacca bits in our wake. Three quarters of the way down, Lily got the upper hand and cracked my skull into the wall, leaving me momentarily stunned. I literally heard ringing in my head.

"Let's unmask you, freak," she snarled, reaching for Chewbacca's head. Seizing her by the underarms, I propelled her heels-over-head into the air. Her feet caught the carpet, and she managed to skirt my hands when I reached for her ankles, shooting down the hall like a bullet. Grumbling at myself, I lurched to my feet and went after her. She hung a right to the balcony.

As I rounded the corner to the balcony, the barbed tip of the harpoon rammed against my stomach, pinning me to the wall.

"You should be impaled like a fish," Lily hissed, grinding the sharp tip into my armor. "You should be dead."

Glaring into the cold, confident eyes of the murderess, my rage that had been at a controlled simmer boiled over. *She murdered Rory Michaels, tried to murder Mrs. Westing, and hurt Clarisse!*

I blinked, and in that micro-moment of time, imagined the snarling, formless beast within me straining at a thick chain I clutched. My hand opened, and the chain slipped over my palm, my fingers, and the shadowy embodiment of everything unnatural in me ran free. My eyelids slid up, and "the beast" looked out at Lily.

I brought my hand down on the harpoon's handle, breaking it in two. Lily stumbled forward and into my fist. The impact snapped her head back, reversing her stumble, which provided me space to rotate my hips and deliver a powerful side kick into her chest, propelling her backwards. She crashed through the balcony's rail and appeared suspended in air, eyes wide, hands desperately grasping at nothing, until gravity grabbed her and yanked her viciously downward.

My heart pounded with excitement as I ran to where she had broken through, and I watched her slam into the coffee table below, smashing it to smithereens. Without delay, she pulled herself up from the wreckage, jerked her chin up to me. For the first time, I saw fear in her eyes. This pleased the beast immensely.

Lily looked at the open front door, preparing to make a run for it. I sprung down and blocked her escape. Her head swung to the ground floor's artery hall, and she let out a furious scream when I suddenly appeared in that escape route, too. Lily might have strength, but I had speed. We both knew she couldn't get past me.

To show her displeasure, Lily chucked a lion's head chair at me. Thrilled, I easily dodged. Next, she snapped up a piece of the coffee table, sending it flying toward me like a Frisbee. I caught it and tossed it carelessly over my shoulder. From that point on, she threw whatever she could get her hands on, all of which I gleefully eluded by sidestepping, ducking, jumping, flipping, and contorting my body in all sorts of weird ways. I was having the time of my life!

Eventually the space around her was emptied, the previous contents lying behind me in a battlefield of broken stair rail, battered walls, and busted furniture, save for a settee alongside the fireplace. This, Lily hoisted over her head and launched high in the air, yelling with frustration when I caught it. Nonchalantly, I lowered the settee to the floor, hopped over the back, and sat down, taunting my opponent with a big smile.

"Think you're funny, freak?" Lily growled, scanning desperately for a weapon. Her gaze settled on the fireplace.

Curious, I watched her fling the fireplace screen aside and snatch up a poker from the tool set, using it to maneuver burning logs onto the hearth. Somewhere in the back of my mind I knew I should feel alarm—Lily plus fire being a bad equation and all—but in my present state of mind I couldn't muster up concern. I was just happy she had found something else to chuck at me.

"Like fire?" she asked smugly, punting a log.

From my seat, I visually slowed down the log en route. Hot embers spun off like fireworks. When the log was a matter of feet away, I sprung up and nailed it with my fist. The log erupted, and sizzling red and yellow chunks of burning wood showered on and around me. Quickly, I brushed embers off Chewbacca's fur and the settee.

"Pity," Lily said, watching me. "You're fire-retardant, but I know from experience that Christmas trees aren't." With that, she kicked a log at the tree.

It disappeared amongst pine branches heavily laden with ribbon and ornaments, and I finally felt proper alarm. Snapping back to my senses, I thought, *She's trying to burn the house down! I've got to get that log out of the tree!*

I shot to the tree and pulled it over. It hit the floor with a crunching thud, spewing ornaments and shiny bits of glass bulbs over the cedar. While I kicked through branches in search of the log, Lily sent another one at the stairs. It docked on the runner, the smell of burning chemicals diffusing in the air.

While the runner diverted my attention, Lily kicked a log toward the front door. I yanked my head around to witness it ricochet off a coat rack and drop into the umbrella stand where I had stashed the gun. I only had time to wonder how extreme heat would affect a loaded semi-automatic weapon when a log struck the base of my neck. Instantly, I saw red.

"Contact," Lily shouted gleefully.

I whipped around to her, fuming. Smiling evilly, she held an open can of lighter fluid, tilting it back and forth in her hand.

"Things are about to get very interesting," she predicted, and we ran for one another.

Faster, I closed the distance in a flying kick. My heel struck her collarbone, sending her reeling into the fireplace, the lighter fluid in her hand. Flames blasted from the firebox. Scrambling backwards and falling, I threw my arm over my face and peeked out at the blaze. It took a moment to make out Lily flailing amongst the flames. A bluish-green aura surrounded her, ghastly and beautiful at the same time.

"Lily!" I screamed, clambering to my feet.

She rolled onto the hearth, and the bluish-green color radiating from the suit turned red-orange like molten hot lava. I froze in horror. She yanked off the hood, ivory ringlets tumbled around her face twisted with pain and fear, as bubbles abruptly formed under the red-orange film. Screaming, Lily clawed wildly at the bubbles, swelling and coursing over her, vanishing as quickly as they had appeared. Then the suit seemed to melt into her, absorbing her skin, defining her every detail with precision. Unfathomably, the suit and Lily had become one.

Howling, she sprinted for the window and dove through the glass. Shards rained down, competing with the torrent the sky released. Lily disappeared from sight, and I heard water splash, felt my feet carry me to the window. Below, a pond rippled wildly from a disturbance.

Moments later, Lily broke through the epicenter of it, smiling and shaking water from her hair. The suit shimmered iridescent again, only the suit was now her. From the collarbone down, Lily was metal.

Elated, she admired her metal arms, hands, chest, giggling over her metal belly button. She slammed her metal fists into the water, sending it shooting around her like a fountain. "Yes!" she shouted in triumph, hitting the water again.

A rapid sequence of pops from the Uzi woke me up from one nightmare and sent me into another. Fire alarms blared throughout the mansion. Smoke and heat choked the air. Flames licked up the staircase. My eyeballs burned and watered, and my lungs felt seared. Having been so fixed on Lily, I had failed to notice the house burning down around me. Hacking, I looked up at the celestial ceiling. It was as if Heaven had become Hell.

I caught sight of her out the front door, strolling to the truck with Axel slumped over her shoulder, raindrops pinging her metal body. Whistling, she tossed him in the truck bed like a sack of potatoes.

The staircase collapsed.

I whipped around to the fiery pile of wood, remembering the woman on the second floor. Lily started the truck, but stopping her was no longer top priority. Rescuing Clarisse was.

I made a running leap to the balcony, catching the edge where Lily had broken through, and pulled myself up. Holding my breath, I ran through a wall of flames and down the hall to the bedroom where Clarisse lay. Gathering her in my arms, I carried her to the room's outdoor balcony, where I stepped up onto a wrought iron table pushed against the rail.

"Be glad you're not seeing this," I told her, and jumped. Due to Clarisse's portliness and the slick mud, our landing was by no means perfect, though I managed to keep my footing and not drop her.

"You're safe, Clarisse," I reassured the unconscious woman, quickly carrying her to the front of the house. Sirens wailed up the mountain. "Hear that? Help will be here any minute. You'll be fine, Clarisse, just fine."

Unable to handle the thought of leaving her in the rain, I carried the housekeeper to the Nativity scene. Ducking into the stable, I pushed Baby Jesus back with my foot and gently placed her at the foot of the manger.

"Look out for her," I requested of Baby Jesus, and backed out into the rain.

The first fire truck swung into the driveway, and I ran for the woods. From behind a tree, I watched two more pull in, firefighters pouring from the cabs. I willed them to look at the Nativity. One did.

"I've got a woman down," he shouted into his headset, running toward Clarisse.

Shifting my gaze to the inferno, I took one last look, then turned and walked away.

Twenty-Three

Revelation

Nate and I sat side by side on the sectional, watching the eight o'clock news, with a plate of freshly baked oatmeal raisin cookies between us, a baking challenge I had taken on the moment I walked through the door after "helping Serena." It had been nice having control over one small corner of the universe for a time, and the cookies hadn't turned out half bad, either.

"These don't suck," Nate praised, taking another cookie. *His fifth*, I noted proudly.

On the news, Detective Adoncia Cruz announced that Ian White, Sam Donnelly, and Wyatt Rent had been charged with the tiger's theft, as well as with attempted murder and endangering public safety.

"Those dudes must've trapped you guys in the auditorium," Nate surmised, motioning to the three mug shots on the television screen.

I smiled grimly at Ian's picture, his jaw swollen and bruised, damage sustained from Axel's fist. *Maybe Ian will look at the bright side of prison*, I thought. *The likelihood of running into a Sasquatch behind bars is slim to none.*

To my brother, I confirmed, "Two of them did. That blond guy was with us. *He's* the zookeeper who brought the python into the auditorium." I said this as if it was Ian White's worst offense against society.

"So, that means those other two dumped the zookeeper, mmm, uh—"

"James Flynn."

"Flynn. Yeah, that's it. Anyway, Flynn's lawyer said in an interview that the guy's last memory of that night was trying to unlock his car at some bar." Nate paused to take a bite of cookie. As he meditatively chewed, I wondered how in the heck I had missed *that* interview. "This is what happened," he announced, cookie in his mouth. "One of those dudes slipped Flynn a 'mickey' at the bar, followed him out to the parking lot, hijacked him in his own car, and then dumped him at the tiger cage thingy."

"Brilliant deduction, Holmes," I teased, though I was actually impressed. "And I agree, with one exception: the bartender drugged James Flynn."

"Of course, Watson!" Nate exclaimed, hacking a British accent. He popped his forehead with his palm. "How shortsighted of me! The *bartender* did it. It's *always* the bartender who done it." He twirled an invisible mustache.

"Sherlock Holmes doesn't have a mustache," I enlightened him.

"Whatever." He took another bite of cookie. "But, seriously, what makes you think some random bartender had anything to do with this?"

Wish I could tell you, Nate. "It's just a hunch."

What my twin and the rest of the general public weren't aware of yet was that the "random" bartender had already been fingered by one of his accomplices presently in police custody. Emery had texted this tidbit earlier from police headquarters, where he was giving an official statement and slyly gathering information. He didn't know which man had ratted Axel out. My bets were on Ian.

Other intelligence Emery had gleaned was that Lily and Axel were still at large, celebrating a bittersweet victory, I supposed. Lily may not be able to build an army of metal soldiers, but she herself was now metal—and maybe undefeatable. When I texted this thought to Emery earlier, he countered: *She is not undefeatable. We will stop her.*

How?

That depends on her next move.

This hadn't reassured me much, but the next thing Emery texted did: *I've concluded William and his mother have no knowledge of the suit or the process. The location of the process probably went to the grave with Michaels and Suttner.*

This was good, in a morbid sort of way. I asked: *How is William holding up?*

His fiancée attempted to murder his mom.

Understood. I'm taking Lily down.

Now I promised myself again, *And I will. I will.*

"Finally," Nate said, pulling me from my thoughts. "Someone interesting."

Wearing his Texan-sized smile, Leroy Rays towered over Paula Kimble, who interviewed him outside police headquarters. Cameras flashed, and microphones from other news networks crowded around them.

Shifting his eyes beyond Paula, Leroy said, "And where do you think you're going?" His arm shot out, pulling Emery into the camera frame. Nate and I busted up at our friend's miserable expression. Secretly, though, I knew that Emery being in the media spotlight yet again was no laughing matter. It was downright dangerous—for us all.

Tucking Emery into his side, Leroy announced into the camera, "This here is the toughest, bravest kid I know. When the Sasquatch shrieked, Emery took off fast and furious—a boy with a mission. I yelled at him to hold up, but he just kept goin', and truth be told, I thought he was goin' in the wrong dang direction. I judged that shriek to be coming from north of us." He squeezed Emery's shoulders, his eyes twinkling with pride. I felt the same pride for my best friend. "But he took us straight to the Sasquatch *and* the tiger, then went after those three punks all on his own." Letting out a boisterous laugh, Leroy gave Emery a manly shake. Turning solemn, he looked straight into the camera and professed, "Emery Phillips is a hero."

After this proclamation, Emery managed to smoothly extract himself from Leroy. "Thank you, Mr. Rays," he said politely, and slipped out of the camera frame.

"Okay. Em is officially the coolest guy I know," Nate declared.

"Me, too," I agreed, giddy with pride.

My brother gave me a funny look, but before I could ask him what the look was for, the phone rang. He grabbed the handset off the ottoman.

"Don't answer it," I quickly advised. "It's Miriam." I guessed she had seen Emery on the news and now wanted to rave about him.

Nate glanced at caller ID and laughed. "How'd you know?"

The answering machine picked up in the kitchen, recording Miriam's high-pitched squeal.

"Emery wore contacts today," I explained.

Nate lifted his eyebrows questioningly.

"This is the first time Miriam has ever seen him without his glasses."

Nate shrugged. "So?"

Do I really have to spell this out for him? "*So*, Emery is totally hot without glasses, not that he isn't hot with them, he's just more hot without them."

The funny look came back. "Cass, friends of the opposite sex do not call one another 'hot.'"

"Of course they do, and so do sisters. Nate, you are *sooo* hot."

"I know," he agreed, and flicked a cookie chunk at my face. I caught it in my mouth. Nate grinned. "Freak."

My mouth dipped into a frown and I glanced away, recalling the last person who had called me "freak." *Lily has taken up enough headspace for one day,* I decided, looking back at my twin. He was frowning, too. "What's wrong?" I asked.

Nate blew out a breath and looked into my eyes. "Straight up. Who do you like, Jared or Emery?"

"Jared," I responded instantly. A sad, empty feeling followed. Despite everything, I was still head over heels for the guy.

"In that case," Nate said, brushing cookie crumbs off his hands, "you leave me no choice but to gossip like a girl. Okay, Jared told me today—"

"No need," I interrupted, knowing exactly what Jared had told him. "Got it. He's angry at me for putting his girlfriend in a hammerlock."

Nate grinned. "Listen to you," he said, wrapping his arm around my neck in a light chokehold. I let him do it, since the gesture was meant in the most affectionate way. "Hammerlock," he echoed, giving me a noogie. "You're so *Crouching Tiger, Hidden Dragon* now. Gotta get Em to teach me some sweet moves, too."

I smiled to myself. Little did my brother know, Bruce Lee, Chuck Norris, and Jackie Chan had more to do with my sweet moves than Emery did.

"And just so you know," he said, "I was beaming with pride when I heard how you humbled Robin. You should have told me yourself, though. Why are you always so tight-lipped about everything?" He gifted me with another noogie before releasing me. I had no way to respond to his question. Was I really tight-lipped about *everything*?

"Now, for the shocker. Cassidy, you really *don't* get it."

"What does that mean?"

"That means you were set up, duped by Robin Newton, and by lame-o me." Nate shook his head, as if disgusted with himself. "It was Mindy Ames who told me about Robin and Jared, and like an idiot I did just what they hoped I would do: I told *you*."

I could feel my face cloud over. "So you're saying it was lie? A trick?"

"Yup. Jared talked to your friends, Katie and Josie, and found out—to his surprise—that he was going out with Robin. He was even more surprised about all the, uh, *activities* they were participating in." Nate wiggled his eyebrows.

Feeling a blush coming on, I protested by pushing him. "I'm not buying it." I crossed my arms stubbornly. "No way he didn't know! Robin was running her mouth every day in the locker room."

"Shockingly, all the graphic details didn't cross over into the guy realm. Jared told me I was, like, the only dude he knew of who had heard anything about it, and I didn't hear all the juicy stuff."

"Be grateful," I huffed, compressing my lips. I had come to grudgingly accept that Jared liked Robin, and now I was having a hard time *un*-accepting it. "They ate lunch together on Tuesday," I challenged, believing I had found a hole in the story. "Sat right across from me. What about *that*?"

"Yeah, Jared mentioned that weirdness. Robin asked him to eat with her, and he didn't see any reason why he shouldn't. He wasn't expecting her to hit on him."

"She hit on him?"

"Big time. The girl has *no* shame. Obviously, this was all for your benefit. You should feel honored Robin hates you enough to go to the trouble. What I can't figure out is how she knew Jared would make a good revenge tool. You haven't even told your friends you like him, right?"

"Right, but I know how." I narrowed my eyes, recalling what had happened at the sports field. "She caught me staring at Jared, or, as Jessica Blanchette put it, *scamming* on him." I dropped my face into my hands. *Must everything always be so messed up between Jared and me?* "How could I let things get this bad, Nate? We were friends, and now—I hate this so much!"

"So change it."

I turned my face in my hands to look at him.

"Time to get over being embarrassed, Cass. Man up and come clean."

"I know, and I will. I really will this time." Jared was long overdue for an apology. Hopefully he would accept one.

~~~

Things ran late for Emery. After news interviews, he had dinner downtown with the members of the NWSA, along with Dad and Serena, who had met them at police headquarters late afternoon. Dad got home about ten-thirty, which in his mind was too late for me to go over to the Phillipses'. So after texting with Emery for over an hour, I headed out when my nightlife began: at the stroke of midnight. Emery was waiting for me at his window.

"What a day," I exclaimed as I climbed into his room. I shoved one of the two storage bags packed with cookies at his chest. "These are for you. I baked, like, six dozen when I got home."

With a thoughtful expression, he studied the cookies through the plastic. "You baked cookies after fighting a tiger and a madwoman almost to the death?" Usually he made such statements in an amused tone, but there wasn't a trace of amusement in his voice or on his face. "I didn't know you could bake, Cassidy. Thank you."

"You're welcome, and I'm pretty surprised myself. Look at the bottoms. They're not even scorched." When he didn't smile, I scrutinized him more closely, while he continued observing the cookies as if they were works of art. Something was definitely wrong.

"Dare I ask whom the second bag is for?" he inquired, not looking at me.

"Oh, that's what's bothering you," I said, relieved. "No need to worry. Joe is a good guy, and my friend." I set both bags of cookies on his dresser, while he silently closed the window and curtains. *He's still worrying about Joe*, I assumed, pulling off my mask. My tumbling hair came alive with static electricity. The night was cold and unusually dry, hence there was no moisture to dissipate the electric charge in the air.

I laughed, turning to Emery. Watching me, he wore a conflicted expression on his face.

"My hair is forecasting no rain," I joked to lighten the mood, watching strands of my hair jump to my palm.

Emery stepped toward me and, to my surprise, clasped my head between his hands and ran them down my hair, neutralizing the electric charge. Speechless, I stared at him. Undeterred by my reaction, he pulled me into his arms.

"What's this for?" I asked, hugging him back, my heart thumping against his chest.

"This is for not letting Roga rip out your throat. I have never witnessed a more terrifying sight. I can't get the image out of my head."

"Oh, please! Compared to Lily, Roga is a pussy cat." I laughed uneasily. I couldn't believe Emery had been this affected. He had seemed all right in our texting and was Mr. Cool after tranking three men. I pulled away to get a look at him, observing emotions warring in his eyes, and understood what he was battling. "Emery, no guilt," I said. "What happened is not your fault."

"I sent you after Lily," he pointed out, furious with himself.

"Yes, you did, but if you hadn't, Clarisse would probably be dead."

"True," he granted, giving the impression that he agreed, which I knew he did not. Agreeing was his way of ending the discussion, something I was unwilling to do until he genuinely relinquished blaming himself.

"Well, if you're going to beat yourself up, then I'm beating myself up, too," I maneuvered. "Confession: I went beast on Lily, and not only did I go beast, I also—" I stopped talking as shame crashed over me. I had enjoyed destroying the Westings' home with Lily. How sick was that?

"Sometimes the beast needs to come out, Cassidy," Emery said gently.

"Funny, Joe said the opposite," I noted dourly, flicking my gaze to the cookies. Tossing the mask on top of them, I felt Emery watching me, strategizing how to get me out of my funk. I had gotten him out of his. Now it was his turn.

"You should know," he said in a markedly lighter tone, "Detective Cruz received an untraceable email this evening detailing Josef Richter's rumored secret weapon, Lily and Ian White's relationship to him, and a very compelling theory of how Rory Michaels and Ernest Suttner may have gained possession of the suit's process. Also included was a short list of poisons that a coroner could misdiagnose as a massive heart attack, along with a strong recommendation to exhume Michaels and test tissues for these poisons."

"Do you think Detective Cruz will take your email seriously?" I asked skeptically.

"No, though she may reconsider the advice when the FBI issues a bulletin regarding an unidentified female suspect in a string of bank robberies or jewelry store heists—or however Lily conducts her reign of terror—who is reportedly made of metal and possesses supernatural strength and speed. Do you suppose Lily still has fingerprints?"

"Definitely. She isn't like Barbie. She's very, you know...*detailed*." I let what I was getting at register for him before adding, "I wish we could do more."

"We will," Emery assured me, as if he had prior knowledge that another run-in with Lily White was predestined. Assessing my grim face, a grin spread over his. "If memory serves me correctly, you were granted an interrogation pass," he reminded me. He knew nothing would boost my spirits more than interrogating him. Flopping on the bed, he folded his hands behind his head and smiled. "Proceed."

I rubbed my palms together, thoroughly cheered up. "Don't think I'm not prepared," I warned, turning the chair to the bed and sitting down. "Baking provides a lot of thinking time."

Emery sighed. "And you baked six dozen cookies. This should be brutal."

"I'll try to make it not too painful. Is Riley your employer?"

His smile widened appreciatively. "You're good," he complimented the ceiling. "Yes."

My heart picked up speed. "Does Mickey work for her, too?"

"Yes."

"Elaborate."

"If I do, does this line of questioning end?"

"No. Tell me vocations. What are their jobs?"

"Riley is a bail bond agent."

"A bail bond agent," I repeated carefully, thinking. "You mean like someone who loans money to criminals so they can get out of jail?"

"So a suspect awaiting trial can get out of jail. Convicted criminals are a little more difficult to release, or more accurately, 'break out.'"

"Like you would know!"

Emery gave me a crafty look,

"Oh, shut up. Is Mickey Riley's bounty hunter?"

"The proper job title is: Fugitive Recovery Agent. Though, granted, Mickey prefers 'bounty hunter.'"

"So that's a 'yes,' and no duh, he prefers it. He doesn't look like a Fugitive Recovery Agent. He looks like a bounty hunter."

"Hmmm." Emery feigned thoughtfulness. "I hadn't realized either had a particular look. Take me, for instance. Do I look like a Fugitive Recovery Agent, or do I look like a bounty hunter?"

"Neither, okay? We're being serious here. No more joking."

Emery shrugged.

"What do you really do for Riley?"

"Presently, nothing very exciting. For the most part she has me 'skip tracing,' meaning I track down defendants who fail to appear in court by running social security numbers, checking credit card activity, and so forth. Once I've located a skip, Mickey, Marky, and/or Marty—those are the other bounty hunters—apprehend the 'no show.'"

"Mickey, Marky, and Marty?" I eyed him suspiciously. "You're making those names up."

"All information imparted thus far has been truthful," Emery vowed, giving me the three-finger Boy Scouts salute. "Riley has had a run of defiant clients lately, keeping Mickey, Marky, Marty, and me extremely busy. Hence, why my wallet has been exceptionally fat, though Jason Crenshaw has done a remarkable job of trimming it down lately." A sparkle came into his black eyes. "I neglected to tell you in our texting that I met with Jason to get squared away when I got home. Just so you know, he received a handsome bonus upon mentioning that you smelled like 'a house on fire' when he picked you up."

I clenched my teeth.

"He then suggested I might like to consider contributing additional funds toward this pending 'car detailing' of his, since removing smoke odor from upholstery requires a series of steam cleanings."

"The scoundrel," I growled, clenching my hands now, too. "And you might like to know that your *henchman* blared the breaking news about Roga's recovery all the way home!"

"Yes, he informed me of the tiger's recovery as well, in case I hadn't heard." Emery grinned at the ceiling and added, "At least he didn't checkmate me."

"Are you sure about that? How big was his *bonus*?"

"A single number, followed by three zeros."

Groaning, I pounded my fist into the mattress. "No more living on the edge," I ordered, shaking my finger at Emery. This made him smile more, of course. "Okay, done with Jason and back to Riley. When can I meet her?"

Emery puckered his lips, contemplating. "I'll weigh out the pros and cons and get back to you on that."

"But that's not a 'no'?"

"Yes, that is not a 'no.'"

I pumped my arm.

"Don't waste precious time celebrating," he advised. "I won't be able to hold this book open for much longer." This was his clever way of saying he was done with divulging secrets.

"Is Riley a blond?" I asked quickly.

After a brief look of surprise, Emery burst into laughter, laughing harder every time he looked at me. I waited patiently for an answer. When he could get a hold of himself, he said, "The answer to your extremely unanticipated question is, no, Riley is not a blond. She is a redhead. Fiery redheads appear to be my lot in life." Sitting up, he mussed my hair and announced, "My turn to interrogate. Something other than Lily White is bothering you. What is it?"

I pushed the hair from my face. "How did you know?"

"I can read your mind, remember?" He tapped his temple. "Well, not really, or I wouldn't have had to ask. Now, are you going to talk, or do I have to put you under a hot light?" He motioned to his desk lamp.

"Not necessary. I want to talk. Actually, I can't wait to talk! Robin made everything up! Jared never went out with her!" While I excitedly shared the good news, Emery's gaze lowered to my mouth, his expression gradually darkening. Assuming his thoughts were elsewhere, I asked happily, "Okay, where have you traveled off to?"

His eyes moved up to mine. "Unfortunately, I'm very present with you."

I shifted uneasily in the chair.

"Yes, Cassidy, I'm about to rain on your parade," he confirmed, reading my body language perfectly. "And know that I take no pleasure in doing so. I see where this story is going. You plan to smooth things over with Jared. For your safety and the safety of your family, I'm asking you not to do that."

My thoughts were swirling. I couldn't fathom how apologizing to Jared would put my family at risk.

"To answer the question written all over your face, simply put, Jared is not someone we want close to our situation."

"Why? Because he's smart?" This was the only explanation I could come up with.

"Not only smart, but Jared Wells is nobody's fool. Frankly, he sees through my act, though he doesn't know what he's looking at—not yet, anyway. Don't offer him a front-row seat. Leave things as they are."

As I opened my mouth to respond, Emery's phone vibrated on the nightstand.

"Hold that tongue-lashing," he instructed—unfairly—since I was merely going to suggest that he stop being so paranoid, because although Jared was smart, perceptive, and absolutely wonderful, he was also only fifteen. No way would he think in a million years, *Ah-ha! Cassidy Jones is a mutant, and Emery Phillips is her trusty guardian.*

Picking up his cell, Emery looked at the caller ID and frowned. "Speaking of tongue lashings, it's my dad. He must be catching up on local news."

"Well, answer it!" I urged. "Do damage control. I'll tell you the what's-what later."

"We'll pick up where we left off in the morning," he agreed, settling against his headboard, making himself comfortable for his talk. In my mind there was nothing further to discuss on the subject. I owed Jared an apology, and an apology was what he would get, regardless of Emery's qualms.

"Hi, Dad," Emery answered the phone, yawning for effect, or maybe the yawn was genuine. It had been a long, eventful day, and Emery was only human, after all.

"Hello, Emery," Mr. Phillips smoothly replied. Hearing his voice made me cringe. "I hadn't realized you had an interest in American folklore."

Emery smiled at me and rolled his eyes. "I've always been fascinated by American folklore," he said, playing the game as I quickly collected my mask and Joe's cookies, ready to vamoose. Even Mr. Phillips on the other end of a phone line was too close for my comfort. Scooting to the window, I tugged on the mask while Emery listed his supposedly favorite folklore characters: "Brer Rabbit, Tommy Knockers, Paul Bunyan, Davy Crockett, Casey Jones—"

I glanced back at him. He winked and gestured for me to tuck in my hair.

"And Sasquatch," Mr. Phillips finished. "You've been a busy boy."

Good luck, I mouthed, rapidly tucking.

Emery gave me a thumbs-up. "A little bit. How are things in China?"

China, ha-ha, I thought sardonically, sliding the window up.

"We'll have plenty of time to discuss China when I'm home in two weeks—"

Air seemed to freeze in my lungs, and for the briefest moment I thought I would faint. *Scary Mr. Phillips, who radiates danger like electricity and watches me like a hawk,* cannot *come home!*

"Son, let's cut to the chase, shall we?" he suggested, as I swung my head to Emery in terror. His fingers already formed the a-okay sign. I shook my head emphatically. His dad coming home would not be okay.

"You tranquilized three armed men, thwarting one of the most bizarre murder attempts that I have ever heard of—"

"Actually, it was the Sasquatch who thwarted the murder attempt," Emery interrupted, grinning big at me.

Mr. Phillips went dead silent.

Outta here!

I hastily waved goodbye to Emery. He held up a finger for me to wait, then pointed at a memory card on his desk. I nodded, understanding that the memory card was from Ben's camera. *Poor Ben! He must be devastated that his Sasquatch shots disappeared*, I thought. After this sliver of a second of devotion to Ben, I went back to worrying about my own butt. *How am I going to avoid a man who doesn't want to avoid me?* I fretted, while the silent standoff continued. *A man who suspects that I'm the reason why he now resides in Queen Anne, why his wife has moved her lab to their basement, and why his college-graduate son attends high school. And darn it, he's right!*

That's it, I'm leaving the country, I decided, just as Emery ended the standoff with my primary threat.

"Dad, I do have a logical explanation," he said.

"Of course you do, Emery," I heard Mr. Phillips reply in his deceptively calm tone as I dove onto the awning, flipping up and over. "You *are* my son."

Twenty-Four

I Am So Dead

*E*ight-thirty, I noted on the mantle clock, pacing the living room. *Not too early to call anymore. Jared is definitely up.* After doing mental aerobics for the majority of the night over Mr. Phillips's imminent return and speculating about how Lily would wreak havoc on society, I had found some peace by resolving to call Jared and apologize ASAP. But peace was at 4:00 a.m., not now at 8:30 a.m. At this present time, I was eager to get the apology over with—or maybe "eager" wasn't the right word, unless you can be eager and terrified out of your mind at the same time.

I shifted my gaze to the handset I had held in a death grip for the last half hour, and thought about how I would rather fight Lily and Roga simultaneously than make this phone call.

Just do it, I ordered myself, looking at the sofa. *After getting comfortable*, I added, delaying.

Gathering throw pillows, I carefully arranged them against the sofa arm, and rearranged them a couple more times after that. After I'd finally had enough of fussing with pillows and procrastinating, I laid back against them, releasing a long breath as I went down. Another calming breath later, I "manned up" and plucked out the phone number I knew by heart. Jared answered after the first ring.

"Hello." His voice was wary.

Squeezing my eyelids together, I silently cursed caller ID. Obviously he had checked to see who was calling prior to picking up the phone. Now, I was committed. There was no turning back.

"Nate?"

"Not Nate," I croaked out, clearing phlegmy embarrassment from my throat, which embarrassed me even more. "Uh, how are you, Jared?"

A silence followed, during which I cursed my voice for having gone up in pitch at Jared's name. Was it possible for me not to make a complete idiot of myself?

"I'm fine, Cassidy. How are you?"

"Uh—" I said, flipping up into a sitting position and curling forward. "Um, okay." I swiped up Chazz's sketchbook from the coffee table. *Best Superheroes Ever* was scrolled in black marker over the cover.

"Sooo—what's up?"

"Uh, nothin' much." I bit my lip hard for my stupidity and began anxiously turning pages. "I want to talk to you about something." The words flew out of my mouth as caped crusaders depicted in crayon flew past my eyes.

"Okay. Sh—"

"But not over the phone," I cut him off, flipping the pages faster. "How about my h—" The rest of the syllables stuck in my throat as a flaming red color caught my eye, disappearing again. I slammed my hand down on the back of the page. Had I just seen what I thought I saw?

"Do you want me to c—"

I disconnected the call.

Dropping the handset, I peeled back the page, holding my breath.

"No," I breathed out, and stared in horror at the superhero girl with flowing red hair, a purple spandex costume and cape, and big green eyes with black lashes curling out like spider legs. One of the green eyes winked in a maddening way. She held a cat or a pig, I couldn't tell which, and a building burned behind her that unnervingly resembled King

Pharmaceutical. And just in case the red hair, the superhero costume, the building, and the wink didn't drill in the fact that my goose was cooked, Chazz captioned the picture in big, rounded capital letters, also purple: *THE AMAZING CASSIDY.*

I am so dead.

Coming Soon
2013

Prologue

Slouching against the concrete wall, Arthur King Junior tore another page from the Bible that had been slipped through the tray slot on the steel door that morning. It was a gift from a well-meaning prison guard who hoped the message inside would reform Arthur.

"Fat chance of *that*!" Arthur said loudly to no one, since he was alone in the prison cell, which was a quarter of the size of his bedroom suite's walk-in closet at his Seattle home. In fact, the dingy mattress on which his backside was now parked filled half of the concrete floor.

"Okay, fellas," he addressed the prison guards who might be listening on the other side of the door. Or maybe they weren't—Arthur really didn't care. "Enough with the 'hot box' already," he blathered as he carefully folded the thin paper into an airplane. "Learned my lesson real good. The décor alone is punishment!"

He glanced up from his creation to look for a target. The sparse space boasted a stained white toilet, wall sink, square barred window near the ceiling, and cream-painted walls. Arthur actually didn't mind the blandness of his surroundings. He liked being the only source of color, which he was, in his bright orange "jailbird" jumpsuit.

"Tell your *colleague* that I'm *sorry* for biting his hand," he rambled on, referring to the prison guard he had sunk his teeth into when the man had ordered him to stop griping about what he was being served and move along in the cafeteria line. The assault had landed Arthur in solitary confinement for five days. He was on day two.

Narrowing his eyes on the toilet bowl, Arthur took aim. "I promise to be a good boy and eat all of my peas." He launched the airplane. Hitting the toilet rim, it joined the other planes that had missed the mark on the floor.

Arthur spat a furious cuss word and savagely ripped another sheet from the Bible. "I'm bored, bored, bored, BORED!" he shouted like a petulant child, scrupulously folding another plane. "Come on! This is prison! Where's the action?"

As if a prayer had been answered—not that Arthur King Junior prayed—the alarm suddenly sounded.

Arthur straightened up on the mattress. Shouts, screams, and cheers could be heard under the blare of the alarm. When the unmistakable rapid pops from automatic weapons added to the commotion, Arthur eagerly jumped to his feet.

"Yeah! This is more like it!" he yelled, pumping his small fist in the air. Gleeful, he listened to the violent ruckus come closer, only feeling apprehension when the screaming, shouting, and gunfire entered his corridor.

Covering his ears, Arthur backed up to the concrete wall, wishing he had been satisfied with "bored."

Then the corridor fell silent. Lowering his hands, Arthur listened. Footsteps echoed; heels clicked against the concrete. The commotion in the distance again sounded like a battlefield.

The clicking stopped outside his cell door.

"Arthur," a woman's voice sang from the other side, "stay clear of the door."

BANG! Something struck the door with the force of a wrecking ball, denting the steel. Flattening his back to the wall, Arthur's heart pounded with a mixture of excitement and fear. *BANG! BANG!* The door flew off the hinges, crashing into the wall inches from Arthur. The thrill of nearly being crushed by it brought a twisted smile to his weasel-like face.

A petite woman who looked like she was made of china, with the palest complexion and hair that Arthur had ever seen, stepped into the doorway. Sapphire eyes cold as glass regarded him from a classically beautiful face, framed by ivory curls. Her attire suggested that she was preparing to have tea with the Queen of England: a perfectly fitted, high-collared dress in dusty rose, a matching hat rimmed with a two-inch veil, pearl earrings, and lacy white gloves. Grinning, Arthur's eyes slid down her delicately formed figure to her shapely calves, which appeared to be made of metal. Metal feet sported dusty rose pumps.

"My eyes are up here," the woman lightly reprimanded.

Grinning like the lunatic he was, Arthur looked up into her icy eyes. "Brrrr." He shivered playfully. "Where have you been all my life, gorgeous?"

"Behave," she scolded, peeling the glove off her left hand, which shone with a metallic gleam. "Time to go." She smiled at him sweetly. "Daddy wants you home for dinner."

Throwing back his head, Arthur exploded with laughter.

Acknowledgments

Many thanks to:

David Stokes for his love and support, savvy business advice, and for being a good sport about demonstrating action scenes for me. I'm a lucky girl!

Julia, Audrey, Catherine, and Ethan Stokes for their zest, sparkling personalities, and willingness to eat cereal for dinner every now and then. You are my life and my inspiration.

Lynne Shoblom for being a fantastic cheerleader, a wise adviser, for always lending a sympathetic ear, and for being the best darn mom in the world!

Peter Loeser for being my very patient "webmaster" and my very diligent "Northern California book distributor." I know I can always count on you, Dad.

My other wonderful family members and friends who have supported me in this publishing venture in a variety of ways: Phaidra and David Campbell, Roya Childs, Wyoma Claire, Shannon Cogan, Charles Engler, Jules Frost, Jill Fuller, Laura Gray, Brant King, Dawn Litterell, Marianne Loeser, Natalia McLaughlin, Robin Moore, James Morgan, Kristen Osland, Electra Redd, Gunner Redd, Elizabeth and Pierre Ribeiro da Costa, Lee Shoblom, Stacey and Anthony Urhammer, and Traci Vujicich. I am blessed to have you all in my life.

William Greenleaf for "polishing" my work so beautifully.

Kelly Carter for another fabulous book cover.

Paula and Katie Young who had read the original version of this book. Paula, thank you for saying, "What's the big deal about Cassidy fighting a tiger?" Due to your candidness, a super villain I can truly be proud of was born.

Steven Krause with Humboldt Herps for confirming that the Burmese Python scene isn't totally implausible.

Chuck and Chandra Meikle, Sergio Michel, and my other Facebook friends who had generously offered information for book content that I wasn't so knowledgeable about. You saved me some headaches.

Last but certainly not least, Cassidy's fans. If it weren't for you, there wouldn't be a Book Two. Happy reading, and I look forward to continuing Cassidy's journey with you!

Elise Stokes lives in Washington State with her husband and their four children, where she is at work on Cassidy's next exciting adventure.

Visit www.cassidyjonesadventures.com
www.facebook.com/Cassidy.Jones.Adventures
www.facebook.com/Cassidy.Jones.Adventures.Series
www.twitter.com/CassidyJonesAdv

Books in the Cassidy Jones Adventures series:

Cassidy Jones and the Secret Formula

Cassidy Jones and Vulcan's Gift

Cassidy Jones and the Seventh Attendant (Coming 2013)